Berkley books by Winston Groom

AS SUMMERS DIE
BETTER TIMES THAN THESE

BETTER TIMES THAN THESE

WINSTON GROOM

BERKLEY BOOKS, NEW YORK

BETTER TIMES THAN THESE

A Berkley Book / published by arrangement with
Summit Books

PRINTING HISTORY
Summit Books edition published 1978
Berkley edition / September 1979
Second printing / December 1980
Third printing / November 1982
Fourth printing / April 1984

ISBN: 0-425-07151-0

A BERKLEY BOOK ® TM 757,375
Berkley Books are published by The Berkley Publishing Group,
200 Madison Avenue, New York, New York 10016.
The name "BERKLEY" and the stylized "B" with design
are trademarks belonging to Berkley Publishing Corporation.
PRINTED IN THE UNITED STATES OF AMERICA

For two soldiers—
My father, who served in a different war
in different times; and James Jones.

Author's Note

This work is fiction. Accordingly, some of the terrain has been altered and military history rewritten to suit the story line. For instance, there is in fact an Ia Drang Valley, but most of the battles there took place a year before this tale is told. There are no such places in the Ia Drang as the "Boo Hoo Forest" or "The Fake," and while there were several Monkey Mountains and Happy Valleys in Vietnam, none that I know of were located where they are put in this novel. Furthermore, there was never a *Fourth* Battalion of the Seventh Cavalry Regiment in Vietnam, and those units of the Seventh Cavalry that did serve there did so, by all accounts, honorably and well. Finally, any character appearing in this book is wholly made up, and no similarity to anyone dead or living is intended.

East Hampton, Long Island
September 23, 1977

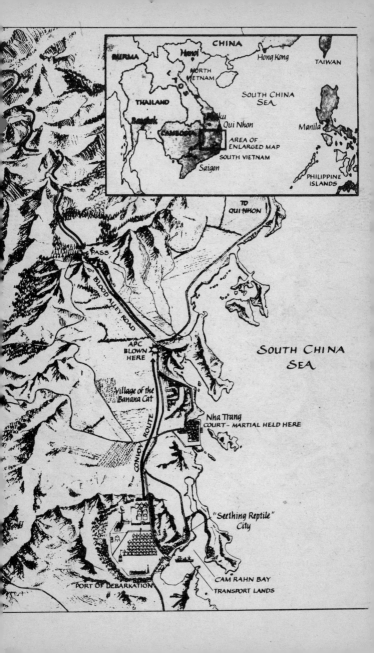

Contents

Table of Organization and Roster
a/o 21 July 1966 (incomplete)

Brigade Headquarters & Headquarters Company	
Butterworth, Samuel G.; Brig. Gen.—Commanding
Dalkey, Robt. C.; Maj.—Aide
Holden, C. Francis, III; 1/lt.—Aide
Dunn, Richard A.; Maj.—Signal Liaison
Greaves, Wilson P.; Maj.—Chaplain
McCrary, Michael T.; 1/lt.—Graves Registration

Fourth Battalion Seventh Cavalry (airmobile)

HEADQUARTERS:
Patch, Jason C.; Col.—Commanding
Flynn, Thomas P.; Capt.—Aide
Kennemer, Frederick N.; Capt.—Adjutant

Bravo Company

HEADQUARTERS:
Thurlo, David A.; Capt.—Commanding
Kahn, William Sol.; 1/lt.—Executive Officer
Trunk, Myron B., Jr.—1/sgt.
Hepplewhite, Norman E.; Spec/4—Clerk
Bateson, Sidney P.; Spec/4—Radiotelephone

PLATOON LEADERS:
Sharkey, Stephen D.; 2/lt.—1st Plt.
Brill, Victor L., Jr.; 2/lt.—2nd Plt.
Donovan, Sean P.; 2/lt.—3rd Plt.
Inge, Cyrus A.; 2/lt.—Weapons Plt.

NONCOMMISSIONED OFFICERS:
Dreyfuss, Leonard T.—plt/sgt, 1st Plt.
Groutman, Gustavus R.—plt/sgt, 2nd Plt.
Moon, Rollie I.—plt/sgt, Weapons Plt.

ENLISTED MEN:
Acquino, R. G.—rflmn
Conway, S. R.—medic
Carruthers, D. C.—rflmn
Crump, Homer R.—rflmn
DiGeorgio, Louis—rflmn
Dunbar, Tyron A.—rflmn
Harley, O. V.—rflmn

Helms, W. R.—rflmn
Hixon, T. G.—ammo brr
Maranto, J. B.—machguner
Miter, Harold N., Jr.—ammo brr
Muntz, Seymour H.—machguner
Poats, Edward—machguner
Spain, B. L.—ammo brr
Spate, Leon—rflmn
Trent, C. T.—rflmn

OTHERS:
Fox, Carter; Capt.—JAG
Gore, Timothy B.; Capt.—JAG
Maitland, Paul, Lt. Col.—JAG
Peck, Oscar A.; 2/lt.—replacement
Range, John T.; 2/lt.—replacement
Sonnebend, Peter; Capt.—Pub. Info. Off.
Spivey, Edward; 1/lt.—aviator
Tolson, Mayon; Capt.—Charlie Co.

There'll be better times than these,
In the Seventh Cavalry,
Just you wait and see,
          GarryOwen!

—*from a song of*
   The Seventh Cavalry Regiment

Part One

THE
VOYAGE

1

THE GRAY hull of the troop transport loomed at
the dock like a ghost ship, and the men, milling around
the olive-drab Army buses that stretched into the fog
nearly half a mile, had been trying hard to get a good look
at it for an hour. Sometimes the fog would thin for a
moment and they could see the gaping square hole in the
ship's side through which men from other buses, carrying
duffel bags and rifles and wearing helmets, were
boarding. Occasionally they could catch a glimpse of the
decks, on which there seemed to be a great clattering of
activity, but it was too fleeting for the men to tell what was
going on, and they had to strain to see what they could
see.

They could hear the roar of big cranes loading cargo into the hold, but they could not see them either. And when the cranes stopped every so often, they could hear the lapping of water against the concrete pier and from the direction of the ship they could hear a great deal of yelling, as though a hundred men were yelling at each other at once, but they could distinguish nothing of what was being yelled. And above this, there was the blaring of voices from loudspeakers and bullhorns which echoed down the canyon of white terminal buildings and blended with the yelling and the roar of the dockside cranes into a single gigantic racket coming out of the fog.

Bravo Company had been waiting beside the buses for nearly two hours, talking quietly, sitting on duffel bags, smoking and cursing the damp Pacific chill which none of them had anticipated in July. Some of the men simply stared out into the fog toward the ocean, or toward where they thought the ocean was—in the opposite direction from where the ship lay—because they did not want to be reminded of why they were here. These few men seemed lost, most of them, in private thoughts about their homes and girlfriends and other things very far removed from this particular dock at the Presidio Army Transport Terminal on this particular San Francisco summer morning.

It was nearly noon when the fog lifted. Almost magically, it simply vanished from the dock and moved off about a mile into the water, lingering as a whitish wall as far as anyone could see in either direction. When this happened, and the men could finally see the ship, everyone got a strange feeling in the pit of his stomach, a feeling which was not exactly fear, though that had something to do with it, but more of excitement, partly because most of them had never before seen a ship this close and partly because they knew it was going to take them across ten thousand miles of ocean and deposit them to fight a war which for the last year they had been trained for, hollered at about and generally saturated with; and yet most of them still did not have the slightest understanding of what it was all about.

In nineteen hundred sixty-six the dark specter of war was moving across America, vexing the spirit that had conquered the tyrants of Europe and Asia. In plush offices and hushed marble corridors of official Washington, older men, many of whom had never heard a shot fired in anger, spoke boldly of defeating Communism and establishing freedom and independence for the peoples of Vietnam. The men boarding the transport were among the first wave of an entire Army that was to follow by the end of the year, and yet to them, all these things mattered little. They knew their departure from the dock would signify that it had begun, and their concerns now were mostly with themselves. Each in his own way realized that this voyage was merely a fortuitous delay of an inevitable adventure from which none of them would return unchanged and some would not return at all.

WORD CAME down shortly after the fog lifted that Bravo Company was to get into formation to go aboard. The men were told this by the noncoms, who had been told by the platoon leaders, who had been told by the Company Commander and the Executive Officer, who had been told by someone else up the line to have the men pick up their gear and get it to hell into some kind of order and sling their weapons and put their helmets over their bald-shaven heads and get ready to move out; but of course they didn't actually move out for another hour and a half.

Private Homer Crump, peeling one of the tangerines his mother had sent him from Mississippi, offered a section to his squadmate Private Louis DiGeorgio, of Bayonne, New Jersey.

"Fuckin' shit, Crump, all you do is eat. Whataya gonna do when we get there—climb up a tree and eat bananas?" DiGeorgio snorted, sticking the whole section into his mouth and squashing it between his tongue and his teeth.

Crump worked the skin from the rest of the tangerine with his big bony fingers; looking a little hurt, he eyed DiGeorgio carefully.

"You always makin' fun of me, ain't you, Dee-Gergio?

You et the tangerine, didn't you? Then you make fun of it. You bolo on the rifle range and I help you get a rating and you make fun of that too. How come you don't never like nothin', Dee-Gergio?" Crump said, stuffing the skin of the fruit into his fatigue blouse pocket.

"Cause yer gonna get yer ass shot off over there and all ats gonna be left is a buncha stinkin' fruits, that's why, Crump. Whatdayathink we're goin' to here—a fuckin' picnic? Ya want 'em ta pack us a box lunch or sompen? Ol' Charlie starts shootin', what'll you do? You'll be runnin' around handin' out fuckin' tangerines to people steda shooting ya blooker, I bet! Yer probably be throwin' 'em steda grenades." He looked up and down at Crump's lanky frame. "That's why, Crump, cause ya don't know what the fuck's goin' on," DiGeorgio said, shaking his head slowly as though he were speaking to a certifiable idiot.

"AWRIGHT, LES GO" came the cry down the line, and the men picked up their duffels and rifles and threw them over their shoulders. "Route step, harch," a voice roared, and Bravo Company moved away from the buses they had learned to loathe since basic training, but which had suddenly become their last remaining link with the world they knew. A few of the men, among them the ones who earlier had stared out toward the ocean, looked back at the ugly, uncomfortable vehicles much in the same way as a prisoner on his way to the electric chair might glance back at his cell.

As Bravo Company moved closer to the ship, the sources of the noise and commotion they had heard through the fog became apparent. The dock was like a crazyhouse. Dozens of men were rushing about moving boxes and crates. One of the cranes the men had heard was lowering huge green metal CONEX containers into the ship's hold. This was the brigade Basic Load, the supplies to keep it going in the field for a month in case it couldn't be resupplied. Another crane was lowering a canvas-covered howitzer. Men on deck with bullhorns shouted instructions down to the crane operators. Rifle companies formed up to go aboard. A dozen men, handcuffed together, these without rifles, filed up the boarding ramp, escorted by MPs in bright black helmets. These men, Bravo Company would learn later, were rounded-up AWOLs, who would spend their monthlong voyage in the brig.

CATTLE, THOUGHT Second Lieutenant Victor Brill, who had spent much of his twenty-three years in and out of military schools for progressively worsening behavior and who was therefore well qualified to form this opinion. After the endless hours of penalty tours and drill he had marched as the result of some transgression or other, Brill knew, or at least thought he knew, what it felt like to be cattle.

He had seen them all his life—from his grandfather's ranch in California to the big pens near Fort Sill, Oklahoma, and at a variety of places in between.

Cattle were stupid. They were not like things actually alive which had feelings and thoughts and could rage against people who abused them and made them do things they did not want to do. No sir.

About the only thing cattle did was breathe and eat and then be eaten themselves.

He had never seen cattle get mad—even when he'd hit them between the eyes with a ball-peen hammer to get them moving. Brill pictured the cattle in the pastures his grandfather kept, waiting to be put into chutes for the slaughterhouse. No matter how hot it was, nor how mean you treated them, the cattle just stood there and took it. And God knew why, but they always wanted to bunch up, usually in a tiny corner of the pasture. It could be a hundred and one goddamned degrees, but there they were, bunched up, fucking lying all over each other in the hot sun, flopping their tails, waiting for somebody to come along with a prod and get their dumb asses moving into the chutes. It reminded Brill of how they'd yelled at him in Infantry at Fort Benning School.

"Goddamn it, Lieutenant, don't let those men bunch up—one mortar round would get every one a you."

Thrashing through those Georgia thickets with a flock of dumbass recruits who kept bunching up against each other; that was when he'd begun to see them as cattle.

As the last of the AWOLs filed aboard, Brill narrowed his skyblue eyes, smiling thinly, and turning to Sergeant Trunk, the Company First Sergeant, he said, "Cattle."

Trunk, knowing what Brill meant, but knowing it for entirely different reasons of his own, replied, "Yessir, that's cattle okay; that's cattle."

IT WAS then that the men heard the music.

At first they couldn't really hear anything they could distinguish as a tune, because of all the racket from the dock and the ship, but after a few minutes they began to pick out the notes in between the racket, and almost simultaneously they recognized it, the forlorn trumpet and drums, burbling above the hubbub. It was their song, "Garryowen"—the battle tune of the Seventh Cavalry, which most of them had sung both drunk and sober for the past year, in the cigarette-stinking, beer-swilling ratholes they had called clubs; the song they had been made to learn, along with their General Orders, when they first joined the Regiment.

The Troop, they had been told, was the only troop to have joined—as if they had had a choice at some point—with a history as glorious as any in the United States Army: the Fourth Troop, now Fourth Battalion, Seventh Cavalry.

"The only difference," Colonel Patch had told them in an uproarious speech at Fort Bragg, North Carolina, "is that the Army has seen fit to dispense with horses, so we shall now descend on the enemy from the air like a swarm of copulating gnats."

Nevertheless, he'd said, this was the same outfit Colonel Custer had taken to the Little Big Horn River a hundred years before, playing this same song, and had been butchered there by five thousand savages, and which had later fought at Wounded Knee, Santiago, Dublan, Luzon, Inchon. All these men, Patch said, choking a bit, had sung the song "Garryowen" ... most of them dead now, as the men of Bravo Company would also be, one way or another, one hundred years hence.

"Whatayawanta do, live forever?" First Sergeant Trunk liked to say, when the men complained that their feet were killing them.

At some point, most of the men had found themselves hearing at least the tune in their heads, if not the words, and they should have known they would have to hear it again for the ten-thousandth time as they too were finally herded up the gangplank onto the transport. A few of them, but only a few, were thinking they were tired of being treated like cattle, but they did not say this out loud.

2

A CHILLY drizzle had been falling on New York City since late afternoon, washing away the spittle and debris and slickening over the chewing-gum wads on the sidewalks. In front of Delmonico's Hotel on Park Avenue, limousines and taxis were disgorging their cargoes of young men in white tie and long-gowned girls and austere, high-coiffed matrons escorted by prosperous-looking, silver-haired men decked out in formal regalia. A cab bounced to a halt and Lieutenant Frank Holden, wearing his dress blue military uniform, dashed under the marquee and joined the throng scuttling through the brass-trimmed doors. Except for its color, the

doorman's uniform looked very much like his own, and
he felt a wry, cynical satisfaction that the formal attire of
the United States Army and the costume of the doorman
at Delmonico's both looked as if they had come from the
wardrobe of *The Student Prince*.

The lobby was a bedlam of gabbling faces, discarded
raincoats and folding umbrellas. A few people stared at
Holden's dress blues, and he couldn't decide whether it
was because they simply didn't know what the uniform
was, or because they did, and felt uncomfortable about it.
He hadn't spent much time in New York since going on
active duty, but he was more or less aware of a growing
resentment here against the war that had not yet
crystallized in other parts of America.

Without stopping to check his cap, Holden brushed
through the crowd into the huge ballroom, decorated in
red and white crepe streamers and flowers. An orchestra
was playing "Moon River," and Holden lingered near the
door for a moment among the fashionable, almost
fashionable, semifashionable and a few unfashionable
New York people who had come to drink and dance and
talk and see and be seen at Cory's debut. There was the
smell of champagne and chafing dishes and roses and
nothing at all to remind anyone of the war, except
perhaps himself.

HE SAW her in a corner, surrounded by half a dozen older
men and women he didn't recognize. Instead of going
straight over, he headed for the bar, feeling slightly
uneasy over wearing the uniform instead of tails. He
ordered a Scotch and soda, standing beside a cluster of
scraggly-looking undergraduates talking about Amherst.
A couple of them gawked at him as though he had just
landed from Mars. One whispered something to the
others, who sniggered and turned the other way. He
wasn't sure it was about him, but he suspected it was, and
it made him feel more uncomfortable in a situation in
which he should have felt completely at home.

Cory was laughing with the other couples, her long
auburn hair piled high on her head, her suntanned face as

lovely as ever. He decided to wait until she was dancing, then sneak up behind her and cut in. She loved that kind of little surprise from him, and he figured it would ease her disappointment that he had come in uniform.

"Oh, Frank, don't be tacky. *Nobody* ever wears a uniform to these things," she'd protested when he'd mentioned it in a phone conversation the week before. "Mother will go through the ceiling. You know she wants to show you off; don't embarrass her.

"You're just kidding, aren't you?" she had asked, when he hadn't said anything.

"Of course I'm not kidding," he teased. "Why should I have to go out and rent tails when I've got this grand uniform? You'll love it, anyway—it's got gold braid on the tunic, and the pants are light blue with a gold stripe down the sides, and—"

"Stop it, Frank. It isn't funny," she'd said quietly.

He'd said nothing, realizing for the first time she was actually embarrassed that he might come in his uniform to her party. Still, he didn't see why he ought to be ashamed to wear the uniform of the United States Army in public. After all, Holdens had been wearing it in some way or other for more than two hundred years, and his father had been one of the most decorated officers in Europe, and after all, he'd paid one hundred sixty-five dollars for it...

"You know you have tails up here," she'd said. "You wont't have to rent them. You look so handsome in tails. Please, Frank, don't kid me like this..."

He hadn't really planned to come in the uniform. He'd meant to stop at home and change into white tie; but they had been on the artillery range until nearly dark that day, and by the time he got back to the BOQ he had known he had better dress now for the evening; he would be just able to catch the last flight to New York, and there wouldn't be time to change there after he arrived.

Normally, the Old Man would have brought them in early on Friday; but three days before, they had gotten their marching orders. Within a few months they would be on the way to Vietnam to join the Division, and they were having to work extra hard to get ready. The little war nobody thought would happen was actually happening, and although no one knew exactly how bad it was going to be, they weren't joking about it the way they had before.

He had saved the news of the overseas orders to tell Cory and his parents in person, because he believed that was the way it should be done—in the big family room, not over a telephone. He had a vision of how it would be: he would call them together as his father had done whenever there had been a family event—except that this time he would do the calling. Everyone would sit down and he would break the news calmly, standing by the fireplace, explaining the particulars. He had planned to do it tonight, before the ball, but the late artillery business had spoiled that, and now he wasn't sure how to tell them—do it here or wait. In either case, he was beginning to regret that he had worn the dress blues, because he knew Cory wouldn't like it, and after all, she was his sister, and this was her big night.

HE WALKED along the edge of the dance floor, picking his way through the whirling couples so that he would come up behind Cory. She was dancing with a balding, fiftyish-looking man Holden recognized from his parents' parties but whose name he couldn't remember. He tapped the man gently on the shoulder and asked, "May I cut in?"

The man quickly stepped away, nodding politely but looking Holden up and down.

"Frank," she gasped, "you—"

"Hi, Button," he said, not letting her finish, taking her gently with the music.

"Frank, you wore it..."

"Hey, listen, Button, I'm sorry, really I am, but we didn't get off till dark. I was lucky to make it up here at all; I had the last flight."

"Oh, Frank, damn," she said.

"It's all right, Button. Honestly. I don't feel very comfortable in civvies anyway," he said, whirling her while the orchestra played a tune from *Cabaret*.

"Oh, well," she said, I guess it doesn't matter.... It's just that..."

"Just what?"

"It's so *military*," she said.

"Well, what the hell else could it be?" He laughed. "It *is* military. I am *in* the military."

"Yes, I know, but you know...the war and everything...killing people," she said.

"I'm not planning to kill anybody tonight," he said good-naturedly.

"It's just that it reminds people of the war," she said.

"Well, they ought to be reminded of it. What do they think, they can get all dandied up and come here and there isn't going to be a war?" He felt a twinge of testiness.

"No, no, that isn't it. But a lot of people are really against the war. Did you know that?"

"Hell yes I know it, but that still doesn't mean it's going to go away, little sister. Anyway, the kinds of people who're against it are sort of nutty anyway...actors and kids...what do they know about it? Huh?"

"Oh, Frank, it's more than that. Let's don't talk about it—it's so stupid," she said.

"Sure, Button. I just hope I haven't spoiled your evening."

"You haven't. Of course you haven't," she said. "Oh, there's Becky, let's go over—don't you want to?" Cory said, taking him by the hand and leading him to a table at the edge of the dance floor.

HE HADN'T seen Becky for three years. She had been so much younger then, a skinny seventeen-year-old with pageboy hair and plaid skirts and knee socks who came to visit Cory. He had always teased her about being skinny and not having any figure, and so he was totally unprepared for the fully blossomed young woman with a long black mane of hair he was walking toward now. She was anything but skinny. She was absolutely devastating in a low-cut green evening gown.

"Becky, it's Frank," Cory said. He felt an immediate attraction to her that seemed out of place. It was hard to understand how this lovely creature had developed from such a bag of bones.

"Hi, Skinny, how's your butt?" he said, deciding to gain the upper hand with a question that had always gotten a rise before.

"My butt's fine. How's yours?" she said smartly. Instantly he realized the tables had turned and he hadn't the faintest idea how to proceed, except that he knew he couldn't deal with Becky the way he had before—and didn't want to anyway.

She was sitting next to a craggy, fortyish-looking man immersed in serious conversation with a fat dowager who seemed to hang on his every utterance.

"Frank Holden," Becky said, tapping the man on his shoulder, "I want you to meet Richard Widenfield."

"Oh, how do you do?" Widenfield said, rising, shaking hands. "Holden—you're Cory's brother, then?"

"Richard is in the Political Science department at Mount Holyoke," Becky said. "Frank," she said, "is in the Army."

"Yes, I can see that," said Widenfield. "You were a big tennis player, weren't you?—I think Cory told me. Brown, wasn't it?"

"Princeton," Holden said.

"Of course; sorry."

"He's a big Army man now," Becky said. "How does it feel to be a big Army man?" She was smiling, but he felt a certain antagonism in the question.

"Not so big, I guess; just doing my time."

"What do you do in the Army?" Her green eyes flashed.

"I'm with the headquarters of an Infantry brigade at Fort Bragg, in North Carolina."

"And what do they do?" she said.

"I don't know if I get you. It's an Infantry brigade. We're a line unit."

"You kill people, right?"

"That's what the Army's for, kid—at least, sometimes. You always hope it doesn't come to that."

Cory interrupted. "Frank went in because he would have been drafted, Becky—he's only in for three years."

"I suppose you're going to Vietnam and kill people," Becky continued.

"Yes, as a matter of fact, I am," he said, the words coming out deliberately, but before he'd meant them to.

"Frank, you aren't!" Cory said. "When?" There was disbelief in her pretty, tanned face.

"Sometime this summer."

"But you can't! Why?" Cory looked as if she were about to cry. "Can't you get out of it?"

"Of course not, Button. I wish I could."

"You haven't told Mother or Daddy?"

"Not yet."

"It'll kill them," Cory said. "They're against the war."

"I doubt it," he said firmly.

"So am I," Becky said, "we all are—and you should be too—we haven't got any business being there."

Holden took a swallow of his drink and looked her in the eyes. "Look, Becky, I don't like it any more than anyone else, but I have to do what they tell me. That's what the Army's all about."

"No questions asked, huh? Just do it. That's exactly what's wrong with this whole thing," she said sharply.

Widenfield had turned in his chair and was watching with interest.

"Well, of course you have questions. I have questions. But once you're in the Army it doesn't matter about that," Holden said.

"Look," he said. "Maybe you don't realize what's going on over there. If we don't stop this thing right now, it's probably going to spread all over Asia—and then what? The North Vietnamese are very ruthless people . . . we've got commitments . . ."

"Did you ever read Bernard Fall?" she said. "Nobody—not the French, not us, not anybody—is going to 'save' that country except the Vietnamese people themselves."

"Becky," Widenfield said, but she waved him off.

"And we're just making it worse. Don't you think Fall ought to know?" she said. "He's been there for years."

"He doesn't know anything now; he's dead," Holden said.

"Are you suggesting," Widenfield interrupted abruptly, "that people's ideas die with them?"

"No, of course not," Holden said, "but Fall only represents a point of view. It's a good point of view, but he didn't understand the capabilities of this country, our counterinsurgency program..."

"There's a new book called *The Village of Ben Suc*," Widenfield said. "It gives a pretty clear picture of our 'counterinsurgency' program: burn everything to the ground and kill off every male between fifteen and fifty. Is that supposed to be the foreign policy of the United States?"

"Well I haven't read that book, but I've heard about it, and I don't think—"

"Let me commend it to you, then, Mr. Holden. It gives a very clear view of what's going on over there. That bunch in Washington is getting us deeper and deeper into this thing, and the entire history of the situation suggests we can never win it," Widenfield said. "You know Schlesinger—"

"I'm in the Army, and there is a very different perspective in the Army," Holden said.

"God," Becky demanded defiantly, "why are we talking this way? The whole thing isn't about 'winning' anything, it's why should we be killing people—any people!"

"Why should the North Vietnamese be killing people?" Holden said, annoyed at himself for getting into this argument. The orchestra was playing "As Time Goes By," and Holden suddenly saw himself blithely standing in the middle of ten thousand dollars' worth of his father's whiskey and champagne and caviar and finger sandwiches arguing with two girls eighteen and twenty years old and a bombastic academic who couldn't, or wouldn't, understand what he was trying to say. But he realized, grudgingly, that it was because he didn't fully understand it himself.

". . . silly," Becky was saying. "It's a silly excuse to take over a country of poor people. You see us killing them on television, don't you know?" she said bitterly.

He gulped from the Scotch. "Look, I'm an officer in the Army—I don't have any choice."

"That's what the Germans said," Becky declared triumphantly, as if she had been lying in wait for him to say it.

"There's a difference," Holden said.

"What difference?" she demanded.

"We aren't Germans," he said, and he walked away.

CORY FOLLOWED him to the bar. "Oh, damn, Frank, see what I mean now? See how people feel?"

"What people? Who cares?" he said. "So some twenty-year-old sophomore suddenly thinks she knows international politics. What else is new?" He ordered a drink.

"She's a junior. And besides, she isn't the only one. Dad talks about it a lot. He thinks the war's a big mistake."

"Yeah, well if he does, it's for different reasons than Skinny-Butt does, I'll bet," he said.

"What difference does it make?" Cory said. "You're just showing off to everybody that you're in the Army. Don't you understand nobody cares about that?"

"So I see," he said.

HOLDEN MADE his way to the far side of the ballroom, looking for his parents, chatting on the way with a few old friends, all of whom commented on his uniform, even though the comments were mostly conversational. Nevertheless, it occurred to him that he couldn't have attracted much more attention by appearing in the nude.

He was about to go back to the bar, where he'd left his cap, when Becky came up beside him and touched his arm.

"Hey, Frank, I'm sorry I gave you a hard time. I really didn't mean it the way it sounded," she said, steering him to an empty table.

"Oh, hell, don't worry about it, kiddo. Anyway, I probably deserved it for all the ribbing I used to give you."

"No, no, that's not it at all—that hasn't anything to do with it. You see—"

"Hey, let's don't get into it again, okay?"

"But it all seems so wrong—all the hating and killing. I'm sorry, but it makes me sick," she said.

"Jesus, I wish I'd never worn this damned outfit," he said. "I'm probably going to stay in some Staff job and fetch ice cream for the general anyway. I probably won't even see a shot fired."

She smiled at him, and he was about to ask her to dance when Widenfield appeared and thrust a glass of champagne at her.

"I thought you said you wanted a drink," he said impatiently.

"Oh, thank you, Richard. I had to talk to Frank for a minute."

"I'll see you at the table," he said, and stalked off.

"Who's he?" Holden asked after a pause.

"We go out sometimes," she said. "Nothing big."

THEY WERE dancing, and the strangeness of holding Becky this way had already worn off. He was pressing her close, feeling her softness, breathing her earthy scent, which he recognized as Jungle Gardenia, a perfume he'd been enlightened about one night in the back seat of a car by a girl from Charleston who'd informed him that *everybody* in New York was wearing it.

"Listen," Holden said. "I know I don't rate very high on your list, but I've got to be back Sunday and I'd like to see you again. Are you free tomorrow night?"

"You rate very high on my list, Mr. Holden...but tomorrow I'm sort of committed to something." She swept a wave of hair away from her face.

"Oh," he said, "well, uh..."

"What are you doing Sunday afternoon?" She looked deliberately into his eyes.

"Seeing you, I hope."

"Yes," she said.

*   *   *

HE PRESSED her close again and was surprised when she squeezed back tentatively. They whirled around that way for the rest of the song, and Holden felt warm and good and comfortable for the first time that day. Occasionally he looked beyond her for some sign of his parents. The room was very crowded, but even so, he was surprised he'd missed them. He tried steering Becky in a 360-degree circle during the last few bars of the song, hoping to catch sight of them, but his thoughts were mostly of her. The soft, comfortable warmth and perfume . . .

Something he saw by the bar jolted him back to reality.

Several of the scraggly Amherst undergraduates were standing stiffly at mock attention while one of them, who had taken Holden's uniform cap from the bar and put it on his head, was parading up and down, his hand tucked inside the breast of his tailcoat like a German officer. He was berating his "troops" loudly with exaggerated military bearing, and the performance had commanded the interest of a few bystanders.

Holden felt himself flush, and as the song ended he took Becky back to her table. He asked if she wanted a drink, and she said she'd have champagne.

She squeezed his hand slightly. "I'll be back in a minute," he said.

HOLDEN STARTED straight for the undergraduates, who were now exchanging the cap among themselves, saluting madly and laughing hysterically at their game. They were still giggling when they saw him coming.

"You fellows having fun?" he said crisply. The laughter and gaiety around him had faded into a bland, unharmonious noise.

Two of them looked sheepish, and the third smirked. The one wearing the cap assumed the position of attention.

"No, no, *Herr Leutnant*, ve vas just doink zome drills," he said, bringing the others to uncontrolled laughter.

"Okay, let's have the hat," Holden said, sternly, as though he were addressing a squad of privates.

"Vat hat, *Herr Leutnant*? Doss you haff a hat, Fritz?" the wearer said, sending the rest into grand hysteria.

About a dozen people at the bar had turned, and Holden noticed that Widenfield was among the on-lookers. He thought he saw a touch of a smile cross his face.

"Look, guys, this has gone far enough," Holden said, "Now give me the hat." He extended his hand toward the boy wearing it, a rangy kid about his own height and build.

"Hey, man," the boy said, "don't get bummed out—we were just kidding around."

"It's not funny anymore," Holden said.

"Look man, be cool, nobody's going to hurt your hat." Holden kept his hand out.

The boy glanced at the others. "Vellll ... how iss ve to know, *Herr Leutnant*, zat you belongs to ze hat?" he said drunkenly.

"If you don't hand it over you're going to find out," Holden said.

By now the crowd had grown around them and it had gotten very quiet. The orchestra was playing "Hello, Dolly!"

Slowly the boy removed the cap and studied it carefully. He looked as if he didn't quite know which way to go, and for a moment he seemed on the verge of giving it back to Holden. Then he looked again at the others and a nasty smile crossed his lips.

"Vhy, *Herr Leutnant*, ziss does not even look like a hat at all! It looks like a bowl—a zoup bowl," he said. "Und a zoup bowl needs zome zoup!" He tipped his drink slightly and dropped a tiny bit of liquid into the cap. "Now *Herr Leutnant*, ze zoup bowl will—"

Holden didn't give him time to finish the sentence. He took one step forward and slapped the glass upward, along with the cap, so that the cap flew over the boy's head and the drink doused his face. He hesitated a split second before throwing a punch, waiting to see what the boy would do, trying to keep an eye on the others, who were looking at each other but slowly closing in on him. He was vaguely aware of a few gasps from the bystanders.

"All right, you bastard, come on—just come on, goddamn it," Holden hissed.

Suddenly a stocky, gray-haired man broke through the crowd into the tiny circle. "What's going on here? What in hell do you people think you're doing?... Frank! Good Lord, Frank, I didn't even see you. What in hell is this?"

"It's, ah, nothing, Dad," Holden said. "It's just a little misunderstanding."

"All right, break this up—you boys be on your way—go ahead, now," the elder Holden said sharply. The undergraduates began to walk off slowly, and the one Holden had hit with the glass looked over his shoulder and grinned. "Vat is das?" he said, but he kept on going.

Holden's father turned to him, bewildered. "This is a hell of a thing to have happen at your sister's party, Frank. What's it all about?

Holden watched the others fade into the crowd. His legs and hands were trembling, and he felt that all the blood had drained from his face—but mostly he felt very much alone.

"It seems," he said unsteadily, "those gentlemen don't have much respect for a man in uniform."

3

ON THE lifeboat deck high above the ramp where Bravo Company was filing aboard, Lieutenant Colonel Jason Patch, Four/Seven's Commanding Officer, adjusted his dark, round sunglasses and leaned out across the gray metal rail so that he could see his battalion go aboard. The Seventh Cavalry battle tune drifted up from the pier and gave him a feeling of immense pride. It reminded him of the last time he had found himself in these circumstances. A different pier and a different ship—but otherwise, things hadn't changed much in fifteen years.

He had been one of them then—simply Lieutenant

Patch, blond hair cropped short, no moustache—leading
a green-grub rifle company aboard an identical gray
transport to Korea. So he knew, really knew, what was
going on in the heads of the men below; the uncertainty,
queasiness, sphincter-pulsating fear, exhilaration, bewil-
derment and discomfort, jumbled into whatever else was
on their minds. All these thing Patch understood, because
when he was a second lieutenant himself he'd been
informed that all second lieutenants were "lower than
whaleshit"—which is at the bottom of the ocean—and
therefore about as close to being an enlisted man as you
could get without actually being one. You ate with them,
slept with them, joked with them, shared their youth, and
everything else. Except for that tiny metal bar on your
collar, there wasn't really much difference.

Patch loved these men. His men.

Even when he was a lower-than-whaleshit second
lieutenant he had envisioned himself as sort of a fatherly
figure, and he liked it when the men came to him with
personal problems. He knew what they really needed was
someone to guide them through their troubles if they had
troubles, and to keep them out of trouble if they didn't.

He did not see the enlisted men as cattle. Patch didn't
like that assessment of enlisted men, because it took no
consideration of the human feelings he knew they had.
The problem with enlisted men was that they had to be
very tightly controlled, so that they did what they were
supposed to do and didn't get into trouble—or at least,
got into as little trouble as possible, under the circumstances.

Now THE little band on the pier was playing the tune for
the third and final time before moving on to something
else. Patch knew it was the last because of the way the
trumpeter went very high on the chorus. Patch liked this,
and he was humming along and tapping his foot when a
froglike voice interrupted his reverie. "Good morning,
Jason; I see you've got your 'special detail' working
again." Without his having to look first, words formed in

Patch's mouth and began coming out even before he'd completely turned around.

"Good morning, sir," Patch said, looking down into the smiling blue eyes of General Butterworth, the Brigade Commander, who had come up behind him with his aide, a plastic-faced first lieutenant who always seemed to Patch like he had just been waxed for display in a museum.

"A nice idea, Jason—the music," the General said.

"Thank you, sir. I thought it might take off the edge a little. I'm glad you like it." He felt relieved, because he knew his little band wasn't supposed to exist under Army regulations, which did not authorize bands for battalions, but only for brigades and divisions. But Patch had ordered one formed anyway because he liked the idea and thought it would add to the esprit de corps which, after all, was the most important thing a commander could give to his troops—esprit de corps. Regulations didn't authorize a lot of things, and he'd be damned if he'd be one of those straitlaced do-it-by-The-Book bastards—not Jason Patch! The men he admired in the history of this man's army, the Grants, Jacksons, Pattons and, yes, even the Custers—maybe the Custers most—were brash, decisive men. Fighters! Men who realized early on that regulations were made to be violated. Framework! Not ends in themselves—and if he'd learned anything at all at The Point and in the fifteen years since, Patch had learned the value of innovation.

It was anything that would make the men get off their asses and do whatever there was to do. Like in any business, those in charge had to motivate those who weren't, and the answer to motivation, Patch believed, was innovation.

The music was a large part of this.

Who could resist it? For four hundred years "Garryowen" had inspired men marching into battle. It had stirred their juices in alehouses and saloons and beer joints on both sides of the ocean, taking its title from an ancient Irish village where it had been the battle song of the Fifth Royal Irish Lancers. Patch, who fancied himself a student of military history, had discovered this wandering through books at the post library just after he joined the Regiment.

Thomas Moore, he learned, had added words to the tune. Other words, some fit only for the beer halls, had been added by the men over the years. Custer had heard it during the Civil War and later decreed it would be the battle tune of the Seventh Cavalry.

And one of the first things Custer did when he became Commander in eighteen sixty-six was to form his own little band, "from the musicians of the Regiment"— despite the fact that a band was not authorized for regiments then any more than it was for battalions now. But that, by God, was Patch's idea of innovation.

"Is it going smoothly, Jason?" General Butterworth asked. "Are there any hang-ups?"

"We're right on it, sir," Patch said, smoothing his blond moustache with a finger.

"Good, good—Second Battalion's coming up next, and we're still going off at oh eleven hundred if this goddamned fog breaks. Navy says it will, but they don't want to get mixed up in the soup with a bunch of freighters coming down the bay, so you let me know if there are problems getting your people squared away." The general's face screwed into a wrinkled smile.

"I don't think we'll have any problems, sir," Patch replied.

"Good—that's good, Jason. Of course, you'll keep me posted," the general said.

The wax-faced aide nodded at Patch. "Colonel," he said, then moved off at the general's heels.

Shitass, Patch said silently, watching the young aide walk away. Just one more regulation-bound school-solution shitass.

Patch had seen his kind before—smug-looking. At The Point, they were the ones who studied day and night, the darlings of the instructors, parroting back exactly what the instructors told them, always giving "the school solution"—as though there weren't ten, or twenty, or a hundred ways of doing something in the Army. The kind of officer Patch liked was a man who would hunker down by the ground and work out a problem by drawing in the sand with a stick.

Not this kid, though. Patch sneered at the stiffness of his gait as the aide walked away. He's going to muddle through a career hiding behind regs and being a general's aide and that kind of crap until he gets a star, and then they're going to cram him behind a desk somewhere so he can screw things up for the Infantry.

Patch had seen his kind before: the anonymous signatures at the bottom of some stupid buck-back form, or a self-important voice at the other end of a phone, saying why this or that couldn't be done or couldn't be done this or that way.

Shitass, Patch said to himself again, turning away from the wax-faced general's aide, whose name was C. Francis Holden and who, before he joined the Army, had been the number-one-ranking tennis player at Princeton University and who had absolutely no intention on earth of making the military his career and who, sensing Patch's animosity toward him, was at that very moment thinking that Patch was an asshole.

4

IN THE enlisted men's quarters on the troop deck, there was grand confusion. Bravo Company was led into a large gray-painted room that smelled of dampness and the sea, with row upon row of quadruple-decked bunks, where it was to live for the next twenty-five days. The room was so full of people it reminded Pfc. Crump of the crowds inside the freak tent at the little carnival shows that brought to Tupelo, Mississippi, such interesting exhibits as the hermaphrodite human and the woman with three tits.

Alpha Company was in the sleeping room already, and part of Charlie Company was backed up at the companionway door—five hundred jammed-up bodies waiting for someone to tell them what to do next. Since that had not happened, Bravo Company put down its gear and milled around with the rest until Sergeant Trunk shoved his way through the door and quieted everybody down.

"Stand by a bunk," Trunk roared, and again there was a great milling around as everyone pressed to find a bed. When it became apparent that there were not nearly enough bunks to go around, the noise and the cursing grew louder as men who were left out scrambled up one aisle and down the next, hoping to find a niche of their own.

Trunk let this continue for a few minutes before he quieted them down again so he could say what he had known secretly since they had left the sand hills of North Carolina: that in fact there weren't going to be enough bunks for each man to have his own, because Division wanted the whole Brigade to arrive at once, and since there wasn't another transport available, these twenty-one hundred men were going to have to go over on a ship built to carry only fifteen hundred of them.

"All right, shitheads, now you see what the problem is," Trunk said, measuring his words slowly.

"Don't fret, girls," Trunk said sweetly, his picket teeth gleaming in a Cheshire Cat grin, "everybody's gonna get to sleep on this here little sail—you're just gonna have to do it different times." He explained how the rotation of sleeping shifts would work—one third of the men would have to be up on deck at all times. There was a predictable chorus of groans.

"Knock it off, shitheads," Trunk bellowed. "You'll get used to it. Now, anybody without a bunk find one to share and stop bitchin' like a bunch of goddamned women. This is just a little pleasure cruise, compared with what you're in for when we get over there."

Slowly, the ones without bunks carried their gear to a bunk that was already occupied. This exercise took somewhat longer than it might have as the left-out men searched the faces of those already with a bunk for any sign of receptiveness and the ones who had already claimed bunks tried their best, without actually saying or doing anything outright, to look as unreceptive as they could.

By 3 P.M., the sun had burned off the remaining haze. The day had turned brilliant California blue, and a perky breeze had sprung up off the ocean. Most of the men were lounging outside on the cargo deck when the first tremor from the big engines shivered through the steel frame of the ship.

DiGeorgio and Crump were leaning against the rail talking to Pfc. Spudhead Miter when they saw the cloud of dirty smoke belch from the forward stack. Moments later a similar cloud flew out of the stack behind it, blowing a gigantic smoke ring skyward.

"Here we go," Crump said, peeling a tangerine and looking helplessly down at the Navy dockhands casting off the thick braided mooring lines. "Here we go."

DiGeorgio's beady little eyes danced wildly, looking up and down at Crump's skinny frame slouched against the rail.

"Goddamned right we do, you dumb ape. Whatja expect, they'd change their minds that last fuckin' minute? You thought Trunk's gonna come running out here and say, 'Okay, shitheads, this here's just a drill'? Jesus, Crump, you're brilliant—fuckin' brilliant!"

"Why don't you shut your mouth up, Dee-Gergio?" Crump said, hawking up a wad of phlegm and blowing it out with his tongue so that it arched in mortarlike trajectory into the boiling water in the fast-widening gap between ship and pier.

Spudhead Miter's big potato-shaped head followed Crump's expectoration until it hit the water, and he gazed down for a while at the spot where the spittle had landed. None of them spoke as the ship shuddered under the strain of 28,000 horsepower, but each felt his own strong sensations. Finally Spudhead jammed his hands into his pockets and said with authority, "We're really in the dogfuck now."

5

FIRST LIEUTENANT Billy Kahn, Bravo Company's Executive Officer, was stowing away the last of eight precious bottles of Cutty Sark he had smuggled into his duffel bag in North Carolina after learning that the Navy didn't allow whiskey drinking on its ships at sea. When the engine tremor reached his cabin, Kahn stopped for a moment and for no reason he could think of glanced at his watch—it was 3:10 P.M.—then finished tucking the bottle gently in with the rest, cushioning it among a dozen or so pairs of olive-drab underwear so that it wouldn't break if the ship started to rock or pound. When he finished, he stepped over to the small porthole next to the bunks to watch the ship pulling away from the pier, and wondered why the Navy wouldn't let people drink on their goddamned old scow. So what if the men got drunked up a few times? So what if they got into a few fights? What was it going to hurt? What'd they expect—their damned ship was going to be torn up by drunks?

Just then the cabin door was flung open and a fireplug-shaped figure with a nose that resembled a summer squash mashed between two wide-opened Jerry Colonna eyes stomped in.

"Shit, shit, shit, *shit!*" the figure bawled, slinging its fatigue cap with a gold second lieutenant's bar onto a pile of gear already lying on the bottom bunk. The epithets continued to fill the air like a fog.

"What's *your* problem, Sharkey?" Kahn said nonchalantly, his back still toward the figure, which was now standing squarely in the center of the cabin, meaty hands jammed on its hips.

"Guess what," the figure demanded violently.

"What?"

"Kennemer's going around with a list from the Old Man. It's the duty."

"Yeah?"

"Guess what."

"Damn, Sharkey, I don't know. What?"

"Guess what I am for the next month."

"How the hell should I know? Tell me."

"The goddamned Laundry Officer."

"You're what?" Kahn said, the beginnings of a snicker welling up from his stomach and spreading along his high cheekbones into a grin.

"Laundry—fuckin' Laundry! Two thousand goddamn grunts gotta have their laundry done and Patch's put my ass in charge of it."

"You mean you have to do their laundry for them?" Kahn asked casually.

"Oh, for crissakes, Billy; there's a big laundry room down there somewhere and a couple of swabbies to help out; but Brigade's gotta staff the whole thing. Patch's put me in charge."

In mock despair Kahn began to bang his head on his forearm on the porthole opening. "I guess somebody heard all your bellyaching about keeping clean after all."

"Can you imagine having to be in there with all that stinking stuff? And Patch'll be chewin' my butt every time somebody complains they didn't get their skivvies back."

"Poor bastard," Kahn said patronizingly. "Did you get a look at what I'm in for?" he asked, and dreaded the answer.

"Nah, I didn't see the list, but Kennemer'll find you sooner or later."

"It's relentless, ain't it, Sharkey?"

"It sucks," Sharkey said.

ON DECK, a stiff, cold breeze, accelerated by the course of the ship against it, whipped out of the west as the transport rounded the bight and cut into the whitecapped chop of San Francisco Bay, heading directly for the Golden Gate Bridge and the ocean beyond. On the port side, where Kahn and Sharkey had found a place at the rail, the city of San Francisco gleamed in pastels like the City of Oz pasted against the blue afternoon sky.

"I'd of liked to have had time to get out to the fault," Kahn said, flipping a cigarette butt over the side.

"What in hell are you talking about now, Billy?" Sharkey said.

"The San Francisco quake, fool—nineteen oh six. Tore this place apart—started a fire that burned it flat. Where you been, man?"

"Jesus, Kahn, you mean you got fuck-else to worry about than something happened sixty years ago? You better worry about your ass and what's gonna happen to it for the next year, that's what you better start worrying about," Sharkey said.

He glared skeptically at the delicate, aquiline features of the company Exec, thinking that he didn't really look much like an Infantry officer; that his lean, freckled frame would probably have been better off in the Finance Corps or Quartermaster, bent over a desk figuring on paper, instead of being second in command of a hundred fifty riflemen headed into jungle combat. It was a sheer stroke of luck that Kahn had been born a year earlier than he, and consequently graduated a year earlier, and therefore outranked him, even though he had gone to the Academy and Kahn was a product of ROTC. It wasn't that Sharkey minded it; it was just that he thought they ought to leave the fighting up to professionals and let the others push paper.

"Nah, seriously, a whole new theory of earthquakes came out of the San Andreas thing," Kahn said, "'Elastic rebound.' The outcroppings are exposed right there."

"Christ, Kahn, you shoulda been in the damned Engineers with all that geology stuff—they coulda got more outta you than they did at Benning."

"I wish to hell I *had* been in Engineers," Kahn said. "I was almost in the Finance Corps."

The bridge was passing overhead, and for a moment his mind wandered back to the ancient geology amphitheater and musty labs at Florida State University and the countless hours he's spent trying to comprehend the forces that created and maintain this planet, and it came to him suddenly and with wry satisfaction that this expedition was simply another clot of man-made stupidity that would scarcely be remembered in the far-distant future of the world. If people then thought about it at all—assuming there would be people and assuming also that they would be thinking—they would see it merely as a tiny spot in backtime, far removed from themselves and whatever they were presently doing. And as far as Billy Kahn's part was concerned, they more than likely would not remember that at all—in the far-distant future of the world.

"Uh-oh," said Sharkey, peering down the line of men leaning against the rail. From this angle, Sharkey's nose reminded Kahn of a banana.

Captain Kennemer, Four/Seven's Adjutant, a clipboard in hand, was approaching, searching the faces for the ones he sought. He spotted Kahn and Sharkey before they could turn around.

"Ah, Kahn, my man, I've been looking for you,"

Kennemer said in the insipid gung-ho way he said everything these days. Kahn had noticed the change in Kennemer ever since Brigade had gotten its marching orders. Before, he had merely been a pain in the ass. Now he was a royal pain in the ass.

He loves this, Kahn thought, looking down at Kennemer's spitshined combat boots. Damned war lover—out for an oak leaf so he can retire and sit on his can somewhere and draw six hundred a month for the rest of his life.

In the meantime, Kennemer was a royal pain in the ass.

"Got a job for you, Kahn," Kennemer said.

"Sorry—the doctor advised me to spend my time playing shuffleboard. I'm up in First Class, you know."

"Don't be a wiseass, Kahn. We're all going to have to pull extra duty because the Old Man's in charge of troops till we get across, did you know that? You know General Butterworth and Headquarters Company went ahead— they're all flying over so they can set things up for us when we get there. The Old Man is senior colonel aboard and he wants Four/Seven's officers to help him out. I've already told Sharkey here what he's got to do."

"I know. He's going to be the navigator," Kahn said unenthusiastically. Kennemer ignored the comment.

"Well, let's see—yeah, Kahn...Kahn...he's got you down for"—a toothy grin spread across Kennemer's pudgy face—"'rumors control.'"

"Say for what?" Kahn asked, squinting at Kennemer.

"Rumors Control Officer. Gotta have somebody to check out the rumors—you know about that—like we did it back at Bragg. Division thinks it keeps the EMs happier if they have somewhere to go to ask somebody official about the rumors—there's more rumors going around here than flies in a shithouse. Hell, I heard we been diverted to the South of France just an hour ago," Kennemer said, winking at Sharkey. "You might check that one out first."

"But what in hell do I do—how do I find out the truth myself? Nobody tells me anything."

"That's your problem, Kahn. Just sit tight—there'll be

an officers' call in an hour; you can find out all about it then," Kennemer said, bouncing off to find another unsuspecting victim.

"I don't believe it. I don't believe it," said Kahn. Sharkey was near hysterics, pounding at the rail with his fist. "This isn't happening," Kahn said. "He's gotta be some kind of nut."

"Heard any good rumors lately?" Sharkey said, breaking again into fits of laughter.

"Shit on rumors—I don't stop em, I start em," Kahn declared sourly. He lit another cigarette and leaned back on the rail, watching the great city of San Francisco disappear forever around a bend as the ship pounded into the blue waters of the Pacific.

"I sure wish I could have taken a look at that fault," he said dejectedly.

"There's a rumor the war's been postponed for inclement weather—mind checking it out?" Sharkey said, breaking up one more time.

6

IN LESS than an hour, the transport was out of the choppy bay, swaying softly on the Pacific swells, bringing on the first wave of seasickness. Many affected by it went below to their bunks, and those who had to wait their turn at the bunks went inside to the enlisted men's lounges or the ship's library, believing this would abate the queasiness. Naturally, it made it worse. Soon nearly twenty percent of the men were ill, and a long line had formed outside sick bay, where corpsmen were dispensing Dramamine tablets.

At the height of it all, the voice of Captain Kennemer blared over the ship's loudspeaker, beginning, "*Now hear this*," and then ticking off the order in which chow would be served. This was received with a flood of horrible profanity from those who were ill, and prompted a further announcement by Kennemer, after a short wait while he sought advice from the Navy officers who had been standing by. Conspicuously missing from this second announcement was the "Now hear this," which Kennemer dropped after noticing titters from the Navy men.

"Ah—ah—it has come to our attention that some people are feeling the effects of seasickness. These people should get the seasick pills from the dispensary immediately and they should refrain from eating chow. The Navy advises us that seasickness is common for the first few hours on the ship but that it will go away in a short period of time.

"The Navy also advises us that anyone who is feeling sick should go out on the deck and not stay below. The Navy also requests that anyone having to throw up please do so in the garbage pails provided on the decks and in the living quarters and they ask that no one throw up over the rail so as not to get the sides of the ship dirty. Thank you."

"That sonofabitch," said Pfc. Madman Muntz, who had been casting about for a quarter of an hour for a good place to heave.

"So that's what the brown shit is on the side of this tub," he said, addressing an enormous black soldier squatting against the superstructure and obviously trying hard not to think of water or ships or anything associated with them.

"What's wrong with you, Carruthers? You don't like the ocean?" Muntz said mockingly.

Carruthers only looked up and around weakly.

"Ah, it'll go away; everybody gets it first time out," said Muntz, profoundly grateful that he was at least in good enough shape to sound authoritative about it.

BY THEN some of those who were not sick were starting to sit down in the mess hall, a huge damp room with long rows of tables end to end. Filipino mess stewards, dressed in white jackets, served the men their food, balancing trays with half a dozen plastic plates on them as though they had been born to walk like marionettes across the swaying floor. To Army men, unaccustomed to being served seated, it seemed a rare treat that they were being catered to this way—almost like a football team before the game, steak and baked potatoes, an offering to the brave. It never occurred to them that the Navy simply didn't trust soldiers walking around with trays full of food on rolling ships at sea. Furthermore, while none of them had actually anticipated steak and baked potatoes, neither were they expecting the kind of meal they received, and their momentary gratitude quickly changed to anger and then despair as the plates were set down.

"Lookit this shit—what the hell is it?" DiGeorgio said, springing back from a heap of gray goo with orange bits of carrots suspended near its surface.

"Who the hell knows what it is?" said Spudhead Miter, poking at the substance with a spoon.

"It's swill," Crump said sadly.

THE MEN picked through the chow as best they could. The only thing most of them could eat was the lukewarm canned pear that had been plopped into a section of their divided plates. It was a disappointing glimpse into their prospects for the next several weeks.

Most of them had never been on an ocean voyage before, and the truth was, they found it a little bit exciting—although they would never have admitted this to one another.

KAHN, WHO had not been affected by the seasickness, had just finished a reasonably civilized meal in the officers' mess. The same Filipino stewards had laid out generous helpings of roast beef, mashed potatoes and gravy, green peas and tossed salad, served on white china—or at least, white crockery—plates on large round tables with white tablecloths. There was ice cream for dessert and iced tea to drink, or milk if you requested it.

Captain Thurlo, Bravo Company's Commander, had taken to his bunk at the first signs of the seasickness, and

when Kahn looked in on him earlier, Thurlo was in such a
state that he did not make sense. The little that could be
gotten out of him was that he wanted Kahn, as Executive
Officer, to run things until he got better, so Kahn had
called a meeting of platoon leaders and told Sergeant
Trunk to have the sergeants there too, at nineteen
hundred hours in his cabin, to make sure things were
going smoothly.

In the meantime, he decided to take a look around the
ship, and staggered off in the sway like a drunken man,
hoping that as time went by he would develop a better pair
of sea legs. The bow was dipping and rising into a golden
Pacific sunset, magnificently illuminated by a bank of
low-hanging gray clouds just above the horizon. It made
Kahn wish plaintively that he had joined the Navy.

THE COASTLINE had long since disappeared from sight,
and the swells had a grayish hue from the angle of the sun.
Kahn was wondering, looking at them, just what he
would find if he could explore the bottom of the ocean
they were passing over right now. He figured the ship
must be somewhere near the edge of the continental shelf,
which could account for these big rollers they were
experiencing—millions of tons of water traveling thousands of miles to pile up against a six-hundred-foot
undersea slope.

Beyond this, the ocean floor dropped down more than
a mile, to the hazy world of the *abyssal* zone, which he had
always called *abysmal*, although actually it was not
abysmal, because it had a bottom of sorts, but then
beyond this the ocean sometimes dropped off again, to
terrific *deeps* which, if they were not literally abysmal,
were at least the closest thing on earth to it, and were
certainly dismal, down seven or eight miles beneath the
surface, where no ray of sunshine could ever penetrate—a
place so hostile to life that nothing except the most bizarre
and primitive organisms could ever exist there.

Watching the huge swells, Kahn mused over what
effects the ship might have down in those deeps as it
passed over them, if such effects could be recorded. It was

an interesting proposition, but given the depth and density of the water and its meager propensity for carrying sound and shock waves, he concluded that the waves would spread out progressively from their source and be totally absorbed before they ever reached the bottom of the deeps. This phenomenon he jokingly named the "Dismal Deeps Effect," and he decided to tuck it away in his memory in case his geology career ever led him into oceanography, which was unlikely—but even if it didn't, it was still an interesting postulation, given his newfound conviction that even with the most sophisticated seismic devices known to man, the passing of the transport over such a chasm would probably have no effect whatsoever.

7

IN THE bow of the ship, Major Richard Arlo Dunn, Signal Corps, was fiddling with his transoceanic radio, trying to locate a certain California station he knew was carrying the Dodgers baseball game. Once he thought he had it, faintly, but then some earthly interference injected itself, and he continued vainly to twist the dial and turn the radio on top of the big ventilator where he had set it down.

This was Dunn's third crossing. The first, in nineteen forty-three, had taken him to New Georgia, in the Solomon Islands, where he received a field commission from buck sergeant to second lieutenant. The second, in nineteen fifty-one, took him to Korea as a captain in the Signal Corps.

This would be his final tour.

He had not succeeded in making the promotion list three consecutive times and was due to be separated within the year. But it really did not matter to Dunn; his life had already fallen apart years earlier, at Mannheim. He wondered now, softly, as he turned the dials, what life would have been like had he gone to work in his father's little radio shop, or to college—where he might have won a football scholarship. . . . But then the war had come, and afterward, with the commission, the Army had seemed like a good career . . . and then he had gotten married— but something had gone wrong with that too. . . .

HE GAVE up on the radio and squinted out toward the fiery sun, which was precisely tangent to the horizon, almost as if it had been brought down in the lens of a sextant. The ocean waves marched by like giant tombstones—at least, that was the way he saw them—and the tombstones reminded him of that day three weeks ago in his little house at Fort Bragg and his German wife, Maria. It had been the Fourth of July, and he had been drinking gin since noon.

Maria made the first one for him, a gin and tonic, but after that he was on his own. He had given up adding a twist of lime after the second, and by the third, the ratio of gin to tonic grew to two to one, and when he finally ran out of tonic he settled for what he called his "very dry martini."

"Is there anything from the mail?" Maria asked, standing in the bedroom doorway in her slip.

"I haven't opened it yet," he said, picking up the half-dozen letters from an end table.

The heat was unbearable. That was why he drank, he decided. Even in their little air-conditioned house on post, the heat closed in on Dunn in a fierce, evil way, driving him first to thirst, then to drink, and then to more drink until the heat and the thirst and the drink finally blended into a warm, soggy mush in his mind. The heat and the drinking—it had been that way for weeks, but the heat really didn't matter until he came home because there were so many other things he hated about his work.

"Please don't drink any more, darling. You know we have to be at the club. Why don't you start dressing?" she said.

"I'd rather open the mail."

She came up behind him and rubbed the back of his head. "Richard, please, we must not be late. Why don't you take a nice shower now?"

"I don't feel like it right now. I'll take one...in a minute. I want to read the mail."

"I must finish getting dressed," she said, drawing her hand tenderly across his shoulder as she pulled away. He looked through the venetian blinds across Ste.-Mère-Église Drive to the field of low scrub brush shimmering in the North Carolina heat. Fourth of July, he thought—the last Fourth of July they would spend together in this house. The Army would permit her to live here while he was gone, but when he returned, if he returned, he would have to move, and he would be "Mister" Dunn, not Major Dunn, or even Captain Dunn. Not even Sergeant Dunn or Private Dunn. Mister Dunn. He wondered if she would understand.

She was so young, and she'd married him in better times, when he was an up-and-coming officer; when it had all been ahead of him. He should have been a colonel by now—maybe a full colonel—but then there had been Mannheim and the board of inquiry...Oh, what the hell, he thought. He picked up the stack of mail and began sorting it.

He went through the bills first—God, that was one thing she'd learned from six years in America: charge accounts. There was Robinson's and Sears and Oinebachs'...

"Oinebachs'—Maria, have you charged something at Oinebachs'?"

"That pretty flowered dress—the one I wore last week—you liked it so much," she said, "that was Oinebachs'—I told you, don't you remember?" she called from the bedroom.

"Oh," he mumbled. It came back to him—the dress she'd worn the night he'd made a fool of himself at the officers' club. The night he'd gotten drunk and told everyone again what had happened—anyone who'd listen. He had started with the ones at the table...

"Darling, please come and dress now," she said. He could see her brushing her short blond hair at the mirror. She was so young, so full, so beautiful, so much stronger than he was....

HE OPENED each envelope with a letter opener, carefully—a habit he'd acquired years before. One was addressed to him personally, by hand, and he couldn't imagine whom it was from.

"DEATH," the letter said in large bold type, "IS SOMETHING WE AVOID DISCUSSING." He read on.

> Sometimes, we feel if it is not mentioned, it will be less of a reality. This, unfortunately, is just not true.
>
> We have long been indoctrinated to prepare for certain possibilities: accidents, extended illness, buying a home, providing an education for our children.
>
> Yet the inevitability of death is often overlooked in our preparation.

He read on.

> You may have drawn a will. You may have life insurance. You may have spiritual coverage to face death.
>
> But have you selected a burial place?

"Darling, you must come dress," she said. "Please don't have another drink."

"Yes, yes, I'm coming," he said.

> As difficult as it may be to think of death, foresight in the selection of cemetery space can save your family a great deal of anguish later. Not only is the family relieved of a major decision at a time when emotional pressures are already excessive, but foresight is also helpful financially.

"Richard, *please*. Don't just sit there. We must be at the club," she called.

He had a vision of her that night at the club—such easy prey for colonels and captains. She had danced and danced, leaving him to deal with the dowdy, sour wife of Major Jacobs. But she was having such fun, it made him feel good just to watch her. Then, when she hadn't returned, he had slipped into moroseness, and when Major Jacobs' wife asked if anything was wrong, he had begun telling her about Mannheim. By the time Maria got back to the table, he was too far gone to stop.

Maria came into the room again. "We must leave by four-thirty," she said. "You can't just sit there and read."

"Future care of the space and grounds of the cemetery which you select is of special importance," the letter said.

He started at the top again. "DEATH IS A SUBJECT WE AVOID DISCUSSING." He sighed and rubbed the back of his neck. It felt numb.

Maybe, he thought, they're right. He had never really thought much about his own funeral before. It had not concerned him because the Army promised to take care of it for him, so long as he remained in the Army. They would plant him with honors in a nice casket with a flag draped on top in a quiet military burial ground, cared for as long as there was an Army of the United States. But within a year, he wasn't going to be in the Army and he would have to attend to his own burial, or at least, make sure it would come off without hitches.

That would be a wry irony—no hitches at his own funeral.

All his life he had tried to bring things off without hitches, but somehow it had never worked out that way. The ideas were good, but in the end he usually bungled them—or let them be bungled for him. Just last week the Supply people had screwed up his requisition forms, and his ass had been chewed royally by the colonel when they'd run out of fresh radio batteries on a field exercise....And then there had been Mannheim....

"DEATH IS A SUBJECT WE AVOID DISCUSS-ING." He had never contemplated his own death before except in the most abstract ways. But now, for the first time in years, there was a possibility he would die—a very slight possibility, but a possibility nevertheless. In two weeks, the Infantry brigade he was assigned to would be leaving. In the Infantry a certain amount of death was inevitable.

"Richard, if you don't begin to get ready now I am going on to the club without you," Maria said sharply. "We cannot keep everyone waiting."

"Come in here for a minute," he said.

He handed her the letter.

"I want you to know that I am going to buy a plot from these people."

"What?" she said. "What people?"

"They're selling plots at a cemetery."

"Yes, I can see that, but ... Oh, Richard, please come and dress."

"I will, damn it, but I want you to know so that if something happens to me I want to be buried there."

"Oh, darling, nothing is going to happen. Are you thinking something is going to happen to you?" She ran her fingers through his gray hair.

"Just in case it does," he said. "I want to be buried there—in this cemetery. I *don't* want to be buried in an Army cemetery—will you remember that?"

"But Richard, what are you saying? Nothing is going to happen to you. I know it."

"Goddamn it, Maria, it might—don't you understand that? Don't you understand Mostellar probably wants to kill me off—that he's going to give me every shit detail in the book? That's a real live war over there now, you know," he said harshly, shaking her hand from his head.

"Oh, darling, why do you think these things? You are only torturing yourself."

"Because it's true, that's why."

"How do you think that?" she asked.

"Because he knows—about Mannheim. Don't you understand I know what he thinks?" He put his head in his hands.

"Darling, you've been drinking. None of this is true.

Colonel Mostellar likes you. He told me that himself."

"No, it's you he likes," Dunn said.

"That is ridiculous," she said impatiently.

"Like hell."

She knelt in front of him, but he would not look straight into her face.

"Richard," she said softly, "you must stop talking about it. Mannheim was long ago, in the past. You have got to stop telling everyone about it. Nobody cares about it. You're only making it worse."

"It can't be any worse than it is," he said.

FAR BELOW, Dunn could hear the prow growling through the seas and see the V-shaped spray of white foam across the darkening waters. The rushing sound, the boiling foam brought it back again. Eight years, but not a week went by... Mannheim...

They had been fording the Neckar during a field exercise in a cold, blue-white German winter.

He had been in charge of a Signal section assigned to lay wire across the river. They had given him a pontoon boat, but the river was running high and the boat, even with an outboard motor, had been pulled downstream into snags. He turned back to shore and ordered half the men out of the boat to lighten it, then sent it back across again. He himself had walked back to an outpost to radio Battalion about conditions on the river. When he returned, the men on shore were frantic. The boat had capsized and those in it carried down toward the snags.

All but two of them had drowned.

There had been an inquiry, and the two who didn't drown testified that they had told Dunn they didn't think the boat could make it. There had been some talk of a court-martial, but the incident got no further than the inquiry, and Dunn was let off with a reprimand in his file, which had been read and discussed by promotion boards for eight years, effectively ending his career.

KAHN WAS still standing at the rail, but his ruminations on the Dismal Deeps had been interrupted by the appearance of Sergeant Jelkes, the gaunt, watery-eyed Third Battalion Mess Sergeant for whose daughter Kahn had manifested a serious case of the hots back at Fort Bragg.

It had surprised no one more than Kahn when she agreed to go out with him. Half the Division had tried to date her; and although the word was out that she fucked like a crazed weasel, she remained inviolate behind her checkout counter at the PX. While they watched painfully, she occasionally brushed her long, auburn hair and sometimes even flicked a piece of lint off her big, tight-sweatered breasts.

One day when Kahn was paying his check, almost without thinking he asked if she wanted to go to a movie with him. She didn't even look up. She simply said yes, and gave him her address, throwing him into a reverie of dreams and schemes for the rest of the day.

He was dressing for the date when a First Platoon man arrived at his BOQ with a package from Lieutenants Sharkey and Donovan. Inside he found a white carnation, a jar of Vaseline, a package of chewing gum and a copy of *The Rubáiyát of Omar Khayyám*. He left the package on the bed and finished putting on his Class A greens with the shiny first lieutenant's bars on the shoulders.

When he arrived to pick her up, Kahn was met at the door by Sergeant Jelkes, still wearing soiled work fatigues, and ushered into the tiny living room, where he was introduced to a plumpish Mrs. Jelkes, who had been preparing supper for the rest of her family. The sergeant was polite and solicitous but seemed uncomfortable and nervous, so Kahn tried to make small talk while they waited for his daughter to come out of her room. When she appeared, Kahn felt as though someone had punched him in the stomach with a broomstick. She wore a miniskirt that would have revealed all in a mild breeze. Her tits poked through a tiny yellow sweater like Coke bottles. Sally Jelkes was the vision every man dreams of at least once in his life.

Kahn felt his cheeks burning and turned quickly to say something to the sergeant. It was then that he saw the embarrassment in Jelke's watery eyes.

Instantly, he realized that Jelkes knew exactly why he was there.

Because evidently, Sergeant Jelkes had been through this many times before. Jelkes knew he had not come to take his daughter on a proper date—to the officers' club, or to a restaurant. Jelkes knew that what Kahn had in mind was a grab-ass session in his car or in his BOQ room—these things were clear in the sergeant's eyes. Furthermore, Kahn suspected that Jelkes knew Kahn realized this, which made it all the more embarrassing.

When Jelkes had approached him just now at the rail, in his nervous, solicitous way, Kahn was polite and inquired about how he was doing, but did not spend much time talking and was glad to see him go. He did not like to be reminded about that night with Sally Jelkes, and was glad, too, that the sergeant hadn't brought it up.

AFTERWARD, KAHN moved off the rail, feeling a little steadier on his feet. He had been watching for signs of seasickness, but he still felt fine. Nearing the bow, he saw Major Dunn, the Brigade Signal Liaison Officer, bent over his radio, his ear close to the speaker.

Kahn liked the major because he was one of the few field-grade officers he felt comfortable around. He didn't know him well, but had spoken to him a few times in the mess, and he'd seemed pleasant and eager to talk. And yet he had the reputation of a loner who preferred to eat by himself rather than with the other officers of his grade. There had been speculation among some of the lieutenants and captains that because Dunn was still a major at his age, somewhere along the line he must have committed a terrible sin.

"Hello, Major," Kahn said.

Dunn looked up from the radio, "Oh, hi, Kahn, How's it going—you all squared away?"

"I suppose so. The CO's down sick, so I'm stuck with the duty."

"Seasick?"

Kahn nodded.

"How about you?"

"Not yet."

"Ever been on a boat before?"

"Nope."

"You'll be all right," Dunn said cheerfully, "This is my third trip over. Got seasick as hell the first time."

"Was that the Big War?" Kahn asked.

"Yep. Left right out of that same dock."

"No kidding! You a second looey then?"

"Nope—corporal. I got a third stripe on New Georgia, and a month later they gave me a field commission. Guess they ran out of people to give them to. How about you—you Regular Army?"

"Oh, no," Kahn said, "ROTC. Just doing my time. I was working on a Ph.D. in Geology when they cancelled my extension."

"Geology, huh? How come you're not in Engineers?"

"Beats me. I was in the damned Finance Corps until the red flag went up. Then they changed me—changed all of us—to combat branches before we went active."

"Yep," Dunn said understandingly, "they have a way of doing that."

"What really pisses me off," Kahn continued, "is I could have been in Germany right now if I hadn't asked to be deferred for a year."

"Germany?" Dunn said. He squinted out over the water.

"You bet. There was a slot open for a Brigade Finance Officer at Mannheim. Can you imagine what that would have been like?"

"I think so," Dunn said. The wind was whipping in his gray hair. Here in the bow, softly dipping and rising in giant swells, they were as alone as two men crossing the ocean in a balloon.

"Were you ever there?" Kahn asked.

"Yes," the major said, "I was."

"I bet it was nice, wasn't it?"

The old major still gazed toward the faint light in the west, all that remained this day of the orange Pacific sun.

"Yes, it was very lovely," he said. "It was the prettiest place I've ever been."

8

IT WAS just past 10 P.M., and the transport knifed relentlessly through the blackness, occasionally wallowing in a trough. Her big engines hummed. After trying the knob once, Lieutenant Brill let himself into Sergeant Trunk's cabin without knocking or announcing himself, and the six men crouched forward over the gray-painted metal floor looked up at once. Beneath one of the bunks was a half-empty bottle of vodka only partly concealed by the legs of Buck Sergeant Groutman, a squad leader in Brill's own platoon. Beside each of the men was a pile of dollar bills.

"Well, hello, Lieutenant Brill," Trunk said—politely,

but not rising or showing any other sign of deference; much in the way a police desk sergeant might react at the appearance before him of an expensively dressed lawyer.

"So, you guys having a little game here, huh, Sergeant Trunk?" Brill said nastily, shoving his hands into his pockets and walking across the cabin to an empty place on a bunk.

"Ohh . . . wellll . . . Lieutenant—we was just discussing what we gonna do with the men tomorrow. You know how it is—gotta plan ahead," Trunk said drily.

The other sergeants shifted in their places and coughed.

Trunk didn't really like Lieutenant Brill. He thought he was crazy and consequently unpredictable, which was worse. The other officers in the company didn't care much for him either, which Trunk knew because he sometimes heard them talking about Brill behind his back. Lieutenant Sharkey, whom everybody liked, had once called Brill "deranged" after he made Hepplewhite, the Company Clerk, run three miles in full pack and weapon for spitting in ranks.

Trunk remembered that day—it was 90 degrees and Hepplewhite had nearly died of exhaustion. Brill had personally followed behind him in his own car—down the streets of Fort Bragg—yelling at him whenever he slowed down.

First, that wasn't an officer's job, and second, that wasn't the way things were done around here—not Trunk's way; the punishment should always fit the crime was his way.

Brill was always telling people about how tough it was in military school. Well, shit on military school, this was the goddamned United States Army, and that wasn't the way things were done here. He had tried gently explaining this to Brill afterward.

"That's what *I'm* here for, sir—to take care of problems like this," But Brill had brushed him off. "Sergeant, what you should have done was stopped that fucker before he spit. After he did it, that's where I step in. His ass won't do it again, I'll bet."

Trunk had never forgotten that conversation.

"I thought you guys might be shooting dice and drinking down here, Sergeant. Did you know that gambling ain't permitted on this ship?" Brill said, testing the charade further.

"Why, sir, I'm surprised at you for thinkin that of us." Trunk said. "Matter of fact, we *was* rolling some dice—but just to see which one of us is going to lead the company in the calisthenics in the morning; we do it all the time—but not gambling, Lieutenant," Trunk said.

The sergeants nodded their heads in mock agreement.

"Well, Sergeant, that sounds like a good way of doing things—sort of democratic, you know. You mind if I sit in a while just to see how it works?" Brill said.

"Why, okay, sir, if you want to. Now, one of the things we do in this little game is to sweeten the pot some while we're deciding who's gonna lead the calisthenics—you don't mind if we do that, do you?" Trunk replied.

"Not if you let me sweeten it some myself," Brill said.

"Of course, sir, you being an officer and all, we couldn't deny you that."

"What's the ante—dollar?"

"A greener to you, Lieutenant," Trunk said.

THEY DRANK and gambled until nearly 2 A.M., and in the end Brill was relieved of his money. Trunk had never seen a worse crapshooter than Brill—he was so bad he didn't even know how to roll the dice, and often as not they wound up under a bunk, so that everyone would have to crawl under it to get a look at the lie.

But Brill was having a grand time with the sergeants, most of them ten years older than himself, sharing their whiskey and stories as though he had forgotten that he was an officer and that they were of a different class. But neither Trunk nor the others had forgotten this, because it was something a man did not forget in the Army. His station. Occasionally there was a misfit of some kind, like Crump's hermaphrodite human or the three-titted woman, born out of place so they couldn't help it; or other freaks of nature, like the orphaned rabbit raised by a bitch hound, so it didn't know what it was and thought it was something else. Maybe that was where Brill fitted in; Trunk didn't know. What he did know was that Brill should have been taught these things at officers' school: that you ought to leave sergeants alone, and that a man was entitled to his privacy. Brill, he thought, wouldn't even be a Pfc. in this outfit if he hadn't of been a officer.

THEY CONTINUED gambling for a while after Brill staggered off, until Trunk decided to call it a night. As they were leaving, Sergeant Groutman thumbed through his winnings.

"The old lieutenant really throws it around, huh, Top?" Groutman said.

Trunk liked Groutman even less than he liked Brill. In fact, he thought he was crazier than Brill, but he'd let him into the game anyway because they needed another player.

"Screw it, Groutman. He don't belong in here any more than them shitheads in troop bay do. Let him play up on officers' deck if he wants."

"Shit, Top, ol' Brill's all right. He must be—'cause them other fucking officers won't have nothing much to do with him."

"Hell, man," Trunk said, "don't you think I know that. That's *his* problem. I don't need no damned nutty lieutenants hanging around here—it ain't natural."

"Aw, Top, the lieutenant ain't nutty. I know him. He just likes to think he's tough, that's all."

Trunk sat on his bunk and began unlacing his boots. "The hell he ain't nutty—you remember what he did to Hepplewhite that day. I thought the poor bastard was gonna have sunstroke. He could of, too."

A sneer crossed Groutman's pudgy face.

"Hepplewhite deserved it. Besides, you ain't seen anybody spitting in ranks after that, did you?"

"Ain't that the point, Groutman," Trunk said. "The point is, *I* should of been the one to take care of that. It ain't dignified for officers to go driving down the street chasing after men."

"What ain't dignified?" Groutman exclaimed. "Since

when you worrying about officers being dignified?"

"I'm not talking about officers, damn it. I'm talking about noncoms," Trunk barked. "What ain't *dignified* is for people to see officers dealing out Company punishment. Makes it look like we can't do it ourselves."

Groutman stuffed a wad of bills into his pocket. "Well, I tell you what, Top, I kind of like old Lieutenant Brill—'cause I know what makes him *tick*."

"Listen, Groutman, you got a lot to learn about this man's army—and one of 'em is, don't fool around with officers," Trunk said, shooing Groutman out the door.

9

PRIVATE FIRST Class Harold N. Miter, Jr., was lying in his bunk playing his harmonica and waiting for the shift buzzer that would send him out onto the decks again. He finished the last bars of "My Old Kentucky Home" and slapped the instrument against his palm, remembering the trouble it had caused him, but still not feeling sorry he'd bought it—though at the time he would gladly have traded it back for the nine dollars and ninety-five cents he had paid for it at a pawnshop just off post.

It had been a sweltering North Carolina night and the barracks had been almost deserted, since almost everyone had gone away on leave for the Fourth of July weekend.

He had spread out all the money from his wallet and pockets and beneath the stark overhead light counted exactly thirty-two dollars and eighty-six cents—all he had in the world until the next payday.

Outside in the dusty Company street there was the glow of a cigarette and the sound of men laughing. He put the money away and stepped into the freshly starched khaki trousers he had laid out, wishing he'd been born a millionaire and silently cursing himself for buying the harmonica when Julie was going to arrive at the bus station in half an hour and he didn't know if the thirty-two dollars was enough to pay for her room and for supper and breakfast in the morning too.

He also remembered finding the letter in his footlocker when he opened it to replace his shoeshine polish, and taking it out and reading it again. Outside, someone must have told a dirty joke, because several men started laughing hysterically.

A large brown sweat stain stretched from "Dear Harold" across the top of the page to the letterhead, which was the great blue seal of the United States Congress.

> I was happy to hear from you last week and I am most encouraged that you are doing well and have been promoted to private first class.

He hated to be called Harold—it sounded pompous and silly. He didn't even mind the rest of the company's calling him "Spudhead," because anything was better than "Harold." Why couldn't his parents have given him a nickname of their own?—a nice one, like "Chipper."

> I do not have to tell you I am pleased to have a son in the service of our country. The news that you are going overseas leaves me with a certain feeling of pride, because you finally seem to have found a place for yourself in our fine Army. Also anxious, for obvious reasons.

Unfortunately, your mother and I are leaving for a three-week fact-finding tour of Eastern Europe, and will not be in Washington during the time you wanted to come home. As you know, I prefer to keep the house empty when your mother and I are away, so it would be best if you remain where you are until we return.

As I understand it, you do not leave until the 26th and we will return on the 22nd. We would like to stop by and see you on our way to the district, so please let me know when it would be convenient for us to arrive.

Your mother sends her love.

Best regards,
Dad
Harold N. Miter
Member of Congress

HNM:sj

Spudhead tucked the letter under some socks at the bottom of the locker. He was disappointed they wouldn't let him come home when he could get his leave, and he was also disappointed that his father had dictated the letter instead of writing it himself. It made him feel like a constituent instead of a son. And he felt funny that some office girl now knew his parents didn't want him in their house while they were away.

Once, when he was home from college, some of his friends had gotten into his father's liquor cabinet and accidentally broken a chair, and since then they hadn't allowed him to stay home unless they were there—but the office girl knew none of this and he wondered what she must have thought.

Spudhead walked to the big mirror by the weapons rack and straightened his shirt.

He wished plaintively his hair hadn't been shaved so close, because it emphasized the size of his head . . . and he wished he were six inches taller and there weren't pockmarks in his face and that he had blue eyes. . . . What he really wished, though he ordinarily avoided thinking it, was that he had been born handsome. It wasn't that Julie cared, because she didn't, but he always felt his father had.

THE COMPANY street had been deserted when Spudhead walked into the soft summer evening across the parade ground, past the infirmary, toward the bus station. Surprisingly, the bus was on time, and Julie was the first one off, lugging her big beat-up suitcase down the steps. She was wearing the pretty flowered dress he'd always liked best, and during those first few minutes he was so thrilled to see her again he felt he was in a dream.

They took a local bus into town to the women's rooming house run by Mrs. Jordan—pronounced Jerden—where he'd rented a room for thirteen dollars. He had wanted to take Julie in a taxi, but he'd worried about the money . . .

He'd also wanted to put her into a proper hotel, where they could spend the night together, but there hadn't been enough for that either, so he'd decided on Mrs. Jordan's because he knew it was neat and clean. There were any number of fleabags in town where they could have gone, but he didn't want it that way with her. They had never made love, though they'd come close a few times, and Spudhead knew she was ready—but he wanted it to be perfect, to happen in a place that was fitting for a nice Midwestern girl.

She snuggled up to him as the bus lurched down Anzio Drive past row after row of wooden barracks and intermittent groups of post housing projects. "You look so healthy," she said. "You look so good."

"How do you like my hiarcut?—It looks funny, huh?" He squeezed her hand, almost petting it.

"Oh, Harold, you look just beautiful; you're the most beautiful man in the world," she said, and for once he didn't mind being called Harold.

THEY STOPPED at the corner near the rooming house and dropped off Julie's bag. They walked down gaudy Fayetteville Main to the Vista-View Italian Restaurant in a motor lodge, where they sat by a window looking out on the pool. The waitress lit the candle in a red bowl between them, and Julie reached over and took Spudhead's hand.

"I love you so much," she said.

"I love you too," he said. "You're beautiful."

She was beautiful, too, he thought. Not pretty, like

some of the girls at the university. Not like the cheerleaders and prom queens and sorority girls. But she *was* beautiful, and as he said it, he realized it was the first time he had ever told her that because up till now he had confused being beautiful with being pretty or being handsome and he knew neither of them would ever be that. But they were terribly in love and it made them beautiful. Perhaps only to each other, but it really didn't matter about anyone else.

They had spaghetti and meatballs with mushrooms and a bottle of red wine by candlelight, and talked about the university and the football team, which might win the conference championship if it got past Notre Dame, and the freshman poetry class where they'd met . . . but after a while Julie grew quiet and began to stare out at the empty motel pool. He sensed what was wrong, because they had been through this before, but he knew she wouldn't let it out unless he brought it up, so he did.

"I'm sorry, darling," she said, "but I'm . . . I'm so afraid . . . I love you so much," she said, looking down into the half-eaten plate of spaghetti as though she were ashamed of herself for saying it.

"It's going to be all right," he said, taking her hand again. "It'll only be for a year, you know; then I'm out, for good. I'll go back and finish school, and we—"

"Oh, damn it," Julie said, and burst into tears.

"It's all right, baby," he said. "It's all right, hear?"

"Can't your father do anything?" She tried to compose herself.

"What do you mean—about what?"

"I mean about getting you out of it. He's a Congressman; he must—"

"Julie, nobody knows about that down here—and I don't want them to, okay?"

"But you could get hurt, don't you know that? You could . . . Oh, damn it," she said, and the tears began again.

"Aren't you afraid?" she asked after a while.

"No," he said.

It was a bald-faced lie.

"But I don't understand," she said. "You mean you haven't told anybody who your father is? They don't even know? Why, they could put you back in the headquarters or something, where it's safer...."

"I just don't want anybody to know, darling—nobody. Do you understand?

"Look, you met my old man. You know how he is. Do you know he even locks the refrigerator when I go home?"

"Locks the... What do you mean?" she said, drying her eyes with the napkin.

"I mean he locks it up at night so I can't get in it and eat anything or drink beer—and he locks the door to the house when he goes to bed and he won't let me have a key."

"A lock on the refrigerator... but why?" She started to laugh.

"Well, he thinks I eat too much—says I get enough at dinner; so he put this goddamned lock on the icebox—he locks it before he goes to bed."

"I don't believe you," she said, bursting into laughter. "A lock on the refrigerator—I've never heard..."

"It's true," he said, laughing too, and for the next several minutes they sat there laughing crazily about a lock on a refrigerator four hundred miles away.

At 1 A.M. he had taken her back to Mrs. Jordan's, just before she locked the doors (proper girls don't stay out past 1 A.M.—that was the rule she had laid down). But he was feeling good, and the wine they had had for dinner hit him hard because he wasn't used to it.

When he arrived at the barracks, there was some sort of party going on out in the parking lot. A dozen or so men were sitting on parked cars or on the ground, drinking beer from several cases iced down in their cardboard cartons. In the middle of this group stood Lieutenants Sharkey and Donovan, both in khakis but stripped to their waists. Sharkey was telling a story, and he interrupted it only long enough to motion Spudhead to the beer cache.

"...So old Donovan here," Sharkey said, "runs into

the goddamn Eighty-second Airborne club, you see—where nobody knows who he is...and the goddamn assholes are lying all over the tables drunker'n goats, right?" There was a chorus of anticipatory laughter. Spudhead opened a beer.

"...And as soon as Donovan hits the door he yells loud as he can, 'When I drink, everybody drinks!' and every asshole in the place runs up to the bar and starts ordering drinks, right?"

Spudhead sat down next to Crump and DiGeorgio, who were enjoying themselves immensely.

"...And Donovan, he orders a drink for himself right off, and drinks it down in a gulp, see, and when he's through he stands back and yells, 'When I pay, everybody pays!' and he throws a buck on the floor and runs out the door—and they're *still looking for him*!" Sharkey was bent over almost double laughing, and there were tears in his eyes. He grabbed Donovan by the shoulder and clanked beer cans with him, and both officers drank deeply, and laughed until they fell down.

This went on for another hour. First Sharkey, then Donovan would recount some escapade, about boxing at West Point or football at Notre Dame, about seducing girls on golf courses or livingroom couches while their parents slept a few feet away. From Crump and DiGeorgio, Spudhead had learned that the two officers had roared into the barracks several hours earlier and rousted out everyone still there. They had formed them up in the Company street and marched them to the parking lot, where the beer was waiting.

At last the beer and the stories petered out and the officers went on their way. Crump, DiGeorgio and Spudhead made their way with the others back to the barracks, Crump and DiGeorgio singing, Spudhead lingering a little behind. Finally Spudhead sat down on a curb and put his head in his hands. It was a few minutes before Crump and DiGeorgio came back and discovered him there, crying softly.

"Hey, what's this?—hey," Crump said. "Hey, what's

wrong, man, you drunk?"

"He's fuckin' stinkin'—lookit him," DiGeorgio said, laughing madly.

"Whataya fuckin' crying about," Crump asked. "Yer girl fuck you over?"

"Nah, nah, just let me be a while...." Spudhead wiped his eyes, looking beyond the dim street lights to the darkened parade ground where they'd spent so many hours in close-order drills and bayonet practice and calisthenics and picking up every scrap of paper and cigarette butt on police detail....

"Hey, say what's wrong, man," Crump said, squatting down in front of Spudhead. "We buddies, ain't we?"

"It's nothing, Crump.... It's just..." He stopped. "I love her so much, and..."

"And what—what in hell is it?" DiGeorgio said.

"Oh, damn, I don't know," Spudhead said. "It's...I don't have any more money.... I wanted to take her to breakfast, you know, and buy her lunch before she has to go back tomorrow, and...I bought that goddamned harmonica, and the dinner cost twelve bucks, and..."

"Well, hell, man," Crump said, "why didn't you say so? We got some money left, haven't we, Dee-Gergio? We got maybe twenty, thirty bucks between us—that'll get you through sure."

"No, no, thanks, I don't—"

"Forchrissakes, Spudhead, don't be an asshole—we'll just lend it to ya till payday," DiGeorgio said.

"O Goddamn-shit-fuck!...Oh, I'm sorry, you guys.... I don't want to...I don't know...I just don't want to go now.... I want to stay here and get married and go back to school and...Fuck the Army...FUCK THE ARMY!—I don't care a shit about the Army—and fuck this war, and—"

"Hey, cool it, man, you gonna wake everybody in the Company up," DiGeorgio said.

"Look here," Crump said, "nobody wants to go over to that thing, but what the hell else we gonna do, huh? We in the damned United States Army, man—we in it now." He stuffed two ten-dollar bills into Spudhead's shirt pocket.

"Come on, now, Spudhead, let's go to bed fore we get ol' Trunk up chewin' our asses," Crump said.

They helped him to his feet, taking him by the elbows and putting their arms around his shoulders.

"Come on, now Spudhead, that's a boy," Crump said. "Everything's gonna look better in the morning."

"Yeah, Spudhead, we gotta war we gonna fight—we need our sleep if we gonna kill gooks," DeGeorgio said.

THE TRANSPORT shift buzzer startled Spudhead out of a half-sleep, and he foggily swung his feet onto the bare metal floor. The harmonica was still in his hand, and he opened his duffel bag and carefully stowed it away. All around him people were stirring, preparing to take their turns up on deck. He thought of Julie and of his father and mother, and wondered what they were doing and if they were thinking of him. He felt a little nauseated, but it wasn't from seasickness; he had felt that way ever since he learned they were going over. He hurried to lace on his boots and get topside. The sea air had been good for the nausea, and this afternoon he might see more dolphins, or a whale.

10

IN SEPARATE auditoriums aboard the transport, two briefings were taking place.

They had been gone five days, and by now most of the men had become more or less acclimated to life at sea. The first wave of seasickness had disappeared by this time, and only those hardest hit, like Captain Thurlo, were still in misery; the rest, while they did not feel particularly good when the ship plowed through an unanticipated series of heavy swells, were able at least to function. The days had broken down to a. boring but predictable regimen: in the mornings, they would eat chow—which rather than improving had become appreciably worse;

there was an hour of calisthenics and laps around the deck; then each company gathered together for instruction: drilling in small-arms assembly, how to avoid getting tropical infections, how to behave toward the South Vietnamese people and how to use the PRC— "prick"—25 radio, over and again until even the dullards and sluggards knew that further repetition was senseless because they had heard it all before.

Whenever these classes ended, the line for the ship's store began forming. As each company was dismissed, at least a third of its number sprinted for the line, or where they thought it was, since they never knew until they saw it how long it would be. Sometimes it was several city blocks long, coiling around the deck like a giant python— hundreds of men in single file, waiting their turn at the tiny counter where they could buy chewing gum and camera film and toilet goods and other little items to make life more bearable. Most precious among these were the candy bars and cigarettes—the cigarettes because men could not live without them, and the candy bars because they could not live with the Navy chow.

The enlisted men were restricted as to how much they could buy at the ship's store at a given time, while officers and senior noncoms had no such quota. As it developed, this quota usually lasted for about two days, after which each man would have to return to the line for more. Since the ship's store was usually open only for half an hour in the early morning and at noon, most of the men in the line did not actually get to buy anything, but they waited there anyway—partly because the sailors who ran the store would sometimes keep it open longer than usual, and partly because they didn't have anything better to do.

This day, however, was different, because whereas before their afternoons had been free, today's briefing had been called in the ship's movie theater—or, more precisely, three assemblies had been called, so as to accommodate all of the men. A briefing was also scheduled for officers in the dining room, and even they had not been told the nature of it but only that they should present themselves with a pencil and pad and be seated by 1400 hours.

*   *   *

THE ROOM fell silent when Colonel Patch entered, a thin
cigar smoldering between his teeth.

"Gentlemen," he said, holding up a sheaf of papers that
had already been passed out to each officer, "our work
has been cut out for us."

At a back table by the dining-hall door, Billy Kahn and
his platoon leaders—Sharkey of First, Brill of Second,
Donovan of Third and Inge of Weapons—were shuffling
through the document, which was titled

INTELLIGENCE SUMMARY
REPUBLIC OF VIETNAM
THE IA DRANG VALLEY CAMPAIGN
ACTIONS IN II CORPS, APRIL–JUNE, 1966

and on which each page was stamped SECRET in bold
red print.

"The shit's hit the fan," Sharkey whispered, saying
what Kahn and most of the rest were privately thinking,
because everybody knew you could get your ass handed to
you in the Ia Drang in a hurry. They had known it all the
way back at Fort Bragg as the first trickle of men returned
from the vanguard of the first wave.

"This is the place—it's the goddamned *place*!" Sharkey
was saying under his breath, jabbing a stubby finger at the
title sheet. "Ohhh, we're up against it now."

Going through Kahn's head was something one of the
newly returned men—a fat, moustachioed helicopter
pilot—had said one night in the officers' club at Bragg:

"Ia Drang—yep, that's a bad, badass place.

"We went in there one afternoon and I never seen such
shit thrown at us, from both sides of the mountains and
below. You get the River Blindness out there—that's what
you get in the Ia Drang Valley."

When they inquired what the River Blindness was, the
fat lieutenant had leaned forward somberly and said
almost in a whisper across a table full of beer bottles, "It's
when you go down to the river and get your *eyes* shot
out," and then had broken into a crazy savage chuckle, in

which he was quickly—if nervously—joined by the other lieutenants who had been listening eagerly to his stories.

Wonderful, Kahn thought darkly—the damned River Blindness.

"YOU WILL remember," Patch was saying, twisting his blond moustache, "that in this operation we will be the pursuers, not the pursued.

"What we will pursue, gentlemen, is asses—North Vietnamese asses and Vietcong asses. These are the same asses the Seventh Cavalry has pursued for exactly one hundred years.

"All of these asses," Patch continued—"Indian asses, Cuban asses, Mexican asses, Japanese asses and Korean asses—have one thing in common, gentlemen: whenever they have been pursued by the Seventh Cavalry, these asses begin to shit, and the Seventh Cavalry has followed the smell and kicked the last remaining ounce of shit out of them.

"And that is what you men are going to do in the Ia Drang Valley," he said, tapping on a copy of the sheaf of papers with a pointer.

"The theory of warfare here, as I have told you before, is just the same as it was when the Seventh Cavalry was fighting Indians—and the Seventh Cavalry was designed to fight Indians." Patch puffed on the cigar.

"Uh-oh, here it comes," Sharkey said, rolling his big eyes toward the ceiling.

"And as all of you know by now, the Seventh Cavalry, with one minor exception, kicked ass on the Indians for nearly fifty years. The results of that effort now live on reservations.

"The only difference is that the bastards you will encounter in the Ia Drang Valley will not be Indians." The Battalion Commander was beaming.

"Jesus fuckin' Christ," Sharkey murmured dejectedly.

"I want you men to take this document back to your cabins and read it carefully. Pay particular attention to the action reports and conclusions, because we're going to discuss each part every day from now on. Your own asses might be saved by somebody else's experience."

"Hey, lookit this shit." Sharkey was punching Kahn on the arm, pointing to a table of figures in the back. "Look at the fucking *casualty* figures."

Two battalions of another division who had been in the Ia Drang had, by their own account, already dispatched some 1,423 North Vietnamese soldiers at a cost to themselves of 231 men killed and 720 wounded.

"Holy Christ," Sharkey said. Studious Lieutenant Inge was studying the document, and the big ex-tackle Donovan was sprawled over the table resting his chin on one hand and scratching his balls with the other.

"The big mistake Colonel Custer made," Patch drowned on, "was underestimating the strength of the enemy at Little Big Horn. We will not have that difficulty, because we have accurate intelligence assessments, extremely good communications and good mobility."

"Lookit *this* . . ." Sharkey nudged Kahn to a paragraph which began: "A majority of the contacts with the enemy have occurred in either jungle or mountainous underbush-type terrain in which visibility is poor."

So THIS was it, Kahn thought: spend a year running around in the deep woods with the River Blindness. The rumors, of course, had been that they were going to the coastal plains, where there were nothing more than a few scraggly VC—certainly not that they were going to be hauled ass out in the jungle damned near to Cambodia to duck with North Vietnamese regulars.

He might have known, being Rumors Control Officer, that the rumor hadn't been any good.

Patch had saved the truth for now, five thousand miles out into the ocean, precisely across the International Date Line, where somehow you were propelled forward a day in time—although in time language, that day was lost to you—except that if you happened to get killed by something like the River Blindness, you would actually get to live a day longer.

If you got killed on Wednesday, for instance, it wouldn't be a lost day at all, because your friends back home would still be living Tuesday while you were getting killed on Wednesday, so in fact it might be better to get killed over here than at home because somehow you got an extra day out of it.

As he listened to Patch's speech, a gloom began to descend on Kahn such as he had never felt before. Not because he was afraid—although he certainly was that—or because he doubted the value of Patch's predictions, which he did, or because he dreaded the rigors of the next year, which he also did. It was none of these; rather, it was the gloom of inevitability about the course his life was taking—or rather, was having imposed on it—and Patch's monolithic predictions, all the inconsequentiality of it, suddenly bore down on him and pressed him down into the Dismal Deeps. . . .

Kahn had always known that someday he must do his part. His father had told him that since childhood—"Every man owes a debt. It must be paid. After that you are free to enjoy what this country has to offer"—and ever since he could remember, Kahn had prepared himself to pay his debt, as though when he had paid it an enormous stone would be lifted off his back and he would be welcomed and congratulated into previously denied regions.

Being a Jew from the South was both a blessing and a curse. For the first few years, except for his family, he had been practically alone in his Jewishness, until just before he entered high school. They had recently moved into the little cul-de-sac by the golf course.

Each year the dozen or so homeowners there erected fancy Christmas decorations on their houses, and people from all over town drove by each night to look at the display. A month before Christmas—and a week after they had moved in—a neighbor came to Kahn's house late in the afternoon. She was in charge of decorations that year and said she needed help.

"We are doing The Twelve Days of Christmas this year," the woman had told his mother. "You will be the Five Gold Rings," she announced. "They're making up the displays in a warehouse downtown.

"I know you and your husband are of the Jewish faith, but this is more than a religious thing," she said. "We have done it for years. Everyone in town expects it. It is a neighborhood thing."

Kahn's mother had listened politely, and when his father came home, she had told him what had happened.

"Sixty-five dollars—for what? Goy decorations?" he cried.

"She says it is not a religious thing," his mother said.

"The hell it's not. Let them have eleven days of Christmas instead—I'm not shelling out for their holiday. What would they do if we asked them to stick a ten-foot candle on their roofs during Passover? They would throw me out the door," he said.

In the end, Five Gold Rings that blinked on and off were installed on the Kahns' roof, but not before bitter argument within the family. "Keep the peace; we've just moved here," his mother said. The passersby oohed and ahhed, and except for an occasional snide comment that the Gold Rings looked as though they belonged outside a pawnshop, the affair by and large had been insignificant—except to young Billy Kahn, who for the first time realized he *was* in fact different from the rest; that he probably *had* to pay that debt to be accepted, the debt of Gold Rings and going out for the football team and joining the Army and now—whether he wished to or not—the debt of killing gooks—or getting killed by gooks in the land of the River Blindness. And later, what then? Was the debt ever to be paid off, as his father had said, or would it hover over him forever, presenting itself for payment, open-ended, in infinite installments throughout his life, administered by some terrible hovering debt bird?

Why did he owe this debt?—and to whom? Was it for being a Jew? Or being a Jew in America? Was it for killing Christ? Was he to be held responsible for *that* by the people who insisted on Gold Rings on top of his home? Was it the reason some girls in high school and college had shunned him, put him off forever with excuses? Was he being blamed as a Christ killer? And if so, would he be redeemed by becoming a gook killer? As if someone would finally say, "Yes, Mr. Kahn, you have paid off your debt for killing the Saviour by killing for your country. You are paid in full; you are free to go."

Well, probably not.

Probably this debt would remain to be administered by the specter of a giant hovering bird, never satiated even after the football, and the gook killing, and whatever came after; which was why, as he heard Patch's speech, the great blanket of gloom had spread itself over Lieutenant Billy Kahn.

"Hey, Billy, lookit this," Sharkey was muttering, nudging Kahn again, pointing to a paragraph which began: "Unlike Viet Cong, the NVA in the Ia Drang region will engage and attack in strength at any time of the day...." Kahn looked at him sourly. "For Godssake, Sharkey," he hissed, "will you keep quiet!"

AT THE same time, in the movie auditorium two decks below, a separate briefing was being conducted for the enlisted men, but the document they were shown was stamped only CONFIDENTIAL and it was much shorter and did not show things like casualty figures or enemy strengths that the officers' report did. But the men felt good afterward because at last the Army had given them a kind of tangible purpose for being here, and they felt a little proud and sort of important that this great army had decided to share its secrets with them and give them a real mission. And because of this, many of the men became more serious during the next few days as they contemplated actually going into combat, and a few of them even took on rough and mean airs.

11

ON THE eleventh day, the sky broke out a thin
ragged gray, and the pallid sun looked as if it would have
preferred to be elsewhere that morning. A heavy swell was
running up from the southwest, taking the transport
abeam and tossing her about just enough to make things
uncomfortable for those who had been teetering on the
edge of seasickness since the first day.

The men were as listless as the weather, lying around
the deck, barely speaking to one another in the clammy
heat that had settled over the ship. A thick mass of clouds
lay on the horizon in the direction in which they were
headed, but no breeze blew. Except for the swell, a sinister

calm prevailed, punctuated only by the throb of the transport's engines.

Spudhead Miter skipped chow and went to the ship's library to see if it had a copy of Hemingway's *A Farewell to Arms*, which he had once started but never finished. He couldn't find it, so he left through an unfamiliar hatchway door located in the rear of the little library compartment. Minutes later, Spudhead found himself in the bowels of the transport.

Past the Navy crew quarters, he went as far as he could go until he was forced to climb down a stairwell even deeper into the ship. Here he was closer to the engines, because he could feel their power vibrating through the steel bulkheads as he passed an open door inside which several sailors in white T-shirts were sitting around a large electric generator drinking coffee. The sailors noticed Spudhead passing by but seemed unmoved by his presence in their domain.

The constant swaying from the swells made Spudhead feel a little nauseated, and sensing that he had gone too far down, he climbed a flight of stairs and went along another corridor and through a hatchway, and then he was alone in a tiny foyer. Suddenly a big metal cover flew up into the air with a rattle that scared Spudhead half out of his wits, and he found himself staring into the scowling face of a sailor standing behind a counter.

"Whatduyawant?" the sailor growled.

"Huh?" Spudhead said, still tingling from fright.

"WHATDUYAWANT—I ain't got all day, bud!" the sailor roared, and then it dawned on Spudhead that he was standing in front of the counter of the ship's store and that outside that door behind him hundreds of men had been waiting in line for God knew how long for it to open and he had somehow found his way in ahead of them.

"Jesus . . . ah, ah," Spudhead said.

"WHAT IN HELL DO YOU WANT, SOLDIER?" The sailor looked frantic by this time. His eyes bugged out of his head. Two other sailors working with their backs toward the counter turned to look.

"Give me a hundred Hershey Almond Bars," Spudhead said weakly, diving for his wallet.

"Box of a hundred—here." The sailor shoved a brown box across the counter without looking at him. "Four bucks," he barked.

Spudhead fled back inside the door through which he had just entered, closing it behind him gently as though it were the gate to Heaven and he did not wish to disturb it. He stole back into the sleeping quarters and stashed the box of Hershey Almonds deep in his duffel bag.

When he returned to the deck, most of the men were still lying or sitting where they had been when he left. The sky had taken on a sickly pinkish tint, and the gray swells had grown ominous. Black smoke from the funnels hung crazily over the transport, settling onto the men in a gloomy kind of pall, but they accepted this without the traditional cursing, because today everyone seemed resigned that his life was to be filled with such indignities.

Several sailors walked down the rail among the men, poking around and fooling with various kinds of gear on the deck. Someone asked the sailors how many days they were from Okinawa.

"Big storm coming," a sailor said, ignoring the question.

Shortly afterward, the afternoon briefings were cancelled and Patch himself got on the loudspeaker to tell the men they were sailing toward some nasty weather. They were instructed to stay in the shelter of the boat deck and not to go outside when the weather got bad. Patch did not go into detail on the storm, which the Navy had already learned about and informed him was a killer typhoon that had wrecked two cities in the Philippines and was now spinning viciously at sea looking for further damage to do, and which the transport was trying desperately to avoid by heading northwest. But it was too late, and the best the Navy was hoping for now was that the transport would hit only the fringe of the storm.

No one actually knew who threw the life ring over, except the man who did it, and he wasn't saying. But if he had been found out he would probably have been torn to pieces by the men themselves, because of the grief it caused.

Patch was on the bridge with the Captain when the signal from the life ring was picked up on the special distress frequency.

"There it is again, Captain," the radio operator said, poking his head out the door of the radio shack.

The Captain immediately dispatched a man to check all the life ring stations on the decks to see if any rings were missing. He seemed clearly annoyed.

"We'd have heard by now if somebody went over. But if some idiot threw that thing in for a joke—and I suspect that's what happened—we're in for trouble, because it has a radio beacon that broadcasts for two hundred miles.

"How long does it last?" Patch asked lamely.

"Five days—a week—who knows? Every damned ship that picks up the signal has to stop and search for four hours. It's the law. We're going to have to turn back and find the sonofabitch," the Captain said. He ordered the transport to come about in a wide circle, and sent two men forward to try to spot the life ring with binoculars.

"It has a strobe light on it, so it shouldn't be too hard to see," the Captain said glumly.

The man who had been sent to check the life-ring stations reported back that a ring was indeed missing from the Number Seven port station. At the Captain's suggestion, Patch had already ordered the troops to form by their bunks for a head count.

It was oppressively hot below, and the heaving of the ship and jammed-up sweaty bodies were taking a toll in seasickness. In fifteen minutes, all companies reported back that all men were present or accounted for. The Navy Captain was getting angrier as the minutes passed.

"What a fool thing to do," he spat. "We're trying to outrun a typhoon here, and some jackass pulls a stunt like this." He looked out toward the gray, lowering weather ahead. "I wish I could lay my hands on him," the Captain said.

Patch knew these comments were for his benefit. Even

though they were not said directly to him, they were obviously meant to chastise him for permitting such vandalism to be carried on by people for whom he was responsible.

"Captain," Patch said, in the awkward silence of the bridge, "I will have the man who did this in less than an hour." He picked up the microphone and ordered an officers' call in the dining room—on the double.

"I WANT," Patch said somberly, "the bastard who is responsible for the life ring. I want his ass in front of me in fifteen minutes. I don't care how you find him, but find him. I simply cannot let this kind of behavior pass." Behind the small, black sunglasses, the colonel's eyes were dark, fathomless tunnels. "Tell them it will go a lot easier on whoever it is if he just comes forward now. But they're going to stand by those bunks down there below until someone does—storm or not; I don't give a damn if it takes all week." He stalked out of the theater, leaving the junior officers on their own.

"Okay, you heard what the man said," Kahn said softly to the cluster of platoon leaders gathered around him. He was in charge again, since Captain Thurlo had taken to his bunk with renewed seasickness at the onset of the storm.

Below, the men had become a confused mob. When Kahn and his cadre entered Bravo Company's sleeping room, they were beseeched for an explanation, because no one had bothered to tell the men that a life ring had been thrown over and what the consequences were. Everyone had been expecting to be told to go back up to the lounges on the boat deck or some place where there was some air, and they were unprepared for the news that they had to remain down here in the heat and pitching.

"I can't promise you anything," Kahn told them, "except if one of you did throw that thing over, it will be a hell of a lot better on you and on your buddies if you tell us about it now."

There was silence, as the men looked at one another and clung to their bunks to keep steady on their feet.

"Did any of you men throw over the life ring?" Kahn asked again. "If you did, say so now."

Again silence.

Sergeant Trunk, who had been leaning against the bulkhead with his arms folded, surveyed the men, "If one of you shitheads did this and you don't step your ass up here now, your ass is grass."

No one stepped forward.

"Well, that's it," Kahn said. "They'll have to stay here until we get back, Sergeant Trunk. You stay too. See if you can find out anything else."

As he turned to go, a weak voice called out behind Kahn, "Suh..." and he turned to the anxious faces.

"Some of us sick; can't we go up to where there's some fresh air?" It was Carruthers, the black soldier who had had the seasickness ever since coming aboard.

"The colonel says you're to stay here until somebody confesses about this. But I think he'll probably let you go up topside shortly—that's all I can say," Kahn said, leaving the men in a state of anger and confusion. Trunk was at his heels.

"Lieutenant," Trunk said, "any of our people didn't have nothing to do with this. I know it—there ain't one of them shitheads got guts enough to throw that thing over. Anyway, I'd know if they did it."

"Listen, you know it, and I know it, but the goddamned Old Man doesn't. And he's in charge. I'll do the best I can do."

"Right, sir," Trunk said.

The officers had been waiting in the dining room for ten minutes when Patch came in again, striding up to the stage in long steps and turning with his hands on his hips; the dark glasses were pushed up on top of his head.

"Well, have you anything to tell me?"

There was silence, the same kind of silence as in the troop quarters. Each of the officers felt slightly guilty himself; there was a kind of collective guilt that had been passed down to them through Patch, then through them to the men, so that even if no one ever stepped forward to admit the transgression, all of the officers and men aboard would have shared in the guilt of it anyway, partially expiating the deed through collective penitence.

"Damn it, I meant what I said," Patch said firmly. "I *WANT* the bastard who did this. I want that man, and I want him now. I know it's rough down there, but they're just going to have to stomach it until somebody steps up. The Navy is furious. Now I want you to go back down there and I want each company commander to personally ask every man in his company—individually—if he was the one, and if not, if he knows anything about it. Somebody threw that thing overboard, and it was somebody in this brigade. Be back here in half an hour." Once again Patch stalked out of the room.

When Kahn and his entourage returned to the troop quarters, they were not expecting the wretchedness that greeted them.

Vomit was spilling out from beneath the locked compartment doors where some of the men had gone to throw up in the little water fountains near the doors because they couldn't make it to the head and they didn't want to throw up on the floor. Other men became ill seeing this, and when Kahn and the rest entered, it was plain in their bewildered faces that Bravo Company did not understand this kind of treatment at all, because if they had understood it, they would have been angry and cursing and resigned to it, no matter how bad. But this was something they had not experienced before, and they were hurt by it and becoming desperate because the storm was heaving the ship about violently now and it was frightening them.

IN THE corridor outside the troop quarters, Kahn and his officers and Sergeant Trunk formed in a small, tight huddle.

"This is crazy," Kahn said. "I think...I mean, somebody ought to stand up and tell him what's going on down here."

"It ain't going to be me," Lieutenant Inge said soberly. "He's mighty pissed off."

"Well, somebody ought to," Kahn said, looking at the others.

Sharkey was leaning against the bulkhead looking slightly green. "I don't know, Billy—maybe Inge is right. It probably wouldn't do anything but get you in trouble."

"Shit on it," Brill said. "They're no worse off down here than anywhere else. Besides, if they had any sense they'd find the fucker who did it themselves."

"Oh, hell, Brill," Donovan said. "You think the guy's gonna speak up now? They'd kill his ass." He turned to the others. "Billy's right. Somebody ought to just stand up and tell the Old Man what's going on down here. Hell, I'll do it myself if nobody else will."

"No," Kahn said, "I'll do it. If we all agree. I'll say that the Company asked me to speak for them, or something like that."

The transport took a long, sighing list to port, then righted itself while they clung to the bulkhead.

"All right, Sharkey, how about you?" Kahn said.

"Okay—but I think it's a mistake," Sharkey said weakly.

"Inge?"

The studious Weapons Platoon leader studied his feet. "I don't think so. I think it wouldn't do any good."

Kahn shrugged.

"Brill?"

"Nah—I say let 'em sweat it out. Why not?"

"Donovan?"

"Yeah—I said it before."

"Trunk?"

"Yessir, I think so definitely, sir. Them men are hurtin' in there. Definitely."

Kahn searched their faces. "Okay, that's it. I'll just say it's what *I* think, so nobody else'll catch any shit."

For a third time the officers seated themselves in the dining hall, and a third time they were ordered below to personally interrogate the men.

By this time, even the most hard-bitten among them felt awkward facing his men. Patch had not been in the

troop hold himself, but had sent his aide Captain
Kennemer down to assess the situation. Kennemer had
reported back that while it was uncomfortable, it was
probably better than letting the men roam about the ship
in this kind of weather.

Patch was beginning to get bad vibrations, yet he was
committed and felt he had to see the matter through. He
hadn't wanted to consign the men to those steaming bunk
rooms, but they had to understand that when they pulled
a dumb stunt like this, all would suffer unless the guilty
man was apprehended. Then because of the theory of
collective guilt, that man would do the suffering for all of
them, rather than the other way around, the way it was
now.

Somebody was lying, but Patch knew these were pretty
good boys. He loved them, and he wished the one who
had done it would come forward so that he could let the
rest go.

The Bravo Company staff sat in the back of the room
listening to Patch's stern admonitions. When he paused
for a moment, Kahn started to get to his feet, but a thick,
meaty hand caught him by the elbow and pulled him back
into his seat.

"No, Billy, I changed my mind. Don't do it," Sharkey
whispered. "I know this bastard. He'll have your ass for
this, and it's not going to do any good anyway. I know."
Kahn glared at Sharkey. He could see West Point written
all over his face. But he did not try to rise.

MOST OF the men were sitting down when Kahn and his
officers and noncoms returned. Sergeant Trunk himself
had been heaving into a waste can in his cabin, and not a
man in the outfit wasn't feeling sick to some degree. Kahn
looked at the white faces before him, heads turned up,
those who were able, searching for a sign of relief. He was
still looking at them, saying nothing, for there was
nothing for him to say, when the first tremendous sea
lifted the transport on her end and smashed her into a
hollow of roiling water as if she were a toy. All of them
simply stared at each other in disbelief as the whole ship

rose up, quivered for a moment, and then whapped down into the chasm as though she had sailed over a waterfall. For an instant, the electrical system wavered, flickering the bunk-room lights. Then the second sea caught them head on with all the unbridled fury of the first, as though the water outside were some savage living thing trying to get at them through the steel hull.

No one said anything during those brief seconds. Everyone, Kahn included, felt panic in his chest, a panic at their utter helplessness before a thing so fierce that for the moment it made every past horror of their lives seem trivial. This was not something that could be dealt with; it was a cataclysmic tumult, as old as time itself, moving against them without reason or mercy.

Gear flew about in the room, and then there was great confusion and swearing. A man who had been trying to vomit behind his bunk threw up on other men. Another, grimacing in pain, had been hit in the shins by a rifle rack that had broken loose.

"Trunk—Trunk, goddamn it," Kahn cried, "get these men to hell topside to the lounges. Now." Kahn heard himself talking, but was surprised, even in this, that he had said what he had said.

The other company officers in the room saw men moving, but they weren't sure what was happening. A lieutenant from Alpha Company cried out across the room, "Do we move them?" and Donovan, showing great ingenuity and foresight, bellowed back, "I think there was something over the loudspeaker. Didn't you hear something like that?"

"I think I heard it too," Sharkey yelled loudly.

Now there was no stopping them. Everyone began clambering into the corridors and up the metal staircases into the troop lounges and dining room, where the big windows gave at least a breath of air. But when they saw what was happening outside the ship, it was enough to make some of them wish they had stayed in their hellhole.

The seas were as high as buildings and utterly chaotic. The air was filled with white spume, and the rain was driving against the porthole glass at a crazy sidewise angle. The transport had changed course slightly, so as to take the seas just abeam of her port side, but the wind seemed determined to shove her bow further down. Each time the ship crashed into a hollow, they could hear her big propellers churning out of the water with an unsteady, unsettling throb.

"Hey, Kahn, you want me to get my men together in here?—they're just sort of all over the boat deck now." It was Brill, and Kahn, who was holding on to a pipe-line support in the dining room watching the storm through a porthole, had to think for a second because the question Brill asked was a reasonable one.

"Damn, I don't know . . . yeah, I guess we should, Brill. Why don't you get them together in here. If you see Inge and Sharkey and Donovan, tell them to get everybody in here over in a corner or something; just keep them together till we find out what's going to happen next."

Kahn really didn't know what to do. He was more worried about his own ass for letting the men out of the troop room. He was hoping Patch might not find out he had started it, because of the confusion of the storm. But if he did, Kahn figured he might just as well have been the one who threw over the life ring, because Patch was going to deal with him worse, if he found out he had let the men go up.

In a corner of the room Major Greaves, the Brigade Chaplain, was praying with a half-dozen men. Kahn could not hear what was being said, but the sober expression on the minister's swarthy face made him feel uncomfortable, because it looked to Kahn as though the chaplain were calling in all his chits with the Big Fellow upstairs.

Brill was herding men into the dining room and making them sit at tables by the door. He came up to Kahn again.

"Hey, Kahn, you want me to send somebody back downstairs to guard the gear they left out? They didn't have time to put it in the lockers before we got out of there. They're afraid somebody might start stealing stuff."

Kahn looked at Brill as if he had just asked permission

to start a bingo game. "Christ, Brill, I don't give a damn. Do whatever you want to do."

Jesus—how do you like that? Kahn thought. Worrying about some fucking cameras and stuff—as though people didn't have anything better to do in a typhoon than sneak around and steal things. Brill actually seemed to be enjoying this. He didn't have enough sense to be scared; he didn't share the terrible aloneness on this puny man-made cork. Brill really was strange, Kahn thought, but so far, thank God, he had been harmless—though there was an undercurrent of meanness in Brill that Kahn didn't like at all.

And Brill, who had just assigned Pfc. Peach to go down and guard the Bravo Company gear, was thinking that Kahn was probably going to fold up the first time they stepped into some shit, because anyone so obviously rattled by a storm was going to be petrified in a firefight. So what, with the damned storm? You couldn't avoid it—and you couldn't attack it—and you sure as hell couldn't go persuade it. So either it was going to get you or it wasn't. In fact, Brill was exhilarated by the storm. He didn't share Kahn's sense of aloneness in it, because he had been alone most of his life—at home, and when his parents divorced, and in the military schools, and every place else—including the Army. The storm actually made him feel less lonely, because the cattle he was in charge of were looking for someone to turn to, and whom else would they turn to but their leader, Brill? Instead of making him feel alone, the storm gave Brill something to do, and in a strange way, he was grateful for it—as he was for the war they would soon be in.

THE FIRST Patch heard of Four/Seven's release was when Captain Kennemer panted up to the bridge with the news that "some people have gone up to the lounges." Asking around, Kennemer had been informed that the Navy had moved them up because of the violence of the storm, and this news came as a great relief to Patch, because it had been getting plainer and plainer that his measures hadn't worked. If the storm conveniently let him off the hook, it was indeed a fortuitous happening, no matter how bad it was otherwise.

Patch instructed Kennemer to tell the officers that the men were to remain in the lounges and dining areas inside, and under no circumstances roam around the ship— which was about as necessary as telling even the dumbest among them not to stand in front of a howitzer when it was being fired. Patch himself decided to remain on the bridge with the Navy in case his assistance or authority was needed in dealing with any problems.

The Captain was feverishly engrossed in controlling the ship, and nodded without expression when the call came in about Pfc. Peach, the man Brill had sent down to guard the gear in the troop quarters. He turned to Patch, who had been sitting pinch-faced on a small bench on the bridge, feeling a little queasy.

"Colonel, one of your men has been hurt. You might want to check on him. He fell down the Number Two companionway just midships outside the enlisted men's lounge."

"Thank you, I certainly will. Is he hurt bad?" Patch said.

"We don't know yet. The doctor is with him now—he may have broken something. He shouldn't have been on those stairs in this weather."

Again Patch shrank from the disapproval of the Navy Captain. Resentfully, he started down the corridor toward the stairwell.

By the time he got to the spot, they already had Pfc. Peach strapped to a litter. He was a smallish pale man anyway, and the shock of his shattered hipbone had turned his face a ghostly white. He was bleating like a sheep. They had cut away his trousers and undershorts, and Patch could see the jagged white bone of the upper thing sticking out through the skin.

A sailor in a white corpsman's jacket was holding a bloody compress just below the wound as they carried Peach away, still bleating, toward the sick bay. Patch and the doctor walked behind.

"I'm gonna have to do something pretty quick about that boy, but I don't know how in hell I can, with the ship bouncing like this—I just don't know," the doctor said.

"We've got our own medical people aboard," Patch said, "Can we give you any help?"

"Yes, tell your orthopedics man I can use him—or at least, he can use me . . . and for God's sake, try to keep these men out of the companionways in this weather," the doctor said, turning into the sick bay, leaving Patch alone in the writhing corridor with only the straining cantations of the engines and the distant bleating of Private Peach.

Damn that little bastard, Patch thought, looking after the doctor. Damn his nerve to say that to me. Patch couldn't figure out at the moment whom he was most mad at, the insolent Navy doctor or Peach, who had caused the trouble in the first place. What a fool thing to try to negotiate stairs in this stuff. And now one less man in the field . . . Besides, Patch thought, he was probably going down there to steal something anyway.

THE FIERCEST part of the typhoon raged through the night and into early morning. There were times everyone truly believed the ship could not stand being dropped into the hollow of another swell. Each time the transport's bow would rise, its cargo of frightened men would brace themselves, stomach muscles tightened, jaws clamped together, chins lowered to their chests as if they were passengers on an elevator broken free in its shaft. Chaplain Greaves continued to pray, and his congregation increased tenfold.

Each time the sea caught the ship up on a crest, there was a terrifying tremor from stem to stern, as though the transport were a patient in an asylum being given an electric-shock treatment, followed by a roller-coaster plunge down into the water with a terrific roar. This went on for hours, but none of the men ever got used to it, and many of their secret prayers dealt only with the hope of getting through the night, leaving the rest to further Providence.

A SICKLY pink dawn brought a slackened wind and an end to the rain, and it signaled that the typhoon itself had passed over. What remained was mountainous seas, higher even than the bridge of the ship, some of them cresting with a great rush of foam and roar of dirty-looking water. But the swells had a definite direction now instead of the chaotic raving at the height of the storm, which gave a predictable and less frightening cadence to the rising and falling of the ship. On the slopes of some of these waves, exhausted gulls and terns bobbed crazily, flying up at the onslaught of a breaker and screeching mightily before settling back down again.

By late afternoon the seas had subsided a little, and down in sick bay the doctor informed the bridge that they were ready to reassemble Pfc. Peach's smashed bones. This was necessary so that the helmsman would turn the transport directly into the waves—a course that would increase the pounding, but negate the rolling which had prevented them from operating up to now. As the ship began to pound once more, the relief of the men cooped up in the lounges and dining room turned to anguish, since again no one had bothered to tell them the reason, and they were not enough attuned to the sea to figure it out for themselves.

Earlier, Kahn allowed some of Bravo Company to return to the troop quarters to look after their personal belongings. They reported back that several packs and duffel bags had been gone through and things had been stolen out of them.

12

SHARKEY SIGNED himself up for the boxing matches mainly to get out of his confinement to quarters following the laundry incident.

"You're crazy. You'll get brained. Don't do it," Kahn told him, secretly wishing he'd had the guts to sign up too.

"I'm so ugly already it wouldn't make any difference. Anyway, I gotta get outta here. I'm getting cabin fever," Sharkey replied.

Four days after the storm, Crump had been leaning on the fantail watching a school of flying fish when he noticed the laundry floating past. At first he thought he was merely observing the flotsam of the sea: green, shapeless blobs streaming past the stern and into the wake. Then he looked down and saw a huge stream of water gushing from a port in the ship's side about ten feet above the waterline, every so often disgorging a fatigue blouse or trousers. Crump looked back curiously along this line of clothing, which stretched as far as he could see into the distance. At that moment a sailor happened to be walking past, and Crump stopped him and pointed out the phenomenon. The sailor's face contorted into a mask of horror, and he dashed off down the deck and disappeared into a companionway. A few minutes later the flow of water and laundry ceased.

No one, not even Sharkey, ever found out how it had happened, but someone had apparently turned a wrong valve, causing the laundry of four hundred men to be systematically discharged into the Pacific. The transport steamed on, however, a destination to reach and a schedule to meet, clothing or no.

Sharkey had been nowhere near the laundry when the mishap occurred, but this did not stop Patch from punishing him, since the Laundry Officer was theoretically responsible for everything that went on in his domain. He was confined to quarters for a week except to attend to his laundry duties and eat meals. After four days of lying in his bunk, Sharkey would have done almost anything to get out.

"I want to see the fights anyway," Sharkey said good-naturedly. "I'll have a firsthand view."

"You're nuts," Kahn told him again. "Don't do it."

Actually, Kahn had relished Sharkey's misfortune in the laundry room as poetic justice for the prank he and Donovan had played on him a week earlier. The two of them had conspired to start a rumor that a sub was following the transport, and within a few hours this news had become so rampant that Kahn, as Rumors Control Officer, was forced to embarrass himself by checking it out with the Navy command and make a contrary announcement over the loudspeaker system.

A week after the storm the sea swells were still running high, but Patch, sensing that the troops were restless and needed to blow off steam, announced there would be fights. On his crossing to Korea, there had also been fights, but Patch had not entered them because he hadn't liked the possibility of getting knocked on his ass by an enlisted man. Now, fifteen years later, he wasn't troubled by it, having decided it was a healthy thing occasionally for his officers and men to engage in this kind of athletic activity. At first he toyed with the idea of restricting the bouts to enlisted men, but later decided to open them to anyone willing to fight.

The response was overwhelming—over a hundred men signed up, and the sergeants in charge spent the afternoon weighing and pairing them against each other. A ring had been erected on the bridge deck, consisting of thick canvas mats laid on the deck and wrapped around four corner posts. Sharkey was fighting light-heavyweight class—in the eighth three-round bout—against a man from Charlie Company, Second Battalion. Sharkey was five feet eight inches tall, one hundred eighty pounds, and had done some boxing at West Point, but seemed like a man better designed to withstand punches than to deliver them, considering his limited reach. He ate lunch but decided against the evening meal, not wishing to hamper himself with a full belly in case he took a punch there.

CRUMP HAD also decided to enter the boxing matches, to the astonishment of DiGeorgio and Spudhead and others who believed it would have been the farthest thing from his mind. When they were convinced he wasn't kidding, they offered to second for him, and after a while everyone became caught up in the idea of the fights.

Crump hadn't been in a real fight since the time he'd whipped another boy in a Mississippi schoolyard. His mother had been furious because he'd torn his trousers at the knees, and he had spent the next weekend at home, picking pole beans. Somewhere in the back of Crump's bony head, he knew his decision to fight had something to do with his mother's not being here now to get after him, because all of his life, even before his father had died, she had gotten after him for something. The only thing

Crump missed about his mother was her cooking. Ever since he could remember, Crump had looked forward to supper at home, with pot roasts and mashed potatoes, home-grown peas and beans, hams, yams, corned beef and cabbage, pork chops with applesauce and beets, and corn bread and fried chicken—she as big as a house, he as thin as a rail. Crump couldn't keep his mind off it, this great mother-cooking, and whenever he got a chance he talked about it as though this would make his dream meals come true.

Like Sharkey, Crump eschewed the evening meal, but only because the food he was offered was so unappetizing; the thought of being hit in the gut never entered his mind. He was lying on his bunk talking to Spudhead and DiGeorgio about the fight when he lapsed into recollections of one of his favorite suppers.

"You guys'd think you was in heaven if you could of sat down to that ol' leg of pork and mashed potatoes—real mashed potatoes with little pieces of hard potatoes in them—and gravy and good hot turnips and greens—and iced tea..."

"For crissake, Crump, you wannta fucking drive us all nuts with your mother's cooking?" DiGeorgio said, "You're gonna get in the ring with some big gorilla and all's you can talk about is your mother's goddamned cooking."

"Everybody's mother's cooking is good, Crump. You better start worrying about that fight tonight," Spudhead said.

"You don't have to worry about that fight—I'll take care of it all right—but damn, I sure wish I had a real dinner before," Crump said. "How da they think you can eat the stuff they give you on this boat? It ain't fit for dogs," he said disgustedly.

"Christ, Crump, will you stop talking about food? You orta go out and punch that bag on deck or somethin'," DiGeorgio said.

"You wanna Hershey Almond Bar?" Spudhead said, his voice almost in a whisper.

"*What*? Whatd'jew say?" Crump sat up on the bed.

"He says you want a Hershey Almond Bar, for crissakes—you got one, Spudhead?" DiGeorgio asked, leaning closer.

"Sure I got one."

"Bullshit—they been outta 'em for a week. They said we won't be able to get any till Okinawa; said some cocksucker bought em all."

"I got one. I got more than one," Spudhead said.

"You lyin', you bastard," DiGeorgio said.

"In my bag—I got hundreds of 'em."

"You lying bastard," DiGeorgio said.

"I ain't lying—I got em in my bag," Spudhead said.

"Let's see," Crump said, "Common, let's see."

Spudhead sidled over to his bunk, reached beneath it and fiddled with the combination lock of his duffel bag. He reached down inside as though he were going to come out with precious jewels. Carefully drawing out the Hershey Almond Bar and sticking it up the sleeve of his fatigue blouse, he walked back and let it slide out onto the wool blanket just beside Crump's thigh.

"Jesus—you really do," DiGeorgio said. "You been saving it?"

"I told you, I got plenty of 'em—didn't I?" Spudhead said.

Crump ripped open the wrapper and devoured the contents like a starved wolf. He even ate part of the paper when it wouldn't come unstuck from the chocolate.

"Christ, Crump, you gonna choke yourself to death," DiGeorgio said.

Spudhead returned to the duffel bag for more bars—one each for the three of them this time,

"Hey, thanks, Spudhead," DiGeorgio said.

"Yeah, thanks, Spudhead," said Crump, wolfing down the second bar as he had the first.

"I thought if you ate something it might help you tonight," Spudhead said.

"It might help," Crump said.

DiGeorgio ate half of his candy, folded the paper

around the rest and stuck it into his blouse pocket.

"Just stop talking about your mother's cooking, for crissakes," he said.

THE MATCHES began after evening chow. It was impossible for more than a handful of people to see much of the fighting, because the makeshift ring was surrounded by such a crush of bodies the only thing a man in the back could see was the tops of the fighters' heads and an occasional aerial blow. It resembled a barracks brawl more than a boxing match.

Brill had been waiting nearly half an hour for the fights to get under way. It amused him that these stupid bastards about to be thrown into a real war would willingly smash each other around for fun—but as long as they would, he was going to enjoy the spectacle. He particularly liked the prospect of seeing officers get the shit kicked out of them by enlisted men, since most of them had made it a point to be so snotty to him.

Standing beside him was Sergeant Groutman, with whom he had shot craps in Trunk's cabin that night. Brill both liked Groutman and also feared him a little. Something about him reminded Brill of himself; yet Groutman, with his big, hulking frame, was more self-assured, and this made Brill uncomfortable. Groutman went out of his way to be friendly, but it seemed to Brill that he wished to manipulate him in some way. Groutman was very much excited over the prospect of the fights and craned forward over people's shoulders, his eyes wild; grinning; yelling, though he didn't seem to care who won.

The first fight was a total mismatch. If it proved anything, it was that people who have had some experience boxing can beat the hell out of people who haven't, this revelation becoming apparent in less than a minute as a thick-necked soldier from Guam destroyed a taller Italian boy from New York in a welterweight bout. After a flurry of fists had pounded his head and body for a few seconds, and the Guamanian stepped back for a breather, the Italian signaled he wanted no more by raising a hand into the air. The second fight was a replay of the first, ending when one of the combatants signified he had no interest in continuing. Between bouts, there was gregarious talking and joking and sizing up of the fighters.

As the names and outfits of the fighters were announced, there would be loud cheering and encouragement from their respective units, but when the bout actually started the yelling became chaotic, as though the men had turned into a crazed mob raging for blood and vengeance. When the third fight ended with a blow delivered so hard the defeated man seemed as though he had been lifted with a kick, everyone felt he had gotten to see what he had come for. And yet amid all the hollering and yelling, there seemed to be a collective nervous tremor, as though the defeated fighter had somehow paid dues for all of them.

Crump and Sharkey fought bouts that were back to back, and Bravo Company nudged as close to the ring as they could. Crump drew a solidly built blond boy who looked as if he had arrived that very afternoon from a Southern California beach, surfboard and all. His honest deep-blue eyes blinked rhythmically as he relaxed against the corner ropes, looking away from the opposite corner where Crump was, into the sea of excited faces around him, but with an expression that suggested he might have preferred to look beyond the crowd, at the real sea instead.

Crump, on the other hand, looked steadfastly at his opponent while DiGeorgio massaged his long neck and bony back.

The brass Navy bell rang, and Crump started slowly toward the beautiful blond boy in an odd, contorted stance, as though he were trying to crouch and stand up at the same time. The blond soldier fought a bobbing and weaving game, and he hit Crump first with a fast combination of left jabs, ducking beneath Crump's defenses. Crump kept pursuing him, and each time he got close the blond hit a couple of licks, then spun away. Crump hadn't thrown a solid blow, and it was already the middle of the round. His nose was starting to bleed a little, and the blood was trickling down to his lower lip, coloring his mouth guard.

Kahn had drunk half a pint of Scotch in his cabin after chow, and was smoking a cigarette in the back of the crowd. He couldn't see much of what was going on, except for Crump's tall head encased in his own gloves, and Kahn thought it strange that Crump should carry his gloves so high. In front of him, Trunk was yelling with the rest.

"Attaboy, Crump, attaboy—kill the bastard. He can't hurt you, Crump—he's a pussy. Go after him, Crump."

Trunk was proud of Crump for getting into the fights. Crump was one of those he never could really figure out, and this surprised him even more than the time Crump had won the mile run on Company field day. Trunk knew the boy was kind of dumb, but you never could tell about these big dumb farm boys. Trunk had first taken notice of Crump after a fifteen-mile forced march when Crump had been brought to him by Sergeant Groutman, the squad leader, who found him in barracks hobbling around in shower shoes with blisters that looked as if they had been branded into the skin with molten-hot quarters. How the hell Crump had ever gotten through that march—and never complained—Trunk never knew; but when they sent him off to sick call, Trunk had said to Groutman, "That shithead's either awful dumb or awful tough," and Groutman had laughed his crazy, snarling laugh and said, "Naw, the fucker's just scared shitless to speak up."

IT WAS the middle of round two before Crump landed a blow to the blond boy. By this time he had been pummeled savagely, and the skin around his face was mottled with reddish-purple marks, as though he were the victim of an awful birthmark. The blond had delivered another vicious combination when Crump heaved out with a right cross that knocked the blond back a couple of steps and stood him up straight. He dropped his guard just a bit, and looked at Crump as if he were hurt: not physically hurt, exactly, but as if his feelings had been hurt because Crump had hit him so hard. His honest blue eyes began blinking rhythmically again, and he lay back in a kind of rocking motion with his knees slightly bent and his muscular tanned arms pressed close in to his sides. Crump bore in and let loose with a powerful left hook that the blond boy took on his glove before backing away, as though he now respected Crump more for the earlier punch.

Kahn was hollering for Crump with the rest. It was obvious everyone felt Crump had the upper hand now, that he had taken the blond boy's best shots and remained unfazed, that it was only a matter of time. Kahn watched, fascinated. Crump—big, muscular, sinewy Crump; lean and mean Crump, the way the Army wanted them. Crump, pressing forward, taking the shots but holding on, the big punch, the killer blow—that was it.

Let the blond boy jab away, he wouldn't last long; he was in a ring twenty feet square and there was no place to hide. And Crump was there, always coming at him, pressing, his big dumb face looking at him, the way the Seventh Cavalry would be, the way Bravo Company would be, pressing in on the gooks, the big punch, moving forward, mortars behind, big artillery behind that, pounding away, a line of Crumps charging in the way Patch had said, colors flying, moving forward, "Garryowen," crush them with the power, the power that stemmed from the almighty righteousness, brushing aside gnatlike punches from blond beach boys or yellow-faced Communist zips.

SHIT! That was what all this was about; what they never really taught you, but you realized it on your own, without benefit of the "school solution": that only America had the Crump-like boring-in stamina to see it through to the end ... and he, Lieutenant Billy Kahn, and the Crumps and all the rest of them were going now to prove that point!

Kahn's head was raised up now, craning to see what was going on in the ring, his heart beating faster at his revelations, and also from the half a pint of Scotch, and he was only faintly aware of the frantic screaming of the crowd.

The blond soldier was circling Crump like a rock 'n' roll dancer, and Crump was standing bewildered in the center of the ring, his head guarded in the same funny way as before, the big gloves about his ears. The blond boy was hitting him at will, moving to his left, circling, lashing out against the side of the head, so that the right side of Crump's face looked as if it had been horribly sunburned. Somehow the second round had passed without Kahn's noticing it, and he wasn't sure how far into the final round this was.

The referee, a sergeant from Third Battalion, was standing in a corner enjoying the spectacle. He had not stopped the fight because Crump was still on his feet and also because nobody had asked him to.

Occasionally, he cast a questioning look at Crump's corner, where DiGeorgio was crouched frantically yelling at Crump to turn head on to the blond. But Crump, either because he could not hear or because he did not care at this point, simply continued, backing around half a step slower than the honest-eyed blond boy, taking a merciless beating on the right side of his face.

The blond, moving rhythmically, began circling in the opposite direction, hitting Crump whenever he felt like it, knocking him back against the ropes. The crowd was at the height of its passion. It was certain Crump was a goner.

DiGeorgio couldn't stand it anymore. He suddenly leaped inside the ring, throwing himself between the blond and Crump, his hands high in the air with the sign of surrender, and it was over. The blond boy backed off astonished, still blinking, and the referee helped DiGeorgio and Spudhead get Crump from the ring. The crowd noise settled to a murmur.

Kahn felt let down. Not so much because of Crump, although he was sorry for him, but because his whiskey had failed him. There had been that fleeting moment when everything seemed to come into focus; but like

Crump, it was gone now, and Kahn was simply a man alone in a crowd.

ON TOP of part of the ship's superstructure, behind the ring, sat gray-haired Major Dunn, his transoceanic radio beside him. Kahn considered going over and talking to him, but before he could make a decision, there was a loud roar from the crowd as Sharkey stepped into the ring, a green Army towel around his shoulders.

In the opposite corner, a tall, powerful-looking black soldier was making his way between the ropes, wearing nothing but his fatigue trousers, not even sneakers. Kahn hadn't realized Sharkey was fighting next, and he suddenly felt uncomfortable that he hadn't offered to second for him, although Donovan had. The black man was at least six inches taller than Sharkey, and he looked as if he could move.

Sharkey could have been chiseled from a sack of cement hardened in the rain. His squat body was so compact it looked as if it had been somehow jammed together from a previously respectable height into this badgerlike mass of muscle now unveiling itself from the towel.

Brill, who had been looking forward to this all night, was reminded of the running arguments he had had years ago over whether or not a lion could beat a tiger. This was going to be good, he thought. Brill suspected Sharkey was going to get the hell beat out of him, which was appealing because it would probably take some of the cockiness out of the sonofabitch. Even though Sharkey was one of the few officers in the company who took the time to talk to him, Brill sensed a kind of condescending attitude. There were times when he liked Sharkey and times when he didn't, and this was one of the times he didn't.

Groutman was still beside him, grinning wildly and offering to take "the nigger" for five dollars. Brill declined the bet, but would have taken it if he could have had the nigger himself.

When the bell rang, Brill worked his way forward, but he was not yelling with the rest of the crowd.

Sharkey met the black soldier in the center of the ring, his chin tucked down on his chest and his elbows bent in tight on either side of his navel. The black man struck out with a frantic combination of punches that rained down on Sharkey's gloves, leaving him virtually untouched, and he waded inside the taller fighter, pounding away at his belly, while the black man, unable to move away, slapped him frantically on the back of the head. The referee stepped in and Sharkey backed off, his chin still down on his chest, looking up at his towering opponent like a man peering over spectacles. The black fighter's stomach had changed color, to a sort of deep purple, and he stopped some of his dancing and began to backpedal as Sharkey stalked him around the ring.

Kahn was yelling with the rest for Sharkey, who seemed to be almost everybody's favorite except those from the black fighter's own company.

"Knock him on his ass, sir; that's it, sir; don't let him get away," Trunk was bawling, jabbing Kahn in the ribs.

"You see that Lieutenant Sharkey, sir? He's gonna whip that motha—that motha can't hit him," Trunk shouted.

The yelling around Kahn became a dull roar from far away. Curiously, what he sensed most of all was the gentle rolling of the transport, imperceptible to most, because everyone now compensated automatically by shifting his weight every so often from one leg to the other. The sky above was very starry, but the ocean around them was black so that it was impossible to see even the water as the ship churned on into the night.

Kahn had a feeling, although he had absolutely no scientific way of knowing it, that the transport was now passing over one of the deeps; that five or six miles below them the bottom of the sea was so still, so dark, so calm, except for the jagged mountains and rocks and crevices where nothing lived—nothing with a brain, anyway—that it was totally unknowing of what was happening here above: that a transport ship with two thousand armed men, some of them fighting each other on the deck, was making its way across the chasm.

*　　*　　*

THE RIGHT hand that stopped Sharkey was so fast only those on the edge of the ring saw it. It lashed out from the tall black soldier like a striking cobra, popping Sharkey's head back the way a man's head will pop back when it strikes a branch in the dark. It took several seconds for Sharkey to realize what had happened, that behind his mouth guard his front teeth had been smashed in by that mighty punch, which somehow was timed, accidentally or on purpose—he would never know—with the rolling of the ship. Both fighters backed away from each other for a moment; then Sharkey looked at the referee and raised his hand high into the air, realizing he could not continue this way.

As the referee held up the black man's hand in victory, Kahn shoved his way toward Sharkey, who was stepping through the ropes, dripping blood from his broken mouth. He'd tongued the mouthpiece out gently, wondering what would come out with it. He knew that feeling no pain meant nothing now. The pain would come later, late at night in his bunk, and in the morning, but it was something he didn't worry about now at all. His gums felt numb and mushy, as though they did not belong in his mouth anymore. Kahn caught Sharkey by the arm, and he and Donovan helped him through the crowd without speaking, and took him to his cabin.

Sharkey plopped down on his bottom bunk, his chest still heaving from the fight. Kahn went to his locker, took out a three-quarters-full bottle of the Cutty Sark and poured a glass full of it. Sharkey sat up and drank half of it down straightaway without a breather. He leaned on the edge of his bunk for nearly a minute, saying nothing, then went into the head and puked. Kahn was tempted to go in after him, but he sensed Sharkey preferred being alone. When he came out, Sharkey sat down on the bunk and drank the rest of the Scotch in a gulp, swishing it in his bloody mouth an instant before swallowing, bulging out his big brown Jerry Colonna eyes and giving out a deep ahhhhhhhh.

"I shuda ta done difs," he said with difficulty, feeling the smashed teeth tenderly with his fingers. "I mighta known thif would happen."

"Ah, hell what can you know—it was a lucky punch," Kahn said.

"Yeaf, lucky—look at my goddamn teef. I gotta gem to a dentist," Sharkey said painfully.

"We'll be in Okinawa in two days. Take the bottle; just keep pouring, Shark," Kahn said. "It was a lucky punch."

THE OVERHEAD lights in the nearly deserted troop quarters below cast a stark shadow on the floor of the dejected head of Pfc. Homer Crump, buried in his sore, bony hands. DiGeorgio and Spudhead Miter sat silently while Crump gurgled pathetic little sobs from the edge of his bunk.

"I tried," Crump whimpered. "I couldn't of tried no more."

DiGeorgio and Spudhead exchanged glances each time Crump spoke. They had said everything they could say to make him feel better, and all they could do now was just stay here with him, although DiGeorgio thought he'd try one more time because he couldn't stand to see Crump cry this way.

"You did the best you could, Crump; nobody could do no better than you did. The bastard was a pro—he wasn't no amateur."

"He wasn't no pro—he just whipped me. He did it fair and square," Crump said, raising his head for a moment.

"Look, Crump, you could've gotten him if they'd been more time—you had him in the second," Spudhead injected.

"Shit, I know I did, I had him in the second. He was running away—he knew he was beat."

"Hey, Crump, you want a Hershey Almond?" Spudhead asked brightly.

"Hell, no, I don't want it. I don't want nothin'. Just leave me be," he said.

"Look, Crump," DiGeorgio said, "We gonna be fighting fuckin' gooks in a few weeks. Them bastards are gonna get their asses kicked. They gonna get the shit kicked outta them by us three. Screw that fight. In two weeks you'll be laughing about that fuckin' fight."

"Hell I will, hell I will," Crump said. "I shoulda beat him, beat him bad. I never lost a fight before—never lost one."

"You didn't lose that one tonight; you woulda had him down if there'd been more time," Spudhead said.

"Yeah, that's right," DiGeorgio said. "If there'd been more time."

13

THE TRANSPORT slipped in before dawn to the concrete piers of the Army Ship Terminal at Okinawa. Everyone knew they were to arrive sometime this day, but it didn't occur to the men as they woke up that they might already be there. It took several minutes for someone to figure out that there was no rolling motion anymore, and no throb of engines. Practically everyone was on deck within minutes after they realized this, because they were excited to see the land again. The transport would be here only a day, taking on fuel and supplies. Then it would steam out, and make a turn southward, two thousand more miles into the South China Sea and the land of the River Blindness.

*   *   *

TODAY THEY had been promised relief from the tedium of twenty days at sea. Provision had been made for their entertainment, and while most of them out of past experience did not expect much from it, they were nevertheless grateful for a chance to drink some beer and be on dry land again. The night before, Patch had announced over the loudspeaker system that they would be taken care of by the Okinawa Army Special Services people. Arrangements had been made for them to go to a local beach, where beer, box lunches and sports facilites would be provided. They could swim if they wished, in the nude, since the spot was remote.

From the deck of the ship the island was a pastiche of brilliant green, with darker, bluish-green hills in the background. It revealed no evidence of the bitter fighting two decades before.

"Jesus, the place is full of gooks," said Madman Muntz, peering down at a cluster of brown-skinned Okinawans feverishly working on the docks.

"Yeah, lookit them shitheavers," said DiGeorgio, who had joined Muntz and Spudhead and Sergeant Groutman at the rail. "Shit, I'll bet they makin' fifty cents an hour wrestlin' those drums," he said.

"Gooks ain't worth fifty cents an hour," Groutman said. "Gooks ain't worth shit."

WITHIN AN HOUR, brown military buses began taking the men off the transport. Officers and senior noncoms were permitted to go on their own, and when Bravo Company was put aboard the buses, the officers signed out and went down to wait in line for one of the tiny taxicabs standing at the dock. Kahn, Donovan, Inge and a lieutenant from Charlie Company went to the village of Nominui to find a bar. Brill joined Groutman to try to find a whore someone had told him about. Sharkey, headed for a dentist, got a lift up to Fort Buckner with Major Dunn, who wanted to try to call his wife, and Captain Thurlo, who had severe stomach pains.

The ride into Nominui took only a few minutes. They passed rice paddies and cane fields and lush bougainvillea and japonica and experienced a variety of smells that had not been smelled in weeks, and it was difficult to tell if they were smells peculiar to this part of the world or simply the normal smells of land. The trip would have been more comfortable had it not been for the bulk of ex-tackle Donovan squeezed into the tiny cab.

KAHN AND his pals had been drinking in the Shan Wan Saloon since it had opened at 10:30 A.M. Before that, they had each gotten a bath and a hand job at the "Geisha House" two doors down. The Shan Wan was about as out-of-the-way a place as a man could find, without really trying hard to get lost, so when Sergeant Trunk came bursting through the cheap plywood doors shortly after 2 P.M., the five officers were completely astonished that he had found them.

"Lieutenant Kahn, I been looking for you for an hour. The Old Man wants to see you," Trunk said.

"What about? Sit down, Sergeant," said Kahn, motioning for Trunk to pull up a chair.

"Well, the Old Man wants to see you about Captain Thurlo, I think. Sergeant Major told me to find you because Captain Thurlo has got appendicitis and he's gonna have to be operated on. It wasn't no seasickness after all—or anyway, he's got appendicitis now, 'cause he's up in the hospital at Fort Buckner, and you gonna have to be the CO, sir, I think."

Kahn said nothing. He looked dumbly at Sergeant Trunk. Inge and Donovan exchanged glances at the new development in the hierarchy, and the lieutenant from Charlie Company drained his beer.

"But that ain't all, sir; there's something else," Trunk said, leaning his fat head across the table, breathing a tobacco breath.

"What else?"

"It's about the men, sir. There's . . . a problem."

"What kind of problem?" Kahn asked.

"I think you ought to come with me, Lieutenant—it's better if you see it yourself."

"What is it, Trunk? Nothing's happened, has it?"

"Oh no, sir, nothing's happened; it's just, ah . . . where they've got them," Trunk said. "Sergeant Dreyfuss is outside with a cab. It won't take long," he said.

"Yeah, okay, Trunk." Kahn polished off his beer. "Hey, you guys, let me know where you're gonna be if you're not here, okay? I'll catch my part of the check later."

The three of them got into the tiny Japanese-made taxi and Trunk directed the driver to the main beach road.

"What's this all about, Trunk?" Kahn asked irritably as the cab flew past the last of the city along the coast road. He was still trying to absorb his apparent new standing.

"If you don't mind, sir, I'd like to wait and let you see for yourself. You gotta see the Old Man afterwards anyway."

Fifteen minutes out of the city, the cab came to the first of the fenced-in compounds. It slowed, but Trunk motioned for the driver to go on. Inside the big chain-link fences, soldiers from the troop transport sat huddled in bunches, many of them with their fatigue blouses pulled up over their heads to keep out of the searing midday sun.

The compound fences reached all the way down from the road into the water, out about a hundred yards or so, so that the men could swim out waist deep but no further. They drove past dozens of idle volleyball nets, and every hundred yards or so there were thatch-roofed cabanas so packed with men they looked as if they would explode and collapse if anyone else was crammed in.

"The men want to go back to the ship, sir," said Sergeant Dreyfuss, a tall black man from Chicago who rarely spoke. "It's damn hot for them out here. The beer ran out in an hour, and they ate all the box lunches, too. The water's full of jellyfish and it's so hot they can't swim. There's not even any fresh water for them to drink."

"Where are we?" Kahn asked.

"They're about a quarter of a mile down," Trunk said.

The compounds they passed reminded Kahn of prisoner-of-war camps. It might have been Treblinka, or Dachau.

"The Old Man know about this?" Kahn said.

"I think he's been out here," Trunk said. "Dreyfuss and me came out to go for a swim till we saw this. I went back to Buckner and ran into the Sergeant Major and he said Colonel Patch wants to find you 'cause of Captain Thurlo."

"Where is the colonel?"

"Up at the officers' club at Kadena Air Force Base. He talked to me from a phone in the bar."

"Pull over by that sign there," Trunk told the driver.

Kahn recognized a couple of men from the Company, but most of them, like everyone else, had their fatigue blouses pulled over their heads like Arabs. As Kahn and the two sergeants emerged from the taxi, the heat engulfed them like a shroud, throbbing up from the white sand and beating down from above, as though they had stepped into some gigantic natural oven.

They crossed the roadside ditch and were close to the compound fence before anyone on the other side noticed them. Then, slowly, the one hundred fifty men of Bravo Company began moving toward them like a flock of caged turkeys at feeding time. There wasn't a whisper of breeze, and Kahn saw in the eyes of the approaching flock the same sad, uncomprehending look he remembered from down in the steaming troop quarters aboard ship during the typhoon; only this time they seemed angrier, perhaps because they were not in danger, only in extreme discomfort. Kahn was trying hard to think of what to say, but it was Spec./4 Hepplewhite, the Company Clerk, who spoke first.

"Lieutenant, we're burning up out here, we can't swim and the beer's run out and we'd like to go back to the boat. This is a bunch of shit, sir," Hepplewhite said, looking at the others beside and behind him for agreement, and while they remained silent, there was agreement in their eyes.

"Listen," Kahn said. "I'm not in charge of this

operation. But I'm going back now to see the CO and I know he'll take care of it." For the first time, Kahn felt he was speaking with newfound authority.

"Let me ask this, though: would you want to stay if there was more beer?"

No one spoke. Then Hepplewhite, who had emerged as the spokesman, finally said, "I don't think so, sir. It isn't so much the beer as it is just being out in the sun. They'd have to get us an awful lot of beer, we told that to Sergeant Trunk before. I think we'd just rather go on back to the boat. Couldn't we drink the beer there?"

"All right," Kahn said; "all I can say is I'll tell it to the Old Man. I don't see any reason why you couldn't go back, but he's the boss. I'll tell him, okay?" and a murmur of "Okay" ran through the crowd as Kahn, Trunk and Dreyfuss made their way back to the taxi.

"Goddamn, Trunk, you mean the Old Man's already seen this?" Kahn said.

"I'm damned if I know, sir. I told the Sergeant Major about it when I went up there, but you know how he is—he don't give a shit."

"Did he say he'd talk to the Old Man?"

"He just said he'd take care of it, but that means he ain't gonna do nothin'. Like I say, he don't really give a shit."

"That's right, Lieutenant, he don't," Dreyfuss said.

"Sir, you can't help but feel sorry for them shitheads," Trunk said.

"I'll see what I can do, Sergeant, that's all I can say."

It had begun to dawn on Kahn that if he was to be Company Commander, there were certain bucks that stopped only with him.

BEFORE HE found the colonel, Kahn found Sharkey. He had gone back to the ship to get his briefcase, since Patch might want to go over some things and he wanted to be prepared.

When he walked into the cabin, Sharkey was sitting on his bunk in his skivvies, spitting blood into a piece of toilet paper and holding another against his upper gums as a compress.

"What the hell happened?" Kahn asked, stopping dead in front of him.

Sharkey raised his gargantuan head, the bloody tissue still at his lips.

"They hada pool ma teeth." His big eyes were bloodshot and his upper lip swollen out from his face. He looked worse than he had after the fight.

"What? You mean the bastards couldn't fix them?" Kahn cried.

"Yeah—they coulda fixed 'em okay—but Patch wouldn't let 'em."

"Patch—what the hell are you talking about?"

"The dentist said I'd have ta stay here ten days—ta wire 'em up and put 'em back right. But that fucka Patch, he said, 'I'm gonna need all my officers when we get there,' and I said I can catch a plane and be there before you, and he said, 'They probably wouldn't be able to save 'em anyway,' and I had to get 'em pulled."

"Jesus Christ, how many?"

"Thefe four—the front onef."

"Goddamn, what do you do now?"

"Juft keep thif up here and stop the bleedin' for a while."

"Jesus, Shark, I'm sorry."

"So am I," Sharkey said. "I'm a tooflef wonder. I could get a job as the Company queer."

"That bastard," Kahn hissed; "that bastard!"

Kahn found Patch where Trunk had said he would, at the bar at Kadena's officers' club.

"Excuse me, Colonel, you wanted to see me?" Kahn said coldly.

"Hell, yes, I wanted to see you. Where've you been? I sent for you three hours ago."

"I was on the beach with the men, Colonel," Kahn said, fudging the truth a little. "I don't know if you know it, but it's pretty bad out there—they're sweltering." Oh, well, here goes, Kahn thought. Patch picked up his cigar and regarded him with steely blue eyes.

"Kahn, Captain Thurlo's out for good. They diagnosed appendicitis and he's going to be operated on, so there's not much chance he'll rejoin Battalion. I'll have to figure something out in the next few weeks, but for now you're *it*. I want you to work especially close with me because you haven't had much experience. But you're going to have to pull it together fast. I don't want you running up and saying you don't understand something or you can't do something, because it looks like we are going to be thrown right into it pretty soon after we get there. You saw the campaign plan. You know what we're up against. Now, I want you ready in every way. Any questions?"

"I understand, Colonel."

"Any problems?"

"Colonel, the men want to come back to the ship. I can't say for all of them, but my men definitely want to get off that beach and I agree with them."

"Lieutenant Kahn," Patch said patiently, "those men are fine out there. I just sent for the Special Services Officer and he's going to take them more beer. I know what's going on; I was out there earlier myself."

"Sir, I don't think you appreciate how hot it really is for them. My men tell me they don't want more beer, or they'd rather drink it back on the ship. Would it be possible to get the buses to bring them back early?"

"Goddamn it, Kahn, those men are fine, and that beach is going to look like a picnic when they get to where we're going. They're going to stay right where they are, because I don't want any goddamn AWOLs on this stopover and that's the best way to prevent it. You understand these men have to be controlled, don't you? Besides, the Navy doesn't want them all over the decks while they're loading stuff aboard." As he was speaking, Patch had puffed up a dense cloud of blue cigar smoke which hung over his head.

"Sir, maybe they could go some place else, then. The flies are eating them up out there, and they can't swim, and there isn't any shade..."

"I told you they are just going to have to stay there. That's it. Is there anything else?"

"Yessir, there is something else—I'm concerned about Lieutenant Sharkey." Kahn was gripping the stool he was sitting on, toying with the idea of telling the Battalion Commander what he really thought of him for doing that to Sharkey, and keeping the men on the beach and down below in the storm—all things that he knew were unnecessary; but since this idea was locked safely in his mind and he didn't really have to let it out, he could think it all he wanted, because thinking it couldn't hurt anything. . . .

"What about Lieutenant Sharkey? They're going to have to pull those teeth, I'm afraid. I'm not going to have him laying up on Okinawa when we're in Vietnam—I told him that, and he understood it."

"They've already done it," Kahn said.

"Did they? What's wrong with him, then?" Kahn began to say something, but Patch interrupted. "Lieutenant Sharkey's a big boy, Kahn. He can take it." Patch twisted his moustache. "I explained to him his men needed him more than his teeth did. He agreed."

Afterward, Kahn left, disliking himself slightly, a little deeper in debt.

THE TRANSPORT was at sea when the men awoke the next morning. Despite Patch's precautions, half a dozen men went AWOL anyway, but they had all been rounded up before midnight and thrown into the brig with the ones brought on under guard at San Francisco. As an example, Patch decided to hold a court-martial of the newest AWOLs in the amphitheater, before as many of the men as possible so that they could see what going AWOL got you. He ordered the troops to watch in shifts, three companies at a time sitting through at least a couple of hours of the proceedings.

Later that day, a few of the men on deck sensed something was a little peculiar but they weren't sure exactly what, until somebody noticed the shadows were different from the way they had been. They were no longer headed into the afternoon sun. Instead the sun was on their right, just forward of the beam, so that the port side of the ship was in shadows from the superstructure. Toward sundown, gray-haired Major Dunn set up his transoceanic radio on the ventilator in the bow, surrounded by a dozen or so men all listening to their first propaganda broadcasts from Radio Hanoi. A woman they had heard about, called "Hanoi Hannah," related in soothing tones how many Americans had been killed that week and how many tanks and planes had been wiped out by the advancing armies of the People's Republic. Naturally, they all laughed at this because it was absurd, but they waited appreciatively for the half-hour of music that followed, since it was rumored to be by far the best music on the air, considerably better than the broadcasts from their own Armed Forces Radio Network.

Kahn was standing in the stern, listening to the propellers churning beneath him. Blue water boiled up, flecked with white, leaving a V-shaped wake behind them which spread out and out until it could no longer be perceived with the human eye. He wondered just how far the shock waves would travel along the surface before they dissipated.

Theoretically, they would go on until they were stopped by something more powerful so that it simply incorporated them into its substance. It was interesting how the waves spread out in a V, though, so that the center, over which the transport had just traveled, became the calmest part...the horizontal corollary to the "Dismal Deeps Effect"—that once you have passed a particular point, either above it or over it or on it or below it, the effect is not necessarily on the particular spot that was being passed. It was kind of an interesting thought, but what the hell did it mean? Kahn mused. Maybe it didn't mean anything, or maybe it was simply beyond his intellectual grasp. He decided to put all this away in his mind for a while and ruminate about it later. It was too pretty a day to dwell on things he had no control over anyway.

For a long time he stood watching the wake, the sun slowly sinking on the left side of him, and although it was still bright over parts of China, which lay somewhere to the west, and beyond that bright in Europe, this particular day's sun hadn't even presented itself to America yet, and wouldn't for hours.

Part Two

THE
IA
DRANG

14

EMERALD MOUNTAINS ringed the harbor where the transport lay, and across translucent waters palm trees rippled softly in the ocean breeze. The sun had not worked into the energy-sapping blast furnace it would become later in the day, and everyone on the beach was preparing deliberately for the unloading before it got too uncomfortable. Except for a sense of dark foreboding among the men on board, it was the picture of tropical paradise.

Bravo Company was among the first to be off-loaded. They stood at the rail in full battle dress, but without ammunition and rations, which somebody had forgotten to have removed from the hold and which would not be provided for hours. A little procession of LCIs was motoring toward them from the beach, and most of the men were watching these and thinking brief, solemn thoughts when Crump noticed the two smoke puffs on the ridge.

Finally they were here. Everything that had happened along the way—the food, the seasickness, the fights, the storm and the rest—all seemed to vanish into the recesses of their minds. Later in their years, children and grandchildren would learn about these things. Each one who returned would have his stories to tell, in cities and towns all over America, the way he had seen it. But these were not things to be worried about now.

The land that stretched before then, peaceful as it looked from here, was what occupied their thoughts.

It took a few seconds for Crump to connect the smoke puffs in his brain, and while he was doing it, two other puffs appeared. They looked very tiny, and the white smoke from the first puffs drifted gently skyward over the crest of the fairy-book mountains before the deep reports reached out to the transport like distant thunder. Bravo Company suddenly stopped talking as though a fearful voice had spoken from the bowels of the earth and told them to be quiet. Everyone turned toward where the sound had come from, except Crump, who was pointing toward the ridge and the puffs of smoke.

"Up there, see—right below that dip," he said. Other puffs were now appearing, and the rumbling continued.

"Jesus," DiGeorgio said. By now the top of the ridge was obscured in white smoke.

Patch was standing at the rail with Kennemer, near Bravo Company, when the sound reached the ship. He watched the little show on the ridge with a detached, superior air, and when DiGeorgio mustered the courage to inquire if the artillery was "ours or theirs," Patch was delighted to answer.

"Damned right it's ours, young man—that's one-oh-fives—and you should thank your lucky stars the enemy doesn't have one-oh-fives, because there'd be hell to pay for it." When the others saw Patch talking to DiGeorgio, they drifted around to hear what he had to say, and Patch, now that he had attracted an audience, was in a talkative mood.

What had evidently happened, he told them, was that somebody thought they had spotted some VC on the ridge and called in artillery to harass them. It was unlikely there was a firefight going on up there, because the artillery had only fired a brief salvo. This, he said, went on all day and night, so that anytime VC moved they could depend on having a batch of 105 rounds lobbed on their asses. "It is your job," Patch said, "to chase these bastards out into the open so the one-oh-fives can blow them away."

The men listened to this eagerly, and Patch was pleased the artillery had provided him an instructive forum. As he was trying to think of other informative things to say, another rumbling of the guns came across the water and everyone became silent again.

"Sir, do you think we'll see any VC today?" DiGeorgio asked tentatively. It was naturally the question on everyone's mind.

"Young man," Patch said, drawing himself up, "we may see VC and we may not see VC. If we do not see them today, we will see them tomorrow, or the next day. . . .

"This is not Honolulu. You did not come here for a rest. There will be no naked dancing girls to greet you here.

"From the time you set foot on that beach until the time you leave it, you may depend on one thing," the Battalion Commander declared:

"We *will* see VC."

LIEUTENANT FRANK HOLDEN was at the dock looking at the transport through field glasses. The Transportation Corps people had told him the unloading would take most of the day, and he was hoping it wouldn't be longer so that they could get away before dark. The artillery firing was much closer to him than the ship, but it scarcely fazed him because he had lived with it night and day for the last month, while they were establishing the Brigade fire base in the shadow of Monkey Mountain. Today, General Butterworth had sent him and a senior aide down to accompany the convoy of Four/Seven to its new home, and Holden was not looking forward to the trip.

All during the month at Monkey Mountain there had been a lot to do, and it was hot, dusty work, but mostly they had stayed inside the compound and had not seen VC or been mortared, although the artillery constantly pounded the hills around then. Once he had accompanied the general in a helicopter over some jungle near the edge of the Ia Drang and they had been shot at, or at least thought they had, but it wasn't the same as traveling over unsecured ground, as he would be shortly, when the convoy left.

The chopper that flew them down at dawn had followed the road they would take back—the Vietnamese preposterously called it a highway. From here it would be one hundred twenty-five miles westward, crossing flat paddy fields along the coast, then up into the highlands, winding through heavily forested hills and mountain passes, then into jungle so deep and tangled the road disappeared into it from the air.

No, it was not a trip Holden looked forward to. There was always the off chance they would be ambushed or run over a mine—incidents that were occurring with alarming frequency as more and more transports and airplanes arrived to pour out thousands of soldiers for the war. Even from his position of relative security at Monkey Mountain, he had heard the stories: the squad that never returned; the dead soldiers with their penises cut off and stuffed into their mouths. He had seen them bring in dead men to the airstrip stuffed in body bags.

It had taken only a few days for him to understand that this was actually a war, a real war, which he had not been able to comprehend before—even after the long hours of training, the lectures, the mock VC villages they had attacked in the pine hills of North Carolina, the night patrols with blackened faces and blank cartridges, the escape-and-evasion course, the live-fire exercise with real machine-gun bullets whining overhead. All of it seemed puny and worthless here, because when you drove up Highway One you didn't know from one moment to the next if you would be blown sky high.

HOLDEN WAS distrubed he hadn't heard from Becky, even though he'd gotten letters from his parents and from his sister, Cory, and from his uncle the stockbroker, who'd offered him a position when he returned. Every day it bugged him, and at night it bugged him worse.

They had met that Sunday after the dance, inside by the ice-skating rink at Rockefeller Center, drinking hot buttered rum and talking about everything but the war and their respective involvements in it. She drove him to the airport at sundown and he kissed her there—gently, politely, at first, and when she responded he felt himself getting excited. At the boarding gate he kissed her again for a long time, ignoring the people filing by, Holden in his uniform, she in a red sweater and tan slacks.

Four weeks later, just before Christmas, she came to see him and they went to the shore for the weekend. There was a fresh blanket of snow on the flat Carolina roads and the hardened, wind-swept tobacco fields that disappeared only when they reached the dunes of the Outer Banks. All the way down he'd avoided bringing up accommodations, but when they got to the deserted little motel it was unavoidable, so he asked if she wanted separate rooms.

"Of course not; that would be silly," she said. He protested clumsily that money wasn't a problem, but she put her hand on his face and said, "That's not what I meant, silly."

There were other visits in the months afterward. Sometimes he went to New York, sometimes she came down. They took excursions into the Southern countryside—along the Blue Ridge Mountains, down to the ocean or occasionally just to quiet back-road inns. Their lovemaking was spectacular, and in time it became that to Holden—lovemaking.

He lived for those weekends—times when everything seemed to go right. The days in between were dreary, tedious hours of paperwork and phone calls, checking and double-checking to make sure General Butterworth's preparations were being carried out, and he phoned her at least once a week.

It was late spring before he found out he wasn't the only man she was seeing.

He'd called early one night, and Becky's roommate said she'd gone for coffee with Professor Widenfield. He tried later—at eleven, when the dorm closed—and she was still out, and again at midnight, and at two and finally at five-thirty in the morning. She had evidently gone out for the night.

Two weeks later he asked her about it.

They had the use of a handsomely furnished cabin in mountains that belonged to the family of a classmate at Princeton. Spring had taken hold earlier that month, and the woods were glorious with flowers and tender shoots. They went for a walk in the sun along the old Appalachian Trail, stopping at lookout points and picnicking on a granite outcropping high above a clear, meandering river. The valley below was alive with sprouting grain and corn in various shades of green, and they ate fat ham sandwiches, cheese and pâté de foie gras and drank a bottle of Saint-Émilion, and when they got back to the cabin it was chilly enough to built a fire. After two brandies they went to bed.

"Do you feel like lying down?" she'd said demurely. There had been that look in her eye.

For nearly an hour they couldn't seem to get enough of each other, and afterward, when they'd napped for a while, Becky got up and began dressing for supper. They'd heard about a little place down the road.

It was nearly dark outside, but he could see her plainly in the fading light and glow of the log fire. She had put on a skirt and was adjusting her brassiere—an operation that intrigued and excited him because it lent an air of mystery to her marvelous, full breasts, though she'd been naked, next to him, only moments before. She was brushing her hair in the mirror and Holden was lying in bed when he finally asked her.

"Sure, I see other people sometimes." She smiled. "You

don't want me to be a dorm flower, do you?"

"What do you mean, 'see'?" he said.

"I just see them—that's all. What do you think I'm doing, bedding down the town?"

"You never came in that night I called. Do you always *see* people all night long?" He was trying not to be sarcastic.

"That was one night. I just went with Richard for a few drinks and we stayed up late—talking."

"You stayed up all damned night *talking*, is that what you're saying?" he demanded.

"Look, I like him—he's been very nice to me. He's a very brilliant person, and he thinks I'm an exceptional student. I'm helping him organize some things."

"What things?—One of those damned protests, huh? What good is that supposed to do? Don't you know that every time you do that it just hurts this country and it hurts me? Did you ever consider that?"

God, he thought, I don't want to get into this. All these months they had avoided talking about the war and her opposition to it, and now it was coming out in a way that had nothing to do with what he really wanted to know. Of course she was involved in the protests, but she was high-spirited and needed to get involved in things. It had nothing to do with them—and she knew that too—or at least, he believed she knew it.

"Becky, I'm sorry, okay?—I didn't mean to go into that. I just need to know if you're involved with anyone else."

"I'm not involved with anyone," she said.

"Not even me?"

"Well, of course you—you know that."

He blurted it out: "Are you sleeping with anyone else? I mean, have you slept with . . . with Widenfield?"

She put down the comb and looked at herself in the mirror for a while. Finally, she threw back her head, still not looking at him, and said it.

"We have slept together a few times. I told you before, it's nothing big."

"Damn," he said. "Damn it to hell!"

"Darling, it's you I care about—really it is," she said quickly. "Can't you see that? Why do you think I'm here? Why would I come here if I didn't care about you? I would be with *him* if that was the way it was." She pulled a gray sweater over her head.

"I don't understand you," he said after a while. "I don't understand how you can sleep with anyone else—especially that bastard—after what we've had."

"He's not a bastard—and don't call him that. I told you, he's a good friend and he's been kind to me."

"You mean you fuck anybody who's kind to you?" he said bitterly.

"I do what I damned well please, Frank Holden. That's what I do—and if you don't like it, well . . . it's too bad." She walked briskly into the other room and stood in front of the fire.

"Screw it, then," he said loudly. He got up and began to dress, feeling self-conscious in his nakedness.

It wasn't a good night. They talked small talk and ate the thick, charcoaled steaks and French fries at the country grill, but much of the evening they avoided each other's eyes. Back at the cabin, they sat apart in front of the fire and they did not make love when they went to bed. Just before he fell asleep, Holden began to wish he'd never brought the business up.

The next morning Becky woke up first and was in the kitchen in her bathrobe making eggs and sausage for breakfast. She stuck the plates into the oven to warm and came back to bed and snuggled under the blankets, kissing him gently on the chest.

"Baby, baby," she said tenderly, stroking his hair and face. "I'm so sorry if I've hurt you—you have to believe that." Tears came to her big green eyes, the first he'd ever seen, and he held her close for a long time.

IT TOOK most of the morning to unload the transport. On one side, the LCIs were taking off the men, while on the other, larger craft were off-loading heavier gear. Bravo Company and most of Four/Seven were ashore by 10 A.M. and were standing or sitting on the beach waiting for orders to climb onto the big open trucks they called "cattle cars" that were lined up as far as anyone could see along the dusty gravel road that ran toward the mountains.

They were inside a fenced-in compound, much like the one on Okinawa, except that this one was rimmed by barbed wire instead of chain-link fence.

Behind the low dunes, two cities existed which they had not been able to see from the ship.

One consisted of tents and tin-roofed buildings, also enclosed by barbed wire. It was laid out in a neat and orderly way, and the sand between the buildings and tents had been raked, and across the raked sand soldiers moved busily on duckboards from one tent or building to the next.

Beyond the barbed-wire perimeter was a second city consisting of shafts built from every imaginable material. It ringed the first city like some giant seething reptile, and its inhabitants were thousands of men, women and children dressed mostly in black, loose-fitting garments. It was impossible to tell what they were doing, because they appeared to be doing many things at once. An unpleasant stench that seemed to be a combination of decomposed food and human waste assailed the men on the beach, but they could not tell at this point which of the two cities it came from.

Lieutenant Brill was annoyed by the waiting.

If there was one thing he could not stand, that was it—and it seemed to be all he had done since he got into the Army. Waiting in line, waiting for orders, waiting for the transport to arrive, waiting now to get where they were going. Hurry up and wait.

On the other side of the barbed-wire barricade, a cluster of children in various stages of dress and undress had gathered, and Brill walked over to them. They were jabbering away at him and some of the other men, holding their hands out for food, cigarettes and whatever else they could talk people out of. Their jabbering was unintelligible, except for a few words like "Ahmercan"; "numba ten," which, they learned later, was no compliment, since it represented the low point on a 1-10 rating scale; "You give me C ration?" and "You VC?" A small naked boy kept repeating over and over again, "Fuck you, fuck you."

The sun was shining mercilessly on the men and they were drenched with sweat. No breakfast had been served aboard the transport, and the rations and ammunition still had not been off-loaded, and by now everyone was hungry.

Since there was no food to give the children, Bravo Company simply stared at them across the wire. Brill had not seen monkeys since he was ten years old, when his father had taken him to the Saint Louis zoo and let him feed them peanuts. But that was what they reminded Brill of, and he wondered what their parents must look like, to have produced offspring that looked like monkeys.

As Brill was meditating on this, Spudhead Miter walked past him toward the wire, with two Hershey Almonds in his hand. He peeled back the paper and broke the bars into small pieces and began tossing them gently underhand to the tiny monkey-men on the other side. The jabbering subsided as they scrambled for the tidbits, but when there was no more left, they broke into a wild, furious cacophony that annoyed Brill even more. If they had actually been monkeys, he might have understood it, but these people were supposed to be humans, no matter what they looked like. When he could stand it no longer, Brill walked to the fence himself and addressed them.

"Hey—that's enough—see—all gone—no more—okay?" he said harshly.

"Okay, okay," they repeated, saying it over and over again until Brill began to get the impression he was being mocked.

"All right—get out of here," he scowled. "Go on—beat it!" He gestured down the rutted track toward the shack town.

"Okay, okay, okay—Ahmercan, numba ten," they cried frantically, still holding out their hands, obviously with no intentions of leaving.

Brill stooped for a flat gray seashell at his feet and drew

back with it in a threatening gesture. "GET OUT OF HERE, GODDAMN IT," he roared.

The monkey-men shrank back and their jabbering ceased. They stared at Brill with the shell still cocked in his hand and slowly began to retreat from the barbed wire, some of the older ones smiling apprehensively and the littler ones cringing in fright. They stopped about twenty feet away, still silent, bunched close together, and looked at Brill.

Bravo Company had stopped talking also and was observing the scene with interest. None of them liked Brill particularly, but they were nervous on this hot Asian morning and the gibberish of the children made them more uncomfortable. The beach was bad, but they knew that what lay beyond it was probably going to be worse, and the general attitude was that they just wanted to be left alone.

Brill glared menacingly at the monkey-men, but they stood their ground across a sort of no-man's-land between themselves and the barbed wire and the men on the inside. The stalemate continued until Brill began to feel foolish, as he realized this could go on and on.

He began to walk down the length of barbed wire, to get closer and force them to retreat even farther, and then the small naked one provided him an opportunity he secretly wanted. "Fuck you, fuck you, fuck you," the tiny creature began again, and immediately Brill fired the seashell through the wire and began yelling and cursing them, hoping it would make them run.

It did not. Instead, several of the older boys picked up some small stones and shells from the sandy road and began heaving them back across the wire. Brill scooped up shell bits and retaliated, still cursing furiously. When some of the monkey-men's missiles began to strike incidentally near men from Bravo Company, they leaped up ferociously and began also to curse the children. In a few seconds a full-fledged rock fight broke out, with men running up from other places on the beach picking up handfuls of things to throw. As the little band of monkey-men began to retire under the barrage, Trunk, followed closely by Kahn—who had been working on getting some water out to the beach for the men—ran up to see what the commotion was.

"All right, shitheads—knock it off!" Trunk bellowed, and the throwing ceased almost immediately. Then Trunk saw Brill, who had been unrecognizable in the midst of the battle, and who had also stopped throwing when Trunk and Kahn arrived.

"Excuse me, Lieutenant Brill, but just what's going on here?" Trunk said. He turned to the men. "Whatdaya shitheads think you're doing—huh?"

"Never mind what they were doing, Sergeant Trunk— these men were helping me after those little bastards started rocking us."

"Lieutenant Brill, let me see you over here for a minute," Kahn said. "Sergeant Trunk, quiet these men down—and get them away from that wire."

Trunk watched as Brill and Kahn walked down toward the beach; then he turned back on the men.

"Get your dumb asses back there to where those packs are and sit the hell down—MOVE IT," he bellowed.

He grabbed the person nearest to him, who happened to be Madman Muntz, by the scruff of the neck and spun him around. "Can *you* tell me what the hell went on here?" Trunk said threateningly.

"Them little gooks was throwing stones at us so we started to throw them back," Muntz said weakly. "They started to throw them at Lieutenant Brill, anyway, and they was hitting us too," he said.

"Well let me tell you something, soldier," Trunk said. "You don't throw no stones at kids—ever; do you hear that?—*ever*. The United States Army don't throw rocks at children."

"Aw, Sarge, they was probably VC kids anyway," Muntz said defensively. "They coulda had grenades or something."

The others agreed. "Yeah, Sarge, you heard about the kids throwing grenades over here, haven't you? Spate's brother got killed by a kid throwing a grenade—didn't he, Spate?"

"Shut your ass up," Trunk said. He scowled at the men, who began to drift off slowly toward the beach. A few of them glanced over their shoulders at the now distant band of monkey-men, who were moving down the road toward another area of the compound. Others broke up into small groups and spent the rest of the hour convincing themselves that they had come very close to being grenaded.

FOR NEARLY an hour, Holden and Major Dalkey, the senior general's aide, had been trying to reach Brigade base camp to find out what they were supposed to do. Their instructions had been simply to go down and bring the convoy back, on the assumption they would get started early enough to arrive at Monkey Mountain before dark. But it was well into afternoon, and if they left now, nightfall would catch them somewhere along the road. Patch had removed his dark glasses and was pacing up and down the little Communications tent while Major Dalkey outlined the alternatives for him: they could either wait to leave until tomorrow—leave now and convoy straight through—or leave now and get as far as they could, then set up for the night somewhere along the way and continue at sunup.

"You see, Colonel," Dalkey said drily, "the country sort of changes hands after dark."

In a way, Patch wanted to make the decision himself. He was in charge of these men—all of them—until he turned them over to General Butterworth, and he felt a certain obligation to make choices such as this.

"If we push straight through," Dalkey said, "we'll lose our air cover at dark. Those gunships can't do us any good at night. If we hole up somewhere along the way, we ought to be all right, but if there's a squad of VC around we'd be sitting ducks for a mortar attack.

"On the other hand, there aren't any facilities for the men here on the beach, and the Old Man is expecting us sometime today—he's got an orientation schedule all set up for tomorrow afternoon," he said.

"Try to get through again," Patch said, looking at his watch.

Holden picked up the canvas-covered field phone and cranked furiously, then waited.

"Torch," he said loudly, "this is Typhoon; get me Wicked Blast. Over."

Something incoherent was muttered from the other end of the line. Moments later, a faint voice identified itself as Wicked Blast.

"Wicked Blast, this is Typhoon; get me Smokey-One. Over," Holden said.

There was a pause.

"No, no—Typhoon—this is TYPHOON," he said.

Another pause.

"TYPHOON—tango-yankee-papa-hotel-oscar-oscar-niner. Over."

"What's he say?" Patch asked.

"He thinks I'm saying 'Baboon,'" Holden said.

"Give me that thing," Patch said impatiently. He snatched the handset and spoke directly into it.

"This is Typhoon-One; give me Smokey-One," he said.

"No, no, TYPHOON—TYPHOON! Over," Patch shouted.

There was a long pause.

"LISTEN, FORGET WHO I AM—JUST GET ME SMOKEY-ONE—UNDERSTAND?" Patch bellowed.

"Sir, I believe you'll be more successful if you hold it a little bit away from your mouth," Dalkey offered.

"Shut up, Major, I'm handling this," Patch said, grinding out his cigar in an ashtray.

After a while there was a squeaking, scratching sound at the other end of the line.

"Now we're getting somewhere," Patch said, sounding pleased.

"Smokey, this is Typhoon-One; get me Smokey-One, Over," Patch said.

Again a scratching, growling noise.

"NO, TYPHOON, I SAY—GET ME SMOKEY-ONE! YOU HEAR?"

Another pause. Patch turned to Dalkey. "Who the hell is this 'Baboon' everybody's talking about? What kind of call sign is that?"

"I think it's something to do with the Navy, sir," the major said.

Patch returned to the phone.

"LISTEN, THIS IS COLONEL PATCH, YOU HEAR—I WANT TO SPEAK TO THE GENERAL," he roared.

More scratching sounds. Patch's eyes suddenly became wild.

"I KNOW COLONEL PATCH ISN'T THERE, YOU IDIOT—THIS IS COLONEL PATCH. GIVE ME THE GENERAL!" he bellowed.

Another pause, and then a thin voice came onto the line.

"Ah," Patch said, "finally."

"General," he said. "We are here at Cam Ranh Bay. We are ready to move out. The situation is this: If we leave now we will be traveling at night, and Dalkey informs me the roads are not secure. We can wait till tomorrow, or we can leave now and push on through and arrive your location by about twenty-three hundred, or we can leave now and set up somewhere and arrive your location approximately ten hundred tomorrow. It is up to you, sir; what do you say? Over," Patch said, breathing a sigh of relief.

"What's that you say, sir?" Patch said, leaning into the phone. "Say that again!" he demanded.

The person on the other end repeated the message.

"WHO IS THIS?" Patch screamed. His face contorted as though he had just stuck his finger into an electric socket.

"JEEP DRIVER! I DON'T WANT TO TALK TO ANY GODDAMNED JEEP DRIVER—I WANT GENERAL BUTTERWORTH, DO YOU HEAR ME?"

The line went dead and Patch slumped down in a chair,

the handset dangling limply in his hand.

"It's impossible," he said dejectedly. "We are on our own."

15

THEY LEFT within an hour. The men were packed into the trucks like cattle, and the incessant jolting and bouncing soon became almost as irritating as the seasickness aboard the transport. Aside from this, their journey into the afternoon sun took on a strange, mystical flavor. The caravan wound its way slowly out of the sand and heat of the beach, past the seething-reptile city; past the artillery site on a low, flat hill; past the dark oil and gasoline storage bins strategically located away from the neat tent town in case someone decided to blow them up, and on into the countryside.

Patchwork rice paddies stretched toward a forbidding

line of trees on their right, and on the opposite side of the road, more rice fields covered the earth all the way to the emerald mountains. Every so often a shining white villa was glimpsed among tall palm trees, and in the fields an occasional farmer, his black pants rolled to his knees, worked behind a large water buffalo. On both sides of the narrow, bumpy road the convoy intermittently passed men and women headed in the direction of the seething-reptile city, some on foot, some riding bicycles and many carrying some kind of produce.

A few were fixed up with a yoke device across their shoulders on which straw baskets were suspended, and they moved in a peculiar, bent-over quickstep as though some mysterious force had catapulted them forward and they were trying to come to a halt. Someone in Crump's truck identified these people as peasants, and after thinking about it for a while, Crump decided that except for the land and the peasants' clothing, it wasn't much different from what went on along the roads into Tupelo, Mississippi. This made Crump wonder if he would be considered a peasant if he had been born here instead of in Tupelo.

They rolled on for another hour, crossing a rickety bridge over a dark, hyacinth-choked stream with banana trees growing on its banks. From a sandbagged rathole just below the side of the bridge, three Oriental men emerged, wearing the green uniform of the South Vietnamese army and carrying carbines. They waved as the trucks went by the same way country people sometimes wave at passing automobiles. Crump was the only one in his truck who waved back, and he felt a little foolish for doing it. All the others seemed slightly on edge and gripped their rifles in a tense way, even though they had been told not to load them or even to open the cardboard ammo boxes stacked on the floor of the trucks.

Kahn, riding in the truck cab, was still thinking about the rock-throwing incidents on the beach. It was the first time he had ever had to chew out a fellow officer, and it continued to nag at him both because of what Brill had said and because he realized he was probably going to have to do it again, and often.

He had taken Brill down toward the beach, out of earshot of the men, and as Trunk was dealing with them, he dealt with Brill.

Brill freely admitted to throwing the first rock, but he argued excitedly that the children were obviously preparing to throw rocks at him and that he wanted only to get in the first lick to scare them away. In other words, Brill saw nothing wrong with it, and as he spoke, in eager, exercised tones, Kahn found himself worrying what Brill might have done if they had had ammunition for their weapons.

At first Kahn had tried to reason with him. He was going to be Company Commander for—well, maybe for good—and he would have preferred to stay on the good side of his officers if possible. So he explained to Brill that they simply couldn't allow this sort of thing to occur, because the fact was, they were all going to be in this country for a long time, living among the people, and the less strained relations were, the better . . . and also that they had just gotten there and really didn't know what was going on, so they'd best not stir up anything unnecessary, and . . . furthermore, that it just didn't look good. . . .

While Kahn was talking, Brill had stared out across the water, his steel-blue eyes narrowed and his thin mouth set tightly, but with almost the hint of a tiny smile. As he listened, Brill took out his custom-made Randall knife—which he had once confided to Kahn he had purchased by selling his stamp collection—and ran the razor-sharp blade ever so lightly across his thumb, which was disconcerting to Kahn, but he ignored it and proceeded with the matter at hand.

When he finished, Kahn asked if Brill understood what he had said. Brill, however, did not look at him, but continued to stare across the water and saw the blade of the Randall knife lightly back and forth across his thumb, and Kahn finally exploded and said, "Goddamn it, Brill, I'm talking to you! Do you understand what I'm saying?" and Brill finally looked up, while Kahn proceeded to deliver a stern warning to him not to do that kind of thing anymore. All during this admonishment Brill nodded as though he did, in fact, understand it, but he never stopped sawing away with the Randall knife, and a thin ooze of blood had appeared on his thumb. Even as Kahn was talking, it began to occur to him that Brill might be disturbed, if not seriously crazy.

At the outskirts of a small village the trucks came to a halt.

Two helicopter gunships rattled by, headed for the front of the convoy, their door gunners peering down curiously at the men in the trucks. Fifteen minutes later word came back that "some kind of accident" had occurred ahead and they would be there for a while. Trunk announced that the men could get out and stretch and relieve themselves in the fields. Many of them needed to take bowel movements but were reluctant because they had sighted women in the village.

There were only a dozen or so houses, set low among coconut palms and built of a white, stuccolike substance. The earth around them had been padded hard and bare, and in the street a few small children played in puddles of green, slimy water. Bravo Company had been told to stay within shouting distance of the trucks, but this still allowed them to go into the village. At the end of the street was a small tin-roofed shack, its front open to display an assortment of shabby vegetables, fruits and other goods, including several cases of American C rations. The proprietor, wearing a conical straw hat, stood at the entrance as Crump, DiGeorgio, Spudhead and Madman Muntz approached.

"Lookit that guy there," Muntz said sourly. "What-daya suppose he thinks about at night?"

"He probably don't think nothin'. . . . He looks like a crook to me," DiGeorgio said.

"I'll bet we can get a soda pop there," Crump said cheerfully. "Anybody want a soda?"

The man began to smile when he saw them headed for his store. His teeth, what there were of them, had been stained a nasty brown by betel-nut juice, and he began to nod and bow as they came up.

"*Lai, lai, sai,* Ahmerican . . . *tune-dok-cat. Ja yo-no we-do woc,*" the man babbled.

"That's what's wrong with these people," Muntz declared. "They're okay till they open their mouths; then they sound so goddamn stupid."

The store owner reached into a box behind him and retrieved an olive-green container of C-ration canned peaches.

"Tun-duc-tan?" he said stupidly.

The men howled with laughter and the proprietor joined in with them, repeating over and over again his singsong sales pitch.

Spudhead recovered enough to proceed with the conversation.

"No-no—soda pop—see—so-da-paahp," he said carefully, shaping his hand to grasp a nonexistent round object.

The man looked confused for a moment, then went to a basket of bananas and held one out to them.

"Oh, for crissake," Muntz said dismally.

"Uh, no-no," Spudhead pleaded. "We want...uh..." He thought for a moment.

"Kok-ah-kola," he said finally. "You got Kok-ah-kola?" Spudhead felt like an idiot.

A broad smile crossed the proprietor's face and he departed into the dark recesses of his shack. Moments later he returned holding two live chickens in his fists.

"Ah—kokahkola," he announced happily.

"Fuck me," DiGeorgio groaned.

From behind them, a raspy voice injected itself.

"You want me to help you, soldiers?"

They turned to find a frail young man balanced on one crutch, his pant leg pinned up just behind the knee where his leg had once been.

"I speak American, I speak Vietnamese," the man smiled. "My name is Bac," he said.

"Uh, yeah—tell him we want soda pops, will you?" Muntz said in an authoritative voice.

"I was Vietnamese soldier," Bac continued, "until VC blow off my leg. I was number-one soldier. I was sergeant in Two Corps. I was decorated by Marshal Ky himself—for fighting bravely."

"Could you just ask him if he has any Coca-Cola?" Spudhead said nicely.

"Oh, Kokahkola, yes." Bac grinned. "Of course."

Bac turned to the store owner and yammered away at him. The store owner yammered back. It reminded Crump of barking dogs.

The proprietor disappeared again, and Bac addressed the men.

"You let me talk with him for you, okay? He say too much money, Ahmercan, but I get good price for you," he said.

They looked at one another and eyed Bac suspiciously, but DiGeorgio said, "Okay."

The proprietor returned with four dripping-wet bottles of Coca-Cola clutched to his chest. He yammered something at the men, but Bac interceded.

"What's he say?" Muntz demanded.

"He say fifteen piasters apiece," Bac said. "Fifty Ahmercan cents."

"Half a buck for a stinking Coke!" DiGeorgio cried. "Tell him he's full of shit."

Bac spoke to the man again. They yammered away for nearly a minute, and Bac turned once again to the men.

"He say twenty-five Ahmercan cents . . . no less. He will not change," Bac said.

They bought the Cokes for a quarter a piece, and as they gulped them thirstily, Spudhead felt a rush of generosity.

"Can we buy you a Coke too?" he asked Bac.

"No, thank you," Bac said. "You are very kind, Ahmercans, but I do this service for you. I do not wish to be repaid." They were astonished and thanked him politely and started to walk away.

Bac hobbled after them on his crutch.

"Please," he said. "There is something I would like to show you. . . . You come with me, okay?"

They stared at him in silence.

"Ah, no, I don't think we can. . . . Uh, we have to go back . . ." Spudhead gestured toward the road.

"Only a moment," Bac pleaded. "Ahmercan don't

come here much.... I think you like what I show," he said. His eyes looked earnest, almost desperate, and a sad grin crossed his pockmarked face.

"Well, what is it you want us to see?" Spudhead asked tentatively.

"Please, you come ... over here," Bac said, pointing to a tiny shack behind a run-down villa. He took a few steps and turned on his crutch, still smiling.

"Well, what can it hurt?" Muntz said. "Maybe he's got a girl back there or something." The others looked nervously at each other but forced obligatory smiles at this prospect. "What the hell?" Muntz whispered. "He don't know these weapons ain't loaded."

"Yeah, why not?" Crump suddenly declared, walking toward Bac. The others followed uncertainly.

Bac limped ahead of them, his pinned-up trouser leg flapping as he walked. They passed a gathering of children and a few older people engaged in various forms of work. Crump thought again of the freak-show crowds at the fair. Each of them felt a queer exhilaration at what they were doing. They had been warned so many times about the Vietnamese ... that they were untrustworthy, that all were suspect, that they would fall on you without mercy at the first opportunity. But somehow they trusted Bac. His pleading grin and sawed-off stump lulled them into a sense of security.

As they walked, some of the older people and most of the children began to follow behind them. By the time they reached Bac's shack they had attracted a small crowd.

Bac ducked inside the canvas door flap and remained there for what seemed a long time. When the flap opened again, it was not Bac that appeared, but a small apelike creature about a foot tall which sprang out on all fours and looked around nervously. A long cord leash was attached to a red collar on its neck, and at the end of the leash was Bac, smiling crazily, coming through the door.

"You see," he said proudly, scooping up the animal and holding it out to them—"banana-cat."

"Hey, lookit ... a monkey," DiGeorgio said.

"I'll be . . . ," Crump said. The creature reminded him of a singed possum. "Hey, don't be scared, little feller." He reached out to touch it, and the banana-cat seized his bony fingers and tried to jam them into its mouth.

"Ah!" Crump cried, drawing back his hand.

"No, please . . . banana-cat very friendly . . . he like Ahmercan . . . not hurt you," Bac said, scolding the animal gently.

"You buy banana-cat from me? I must sell . . . not much money, okay?" Bac said.

Crump, DiGeorgio, Spudhead and Madman Muntz looked at each other and a wistful grin came over Bac's face. The banana-cat glared at them resentfully. Suddenly it began to cheep loudly and struggle in Bac's arms. He petted it and it calmed down.

"Uh, I don't think we need no monkey, Bac," DiGeorgio said finally.

"Please," Bac said. "Not much money . . . I give you for only one hundred Pee . . . you take, okay?"

"Ah, no, thank you, Mr. Bac," Spudhead said. "You see, we really don't have any place to keep a monkey."

"Ahh . . . banana-cat very clean," Bac pleaded. "Catch mice and frogs . . . keep your house clean."

"We ain't going to no house, Bac," Muntz said. "We gonna live in the woods . . . out there, see?" He gestured into the distance toward a dark stand of jungle across the paddy fields.

"Oh, yes, yes . . . banana-cat very good in jungle too, eyes wonderful at night . . . smell VC long time away. . . ."

"You see," Bac said, "I have banana-cat long time, since he very tiny. But I must go to Nha Trang soon . . . for *proslectic*." He pointed down at his missing leg. "Very expensive; you see, I must buy from doctors there. . . ."

The banana-cat began to chirp again, and Bac stroked it into silence.

"You take, okay?" he said. They felt embarrassed.

"Well, how much money is this one hundred 'Pee' . . . American money?" Crump asked quietly. Di-Georgio looked at him as if he were going to faint.

"Ah . . . one hundred piasters is three of your American

dollars...here," Bac said. "In Nha Trang, Saigon, you see one hundred Pee worth only half of that. But here it worth more...you make twice as much for your dollar."

Crump turned to the others. "Three dollars...that ain't much for a live monkey, trained an' all."

"Jesus, Crump, you gotta be outta your mind. You can't buy no fuckin monkey.... What'll you do with it?" DiGeorgio rasped.

"Never mind what I'll do with it," Crump said. He reached into his pocket and drew out three dollars. "Here." He gave the money to Bac, who stuffed it into his shirt pocket and handed Crump the banana-cat, collar, cord and all.

"Well there, little feller," Crump said soothingly, "you and me gonna get along just fine." He patted the banana-cat tenderly on top of its head. It seemed to go to sleep.

"One moment, gentlemen," Bac said as they started to walk away. He looked sadly at the traded-off banana-cat cradled in Crump's arms.

"I think there is something else I can do for you...perhaps a favor for both of us," Bac said.

"What's that?" DiGeorgio asked.

"It is about money...your money and mine," he said. "You are in luck you come here today, because things will not last as they are."

Bac began telling them a story—about Vietnamese money and American money. About how the values were changing every day as more and more Americans arrived. Once, he said, American dollars were worth a great deal in Vietnam. But as the Americans arrived in force, they spent more and more dollars, thereby driving the worth of the dollar down in relation to the Vietnamese piaster. There had been a time, he said, when the dollar was easily worth three hundred piasters, but that was rapidly changing...especially in the big cities like Saigon, and in places where there were many Americans...like the places Bravo Company was going....

Bac's theory of economics was that as the war progressed, corruptive influences like the black market and inflation would soon render the dollar practically worthless. Then, he said, they would be unable to buy certain necessities . . . girls, souvenirs, decent food . . .

However, he told them, these corruptive circumstances had not yet reached this village, and the dollar was still worth what it should be, although most Vietnamese here had no way of converting it to piasters and consequently did not want it. Bac, on the other hand, had a brother in Qui Nhon who could still turn dollars into piasters for a slight profit. Therefore, Bac said, he was in a position to make some money for all of them.

"I will buy your American dollars for their value of thirty-three piasters each. You will then have many more piasters than you could buy where you are going, and I will be able to make a few cents on them through my brother toward the purchase of a new leg."

Spudhead, Crump, DiGeorgio and Madman Muntz went into conference.

It sounded plausible. After all, hadn't Bac been straight with them so far? Hadn't he talked the proprietor down on the sodas? Hadn't he let his banana-cat go for a measly three bucks? What did they have to lose?

After talking it over, each of them drew into his wallet for bills. Spudhead turned over twenty-five dollars, Crump ten, DiGeorgio thirty and Madman Muntz, ordinarily very parsimonious, forty-five.

Bac carefully doled out three thousand, six hundred forty piasters.

POCKETS FULL of the valuable piasters, they started back down the pressed-earth street, Bac tagging behind on his crutch. It was late in the afternoon, and a cool breeze was blowing in off the ocean, which they knew lay somewhere beyond the line of trees opposite the emerald mountains. Crump, using a trick he had learned with flying squirrels, had tied the banana-cat's leash through his belt so that it wouldn't get away. The village was full of other soldiers from the convoy now, and nearly a dozen of them were bargaining with the proprietor of the store.

A battered stucco house was situated among some

coconut palm trees. Candles flickered inside, and through the windows and door a strange wailing sound wafted out into the street. Muntz walked closer and tried to peer inside and Bac caught up with them.

"A funeral," he said. "There were killings here last night."

"Killings," Spudhead said, "What do you mean ... murders?"

"Oh, no, no ... killings ... not murder. It was VC," Bac replied nonchalantly.

"You mean there are VC here?" Muntz demanded, looking around quickly.

"No ... no VC here ... down there," Bac said, nodding toward a dark lane through some palm trees.

"What? You mean VC killed people here yesterday?" Muntz cried, his eyes getting big.

"No, VC not kill. Ahmercans kill ... Ahmercan artillery. They think VC here, but VC already gone. This man's family all killed.... Come, I show you," Bac said offhandedly, going toward the dilapidated little house.

Hesitantly, they followed him inside. Shades had been pulled over the windows, and in the dim light of the candles they could see three rough wooden coffins, one large and two small, resting between two crude tables. Squatting on the tile floor, six or eight women dressed in loose black garb raised a constant, pathetic wailing. Beside a stand of candles, a crucifix leaned crazily to one side, the bottom of its cross stuck into a box of sand. No one seemed to notice the intruders, and they stood reverently near the door as the wailing continued.

"See," Bac said, "all dead."

"Holy Christ," DiGeorgio whispered. "I think we ought to get the hell out of here."

"Yeah," Muntz muttered quietly, "this place gives me the heebie-jeebies."

Spudhead was gawking goofily at the coffins when the man threw himself upon him.

None of them had noticed him standing in the shadows behind the door when he came in.

He seized Spudhead first by the shoulders and then slid

down to his feet so that his arms were entwined around Spudhead's knees. The man howled like a dog.

Spudhead was frozen in terror. The others sprang back, nearly knocking over a coffin. As DiGeorgio instinctively drew back his rifle butt to brain the man, Bac recovered and restrained him.

"Please, no," Bac said. "He mean no harm."

"Jesus," Spudhead said. He felt as if he were going to throw up. The man continued to howl and wail awfully and kept a lock on Spudhead's knees so that he couldn't move away.

"What's wrong with him?" DiGeorgio asked fearfully.

"That is his family," Bac said, nodding at the coffins. "He believe you have come here to pay him."

"Pay him . . . pay him for what?" Muntz said.

"The reparations," Bac replied. "When Ahmercan kill, they pay, you know? . . . You are Ahmercan . . . he think you sent by Army to give him money."

"Jesus," Muntz said.

"Tell him we didn't have nothin' to do with this," DiGeorgio said. "You tell him that, hear?"

Bac said something to the man, and he quit wailing and looked up at Spudhead and then to the others. He seemed bewildered and babbled something to Bac.

"What's he say?" Muntz asked.

"He want to know why you come here then," Bac said.

"Tell him . . . uh, tell him we was just passing through or something. Tell him we're sorry about his family," DiGeorgio said.

Bac spoke again to the man, who looked even more bewildered and put his head back down and began a low moan, still clinging to Spudhead's knees.

"He not understand. He want to know when he get paid," Bac said sadly.

"Ask him to let go of me," Spudhead said.

Bac spoke to the man, who slowly released his grip and stood up. He looked plaintively at Spudhead and searched the faces of DiGeorgio and Madman Muntz. They looked back sympathetically. Then, without warning, he flung himself howling at the feet of Crump, who had been gazing idly at the crucifix and stroking the banana-cat.

Crump leaped back in fright and nearly fell down because the man had hold of his knees. Instantly the banana-cat flew at the man's head with a wild, screeching noise and began to tear at his hair.

"Aiiiieeeee," the man cried, and beat madly at his head to drive the monkey away. The banana-cat sprang back and forth on its leash like a living yo-yo, using Crump's chest to carom off between the man and the ceiling and the little table where the crucifix was. The wailing women jumped up hysterically, and the man began to shout what were unmistakably curses.

"Oh, my God," Spudhead said frantically.

Bac seized the banana-cat in midair as it was headed back to Crump's chest.

"Please, we go now," he said, gripping the animal by the neck, pulling Crump, still with the leash tied to his belt, behind him. They hurried out the door, pursued by the cursing man and the band of shrieking women, who stopped at the steps and continued to hurl what sounded to the men like oaths as they walked quickly down the street.

As they approached the convoy, Bac slowed behind them and stopped.

"I must go now. I am very sorry..." he said, nodding back toward the house where the funeral party still clustered on the porch, gesturing furiously to each other.

Spudhead, Crump, DiGeorgio and Madman Muntz thanked Bac awkwardly. He winked at them and hobbled off down the dark lane through the palms. When they got back to the trucks, word had just come down that the convoy was ready to move again. As they pulled out, each of them began eagerly relating to others what had happened in the village... about the sodas and meeting Bac and the acquisition of the banana-cat and the killings and the horrible scene at the funeral house. However, they had all agreed to keep quiet about the deal they had made for piasters, and it wasn't until two days later, during their orientation, that they learned a dollar was worth over two hundred piasters and they had been gypped out of their money.

16

SEVERAL PLASTIC ponchos had been set out in a neat row, and as the convoy crept by, a Graves Registration squad was diligently sorting out what was left behind. Remnants of watches, wallets, pens, rings and other personal effects were tossed into one pile.

The personnel carrier lay in the rice paddy like a dead elephant. Its undercarriage had been ripped open as if by a huge can opener, the thick armor plate peeled back in jagged edges. A side upturned crazily toward the road was bulged outward by the blast, and the rear door rested in mud twenty yards away.

A second pile contained shattered helmets, packs,

boots, canteens and torn flak jackets. On the third, rifles, ammunition bandoliers, a cracked machine-gun stock and a few grenades had been heaped. All of this would be sorted again, resorted, and the personal effects packed into brown cardboard boxes and shipped to the next of kin. The remains of the vehicles occupants had already been removed by helicopter.

MPs directed the trucks past a preposterous-looking tank extractor which sat by the crater where the mine had exploded, waiting to remove the APC with its crane. Two mud-covered tanks crouched in the fields like sullen monsters, their sweat-stained crews standing glumly by, watching a gunship fly along the edge of the distant line of trees, looking for an excuse to open fire.

Bravo Company viewed all this with a macabre fascination, as though they had happened by the scene of a brutal automobile accident.

Because they had not yet experienced the war itself, they had not come to terms with its essential scheme— that this was an act carefully planned and executed, with no particular malice toward those aboard the APC, with no thought of gaining their immediate possessions, with no hope of bringing the conflict to an end by this individual deed.

So they looked upon it as an act of fate. Long ago, most of them had begun to accept their own fate. In the teeming cities of New York, Detroit, Los Angeles, Houston; and small towns like Orangeville, Waycross, Poplar, Tupelo; in villages in New England, the Prairie States, the South and Far West; in the kitchens of carry-out restaurants, mechanics' shops, stockbrokerage houses, pool halls, high schools, truck stops and universities—all of their lives this sense of fate and destiny had been working itself into their minds, and they were slowly beginning to understand it and deal with it and sometimes use it to their advantage. Buddies and girlfriends had been killed in car crashes; relatives had died of cancer, heart disease and old age. They had attended the funerals in Sunday-school suits, shaken, but reaffirmed in their belief that fate had called. They had also known the rewards for jobs well done: the winning of a basketball game, passing tests, the paycheck at the end of the week—and the penalties for failure: the silence of a locker room, an instructor's scorn, no paycheck. They accepted these things, most of them, because it gave an order to their lives, and they had worked a place for fate into the scheme, the random happenstances that would inevitably select some of them for its mysterious purposes, although none of them accepted the idea that he might be the one.

Though few of them realized it, they were about to enter a new period in which these rules of fate would not apply. Very soon, in fact, they would be living by instinct.

AT A crossroads past the mine site the convoy turned sharply westward, and the terrain began to change. They were headed directly into the emerald mountains, but the sun had dipped behind them and the emerald color had given way to stark, black silhouettes against a brilliant yellow sky. They were moving across a vast plain where uncultivated rice fields were overgrown by a tall brown saw grass that stretched as far as they could see in the fading light. Out of this, the twisted skeletons of burned and rusting vehicles began to appear on both sides of the road. As they approached the mountains, more and more of these loomed out of the saw grass. Automobiles, jeeps, trucks, personnel carriers, an occasional tank, some dismembered beyond recognition. A few were unmistakably American, others appeared to be French and the older, battered ones looked as if they might have been Japanese. Bravo Company stared at them wordlessly in the gray twilight, realizing they must be crossing what had been and was now a great battlefield.

Junk, Kahn thought. All junk. Scrap iron at two dollars eighty cents a pound. Rubber at forty cents, tin at two seventy-five, copper from wiring at five dollars, ball bearings, rods, ties, shafts, axles, glass—all of it salvageable, here for the taking.

"What about this place?" he asked the driver as they bounced along in the cab of the truck.

The soldier's eyes were glued straight ahead and he

gripped the wheel tightly. "Well, sir, the gooks call it the Plain of Elephants or something, but what we're on now, we call this the Blood Alley Road. There's about six more miles before we get to the pass."

Kahn suddenly remembered the conversation he'd had with his father's business partner, Mr. Bernard, a few weeks before they left, the night before his leave had ended. It had been the Fourth of July, and his father and mother and some friends were having a cookout in the backyard of their little house on the edge of the country-club golf course. Mr. Bernard had cornered him as Kahn walked down the steps to rejoin the party. His breath smelled of beer and shrimp, and he peered crookedly over horn-rimmed spectacles. He appeared to Kahn like a half-capsized owl.

"Say, Billy," he had said, "I don't know what your father has said to you about this, but I want you to know that when you're out of the service, you should think seriously about coming into the company. The junk business is a pretty good way to make a living. Your father and I, we've done pretty well, wouldn't you say?"

Kahn had nodded politely but said nothing, and stared down at the little picnic table where his parents and the others were watching the fireworks and eating seafood—less than fifty yards from the manicured golf course on which neither his father, nor any of them, for that matter, was allowed to play because they had had the luck, good or bad, to be born Jews.

"I know it might sound odd to a young man like yourself," Bernard had said, "but this war could be a good thing for us—all of us—in some ways, providing we do the right things. During a war, the military is nothing but waste. That's how we got started in this game, your father and I, twenty years ago after the last war.

"We know there'll be enormous amounts of surplus when this is over—heavy construction equipment, stoves, motors, clothing—stuff the military no longer wants. Some people call it salvage, but it's junk. Your father and I are not ashamed to call it junk. Nevertheless, there's a great deal of money to be made..."

Kahn continued to listen politely, but was more interested in watching the fireworks display which was now exploding in a kaleidoscope of noise and color all across the muggy Georgia night. It reminded him more of a mortar barrage than of fireworks. A red star cluster—that was nothing but fireworks, really; only the wrappers were different—one for fun, the other not so much fun. His profundity amused him. He had stopped listening to Mr. Bernard completely. Instead, Kahn was thinking about his father and wondering how many times he might have wanted to play a few holes on the golf course instead of driving all the way to the public course on the other side of town. Once, he had asked his father about it and had been told simply, "We don't play there"—not that "We can't," but that "We don't." Kahn knew his father must have wanted to, though, because it was right there, every day, in his own backyard.

"I want you to think about this, Billy," Mr. Bernard was saying. "While you're over there, you will see many things. You will be in a very good position to keep your eyes out for certain opportunites. The war won't last forever...."

THE TRUCK jolted over a huge pothole. "You know, sir..." the driver said. The driver's eyes were narrowed. His hands and face were filthy.

"...there ain't been a convoy across here in four months they don't try to mine or ambush somewheres along the way. The gooks don't even use this road no more. They say they ain't used it since the French was here."

Kahn looked out over the enormous junkyard/graveyard, where the unseen traces of human wreckage—bits of bone, teeth, blood and so on—were lumped in with the other junk. What was a human body worth these days? Ninety-eight cents, if you could break it down and process its precious metals and deposits? Maybe more, he thought.

Ahead, the jungle sloped down toward the plain from halfway up the mountainside. In time, he decided, if the fighting ceased, it would probably creep out of the hills and overtake the Plain of Elephants. The roots would embed themselves in the earth, hold soil, rot and then be reborn again until layer after layer of dirt and compost would cover the Blood Alley Road where so many battles had been fought. Later, in thousands of years, other processes would occur. Perhaps the ocean would rise and deposit sediments, or the forces of erosion would slowly bring the mountains down, pressing it all deeper and deeper into the earth's crust, and the bones and iron would disintegrate under the weight until nothing remained but their fossilized impressions. Then eventually, in the far-distant future of the world, a geological sleuth might uncover all of this—and wonder for a while what in hell had gone on here. In the end he would probably figure it out and write about it in a book, and then they would learn what had happened. In the far-distant future of the world.

THE TRUCK rocked along madly, and Kahn's thoughts continued to return in bits and pieces to the night of the family picnic. After the conversation with Bernard they had all sat down again, and after the food was gone they had drunk more beer, and the women had gone inside, but the men had stayed on and talked, and Kahn had stayed with them, because there hadn't been anywhere else to go. At one point, Mr. Bernard had peered at him across the table and said, loudly, "You know, Billy, I want you to know we are all proud of you for what you're doing. . . ."

Kahn remembered that his father had looked up at him from picking the last of a steamed crab, and smiled, and Bernard had gone on about how he and Kahn's father had enlisted in the service in nineteen forty-two and how they had been in the Quartermaster Corps but nevertheless had seen some of the fighting in Europe and how it was such a fine thing that Kahn was going over now. . . .

And he had begun to wonder then, actually for the first time, *Why?* Not that it made much difference, because the fact was he *was* going, but it had still set him to thinking. He had tried to imagine what it would be like, and found that he couldn't. He found, in fact, that he had utterly no idea, either of what it would be like or of why he was going, and from time to time until they left, and also on the transport, he had stil wondered and still come up with no answer he could make sense out of, and it bothered him still even now, in the cab of the truck, and his head began to ache, and he had a tingly sensation in his hands and feet as though his brain were trying to tell him something and he couldn't figure out exactly what it was.

It did not come to him quickly.

It took another mile for him to realize that he no longer cared why he was *going* here, and that what he was feeling now was fear, and that for the past ten minutes he had been asking himself over and over in the deep recesses of his mind, Why am I here?—Why the hell am I here?

ALL OF them were glad to see the dawn. Beyond the pass through the mountains, they had bivouacked for the night in a quiet green valley, although some of the trucks had had to pull off in the pass itself because their timetable had been upset by the mining of the personnel carrier. Patch considered this insecure and would have much preferred to circle up like a wagon train instead of being strung out along several miles of road, and he had radioed an Artillery battery in the area to put up flares during the night.

They had slept, or tried to sleep in or under the trucks or on the ground beside them, but the flares kept them awake most of the night. The banana-cat was edgy because of its change of ownership, and Crump finally had to tie it to the wheel of a deuce-and-a-half so he could get some sleep. Once they observed a firefight in progress on some low hills at the end of the valley. Red tracers arched out from a machine gun, and they could hear the distant pop of small-arms fire and the dull thud of mortars. Rumors abounded about the circumstances of this engagement until word got back that a South Korean unit was operating somewhere in the valley.

In the predawn blackness, which seemed the darkest of all, they were roused and loaded again into the trucks, and at the first sign of light the convoy lurched toward the second line of mountains; then upward over them, across awesome, winding passes, and along thin gravel roads where the endless jungle rose above them in tangled shades of green; then onto a high, open plateau where everything was brown, with scrubby, broken trees; past strange huts of straw and thin timber shimmering in the noonday heat, and through filthy roadside villages of tin shacks so flimsy it was hard to see how they were still standing. In late afternoon they reached the Base Camp at Monkey Mountain.

17

"You're supposed to bring them out head first," the Graves Registration lieutenant was saying. "Everything has to be done a certain way.

"It's easier, especially if you're going uphill, because the weight of the body is mostly in the trunk—but that's actually not the reason."

He took another swig of beer. . . .

"It's something that started in the First World War, I think—it's a matter of showing proper respect. The theory is, the men feel more comfortable if they see it done properly instead of just dragging them off like flour sacks."

Kahn liked the Graves Registration lieutenant—and he liked the other guy sitting at the table, whose name was Holden and who worked on the general's staff. He had seen Holden around before back at Fort Bragg, and also during the convoy, but never actually talked to him until tonight, when they'd both happened about the same time into the tent set up as an officers' club. Now here they were, he thought, sitting together on the night of his arrival, three first lieutenants: one who worked where the orders originated; himself, who was destined to carry the orders out; and another whose job it was to deal with the results of the carried-out orders.

At first Holden seemed aloof, and Kahn had tried to decide if it was because he was a general's aide or because he had grown up that way. In the end, he decided it was both, for Holden's speech, like his face, was patrician, and it was somewhat mannered; but the face was handsome—though not in the way Kahn thought his own was—and he was drawn to him in the way good-looking men are often drawn to each other because they share a bond of having it easy with women. After a while Holden seemed to become more natural, and Kahn was duly impressed when he learned Holden had gone to Princeton. From the point of view of a Florida State man, they did not let fools into Princeton.

"THE TROUBLE," the Graves Registration lieutenant said, "is after they've been out there for a while.

"At Fort Lee we used dummies in the fieldwork, but it isn't like that here. You don't find remains just lying in an open field—they're in all sorts of damned places."

Holden also liked the Graves Registration lieutenant. He was a cheery sort of fellow who had an awful job and was making the best of it.

But Holden hadn't made up his mind yet about Kahn. He was a little put off by what he took for cockiness. He had learned Kahn was from the South and he suspected he was a Jew, and while the first enhanced his interest, the second diminished it just a bit—but that wasn't what troubled him. It seemed that behind Kahn's apparent cockiness there was a great deal of uncertainty, and it bugged Holden a little because it was a weakness of his own.

"Last week, for instance," the Graves Registration lieutenant continued, "we had to go into the Ia Drang after three guys from the Twenty-fifth Division who'd been there sixteen days. Boy, was that a mess. . . .

"They were at the bottom of a little ridge that had been taken by us and then taken back by the gooks and then taken back by us again. These guys got it when the gooks took it back the first time, and the gooks just shoveled some dirt over them after a while so they wouldn't smell. . . .

"Well, let me tell you, when they've been under for a while—I mean, that shallow—they fill up with gas and they just come up to the surface—a hand or a leg will just pop out, you know? That's how we found them, but it took nearly four hours to find the last one. . . ."

From the distant mountains came a deep grumbling of artillery, and a thin tremor ran through the plank floor of the tent. Kahn looked up from his beer.

"You gotta get used to that," the Graves Registration lieutenant said. "Goes on all night."

Holden went to get them more beer. While he waited at the bar, he took out Becky's letter and looked at it again. He had a sudden urge to put it to his nose to see if he could recognize her smell, but instead simply ran his fingers over her signature several times. After the convoy arrived, he had hunted down the mail clerk and persuaded him to open the mail tent. The letter was there, but it took him a long time to find it. . . .

"Oh, here you are, sir," the mail clerk said. "It must have come in yesterday."

Holden thanked him, and as he was leaving, the mail clerk said, "I know how it is, sir; I got a girl at home too." Holden made a mental note to do something nice for the mail clerk. Because of his job, the mail clerk was the most popular man in the Brigade.

He went off alone to read it.

The sun was low behind the mountains, and Holden

found a knoll at the edge of the compound where he sat down and opened the letter carefully. The first thing he took out was a *Time* magazine photograph in which Becky, beautifully defiant, was featured with five or six others in front of an academic-looking building. In the background, a crowd of students help up antiwar signs.

"Hi, love," the letter said. *"This is my latest photograph."*

The accompanying clipping described a demonstration in Boston to protest military-type research being performed in various departments of the consortium of universities. Quoted prominently was a Dr. Richard Widenfield, who was described in the article as "the emerging leader of the growing antiwar movement."

He stared at the clipping a long time before reading the rest of the letter, anger and fear and jealousy and hatred welling up inside him. Widenfield again. It was always Widenfield somewhere, waiting in the wings. He resented him, resented him because he was there, and because he was older, damned near old enough to be her father—and because he had had her; but mostly, right now, because Widenfield was there and he was here and there was nothing he could do about it except maybe get himself shot up and sent home.

At the table, the Graves Registration lieutenant was still holding forth:

"Did you know it takes four men to carry one remains? You'd think it would only take two, but it takes four—especially because of the jungle and underbrush."

The Graves Registration lieutenant's face was white and long, the kind of face that never tans, and his thin blond hair was receding at the temples. Kahn asked him what happened if they got shot at while they were doing their work.

"You drop him right there and hit the dirt," the Graves Registration lieutenant replied cheerily. He seemed pleased he'd been asked the question.

"Now, that isn't the school solution, but I don't want any of my men killed. And he's already dead—what does it matter to him?"

*   *   *

HOLDEN SUDDENLY wanted to read the letter again; to study it closely; weigh it against the implications of the photograph and clipping; search it for any sign she might be involved with Widenfield again. Why had she sent it? The uncertainty was maddening. Even though they'd tried one weekend before he left, they hadn't really resolved it to his satisfaction.

It had been the Fourth of July, two weeks before he shipped out, and he had invited Becky to his parents' summer home near Southampton, Long Island, They sneaked away early from a big fireworks beach party and walked down a dark, sandy lane until they found their car. She touched him and kissed him, and during the ride back she had slowly taken off her clothes and begun taking off his, and they had driven the last five miles completely naked, laughing drunkenly and hysterically through several historic villages where Holden was mildly concerned that if a local policeman should stop them for something they would be thrown into jail forever.

They pulled the car close behind the guest cottage where Becky was staying and dashed madly for the bedroom, where they spent the next hour doing practically every imaginable erotic act. They did things Holden had never dreamed he would do, could never have pictured himself doing and would have felt extremely uncomfortable doing—except with her.

She was a good, dirty woman.

Afterward, he made them tall glasses of daiquiris, which they took back to bed, lying on top of the sheets. Through the French doors they were bathed in light from the silver moon that hung over the dunes and the flat potato fields which stretched from the ocean to the edge of the lawn.

It had come up again when he had asked if she was coming to North Carolina the next weekend.

"Oh, baby, I can't—Richard's called a meeting in New York to plan what we're going to do in the fall. They're counting on me—I just have to be there," she said.

Holden got up and put on his pants and went into the

small living room. She came in after a while, wearing a terry-cloth robe, and sat on the sofa across from him, her legs tucked beneath her.

"Frank," she said finally, "we're going to have to do something about this."

"You bet we are!" He said it as though he had a mouth full of ashes.

"I'm not doing this against you—any more than you're doing what you're doing against me," she said. "We both have to do what we think is right."

"That's not what I'm talking about," he said. "If you want to make a fool of yourself with this protesting business, it's okay by me. But I don't like it worth a damn that you're fooling around with Widenfield. I mean, how do you think it makes me feel?"

"Look," Becky said sharply, "he's a very important person in the movement—maybe the most important. Every day there are people—you'd be surprised who they are: politicians, and writers and actors—who phone up or write to ask him how they can help. You really would be surprised. . . ."

"I'll bet. But that doesn't have anything to do with what I'm saying. I'm saying I don't like him trying to get into your pants, that's what I'm saying."

She went to the bar to get a drink.

"You know that Richard and I felt a lot for each other at one time—I've told you about that. And he knows about you and he understands and he isn't always running you down like you do him. As a matter of fact, he asks about you sometimes—in a nice way. He wants to stop this war before you have to go over there and get yourself hurt," she said.

"You're still sleeping with him, aren't you?" he demanded.

"That's really not any of your business, Frank Holden." There was anger in her eyes—the first he'd seen since their time in the mountains.

"If you want to believe it, then do. I might as well say this, too: My sex life is my business. If you want me to say my sex life is going to stop while you go over there, I'm not going to. I don't know. I like sex too. With you it's been different, you know that; but you might just as well know right now I'm not making any promises. I'm going to be completely honest about it. I've said I love you and that's all that ought to matter.

"Listen," she said after a silence, "I'm going to take a walk on the beach."

He didn't wait for her to dress. He stormed out to the car and took off down the road at high speed, back toward the big fireworks beach party, where he intended to get very, very drunk and, if possible, get laid.

"YOU WOULDN'T believe the paperwork it takes to process a remains," the Grave Registration lieutenant said. "That's probably the worst part of the whole thing.... The smell of the dead isn't as bad as most people think...." He looked as if he were getting a little drunk, and Kahn thought his tone was slightly apologetic.

"It's just a job," the Graves Registration lieutenant said. "Somebody's got to do it....

"The thing about it is, you gotta take it seriously—it's all a matter of respect." His long face grew suddenly serious.

"You know, when we went out there to get those guys from the Twenty-fifth Division, a wiseass I've got working for me installed a sign over my morgue that said, 'Three two eight GR Company—We always get our man.' Jesus! You never heard grief like I got when we came back. The G-Three saw it and came down and chewed my ass for half an hour. He says, 'What do you think this is, McCrary, a joke? Would you find it more amusing to spend a couple of weeks as point man out there?' It took some fast talk to convince him I didn't have anything to do with that damned sign." The Graves Registration lieutenant went to the bar for another round of beer.

"I'd hate to have his job, wouldn't you?" Kahn said to Holden, who was looking despondent.

"Yeah, but I'm not sure I'd want yours either," Holden said.

His mind was still far away, wondering what she was

doing tonight, or this morning, by her time, and if she was thinking about him, if she was with Widenfield, twelve thousand miles away—the difference between night and day. He wanted desperately to talk to her now, to tell her he loved her, to hear her say it to him, even though he might not believe it—not that she told him lies, but he felt she was keeping something from him.

But he knew there was nothing he could do about it. Because he was up to his neck in this now. There was no quitting, and no turning back and no place to hide. Secretly, although he would never openly admit it to himself, he wished Widenfield had been successful and that the war *had* ended and that he hadn't had to come here.

"You know the bad thing about this job?" the Graves Registration lieutenant said. He took a long swallow of beer and peered at them through watery eyes.

"Sometimes people look at me like they think I'm some kind of ghoul."

18

THEY HAD been there a week when Spudhead burned the shithouse down.

It was a week of lectures and endless drilling in do's and don'ts delivered morning till night by tan-faced sergeants fresh from the fighting.

They told them how to stay alive:

"Don't touch nothing you don't know exactly what it is...."

And how not to get the clap:

"All these gook women got it, so you don't want it, you stay the hell away from them. Wait till your R and R—there's good clean whorehouses in Bangkok and Hong Kong...."

And how to use proper radio procedures:

"I don't want to hear nobody saying anybody's name over the radio. I catch anybody saying anybody's name over the radio, his ass is in big trouble...."

And how to behave toward the Vietnamese people:

"Grab 'em by the balls; their hearts and minds will follow...."

It was a week of being issued more equipment, of interminable lines into hastily thrown-up sheds and tents wherein lay mountainous piles of canvas-covered steel-soled jungle boots, lightweight poplin jungle fatigues, heavy green socks, black face paint, insect repellent, poncho liners, ponchos, camouflage underwear, malaria pills, sunglasses, toothbrushes, shaving cream, entrenching tools and every other conceivable item to keep a moving army on its feet. They were even issued military scrip in exchange for their American dollars. This was promptly dubbed "funny money."

The same tan-faced sergeants told them how to use all their new gear.

They said:

"The M-sixteen rifle is an outstanding weapon. But you got to keep this weapon clean. If you don't keep this weapon clean, this weapon will not fire. If this weapon does not fire when you want it to, you might as well just take out your dick and play with it till they come and kill you...."

And they said:

"Everybody wants to carry a roll of this here green tape. Green tape can fix anything. Some of you don't know it, but the world is actually held together with green tape. Without green tape, the world would fall apart...."

And they said:

"These here boots are made to dry out fast, but they ain't magic, so you always carry two extra pairs of dry socks. If you walk around with wet feet, you gonna get immersion foot, and if you get immersion foot, you gonna be one sorry asshole...."

THE SHITHOUSE had been the subject of bitter controversy ever since they had arrived. It was an officers' shithouse, consisting of a long wooden shed inside which half a dozen round holes had been cut in a long plywood board. Beneath each hole was a sawed-in-half fifty-five-gallon oil drum filled with low-grade kerosene. Every day, the shithouse detail would pull out the drums and light a match to them, and whatever was inside would burn for half an hour with a foul, black stench.

The trouble was that the shithouse had been established very close to where Bravo Company was billeted. When the convoy arrived, a grinning, red faced Quartermaster sergeant had ushered them to a line of newly erected wood-floored forty-man tents, with rolled-up sides and mosquito netting, where they would live until they went into the field, and where they would stay whenever they returned to pull palace guard, and where they would store all their regular gear. It was their permanent home as long as the Brigade stayed at Monkey Mountain.

The morning of the second day, they discovered the location was not ideal.

Shortly after sunup the shithouse detail went to work, and soon great billows of black smoke wafted through the tents of Bravo Company and part of Charlie Company as well, and the men, who had just gotten up and were performing their morning regimens, began gagging and coughing and cursing fiercely at the indignity of the consumptive shitsmoke. Even the banana-cat was outraged, and it screeched and chattered and batted furiously at its nose.

Trunk was infuriated and stalked off to find the red-faced Quartermaster sergeant who had put them there. When he was unable to locate him, he went to the Brigade Sergeant Major, who was eating his breakfast in the senior noncoms' mess. The Brigade Sergeant Major looked at Trunk with dark, cobralike eyes as he explained the situation, and when he had finished, the Brigade Sergeant Major put down a forkful of watery eggs and stared silently out the tent flap as though he did not need to deal with such problems so early in the morning.

"Well, Trunk," he said in slowly measured words, "why don't we give it a while? The wind doesn't always blow in your direction—maybe it's just a fluke.

"The trouble is, we had the damned thing up on the north perimeter, but the wind that comes out of the valley blew the smoke into the general's tent, and he raised hell with me for it. I'd like to move it to the other side of the compound, but it's gotta be close enough for the officers to get to it or they're gonna raise hell with me again. I'm in a bind over this, Trunk—we can't go moving the thing all over hell's creation. Besides, you guys are going into the bush in a few days and you won't have to worry about it no more anyway," the Brigade Sergeant Major said.

Trunk tried to gloss over the bad news, but after a week the projected wind shift had not occurred, and the tents and the men in them were beginning to take on a smell of their own. Every morning they spoke of taking matters into their own hands—and then Spudhead's name came up on the duty roster to burn the shit barrels in the officers' latrine.

No ONE in charge ever knew if it was accidental or on purpose, but the latrine went up like tinder when the barrel of kerosene Spudhead was lighting tipped over, spilling its flaming contents against the shed.

The latrine's lone occupant, a second lieutenant of Engineers, had gone unnoticed by the shithouse detail, because they were working strictly from the rear of the shed. The first they learned of his presence was a muffled cry from within: "Hey, what's going on out there!"

But before anyone could answer, a great rush of fire and smoke lapped through the dry-board wall, and the lieutenant of Engineers bounded out of the flaming latrine like a man in a sack race, his bare ass gleaming in the morning sun, shouting disjointed curses at Spudhead and the others.

"Are you goddamn bastards crazy?" he bellowed. His eyes were wild, as though he had been raised from sleep by a trombone played in his ear. "I could have been burned alive in there!"

When he was partially recovered, the Engineer lieutenant took charge of the fire-fighting effort. But by then it was too late, since the detail had no tools with which to extinguish the blaze; the most they could do was try to stomp out some burning grass around the edges, and in the end they just stood around and observed the immolation.

"You bunch of fucking numbnuts," the lieutenant of Engineers said sourly. "If you were in my outfit I'd have your asses courtmartialed.

"I might even do it anyway," he said. "That was a damned fine latrine."

Spudhead looked like a man who had just been fired out of a cannon. His face was black and his eyebrows singed off. Miraculously, he wasn't hurt badly, and when he came back from the infirmary that afternoon, Spudhead had already become a sort of folk hero to the rest of the company.

That evening in the mess tent, he was seated at a long table with Madman Muntz and Crump when DiGeorgio stood up from his table at the other end of the tent and shouted:

"WHO BURNED THE SHITHOUSE DOWN?"

At once, an obviously orchestrated chorus of a hundred men began chanting:

"SPUDHEAD, SPUDHEAD, SPUDHEAD," over and over again, and this was repeated at various times each day: at chow; at the outdoor movie at night; in lines where they waited to be issued equipment and sometimes in the tent after lights-out. Finally, Spudhead began to wonder if the cry would follow him around the rest of his life.

TWO WEEKS LATER, Bravo Company saw its first action, killed its first enemy, suffered its first casualties and got a slight glimpse of what was to come.

Several days earlier, a patrol operating near a village not far from Monkey Mountain had killed a North Vietnamese officer and removed two documents from his body. One was an important-looking paper, sealed and signed by some high-ranking official. The other was an almost illegibly scrawled note on a piece of rice paper.

Both were sent back to Intelligence headquarters, translated, assimilated and presented at the staff briefing the following day. The official-looking document turned out to be a plea from the Assistant Chief of Political Operations saying North Vietnamese soldiers should refrain from defecating in the rice fields because it was creating ill will among the people. The scrawled note, however, indicated that the enemy had established a staging area in the village near the spot where the officer was killed. It was to be Bravo Company's baptism of fire.

IN THE dark stillness of early morning, they slogged across the rice fields like a gang of New Year's drunks, muttering bitten curses at the muck and unseen lumps of earth that caused them to stumble and slip. They had been walking for nearly an hour since the trucks had let them off by the roadside several miles away. Anything that might rattle, including their dog tags, had been fastened in place by the green tape. The M-16 rifles had been meticulously cleaned and loaded; the canvas-covered jungle boots were completely soaked, but extra socks had been stuffed into packs and pockets. To the smallest detail, every preparation had been taken and with the kind of care and thoroughness they would not take again to quite the same degree.

It was a one-shot deal, Patch told the officers' briefing the night before. "A live-fire exercise," he called it.

Two platoons from another battalion which had been in the bush for nearly a week would begin before dawn to close in on the village from some hills to the west. The theory of attack was that the two platoons, known as Charlie Force, would drive the enemy out of the village and Bravo Company would act as a blocking force to gun them down as they ran away. It was as simple as that—but of course, it wasn't.

A little light finally appeared from behind the eastern ridge, and Kahn halted the line to get his bearings. A stand of trees was barely visible ahead of them, but there was no sign of a village. It took ten minutes of precious darkness to locate it. Sharkey, on the left flank, got word down that his men had it in sight far to their left, which meant the whole line had drifted nearly a quarter-mile out of position. Kahn had just hurriedly ordered the line to move left when Bateson, his radio operator, handed him the handset. "The colonel wants you, sir," the radio operator whispered.

Kahn identified himself, and Patch's voice came back in his ear, clearly irritated.

"Why haven't I heard from you?—You were supposed to be in position fifteen minutes ago. What's going on down there?" he growled.

"We have it in sight and are getting into position now," Kahn replied.

"You get moving and get back to me on the double—do you understand?" Patch said.

By now they could see the village among the trees—ten or fifteen thatched-roofed huts that looked deserted in the thin gray light. Kahn arranged the company in a slight arc behind a low dike in the paddy and informed Patch, who was in the command post at Monkey Mountain, that they were set up.

"Okay, okay," Patch said. "Anything that moves now—anything that moves . . ."

THEY WAITED for a long time. Nothing stirred in the village or the rice fields, and there was no sign of Charlie Force. As the light brightened behind the eastern mountains, each of them was deep in his own thoughts: some about what might be forthcoming from the village, some about homes and friends and some, more immediately, about their present condition, especially those unlucky enough to be lying in a watery part of the paddy.

Today they had reached the ultimate milestone in their soldiers' careers. The first had been their induction into the service, passing the requisite physical and mental and moral tests. The second had been their completion of basic training: the long, rigorous hours of drilling and instruction and cleaning their barracks and themselves and learning to live with the Army and with one another to the satisfaction of their superiors so that at the end they were awarded the privilege of contributing to the service of their country and not merely taking from it. Third was their delivery to this war in which the elected leaders had seen fit to engage. Now, at any moment, each of them would become an individual, final extension of a great policy-making scheme that involved the entire political, social and economic fabric of the most powerful nation in the history of the world.

Looking out at the village, bathed now in the glow of a warm morning sun, few of them saw it that way, but they were all aware, more or less, of what was expected of them; that their duty here was to kill on sight anyone who ran out of that treeline, because they had been informed in no uncertain terms that whosoever did would be no friend of the United States of America or of theirs. . . .

Bateson, lying with his ear glued to the radio handset, started for a second, then handed it to Kahn. "It's the Old Man again, sir," he said.

"They're moving in now," Patch said; "be ready."

As he finished the sentence, there was the sound of rifle fire popping across the paddies from the other side of the village. It began as sporadic bursts, but quickly increased to a steady cacophony. From behind the dike Bravo Company could distinguish two different types of fire, although one type, louder and slower, was less intense than the other.

Kahn had a sick knot in his stomach, not so much from fear as from uncertainty. He worried that he might not do the right thing. Today he could see in the eyes of the men that they were looking at him in a different way than before—he was now their sole leader, guide and savior—and he knew that he somehow had to get over the urge to save his own skin he had felt ever since the sun came up.

He was scanning the village intently through his field glasses when he saw the man run out.

The man was dressed in standard black peasant's clothing, and from this distance he seemed to be running in a jerky, pantherlike way, crouching every so often behind a dike. It was impossible to tell if he was armed, and Kahn figured that if he kept his course the man would run right into Brill's lap.

Brill's platoon had the right flank, and when Brill saw the man running he frantically motioned the platoon to scrunch down lower so as not to alert him. Crump took a final look and simply turned over on his back with his head resting against the dike, and began counting. It was just like hunting deer, Crump thought as he lay there, barely breathing, remembering the lessons he had been taught in dark Mississippi forests: "Just take a look and drop down, count the seconds it'll take till he gets into range, then rise up slow and bring the barrel down on him. Either he's coming your way or he isn't. Watching ain't going to change it."

Patch was on the radio again, and there was a coolness in his voice as though he were deliberately trying to keep himself calm.

"Charlie Force has contact," he said. "I want you to be ready to advance at my command."

Kahn had his glasses on the spot where the running man had crouched last, and the handset was tucked under his chin. He had just pressed the transmission bar to tell Patch they had a suspected VC in sight when the man leaped up and began to run again toward Brill's position. Why don't they shoot? Kahn thought. He's clear in range by now. Is it because they're waiting for me to tell them? Hadn't it been clear? Maybe not—maybe they were waiting for him to give the order, the order to execute the Running Man. But he had said it already: "Anything that moves . . ."

The single crack of Crump's rifle jarred everyone down to the last man on the farthest flank of the line.

The Running Man stood upright for a moment, then began to waver sideways in crablike steps, his entire body twitching and jerking like a man with Saint Vitus' Dance. He took about ten of these steps before sinking to his knees, creating in the final seconds of his life a brief little spectacle that commanded the undivided attention of the entire Company.

Kahn watched in frozen, rapt fascination, Crump's shot still ringing in his ears, trapped like a fly in amber on a warm Asian morning. Then it dawned on him that his hand was still pressing the transmission bar on the handset. Quickly he released it and received the last sentences of furious monologue by Patch, who had been trying to get through to order the advance. Kahn was waiting for him to finish when the enemy mortar fire began dropping in around them.

Two rounds came in first, shooting high geysers of paddy mud and water and smoke just behind Sharkey's position. The third, nearer the center, was close enough for Kahn to feel the concussion, as though someone had blown a strong, warm breath on his face.

The silence rolled back in, and there was yelling and confusion down the line where the last round exploded, and Kahn was frantically pressing the transmission bar on the radio and yelling into it as if it were a magical instrument of their deliverance. When he finished, Patch's voice came over in the same cool way it had at first, but sternly this time, as though he were talking to a child.

"I want you to get up and move forward. I want you to get up out of there right now. Move toward the village—do you understand me?" he said.

A second salvo of mortar fire burst behind them, and Kahn squeezed down as tight as he could behind the dike, where he found himself face to face with Sergeant Trunk, who also had been listening to Colonel Patch's vituperations over the radio. Beyond them, a vicious rattle of gunfire issued from the village, and again, for a moment, Kahn felt frozen in time. Trunk's voice came at him extraneously, and from a great distance away, although Trunk was leaning toward him, only inches from his face.

"We going on now, Lieutenant?" Trunk asked. Kahn nodded dumbly, but didn't move, and for an instant his eyes locked with the First Sergeant's in a strange, silent, desperate query. Another mortar round blew up mud and water somewhere to their front.

"Lieutenant," Trunk said fiercely, "we got to move. We got to get up out of here."

Kahn suddenly felt short of breath. He was trying to picture what might happen when they got up. They could make a dash for it, toward the village, in between salvos—but suppose they got up just as the mortars landed...suppose...

Then Trunk was on his feet, yelling, and dragging people up all along the dike and moving them out. Instantaneously Kahn joined him, standing on the dike, signaling with his arms for them to advance. Another salvo caught them in the open as they stumbled forward.

Two men from Sharkey's platoon fell. Other men went to them, but the line continued to advance, and Kahn gave the signal to advance on the run. The Company lumbered forward under its heavy gear, past the body of the Running Man, leaving the injured and their helpers to their fate. As they approached the village, a patch of woods on a hill suddenly exploded, and Kahn guessed that Charlie Force had spotted the mortars and called in artillery.

No more mortars fell, and when they reached the treeline, Kahn signaled to stop, and they knelt down on line, giving the stragglers a chance to catch up. The firing in the village seemed to have ceased, and through the trees they could see the green forms of Charlie Force moving down the paths and among the huts. The radio operator handed Kahn the handset again.

"What is your situation down there?" Patch demanded.

"We need dust-off ASAP. Charlie Force is in the village now. The shooting has—ah, seems to have stopped," Kahn said.

"I know about Charlie Force. I have been in contact with them," Patch said crossly. "I want to know where you are and what your situation is. Can you tell me?"

"Ah, roger," Kahn said. He noticed that his hands were shaking violently, and he was having difficulty holding down the transmit bar on the radio.

"We are on line just outside the village—we are about fifty meters away from it. We have several men injured and request dust-off immediately," Kahn said.

"You are on line at the village—fine," Patch said. "Now I want you to move forward slowly into the village until you link up with Charlie Force—and be careful who you shoot. I have a bird waiting and I'm on the way down there now. Your dust-off is in the air."

They moved into the treeline, rifles at the ready, searching every hut for possible enemy supplies or people hiding. All they found was old men, women and children. They met Charlie Force near the center of the village.

Kahn told Bravo Company to take a smoke break, and then he sat down on a log next to Trunk, who had taken off his helmet and removed from his little knapsack a hopelessly stained and battered coffee cup. Trunk opened his canteen and poured the cup half full of water and set it down in front of him, stirring it slowly with a stick.

"Sergeant," Kahn said, "I want you to know that out there in the paddy... I don't know what..."

"We got their asses outta there, didn't we, Lieutenant? I thought it was pretty damned good for their first time, huh?"

"Yeah," Kahn said numbly, "I guess so. It was mine too...." He felt a sudden rush of blood to his feet, and the sweat in his fatigues became cold on his skin. Somewhere along the way he had twisted his ankle and it was hurting a little bit. Hazily, he watched Trunk stir the water in the coffee cup, which had now turned a dark, chocolate brown.

Kahn wondered what might have happened if Trunk hadn't stood up and made the first move. How long would he have lain there, hugging ground, while the mortars rained down on them? Well, he just didn't know. He wanted to believe he would have jumped up by himself in a few seconds and gotten them going. But he just didn't know, and now he never would.

What he did know for sure was that he'd felt as helpless as a sailor in a fog. Not a captain, but a sailor, waiting for someone to tell him what to do, and when that finally happened, in the form of Patch's orders, there had been a strange, two-way pulling, one way going with his instincts and another going against them, but the one against them—the moving out—was what had saved their asses, although he hadn't seen it that way then. What bothered him most was that this two-way pulling had damn near thrown him into a panic, and made him wonder now if he was really fit to run this or any other outfit.

Trunk tossed his stirring stick aside. "Want some mocha, Lieutenant?" He offered the cup to Kahn.

"What is it?" Kahn asked. He peered at the substance inside the cup.

"Sort of like coffee," Trunk said. He took a swallow himself and shuddered.

"Where'd you get that cup, anyway? It looks like some kind of relic."

"Korea," Trunk said proudly. "Somebody hit me in the head with it, so I kept it as sort of a souvenir."

The cup had no handle anymore, and it was stained and chipped beyond belief. Kahn was barely able to make out the insigne of some long-forgotten tactical fighter wing. There was a thick crust caked inside, almost like the charring inside a well-used smoking pipe.

Trunk explained that he'd kept it for ten years without washing it, so now he could simply pour in water and it automatically became coffee—or mocha, as he called it. "Sure you don't want some, Lieutenant? It'll lift you right off your feet."

"That's what I'm afraid of," Kahn said. He stood up, testing the soreness of his ankle and looking around for a place to take a leak. He was goddamn glad to have Trunk around.

MEANWHILE, SOME of the men had been taking a look at the bodies of four or five VC killed by Charlie Force. They were sprawled on the ground in odd positions, limbs askew, like preposterous rag dolls, the blood already drying on their clothing and dark yellowish skin. The men of Charlie Force had already stripped them of possible souvenirs.

Bravo Company gawked at the corpses with nervous exhilaration. Most of them had never seen dead men this way, and lying as they were, they looked like so much subhuman meat—but nevertheless remained testimony to the fact that there was an enemy here who would try to kill them if he got a chance. There was satisfaction in it—though it was an uncomfortable satisfaction, standing this close to the corpses—that they had come through the day properly. They had faced the enemy, in the form of the Running Man and these dead—who would surely have shot at them if they had seen them; had suffered the terror of the mortar fire and had moved forward through it and taken the village, so that for the time being it was theirs. But most important—and most of them knew this, because they had discussed it for days before the operation—each one of them was now entitled, by virtue of the fact that he had come under enemy fire in a combat situation, to wear the great prize of honor: the Combat Infantryman's Badge.

—One who didn't feel that way, however, was Sergeant Groutman. Badges didn't mean shit to him. Like the bodies, he could take them or leave them, and while most of the others were taking a smoke break or gawking at the bodies, Groutman had been negotiating with one of the village girls for a quick piece of ass.

Half of Brill's platoon, including Brill himself, was watching as Groutman bargained with the girl for her services. She was young and frail and her black peasant's clothing soiled. Her face had been pitted by smallpox. The two of them were standing away from the rest, near a clump of foliage that opened into a trail to another part of the village. The girl seemed nervous and giggled, as she grappled in pidgin English, but she was not smiling as Groutman pressed his offer.

"Fifty Pee," he said.

"Two hundred Pee," she countered.

"Fifty," Groutman declared.

"Two hundred."

"Okay, cunt—seventy-five piasters."

"Two hundred," she chirped.

"You sow!" Groutman cried, using the Vietnamese word for bad.

"Me no sow—you sow!" the girl spat.

"Piss on that!" Groutman said nastily. He pushed his face close to hers. "Seventy-five Pee."

The girl turned haughtily away, but as she did the sergeant grabbed her by her blouse and pulled her backward, and when she turned, her eyes were wild and frightened.

He released her and she began to back slowly down the trail. Brill and his men were sitting, watching with interest about ten yards away. Suddenly Groutman lunged for the girl, but she jumped out of reach and turned just in time to run smack into the huge bulk of Lieutenant Donovan, who appeared unexpectedly from the other direction with a squad of his men. The girl let out a shrill cry and started to go the other way, but Groutman was right in front of her. Sandwiched on the tiny path between the two large Americans, the girl began to back off into the bush and she nearly stumbled in some vines.

"What's going on here?" Donovan said.

Groutman grinned sheepishly. "The lady and me was having a conversation, Lieutenant, that's all."

"It doesn't look like it to me," Donovan said. The squad of men behind him had crowded forward to see what was happening.

"Come 'ere, little lady," Groutman said. The girl's face was set in fear. She had backed as far as she could into the underbrush. Groutman took another step toward her.

"Oh, knock it off, Sergeant," Donovan said.

"That's what I'm trying to do, Lieutenant." He grinned.

"I mean it, Sergeant. Go on back to your platoon," Donovan said sternly.

Brill, who had heard but not seen all of the confrontation because they were halfway down the trail, suddenly arrived on the scene.

"Brill, if this man belongs to you, you better get him squared away," Donovan said.

Brill turned to Groutman, who had abandoned his interest in the girl. "All right, Sergeant, what's happened? What are you doing?"

"Nothing," Groutman said darkly. "I was just trying to

make a deal with this gook when the lieutenant here—"

"Deal, hell!" Donovan said. "He's fooling around with her. You know we can't—"

"Go on back to the platoon, Ed," Brill said. Groutman glanced at him sourly, but said nothing and stalked back down the trail. When he had disappeared, Brill turned to Donovan.

"Look, Donovan, the sergeant wasn't hurting anything. I saw most of it until you came up. He was just—"

"Like hell," Donovan said. "I saw what was going on."

"Listen, I can take care of my platoon, and if there's any problem you ought to go through me instead of—"

"Oh, fuck off, Brill," Donovan said. "You can't clean your own shoes." He walked away, the squad following behind him.

Brill stood and watched them go, and afterward, instead of returning to his platoon right away, he went down the trail a little farther and took out the Randall knife, and when he was certain he was alone he seized it by the blade and threw it savagely at a thick-trunked tree.

19

"I'M SURE glad you guys didn't give me any business out there today," McCrary, the Graves Registration lieutenant, said. They were plodding in the darkness from the officers'-mess tent up the rise where the Tactical Operations Center was situated.

"Heard a couple of your men caught something—but they're going to be all right, huh?"

"They'll be all right," Kahn said. "One's going home, though." He shoved his hands deeper into his pockets and leaned forward, boots sinking into the soft earth. He was dead tired and his ankle still hurt and he had planned to get some sleep until Patch sent word he wanted to see him in the TOC after chow.

"Heard you really did a number today," McCrary said. "Mostly all you come up with out there is a mouthful of wind...." Kahn noticed that McCrary, whom everyone called "Digger," was breathing heavily as they trudged up the hill. Evidently they didn't get much exercise in Graves Registration.

"The Ia Drang, now—it's something else," McCrary continued. "When it's hot out there, I'm all over the place. They get too busy to police up their own dead. Usually it's just one—maybe two—they can't find...."

McCrary looked forlorn. In the weeks he had known him, Kahn had noticed that McCrary talked incessantly about his work—as if by sharing the experience he could somehow be relieved of its burden.

McCrary continued to talk, but Kahn was barely listening. He was thinking about earlier, when he and Holden had been drinking beer alone in the mess before McCrary came in and Sharkey and Donovan had passed by the table where they were sitting. Kahn had motioned for them to sit down, but Sharkey told him, "No, thanks, sir, we're going to play cards," and had gone on by to join a group of second lieutenants in a poker game.

That, of course, hadn't bothered Kahn, but the "No, *sir*" had. Ever since Okinawa, when Patch had given him the Company, and during the rest of the trip on the transport, and the weeks at Monkey Mountain, Sharkey had been gradually putting a certain distance between himself and Kahn. Kahn hadn't noticed it at first, but pretty soon Sharkey had stopped calling him by his first name, and he hadn't been as loose around him as he used to be.

It wasn't that he wasn't friendly or anything, because he still was, but in front of the men he had begun addressing Kahn as *sir*, which was absolutely proper, though he hadn't done that when Kahn was Exec. Now that Kahn was CO, Sharkey's West Point drilling had begun to take hold of him, or at least that was the way Kahn figured it. And then, a few days back, Sharkey had called him "sir" for the first time in private, though even that hadn't been clear until now.

It had been when Kahn inquired about Sharkey's new teeth, which had been fitted and ordered but had still not arrived. Sharkey said he had no word when the teeth would be forthcoming but wished the hell they would because he was having trouble eating. When Kahn asked if there was anything he could do, Sharkey smiled his toothless grin and replied, "Yessir, you can put an end to these rumors that I'm sucking cocks on the side; you're still Rumors Control Officer, right?" Kahn didn't know about the "Yessir" then, because it might have been just a figure of speech or whatever, but this time there was no mistaking it.

If that was the way Sharkey was going to be, then all right, Kahn thought. Let him pal around with the second lieutenants and call me "sir." Kahn had found new friends in Holden and Digger McCrary—unlikely as they were: the mortician, the stockbroker and the geologist—and if his old friend Sharkey couldn't understand that Kahn's new status shouldn't have meant squat to their friendship, to hell with it, then. But he still missed having Sharkey to kid around with, and now he felt a little uncomfortable about it, because he was starting to feel the distance too.

AHEAD, THE TOC glowed like a huge jack-o'-lantern.

Far to the west, the sky flickered with lightninglike flashes from an Artillery battery, silhouetting the two men against the top of the rise. Moments later the muffled *whump, whump, whump* rolled across the rice fields as if someone were dropping huge anvils in the mountains.

"Well, I guess I'll go down to the morgue and catch up on some paperwork," McCrary said. "Why don't you drop by later?—I've got some vanilla ice cream in the cold locker; it keeps great in there...." He waved and stumbled off along a rutted path behind the TOC.

More flashes appeared behind the western mountains, and Kahn paused before going inside. He had a sudden compulsion to experience the completed act, the sound being a final confirmation of an event that had already occurred seconds earlier, a dozen miles away.

Whump, whump, whump, whump. The explosions

finally reached him, distorted by time and distance, leaving the results to his imagination. I am, he thought, the apex of a very odd triangle.

The triangle he saw was marked at one of the angles by the men who fired the artillery, at another by the men who received it and at the third by himself—three vastly different views of the same event, distinguished merely by a factor of relative proximity. In a way, it was like the Dismal Deeps Effect aboard the transport, except that here the effect was perceivable—but only because it was not deep enough, or far enough away. God, Kahn thought, I am going nuts.... This is ridiculous nonsense.... I am so tired ... so goddamn tired ...

THE TOC was a place of high-pitched tumult, the kind of formless clamor one might expect during a panic in a stock exchange.

Rows of enormous terrain maps stretched from one end of the tent to the other, held in freshly built wood easels. The acetate overlays that covered them were a maze of black, red, orange and yellow grease-pencil markings showing friendly positions, enemy positions, free-fire zones, artillery targets, aircraft landing strips and dozens of other things not indicated in the brown contours and green terrain features originally reproduced in the basement of a government building in Washington, D.C. These markings were continually being fiddled with by bored-looking enlisted men who moved among the maps erasing and redrawing as the situation changed.

In the background, a dozen radios crackled— monitored by stern-looking officers attentive to the nervous chatter of commanders reporting in from the blackness, asking for things, giving positions, wishing for the sun to rise. One radio carried a frantic conversation between a platoon leader under fire and his Company Commander. A staff officer who had been listening for several minutes finally threw up his hands in despair. "Why don't they shut the hell up so we can see what they need?" he cried. "What do they think—talking is going to help?"

Outside, diesel-driven generators hummed and growled; their thick black cables snaked into the TOC like garden hoses. Here was the nerve center of the Infantry brigade: a clearinghouse for three thousand armed men; for artillery—the 105s and 155s and the big 175-millimeter guns posted on hillsides miles away, poised to deliver fire on a moment's notice; for supersonic Air Force fighters carrying two thousand pounds of deadly explosives; for huge B-52 bombers which, summoned under the code word "Arclight," flew in nightly from Guam and the Philippines so high it was impossible to see them, unloaded destruction enough to wreck a small city, then flew homeward again, their weary crews joking, drinking coffee and eating sandwiches—oblivious to the effects of their deposit. All of this was presided over by smartly schooled officers in starched fatigues, carrying .45-caliber pistols in brown holsters, moving briskly about the wood-floored tent, providing wonderfully skilled administration to this vast armament—the best, in fact, that money could buy.

And it was massed, the whole of it, against a shrewd army of little brown men, largely unseen unless they wanted to be; dressed in shoes made of discarded automobile tires; employing every crude device at their disposal—bamboo stakes and tin-can mines and water buffalo...And in the end, all the awesome power of planes and cannon and bombs dispatched by the TOC would be reduced to one simple, time-honored military equation: men would have to fight other men, measuring each other, sweat for sweat, blood for blood in the deep tangled jungles, craggy mountainsides and steaming rice paddies. And the men selected for this task—Bravo Company among them—were known, in the lingo of Monkey Mountain, as "freshmeat."

PATCH WAS alone in a corner of the TOC, studying a map of the eastern sector of the Ia Drang. A cigar protruded beneath his blond moustache, which he had allowed to grow longer, Cavalry style. Kahn reported in.

"Ah, Kahn," Patch said. "Good." He seemed less

animated than he'd been earlier when he had landed near the village and taken charge of the mopping-up operations. Kahn was surprised at his efficiency in directing the search for enemy arms and supplies. Patch had taken time to talk to some of the men and officers and had moved them out quickly when the work was done. Later, when they returned muddy and exhausted, Patch had arranged for ten cases of beer to be sent to the billets with his compliments.

"Sit down for a minute," Patch said. "I want to talk to you."

Kahn sank into a crude wood chair. His whole body ached and he was grateful even for this brief rest. Patch sat on a table beside him.

"I want you to know," he said, "you did a hell of a job out there today. The general wanted me to convey his appreciation. He said you played it very nicely." Kahn was dumbstruck, but managed to get out a weak "Thank you."

"Yes, I'm proud of you, Billy," Patch said. "You made a few mistakes, but we had ourselves a hell of a day."

"Thank you, sir," Kahn said appreciatively.

"I'm sorry about your two men—but they'll be taken care of."

In the background, the radio conversation between the platoon under fire and its Company Commander flared up again. They could hear the sound of shooting and the desperate shouting. Patch glanced toward the radio bank. "Trouble there," he said. Kahn nodded.

"Now," Patch said, removing the cigar from his teeth, "there are some very basic things you have got to remember. First, about that mortar fire. You know what you should have done, right?"

"Moved out," Kahn said. He felt a lecture coming on.

"Moved out—damned straight. Get the hell out of there. When they have your number out in the open like that, they'll blow you to bits."

"Yes, sir," Kahn said.

"And you've got to keep me better posted. I don't know what's going on unless you tell me, right?"

"Yes, sir," Kahn said. "I guess I was kind of jittery."

"We all were," Patch said solemnly. "But we have to get over it."

"Yes, sir," Kahn said. Patch was being very gentle. He didn't know why.

"Come over here for a minute. I want to show you something," Patch said.

They walked to one of the big terrain maps which was covered with a large white cloth. On top of the cloth, red stickers were pasted. They said TOP SECRET. Patch threw the cloth over the top of the map. The overlay was marked in black and red grease pencil. The legend at the bottom said, *Sector II, Ia Drang Valley, western approaches. Estimated enemy strengths, a/o 10 Sept., 1966.*

The map, if you stood back from it, was a blur of green and brown thinly spaced contour lines showing the extent of the elevation. Imposed on the acetate were dozens of red rectangles with numbers drawn above them. Each represented an enemy unit, its probable designation and the date it had been sighted. At the top of the map, in large black letters, the words OPERATION WESTERN MOVIE had been carefully inscribed.

"This is our show," Patch stated proudly. "At least, a big part of it will be. We jump off next Sunday."

Kahn looked at the map again. He had never seen such dense vegetation depicted on a map—even at this scale.

"If Intelligence is half right, you can see what we're likely going to find in there," Patch said. He kept his eyes on the map. Kahn did not say anything. His mind was numb with exhaustion, numb even to this, as though it were slipping into a frameless void.

"There's an old French landing strip here." Patch put his cigar on a gray line with a tiny red airplane printed above it. "I had a look at it from the air the other day.

"A South Vietnamese outfit is there now but about to move out. We're going to call it 'Firebase Meathead,'" the Colonel said grandly. Four/Seven would use this as a staging area and push out from there into a large green area bordering the Drang River, which meandered down the center of the valley. The green area was identified on the overlay as the *Boo Hoo Forest*, but on the map itself the area was marked in print as the BUTT SUIT, which Kahn gathered was a Vietnamese term for forest.

Patch described a circle with his cigar on the center of the green area.

"Now, this Boo Hoo Forest is where Intelligence says the NVA Three Forty-two B Division has been living. If their assessments are correct, it might be very hot in there. The ARVN has already been kicked out twice, but of course you know how they are."

Kahn listened.

"The thing," Patch said, "is that we have to clean out this whole sector. Just annihilate the bastards and drive them up these mountains. It's already shaping up as one of the biggest operations of the war; a lot of people are going to be watching us, all the way back to Washington.

"I've got a plan worked out that is going to save us time and lives, and I'm going to brief everyone on it in the morning. What do you think?" Patch said, sticking the cigar back into his mouth.

What did he think? Kahn thought. What the hell *did* he think? For the first time in months he'd actually been asked what he thought about something.

I am so tired I must be dreaming. That was what Kahn thought.

"Uh, well, Colonel . . ." He struggled for words. "From the looks of it, the terrain is pretty rough. We might need some special equipment."

Patch's face lighted up. "Indeed you will—indeed you will," he said cheerfully. "I've laid it all on—or at least, it's been promised. There will be an Engineer detail with a chain-saw squad and two explosives teams. Anything we can't get through with that the Air Force has promised to blow out of our way."

Kahn nodded stupidly.

"The trouble is, we really don't know what we're going to find in there. The patrols that have gone in have only penetrated a little way, but it looks like there is an outer perimeter here"—he made a line with the cigar just inside the green area. "This seems to be the forward position of a big base camp. They say the whole area is mined and booby-trapped and they have fortifications laid out."

The radio conversation between the platoon under fire and its commander had died down to an occasional exchange as they tried to direct two Medevac helicopters to a cleared landing space. Patch turned to Kahn and put his hand on his shoulder.

"You know, you look pretty tired, Billy. You ought to get some rest. There's a briefing at oh eight hundred; I'll see you then." He walked him to the flap of the tent.

"By the way," Patch said. "What we talked about here is just between us. I'll spring it on the others tomorrow—understand?"

"Yes, sir, and thank you," Kahn said. He walked out into the dark, alone with the deep, starry sky, and the first thing that crossed his mind was that he sure would like to have some of that vanilla ice cream McCrary was keeping cold down in his morgue.

20

THE MIST lay like white chalk across the valley floor, and above it the treetops of the Boo Hoo Forest loomed like strange, stark sentries. Beyond rose the blue-green peaks of the Drang Mountains, one after another as far as the eye could see, looking the way an enormous cloud bank might appear from above.

They were moving across a marshy depression west of the river, a mile from where the helicopters had set down. The cleared spaces once had been farmed for rice, but were now overgrown in tall brown elephant grass. Beside them and ahead, they could hear the sounds of other men, but because of the mist they could not see them any more than they could the treetops or the mountain crests. They could barely make out the pale, white sun, low in the eastern sky but rising quickly to turn their day into a sweat-drenched, steaming nightmare. Already they had an inkling of this, and they sensed what to expect, because by now they had been here long enough to know.

The order of march was Alpha Company in the lead, Charlie Company behind on the right flank and Bravo Company behind on the left. Weapons Company, with its heavy mortars, was in the rear, as were two companies from another battalion who were in reserve. Behind all of this were various support units.

This moving mass of flesh and metal, if it could have been seen from the air, might have appeared as a giant arrowhead, half a mile across at its widest point and nearly half again that long from end to end. Patch had likened it to a ball-point pen, the tip being Alpha Company and the sheath being Bravo and Charlie companies and the reserve and support units. His plan was that the tip would penetrate into the jungle until it met resistance, then withdraw into the protective sheath, which would move up and envelop the enemy.

THEY WERE still a distance from the outer edges of the Boo Hoo Forest, moving across the hummocks and swamps to ensure that the North Vietnamese were not in fact here, instead of where they were supposed to be.

Brill swatted at a ball of gnats that had risen out of a mud heap and were swarming around his head. He felt a strange elation in all of this and for the past half-hour had been thinking about a girl he had screwed Fourth of July night, just before they left. There had been a big party at Laguna Beach, and he had driven down with some people he barely knew. In fact, Brill hadn't even been invited to the party, but heard about it and hooked a ride.

The girl was about eighteen and sort of flaky, with long blond hair and a tight-looking ass in cutoff blue jeans and a tied-up work shirt. She was sitting on a big red cushion on the floor, stoned out of her skull. He hadn't spoken to her all night, but now that they were the only two left in the room, Brill took a swig of vodka and orange juice he had been sipping since sundown, walked over to her and said as firmly as he could, "Why don't we get out of here?"

Blearily she looked up, her bored expression never changing, and said, "Yeah, why not?"

He had no idea where to take her. He was considering a walk to the beach when she said, "You want to take my car—it's a faaaaast muthah" and led him to a silver Porsche parked on the lawn.

Brill figured he was ninety miles an hour even before he got into the driver's seat.

He spun the Porsche onto the winding highway and headed south for his uncle's beach house forty miles away. His uncle was probably still in New York, and he remembered that the key was hanging inside the pumphouse. When they walked inside, he turned on the lights, and the Porshe-driving eighteen-year-old sucked in a deep breath and let it out with a sigh. "Oh wowww," she said.

She didn't seem to need warming up, so Brill told her to take off her clothes. Moments later she reappeared from the bathroom unashamedly naked and slid under the covers of the big round bed. Brill had stripped too and threw the blankets off immediately. Without further ceremony he mounted her savagely, and she began to cry out in the brightly lit room, "Oooh, please don't be so rough," but he did not stop or slow up, and instead continued pounding her and pounding her until she started to scream—not screams of joy but screams of agony—and tried to struggle upward toward the head-board, but he pulled her down roughly and banged her mercilessly; which was what he was remembering now in the heat of the jungle morning—her face contorted, her hands grasping the headboard trying to escape the pounding. He remembered thinking, She's dry—why the hell is she dry? Then he'd said it aloud: "You're dry—damn it—*why are you dry*?" and kept banging away and saying it over and over in a bitten, deliberate voice, oblivious to her replies, and toward the end, when he felt himself coming, he had taken her hair in his hands and lifted her head and pounded it against the pillow again and again, bellowing the question *"Why are you dry?"* until she was nearly hysterical, screaming and sobbing some answer he did not understand because he wasn't listening.

Brill wiped sweat from his brow with the back of his sleeve. The ball of gnats had disappeared, and he reached to his canteen for a swallow of water.

He remembered the girl lying in the darkness afterward when he had finally turned out the lights. "You never even kissed me," she had said haltingly. He had said nothing but had lain there next to her, eyes wide open, staring at the ceiling, wishing she would shut up. After a while, she turned to him in sleep and threw an arm across his waist. He threw it aside and turned over toward the edge of the bed, eyes still wide open, staring at nothing. The next morning he sent her on her way in the silver Porsche, and as soon as she was out of sight he straightened up the bedroom and walked out into the warm California sun, without showering, or shaving, or having coffee or even so much as a glass of orange juice—even though all this was available—and stuck out his thumb on the highway, northward toward LA, feeling elated, feeling mean, the same as he was feeling now.

THE LEAD elements of Alpha Company had disappeared into the jungle, and within minutes the entire formation began to jam up like a coiled-down spring. The sun, having burned off the morning mist, was now in the process of broiling Four/Seven, and a fearful uncertainty had spread over everyone. Somehow being in the open had not been so bad, but going into jungle was a different matter. Days before, word had gotten around that a certain number of casualties were anticipated and, in fact, had been planned for and counted on. Rumor placed this figure anywhere between 10 and 25 percent, depending upon who was telling the story. But whatever it really was, each of them was aware in some way that men were going to die here, possibly today, and maybe even in a few minutes. In many cases, the uncertainty had manifested

itself in the lower bowel and worked from there into a
general feeling of nausea and weakness that tended to
drag them down under their already heavy loads. The
climate and the food, in the weeks since their arrival, had
thrown their stomachs into a constant state of turmoil,
and each morning they would return from the latrines
with passionate oaths against an affliction called "Ho Chi
Minh's Revenge." For many of these men, a brighter part
of their day had been the relief of a good, clean shit, and
now even this simple pleasure had been denied them.

The line began to advance again, and the first elements
of Bravo Company were swallowed up in the Boo Hoo
Forest. As they moved through the first scrubby jungle
brush, Madman Muntz, shouldering the big Colt Arms
M-60 machine gun, turned to his squadmate Spudhead
Miter, who was carrying belts of ammunition for it
draped around his neck like some absurd Mexican
bandit, and said with a dour grin, "I hope you got
insurance," and Spudhead, thrashing his way through
some waist-high kupi plants, called back, "Lot of damned
good it'll do us now." It was 10:35 A.M., and they were
whistling in the dark.

By THE end of the hour, they had advanced only a few
dozen yards. People were confused and cursing with
mechanical passion. The swearing had improved dra-
matically since they had left the billets at Monkey
Mountain for Firebase Meathead, the abandoned airstrip
near the Ia Drang.

If the shitsmoke from the officers' latrine had been a
nuisance, it was nothing compared with what they had to
deal with at Firebase Meathead. As their convoy had
descended over the last low hills, they got their first look
at their new home from several miles away. All they could
see of it was a gigantic cloud of red dust, swirling
hundreds of feet into the air, blown up by arriving and
departing helicopters. Later they were let out into the
cloud of dust, and covered in seconds with a thin sienna
grime that stuck to their sweat-stained flesh and stung
their eyes and clogged their lungs.

Almost immediately everyone's nose was assailed by a new and horrifying stench which, they soon learned, emanated from the corpses of several dozen South Vietnamese soldiers which had been neatly stacked at the end of the runway like so many cords of firewood. The South Vietnamese unit that had evacuated the strip a week earlier had simply left the corpses behind for the Americans to deal with, and they had been roasting in the sun inside their flimsy black body bags long enough to produce an awful collective aroma that mixed with the red dust and stifling heat to spread an atmosphere of vileness over the whole encampment.

During the next two days, Firebase Meathead began to take on the appearance of a hobo jungle. The men lived in scrubby dirtpacked areas on both sides of the landing strip. They erected whatever shelters they could. Some put up two-man pup tents and others erected more elaborate affairs, but most merely staked out their ponchos a foot or so above the ground and lived under them. Beginning just after dawn, helicopters and the big cargo planes began landing, delivering supplies and more men. Convoys arrived later in the day with other cargoes, joining with the aircraft to produce an earsplitting roar and raise the cloud of red dust to its most impressive bloom.

Bravo Company, like the rest of Four/Seven, was put to work much of the time stringing concertina wire, setting out claymore mines, arranging aiming stakes, digging slit trenches and latrines, burying garbage and performing other duties attendant to the war. When they were not doing these things, most of the men spent their hours scrounging anything they could lay their hands on to make their lives more comfortable. Sometimes piles of lumber would mysteriously disappear after being off-loaded from a truck, then reappear just as mysteriously in the troop area beneath a siding of tin that had also disappeared without explanation. Large pots and pans would be found missing from the field kitchen, only to turn up a few days later in someone's tent. Even though they knew these accommodations were very temporary, and that they would be moving on in a few days, almost all the men took part in the scrounging because, in addition to its being a good way to pass the time, by improving their condition—if only a little—they were able to bring a sense of order and permanance to their lives.

CRUMP AND DiGeorgio shared a shelter with the banana-cat, and by the end of the second day, thanks to DiGeorgio's prestigious scrounging, they had erected a small but very livable house of wood, tin and canvas. Crump had already made arrangements with three men from the Engineers company to turn over the house to them when he pulled out, in exchange for which they would keep and feed the banana-cat until he returned.

Also on the second day, the pile of corpses was removed by an infuriated deuce-and-a-half crew whose instructions from Colonel Patch were to "take the whole load of them back up to Pleiku and dump them inside the ARVN compound."

On the third day, just after sunset, they were mortared briefly and a man in Alpha Company was wounded in the buttocks as he waited in the chow line.

On the morning of the fourth day, as the trucks and aircraft began bringing in their supplies, Four/Seven jumped off on Operation Western Movie. While they stood choking and gagging on the landing strip, waiting to board the helicopters, somebody was heard to complain loudly that the Army could have selected a more agreeable site for its firebase.

"Bullshit," someone grumbled back through the haze. "If there wasn't no dust here, the Army would truck it in and have somebody to stir it up."

NONE OF THEM, not even the few tough sergeants who had served on Guadalcanal or Bougainville twenty-five years before, were prepared for the Boo Hoo Forest. It was a dark, unwholesome place bathed in an awkward kind of twilight on even the brightest days.

A few yards in, the growth became triple canopy. The bottom layer was an almost impenetrable wad of underbrush and deadfall, as tall as a man or taller. Out of this grew a second canopy of trees, perhaps thirty or forty feet high. Above everything else, a third layer of trees—a hundred feet or more in height—sealed out the sky and the rest of the world.

They had been at it for more than five hours, and had advanced less than six or seven hundred yards. Ahead they could occasionally hear the cursing voices of Alpha Company and the drone of a chain saw. One thing was for certain: their arrival in the jungle would be a surprise to no one.

Each man had been told to carry only four canteens of water and two socks stuffed with as many C rations as they would hold, but no packs. A few men did bring packs, but quickly discarded them when the going got rough. The heat was staggering, even without the direct sun. It was as though they had entered a gigantic steam bath where every breath sucked moisture into their lungs. Dampness was everywhere, and the ground, where it was not covered with deadfall, was an oily mush. Beads of water lay on every piece of vegetation, and this was absorbed by clothing along with the sweat until many of the men felt they would never dry out again. Here and there a man would collapse from the heat or from exhaustion and be marked by his companions until the medics either revived him or dragged him back to the aid station that had been set up at the edge of the jungle.

For Kahn, the situation was impossible to control. Since he couldn't see more than a few yards in either direction, he had constantly to get word by radio for the platoons to try to stay on some kind of line. The needle of the compass seemed to lead them maliciously into walls of stuff a snake couldn't wriggle through, and the line kept tipping one way and then the other. Finally, his mouth dry as cotton, Kahn gave up except for an occasional radio check, clinging to the hope that at least they seemed to be going in the right direction. If it could have been seen from the air, the advance of Four/Seven would have appeared now as a large anvil instead of an arrowhead, but with a little knot in the middle where the point of

Alpha Company was poking its way through with the aid of the chain saws.

THE FIRING began on the right and forward, on Charlie Company's flank. It grew to be a steady din, punctuated occasionally by a muffled explosion. Without being told, every man in Bravo Company stopped dead in his tracks for an instant, then just as quickly crouched down and began to look around in the jungle as far as he could see, which was not very far at all.

Kahn had the radio operator, Bateson, switch to the Command net so that he could hear what was going on. He recognized the voice of Tolson, commander of Charlie Company, who was calmly informing someone that one of his platoons was receiving heavy fire.

"Whipcrack three, this is Backlash. Over," Patch's voice crackled over the radio.

"This is Whipcrack Three; go ahead," Tolson said serenely.

"Can you estimate the strength of your contact?" Patch asked.

"Negative at this time," Tolson said. "All I know is it's raining on us pretty hard."

"Ask the platoon leader," Patch said sternly.

"I am not in contact with him," Tolson said almost dreamily.

"What do you mean you're not in contact with him?" Patch demanded incredulously. "Haven't you got radio contact with him?"

"Negative at this time," Tolson said. "He isn't answering the phone."

"Have you tried your Two-B element?" Patch said, referring to Tolson's second platoon. "Do they have contact?"

"With who?" Tolson said. "Over."

"With the goddamn enemy," Patch roared, "Who else?"

"I thought you meant contact with the One-B," Tolson said. He sounded as if he were falling asleep.

Kahn felt himself getting mad at Tolson. Dumb

Arkansas bastard—why doesn't he even seem upset? What in hell is going on over there?

"I want you to get ready to send us green smoke," Patch said. "Put it as far in front of you as you can and send someone to find out what the hell is going on with your One-B element. We are going to bring in some air on this, you read? Over."

"Roger," Tolson said. "Green smoke forward. What do you want us to do, pull back?"

"I want you to sit tight," Patch said gruffly. "Just sit tight and get support to that platoon. Throw the smoke when I say so." He sounded very unhappy.

The firing from Tolson's direction seemed to become more intense, and there were more explosions. Bravo Company waited, trembling and frightened, hoping none of this would involve them, but their hopes were quickly dashed as Patch ordered Kahn to saddle up and begin a wide sweep toward the fighting so as to put some pressure on the enemy flank.

THE FIRST burst of machine-gun fire should have killed Lieutenant Donovan outright, but he lingered on for a few more minutes. It caught him in the chest with two loud "whacks" that reminded Spudhead—idiotically, he thought later—of someone whacking his fist into a baseball glove, and propelled Donovan backward several steps into a huge tangle of deadfall covered with the leaves of some creeping green vine. He was only five yards or so from where Spudhead and Donovan's radio operator, Spain, had crouched when the first burst went off. Spudhead stared mindlessly at Donovan, because he was the closest human to him and also because he didn't want to look ahead.

The machine gun was still laughing hideously and spraying little showers of mulched leaves and twigs gently to the ground around them.

Donovan's rifle lay a few feet in front of him where he had dropped it when he was hit. His head rested peacefully in the creeping vine. There was an astonished look on his face, but wary too, as though he had heard a strange sound in the dark and was trying to adjust his eyes to see its source. Both hands were at his chest, and blood, in a bright, fine spray from his mouth, had stained his chin and nose.

"Oh, oh Christ—I'm hit," the big ex-tackle said, almost matter-of-factly, but he did not look at Spudhead or Spain or anything else. His head was tilted upward a little bit, and his breath came in sucking, whistling gasps as though he was suffering from a severe chest ailment— which, in an odd sort of way, he was. Then his eyes closed and he settled down to a low humming moan.

As Spudhead watched in helpless terror, the machine gun barked again and continued to rain down its little residue, and Donovan quietly died.

The machine gun chattered madly again, and Spudhead slowly became aware of people dashing around in a wild panic, yelling and cursing and shouting. All of them, except Spain, seemed to be going somewhere, popping up and down, moving around, and this had been going on while he had been gaping at the last breathing seconds of Lieutenant Donovan, which actually was not a long time at all, but in Spudhead's mind it seemed to have consumed a large, if not a major, portion of his life.

Spain was crouched about ten yards away, his face frozen in terror, his eyeballs white. His rifle was lying beside him, and the radio on his back was grumbling frantically with a voice Spudhead recognized as Lieutenant Kahn's. Spain made no move to pick it up.

"Spain, *Spain*!" Spudhead's words came out in a deep, hoarse whisper, but Spain continued to crouch like a terrified rat. Bullets whistled overhead.

This is insane, Spudhead thought. *I've got to get out of here!* The radio crackled again, and without thinking about it, Spudhead was at Spain's side, tearing the handset from its holder, desperately squeezing the transmit bar and yelling into it.

"Lieutenant Kahn, sir, Lieutenant Kahn! Lieutenant Donovan's been shot and they're shooting all over the place—what do you want us to do?" Again, he thought, This *This is crazy. I've got to get out of here!*

At the other end of the line, Kahn heard Spudhead's message. He knew it must have been Donovan's platoon catching it, and now that it was confirmed he had to make a decision—the decision Spudhead asked about. What in hell *did* he want them to do? It dawned on him that he really hadn't the slightest notion, because he didn't know what was going on over there. While one portion of his mind worked on the problem, he felt compelled to say something immediately in reply. Reflexively he said the first thing that came into his head, which was *"Soldier, I don't ever want to hear you using my name over the radio again. You do, and I'll ... I don't know what I'll do, but I'll do something. ..."* Before he finished the sentence, Kahn knew it was a foolish thing to say.

When he received this message, Spudhead took the handset away from his ear and stared into it quizzically. This is all very strange, he thought. Maybe it is just a dream. He felt an urge to stand up and laugh until his sides split. His brain began to shift around crazily, as though it were changing gears from reality to unreality. Momentarily, he felt a rush of terror that he was losing control of his mind.

Through the brush a large figure, half crawling, half crouching, sprang toward him, landed noisily by his side in a spray of dirt and twigs, and hastily looked around, surveying the body of Lieutenant Donovan and the lie of the land and Spudhead himself. Spudhead found himself looking into the scowling black face of Sergeant Dreyfuss, who had come out to the beach at Okinawa that day with Kahn and Sergeant Trunk. Dreyfuss snatched away the handset and punched the transmit bar and spoke firmly into it. In the seconds it took for a reply, he seized Spudhead by the shoulder and shook him.

"Where's your gunner? Get that ammo to him! Get your ass going! Return fire, goddamn it—*return fire!*" Dreyfuss spat through clenched teeth.

Grateful in a way that someone had finally told him what to do, Spudhead exchanged a last frightened look with Dreyfuss and leaped out into the brush to his right where he figured Madman Muntz would be. On his hands and knees he fought his way over a large tangle of deadfall, oblivious to what might be living beneath it, his hands and feet punching through. He cried out through the gloom for Muntz, and above the racket Muntz's hoarse voice came back.

"Over here!"

Muntz was huddled in a nest of underbrush his body had formed when he had hit ground. Hixon, the other ammo carrier, was beside him, flattened out fearfully.

"Cain't see nuthin' through this stuff," Muntz said grimly.

"Can't see over there either," Spudhead panted. "But they're just into those trees."

"What trees?" Muntz demanded. The shooting in front of them had stopped, but the battle continued to their left.

Spudhead pointed upward where the tops of several second-canopy trees loomed above the brush. "I think Lieutenant Donovan's dead," he added, almost as an afterthought.

"Fuck this," Muntz growled. "What the hell do they want us to do?"

Two single, well-spaced shots cracked out on their left.

"Dreyfuss says return fire," Spudhead said.

"How the goddamn fuck are we gonna do it? You can't even ..." His words were lost in two terrific explosions somewhere far to the right where the shooting had first started. The air seemed to rush out of the jungle toward the sound of the explosions with a deep sucking noise and then just as quickly rush back in with the fierce, warm breath of an ocean breaker in a heat wave.

"Napalm—they're napalming the bastards!" Muntz cried.

As if to confirm his declaration, they could just see through the cracks in the topmost trees an orange fireball and black smoke and faintly hear the screaming of a jet fighter somewhere above. Suddenly a vigorous firing poured into the jungle in the direction of the enemy positions. Above it, someone's voice screamed loud and clear, "Return fire! Return fire!"

Muntz grabbed the machine gun and leaped up, his knees bent, and propped himself against the trunk of a tree. *"Keep me fed,"* he bawled, and let loose a burst in the direction of the trees ahead, holding the weapon as tightly as he could against the tree trunk. Spudhead and Hixon crouched beside him holding more ammunition. Muntz's jaw was set like that of a man being kicked in the shins as the gun jumped spasmodically in his hands, spraying the line of trees Spudhead had pointed out before. Ahead, there was a flash of bright light followed by a black explosion. Two more explosions followed, and when Muntz crouched back down, all firing but their own seemed to have ceased.

A voice swelled out of the jungle ahead and from their right: "Machine gun, move up." The voice died into an echo that reverberated all around them in the thin light. Muntz wilted into the ground.

"Come on, Muntz. We better get up there," Spudhead said.

Through the brush they glimpsed an occasional helmet or the backs of other Bravo Company men, and the three of them warily set out toward the source of the enemy fire. Far off, there was still sporadic shooting and the sound of distant explosions. So far, they had yet to see their first live North Vietnamese soldier.

HIGH ABOVE the Boo Hoo Forest, Colonel Patch and several of his staff aides were cruising in a helicopter. Seated near the right door, Patch was listening intently to what his commanders below had to say.

From this perspective, the scene of battle was vastly different from what it was to the men on the ground. An enormous cloud of black smoke drifted over the tops of the tallest trees, and below this, huge chunks of jungle had been blown open and were still smoldering. From other spots beneath the trees, wisps of white smoke drifted skyward, indicating the various points of contact. Several single-engine spotter planes swooped up and down, occasionally tossing out canisters of red or green smoke which streamed downward and mixed with the rest into an incongruous Technicolor mélange above the jungle.

Not being able to experience the sounds, it was impossible from this height to know the fury of the battle below, except through the intermittent yammering over the radio. What was obvious, Patch saw, was that his ball-point-pen formation had now assumed the shape of a large horseshoe. Most ominously, from the outline of the horseshoe it was apparent that what they had encountered was a full-fledged line of resistance and not just some idle skirmishers. The tactical problem was imposing. How deep, for instance, did the line of resistance go? How wide was it? How well fortified? Artillery and the Air Force could do only so much—after all, they had been blasting this place night and day for the past few weeks, and look what good it had done. Somebody was alive and kicking down there.

Still, Patch thought, it really wasn't much different from the situation with the Plains Indians a hundred years before. What counted here was punishment, the same as it had taken incredible punishment to drive the Plains Indians back to their reservations. The secret was not to get dry-gulched in the process.

CRUMP'S SQUAD was the first to reach the bunkers where the North Vietnamese had been. The last twenty-five yards had been thoroughly cleared of underbrush, and some of the trees had even been chopped down and used in the fortifications. Exactly who had first started the shooting was not certain, but it was plain to everyone that if they had advanced into this cleared space the casualties would have been far greater than they already were. As it was, three men, including Lieutenant Donovan, had been killed and seven wounded, and one man in the Weapons Platoon had broken his wrist running into a tree during the confusion.

The North Vietnamese bunkers stretched in a zigzag line in both directions far into the jungle. They were remarkably elaborate affairs, dug out of reddish clay and mud and packed down on top with logs and branches. Some of them emptied into man-sized tunnels, and here and there was a piece of crude furniture for sitting or eating. Two bodies were found, both in the same bunker, evidently victims of a lucky shot from a blooker-gun grenade. There was also evidence that others had been hurt or killed. Blood stained the ground in several places, and there were markings in the bare earth suggesting that men had been dragged away.

The two bodies were pulled from the bunker and laid on the soft earth. Most of the company had reached the bunker line by now, and a crowd gathered to look at them. Both were torn up rather badly from their chests upward, and someone volunteered that because of the lack of bleeding they had probably died instantly. Neither appeared to be over twenty years old, and they were scrawny and emaciated. But in the green-brown uniforms of North Vietnamese regulars they seemed far more dangerous, even in death, than the sorry spectacle of the dead VC the men had seen after the village attack.

Pulled out of the bunker also were two slightly damaged Russian-made AK-47 automatic rifles, the first Bravo Company had seen, although they had heard stories enough about this weapon for it to be almost legendary. There was some grumbling disappointment that the rifles were not the older SKS semiautomatic variety, which, because they were not full-automatic, could be taken back to the States as souvenirs or traded to the Air Force for other loot.

Sporadic firing continued from the far right where Charlie Company was positioned, but it appeared the North Vietnamese had pulled out of here lock, stock and barrel. Patch's new instructions were to hole up here for the night, and Bravo Company began combing the bunkers like derelicts, taking anything they might be able to use or trade at a later time. Only Crump remained aloof from this, sitting quietly atop a mound of dirt, cradling his blooker and wondering how the banana-cat was faring with the men from Engineers company.

Kahn made his way down the line of bunkers, followed by Trunk, Bateson and Hepplewhite, the Company Clerk, stopping occasionally to check dispositions and see that a proper perimeter had been set up. When he arrived at Third Platoon's position, Sergeant Dreyfuss rose from the ground, where he had been eating a C-ration tin of peaches. He drained the delicious nectar from the can, which immediately made him thirsty again. Their canteens were dry already. Kahn asked about Donovan.

"He's over there, sir," Dreyfuss said, nodding toward a bamboo thicket. "Lieutenant Sharkey came over here a few minutes ago. He's there now."

They walked down the slope of the bunkers and shoved their way through the brush toward Donovan's body. Someone had covered it with a poncho. Two men, haggard and bleary-eyed, sat on a log next to the corpse. One of them stared off into the jungle, and neither made a move to rise or acknowledge Kahn's presence, and no one in the party suggested that they should. Sharkey was standing five or six feet away in the clearing, his eyes fixed on the body. His face was pale, and he was biting his upper lip with his lower teeth, which had not been damaged in the boxing match.

"Any sign of that stretcher and stuff?" Dreyfuss asked. One of the two enlisted men on the log shook his head.

"I guess he never knew what hit him, sir," Dreyfuss said. "I sent back for the stretcher. It ought to have been here by now. We have to send back for some water, too—we're nearly dry," he said awkwardly.

Trunk had been watching the other man seated on the log. Finally he squatted down in front of him.

"Hey, Miter," Trunk said softly, "you all right?" Spudhead did not look up.

"Hey, Miter," Trunk said. He tugged at Spudhead's fatigue collar. "I'm talking to you."

Slowly, Spudhead raised his grimy face and looked at Trunk.

"I said, are you all right?"

Spudhead looked drained and bewildered.

"The lieutenant..." he mumbled. "He was the only officer I... and now... he's... dead." He seemed on the verge of tears.

"Okay, let's go," Kahn said. Trunk rose up, and

Sergeant Dreyfuss turned to go.

"I'm sorry, Shark," Kahn said, but Sharkey did not say anything, and he remained there long after Kahn had gone.

DiGeorgio HAD been struggling back through the jungle for half an hour with instructions to bring back some water. When at last he emerged into the sunlight, it was like walking out of a darkened room. The only good thing was that because of the trails they had hacked out earlier, it had been easier than going in. DiGeorgio was looking for the water point, but what he saw in front of him startled him.

Two large tents had been erected at the edge of the jungle. Nearby, a helicopter with a large red cross painted on its side waited silently, its blades drooping like fronds of a wilted plant. Several mud-spattered tanks and half a dozen personnel carriers baked in the late-afternoon sun. Beyond the helicopter, several hundred men in combat dress sat on the grass or milled around. All of this looked as if it had been here for weeks.

In one of the tents, men were working feverishly over other men lying on tables. Outside this tent were perhaps a dozen other men, most of them sitting or lying on stretchers, shading their eyes from the sun. Some were smoking cigarettes. All had white gauze compresses on some part of their bodies, and some had more than one gauze compress. Some of the compresses were soaked with bright red blood. DiGeorgio had to walk by them to find the water point. A few men moaned audibly, but most simply stared blankly. Some carried on conversations with others. Stretcher bearers periodically moved someone from the tent and loaded him aboard the helicopter. Medics moved here and there among the men outside the tent, methodically examining them and attaching paper tags to their fatigue blouses, not unlike the paper sales tags on large appliances.

The water point was a collection of dozens of fifteen-gallon jerry cans, some standing and some lying on the ground. Distribution of water was apparently being administered by a specialist fourth class who walked among the cans with a clipboard. When DiGeorgio attempted to take one of them, the specialist fourth class addressed him in a tone that sounded very much like the bark of a large dog.

"Hey, soldier, whatdaya think yer doin?" he demanded.

"Getting some fucking water—what's it look like I'm doing?" DiGeorgio retorted.

"Unh-uh—not till you check in with me. This water is strictly rationed," the man declared authoritatively. "Who you with?"

"Bravo Company, Second Platoon," DiGeorgio said, glaring fiercely. He suddenly felt like slugging the specialist fourth class, right in his big, fat gut. He hadn't slugged anybody in years, because he was so small, and secondly, because despite all his bold talk he was really a coward; except now he didn't feel like a coward anymore—at least, not back here by the aid station.

"Lemme see here a minute—Bravo Company, you said?" The man ran his finger down the clipboard.

"Damn straight that's what I said," DiGeorgio spat, stepping close to the man's face. "You know, Bravo Company—the one's that's been doing the fucking fighting while you route-step bastards sit on the water so's we all die of thirst."

The specialist fourth class in charge of water did not answer but continued to check his clipboard while DiGeorgio stood in front of him, hands on his hips.

I *will* punch him, I think, DiGeorgio thought.

He was about ready to throw the punch when the man saved himself. "Okay, Bravo Company, only got four cans so far—you're allowed eight. How many you taking?—One, right?"

"Screw you, Jack," DiGeorgio said. He seized two of the huge cans by their handles and lurched back toward the jungle, half dragging them behind him.

"Okay, okay, wiseass," the specialist fourth class called out, "but you get tired, don't you go leaving one of them cans behind—there's other people need water bad as you."

DiGeorgio paid him no attention. He smiled a dark, wolfish grin as he struggled past the hospital tent where the wounded men were. A few of them looked up at him, because he was talking to himself and cursing loudly. He felt the new, savage abandon that all of them felt now. After all, what else could happen? The fact that he had been prepared to punch the man at the water point—even though he did not actually do it—was cause for a moment of inward celebration. In his own mind it was an act at least as bold as his participation in the firefight.

21

THE COUNTERATTACK against Bravo and Alpha companies came just about dusk and took them completely by surprise. As such things go, it wasn't much of a counterattack, insofar as the North Vietnamese did not attempt to retake their lost positons, but contented themselves with directing a murderous fire from the jungle on the American soldiers, most of whom were sitting or standing or walking around on the bunkers when it began.

DiGeorgio, still seething over the water-can dispute at the aid station, had finally arrived back at the Company with the jerry cans. Several thirsty men had clustered around as he opened the top on one can, and other men with ready canteen cups were on their way over. The first burst of fire stitched a line of bullets into the legs of two of these men, who went down hollering, and then smacked a neat row of holes into the opened can, which did not budge but gently began to spill its contents onto the soft red earth, creating the effect of some bizarre fountain in an Art Nouveau display.

DiGeorgio leaped back in horror. His hand had been on the lid when the bullets hit. He tumbled backward down the far side of the bunkers, sliding and groveling to the bottom, frantically trying to unsling his rifle, which had become entangled around his shoulder.

People were shouting and scrambling pell-mell for a safe spot when the mortars began bursting in the trees above them. Everything was roaring and flashing in the dim remaining light. Dirt and debris flew all around them, and the air was filled with a thick, whooshing sound as though someone were swinging a large fiery broom around and around above their heads. The trees and earth shook. The jungle jumped and trembled as though it had gone mad with fright.

Kahn was on the Artillery net, yelling into the radio handset. "They're using rockets," he screamed. Earlier he had radioed back preset firing coordinates, and while he wasn't sure they were correct for what was going on now, it was clearly the place to start. At the other end of the line, a calm voice reassured him that fire would be on the way shortly. As the explosions from the rockets burst around them, Kahn lay as flat as he could possibly get against the soft earth. All his instincts told him to stay put and not move. Every fiber of his brain fought against his raising himself even a fraction of an inch or turning his head or even breathing heavily. It was as though he had become a part of the earth he was lying in.

A few feet away, Sergeant Trunk was burrowed into a little mound of dirt, facing in the opposite direction. Kahn heard him yelling something, but could not hear what it was for all the racket and confusion. The back of Trunk's neck convulsed with each yell, and Kahn finally craned toward him to find out what he was saying. Suddenly, Trunk turned and shouted in Kahn's face, "They ain't firing, Lieutenant—we gotta return fire!" They stared at each other for a moment; then Trunk was on his hands and knees crawling off down the line toward the other men, still screaming through the boiling, smoking gloom.

Oh, Lord, Kahn pleaded. *Oh, please God.*

He was not a religious man. They hadn't made him go to Temple after he was sixteen. And he had done bad things in his life. Some of them came to him now. Why should God help him? What had he done for God? Not a goddamn thing. . . .

A huge explosion cracked behind him, and there was a fierce whirring sound in the air. Something hot stung the back of Kahn's hand, and he recoiled from it. A thin stream of blood ran down his fingers, dripping into the dirt.

Oh, God, he thought again. I'm hit! And suddenly his mind was filled with the fat, chortling face of the helicopter pilot back at Bragg who had told them of the River Blindness. Ha, ha, very funny. Go down to the river and get your eyes shot out. His face felt numb. He pinched his cheeks. They were numb. Oh, God, I have got to do *something*! A kind of fear-anger swept over him, and he raised himself up on his knees. Oh, God, he thought, here goes.

"Are we going to take this?" Kahn bellowed.

Bateson, the radio operator, who was huddled beside him, looked up in astonishment. Kahn's eyes were as wild as those of a panicked racehorse. *"Get up and return fire,"* he roared. He got to his feet in a half-crouch, bent over at the waist, still yelling at the top of his lungs, and took off down the line in the opposite way from the direction Trunk had gone. He came to a pile of white-faced men who had pressed themselves into the ground about ten yards away.

"Off your asses!" Kahn bellowed. "Get up there! Return fire!" He seized one of the men by the back of his flak jacket and pulled him upright. It was Carruthers, the giant black private. Bullets cracked around them. A look of utter horror crossed Carruthers' face and he struggled to press himself back into the dirt.

"Get up there, I said!" Kahn raged. He kneed Carruthers in the buttocks and jerked him up again and screamed in his face, *"Return fire, you sorry bastard!"* The bullets above their heads continued to whizz and thunk into tree trunks. Carruthers' eyes bugged out, but he slowly began to crawl to the top of the bunker. The two other men were watching with strained faces. Kahn glared ferociously at them and they too began to crawl up. Carruthers peeked over the top of the earth pile and stuck his rifle out and fired a burst into the jungle. The others did the same as Kahn stood, bent over, watching them. When he was satisfied, he took off again, followed by Bateson with the radio, who was crawling on his hands and knees. *Why am I here?* Kahn thought. *Oh, God, why am I here?*

Ten yards farther down he came across a lone dead man, shot through the throat. The dead man's legs and buttocks were on top of the bunker, but his trunk and widespread arms lay on Kahn's side of it. A large pool of blood had drained from the wound and settled at the bottom of the slope. Kahn grabbed the dead man's arm and yanked him down out of the field of fire, and he rolled face down into the pool of his own blood. Kahn thought he recognized him as Spate, one of those involved in the rock fight on the beach, whose brother had been killed by a grenade in the Marines.

Oh, God, why am I here?

A searing flash and a gigantic cracking blast ahead in the jungle announced the arrival of the artillery.

"That's it," he yelled to Bateson. "Put me on!"

Kahn grabbed the handset. "Okay, okay, no corrections, shoot again."

Seconds later, there were more thunderous explosions. The jungle lit up like a neon light. "Keep it coming," he shrieked into the radio. The rounds continued in salvos of three, at intervals of about forty-five seconds. Finally Kahn pressed the transmit bar again. "Okay, hold it up," he panted. A final salvo burst into the twilight. For a few moments, uncanny silence unfolded over the Boo Hoo Forest; then the first painful moans and some low cursing rose into the darkness.

AT THE same time Kahn's company was being counterattacked by the North Vietnamese, Holden, Major Dunn and Captain Sonnebend, the new Brigade Public Information Officer, were sitting down to chow in the tiny officers' mess tent at Firebase Meathead. They had driven down from Monkey Mountain that afternoon, Dunn to check his communications setup and Holden to escort Sonnebend closer to the action—a suggestion, if it could be called that, of General Butterworth's.

Holden had brought Sonnebend in to introduce him to the general that morning, and after a brief talk, the general had declared that if Sonnebend was to be Brigade PIO, he ought to see some of the countryside.

"There's a hell of an operation going on out there now—might be the biggest of the war," the general had said. Then he had turned to Holden: "Frank, it might be a good idea if you went along too and introduced the captain around." It seemed to Holden that the general was very cavalier about getting people into dangerous situations.

Sonnebend had been talking continuously since their arrival at Firebase Meathead, giving his theory of how the war should be fought, while Holden and Dunn sat silently across the table, chewing their food.

Holden didn't like Sonnebend. The impression he formed during the ten-mile ride down from Monkey Mountain was that the new captain was fatuous, and thoroughly out of place in the military.

As their jeep bounded down the rutted jungle road, Sonnebend had been a nervous wreck. Once, when they slowed behind a deuce-and-a-half full of soldiers, Sonnebend had extended his hand, plam up, beneath Holden's chin.

"Say, Holden, did you ever stick a pencil point in your hand?"

Holden looked and saw nothing. "Where is it, Captain?"

"There, just under the thumb," Sonnebend said. "I tried to get most of it out, but I've heard you can get lead poisoning from pencils if you aren't careful."

Holden took a closer look. He couldn't tell if the black dot was actually a piece of pencil point in the skin or just skin made black when it had gone in.

"I wouldn't worry about it, Captain," he said politely. "It'll probably work its way out by itself in a day or so. Doesn't hurt, does it?"

Sonnebend seemed disappointed. "No, it doesn't hurt, but I'm worried about the lead poisoning."

Ahead, a truck growled in the mud.

"There are a lot of things you can get lead poisoning from around here, Captain, but I don't think that's one of them," Holden said. He exchanged glances with Major Dunn, who was sitting in the front of the jeep.

"Why do you think we've stopped?" Sonnebend asked furtively. He had been staring down the road, which ran straight for a hundred yards or so, then dipped down and out of sight into a dark stretch of jungle. "You don't think they've seen an ambush or anything down there..."

"Nothing to worry about, Captain," Major Dunn said patiently. "I've been down this road before. We have a checkpoint at a little bridge just below that curve. All the fighting is way to the west of here."

"Ah, yes," Sonnebend said. "I was just wondering." His face was covered with sweat, and there were dark stains under his armpits. Already the temperature was above 100 degrees. "I'm not feeling very well," he said. "It must be the heat."

The truckload of men ahead began to move again, and the driver put the jeep into gear. As they lurched forward, Captain Sonnebend resolutely fingered his holstered .45 and alternately looked at his palm. Holden leaned back in the low, uncomfortable canvas seat and closed his eyes. No wonder the Army is screwed up, he thought, with straphangers like this in charge of things. The hot sun baked through his closed eyelids, and his world became a swirl of black bugs moving against a brilliant yellow frame. Soon he indulged himself again and began thinking about Becky, and the pain returned, as it had many times each day, ever since her letter had arrived last week.

It had been the last of four in a row he'd received. Each of the others had been the same—filled, unavoidably, with her antiwar activity. She rarely mentioned it outright, but of course, he'd read between the lines. When she spoke of the "work" she had to do, Holden knew it wasn't schoolwork. And when she'd been in "the city" for a few days, she sure as hell hadn't been shopping at Bloomingdale's. Over the weeks, the language in the letters had become stronger. Where at first there had been a hell or a damn, now there was shit or fuck, and she spoke of "pigs" and "us" and "them."

Then she lowered the boom.

It *was* Widenfield. At last his suspicions were confirmed. She *was* still seeing him, though she still claimed the relationship was platonic. But for both their sakes, she could not keep up the charade any longer.

In spite of what she'd told him before he left—with all of its brutal honesty—he now felt deceived.

She was terribly sorry, she said, but they had gone in "different directions"—that was how she had put it.

Different directions, he thought bitterly. That was quite literally correct.

She begged his forgiveness, but he simply no longer fitted into her life, she said. All her energies now had to go for the cause.

It was a short letter, and when it came he knew at a glance what it was. It did not open with *"Darling,"* and it did not close with *"Love,"* or *"I love you."* It opened with *"Dear Frank"* and it closed with *"Sorry."* When he read it, a sick knot of hurt had welled in his stomach, and then turned to despair and finally to rage. Afterward, he tried to imagine her writing it, and the face he saw was of a very determined woman.

Two emotions had tugged at him constantly since the letter had come. One was to go AWOL and see her, for he believed thoroughly he could make it right again; the other was to get the hell off Staff and into the fighting and take his mind off it.

*   *   *

CAPTAIN SONNEBEND forked up another piece of tough fried steak. "You know," he said, "I've given this a lot of thought. I mean, about how to win this war." Holden and Dunn sat across the table, saying nothing, but thinking the same thing.

"The problem isn't the VC anymore—they're about licked, right?—it's the North Vietnamese. . . ."

Holden shrugged. Dunn shifted in his seat but remained silent.

"So the exercise is to keep the NVA out. But we can't just patrol eight hundred miles of jungle between the DMZ and the southern border—right?"

Dunn grunted and sawed at his own steak.

"Well, how's this for a solution. We defoliate a strip along that whole jungle, or blast it, or whatever—maybe a hundred yards wide—all the way from the Gulf of Tonkin to the southern tip of the country. Then we string wire along it and man it with machine-gun posts every fifty yards or so and patrol it with gunships, and we have strike forces ready in case they try to break through. Anytime they do, we could blow them right out of the tub. . . ."

An Artillery battery at the edge of the perimeter unleashed a furious barrage that left Holden's ears ringing. He had no way of knowing this was the one so desperately requested by his friend Kahn. The dim light inside the tent hurt his eyes, and he let his mind return to Becky and what she probably was doing now. . . . It would be, what?—7 A.M., her time?

He wondered if she was asleep in her dorm . . . or was she asleep with Widenfield. The vision had been driving him crazy for days, but in a perverse way he enjoyed it. In fact, he indulged himself in it so much he had invented a picture of Widenfield's apartment near the campus, a place furnished in leather chairs and books stacked high everywhere. It was October, and there was frost there now. Becky loved fireplaces. So Widenfield had to have one. If it was 7 A.M., he thought, she would be awake soon. But he would probably be up first—she was so damned hard to get up in the morning. And she never slept with anything on. He pictured her in Widenfield's bed, alone while he took a shower or made coffee, murmuring softly whenever he tried to wake her up. . . . Finally she would sit up on the edge of the bed, a blanket wrapped around her full, soft body, and stumble into the bathroom. She didn't like to make love in the morning. Strange, he thought; that had annoyed him before, but he was grateful for it now because even if she was sleeping with Widenfield, chances were they weren't making love at the moment, so at least he didn't have to picture that too.

"WHAT I MEAN," Sonnebend said enthusiastically, "is that we just build a big fence around the whole damned country—I know the comparison isn't good, but it would be sort of a Berlin Wall; then all we'd have to do is rout out whatever VC are left."

Dunn was through eating and stared thoughtfully into a cup of green Kool-Aid, known as "bug juice" because it invariably attracted gnats and other insects, which died immediately upon touching it and then floated around on top. His mind was making calculations, the kinds of calculations an electronics man might make when presented with such a theory.

"You say you want to put a guard post every fifty yards along this border, right?" Dunn said.

"Yes, about that," Sonnebend said cheerfully.

"And there are roughly eight hundred miles of border, right?" Dunn asked.

"Roughly," Sonnebend said.

"So that would require approximately thirty thousand guard posts, wouldn't it—all manning machine guns?" Dunn said.

"Thirty thousand . . . well, I hadn't exactly thought of that, but I guess so," Sonnebend said.

"And every guard post would have to have at least two men for the machine gun, right?"

"Yes, two men. That would be correct." Sonnebend had begun to sense that Dunn's tone was not sympathetic to his plan.

"And they would work in shifts of eight hours each.

That's about as far as you could stretch it, right?" Dunn said.

"Ah, yes ... eight-hour shifts I suppose. ..."

"So," Dunn said, "your plan calls for a hundred and eighty thousand infantrymen manning these guard posts, doesn't it?"

"Well, they don't have to be infantrymen," Sonnebend said. "They could ..."

"If you're going to have machine guns, man, you've got to have infantrymen at them—you can't have Transportation Corps people doing it," Dunn said. He seemed to be getting peevish.

"And how many people would be in these strike forces you talk about? At least another hundred and fifty thousand, right?—at least a battalion every fifty miles?" Dunn said.

Sonnebend realized he was being pushed into a corner.

"So what you are saying," Dunn said, "Is that you want nearly half a million infantrymen, Captain. Do you know how many support troops you would need to keep that kind of force in the field? *Do you have any idea?*"

Sonnebend knew he was trapped. "Well, maybe you wouldn't have to have a guard post every—"

"What you are proposing is that we place nearly five million men here to patrol those borders or to support those who patrol it. Do you actually think anyone's going to throw that many troops into this shitty war?" Dunn declared.

"Well, sir, I—"

"Well, *nothing*, Captain. Do you think that or don't you?"

"I guess I never thought of it that way," Sonnebend said.

Dunn finished off the last swallow of his bug juice.

"The idea is preposterous. The best thing you can do, Captain, is keep your ideas to yourself until you understand what's going on here," Dunn said. He rose abruptly from the table and stalked out of the chow tent.

"Well ..." Sonnebend said sheepishly. "Well ..."

Holden excused himself too, and walked out into the

cool evening. Around the horizon he could see the faint
flashing red lights of several helicopters, all of which
seemed to be going in different directions. The Artillery
battery had stopped firing for a moment, but through the
darkness Holden could make out feverish activity in their
area. Men were running with flashlights, others were
carrying the big 105-millimeter rounds, and he could hear
shouting and cursing. A dozen yards away at an enlisted
men's chow tent a platoon waited in line, every man
armed to the teeth. There was no saluting here or other
Mickey Mouse, the way there was at Monkey Mountain.

Somewhere to the west, but not far away—perhaps five
miles—a great battle was raging. This encampment with
its artillery and communications and ammunition stock-
piles, its food supplies and its reserves and medical staff,
was the main lifeline to it. No Mickey Mouse here. This
was what the Army was all about. No pressed and
starched fatigues, no thrice-daily briefings, no eating in
tents with wood floors and electric generators and movies
at night and ice cream, even if it was kept in the cold
locker in the morgue....

HOLDEN STOOD near the edge of the barbed wire looking at
the dark stand of jungle in the distance, and the enormous
mountains that rose behind it. He knew Kahn was out
there somewhere and in a way envied him. He looked to
make sure no one was watching, and then drew his .45
from its holster, running his finger along its smooth, oily
barrel. For so many months he had persuaded himself
that he really was a Staff man. That he disliked the notion
of war. That he agreed with her. That it was, if not wrong,
at least foolish. He pictured what their life might be like
together: brilliant autumn weekends—he playing tennis
on grass courts at the club; she watching from beneath an
unmbrellaed table; a cozy apartment in the city; plays and
parties; the brokerage firm...

Well, she had torn it now, and suddenly he had no urge
at all to go back to the Mickey Mouse bullshit at Monkey
Mountain. The farther back you got, the more Mickey
Mouse there was, and during the nearly two years he had

been in, most of what he had done was kiss ass. Kiss the general's ass, kiss the general's staff's asses. Now it became clear that this was not any way a Holden should serve in the Army—and Holdens had served in the Army ever since Holdens had lived in America, and they had lived there for a long, long time.

Half in and half out of a devilish dream, Holden saw himself in command of a rifle company, far away from the ass-kissing and Mickey Mouse of Monkey Mountain. If I ever have children, he thought, I sure as hell don't want to have to tell them I spent the war fetching cigars and Coca-Cola for a general. On the spot he resolved to speak to General Butterworth when he got back and ask for a field assignment. As it turned out, it would not be long before he got one.

THE COUNTERATTACK had been much more costly than Bravo Company's initial engagement at the bunkers. Everywhere in the dark, men moved about busily collecting the wounded and reestablishing their perimeter. Eleven men had been hit badly enough to be evacuated; but since there was no place for a helicopter to land, they would have to be carried back to the aid station. Because there was conern that other Four/Seven men might mistakenly fire on them in the dark, it was decided to bring the wounded to a collection point at the company CP and move them back through the lines in a single group. The dead, of whom there were seven, could wait till daylight and be picked up by Graves Registration.

It was an eerie spectacle. For nearly an hour they searched for casualties. Flashlights jacketed in red flickered among the trees and underbrush. A few strange jungle birds had returned to their roosts and began calling out in shrill, disturbed voices. The mutterings of the searchers and the groans of the wounded rose to meet them.

Kahn, his wrist bandaged tightly in gauze and tape, moved among the wounded, offering them cigarettes and encouragement. The shrapnel had barely skimmed the back of his hand, digging out a little half-moon chunk of skin. Another eighth of an inch and he might have been out of it himself with a severed tendon or splintered bone.

There were many men, officers among them, who would have given a lot at this point for such a wound, but Kahn wasn't thinking about that—one way or the other. He was consumed by a deep, yet controlled rage; an anger so fierce he probably could not have expressed it in words even if he had sat down and tried. It was as though he had spent the past three hours of his life in a slow-motion automobile wreck, in which he was able to experience the terror of going out of control and still observe, at the same time, the injuries to other occupants. It was a hateful, helpless feeling.

No one slept much during the night. In addition to the evacuation detail, teams of men had to be sent back for more water and ammunition, and there was a lot of idle firing by nervous sentries.

MEANTIME, Colonel Patch had revised his ball-point-pen assault plan.

The point and sheath would continue to press forward, but if and when they made contact, the point would withdraw, and instead of the sheath's moving up to envelop, a rolling artillery barrage would be laid down. Then they would all move forward together. This, Patch calculated, would be slower, but with the lessons learned from the day, he figured it would save lives. Furthermore, when Patch returned to Monkey Mountain late in the afternoon, he learned that other fish were being fried.

Since it was apparent that the fight was growing bigger, General Butterworth had consulted the Field Force Headquarters at Nha Trang and it was decided to throw more men into the battle. An Airborne battalion and a Mechanized Infantry regiment were detached from nearby and the whole shebang placed under the command of a two-star general from Headquarters.

The valley itself was twenty miles long, and nearly half that across, but the present fighting was contained in the eastern half, bounded on the north and south by tall mountains. The overall idea now was that the Brigade would continue to press forward in a giant wheeling motion to the north while the Airborne battalion drove straight across the valley from the south, toward the northern mountains. The Mechanized Infantry would work its way down an overgrown road near the base of these northern mountains, and with any luck the retreating North Vietnamese would be pushed right into their laps and the area secured within two weeks. With any luck at all. Privately, Patch fumed at the loss of his authority, but he played the good soldier and kept his counsel and chewed on his cigar.

When the new instructions were received by Bravo Company at about 0200 hours, Kahn and his officers spent the next couple of hours in one of the bunkers poring over maps and lining out their formation for the following day. Trunk was there too, working on his morning report, recording casualties and other odds and ends.

With a few hours to go before daylight, Kahn called it quits and sent everyone back to get some sleep. As he curled up on the damp floor in his poncho, Sharkey stuck his head back into the bunker. The only light he saw was the glow of Kahn's final cigarette.

"You know the hell of it?" he said solemnly.

"No, what?"

"We ain't gonna get to take a bath for two more weeks." Kahn was grateful for it—that Sharkey had stopped back in that way. Like the old times. Still, as he lingered on the edge of sleep, Kahn could not understand how a man who planned a career in the Army could continue to worry so much about staying clean.

22

THE NEXT DAY, Bravo Company was assigned the point of the advance, and Operation Western Movie pressed forward again. Dawn did not come to the jungle in a rose pink glow, but was announced by a few shrieking birds perched high enough in the trees to actually see first light. The men—who had been in various stages of rest or, in some cases, anxious, lonely terror—began to stir around in the cool gray light and raise harsh morning noises that blended into a single, if unharmonized, symphony. First there was coughing and spitting, followed by farting and belching and the sound of noses' being blown. There was the spatter of urine striking the ground and drowsy mutterings and low oaths, the rattle of steel against steel and the slapping and flapping of clothing being shaken out. The sound of a rifle company rising to greet the day is like no other sound in the world.

Cautiously, they moved through the trees toward, and then beyond, the source of yesterday's fire. The jungle became sparser than what they had had to thrash through the first day, and it was naturally thinner—not deliberately cleared away, as it was near the bunkers. When they reached the positions where the North Vietnamese had launched their counterattack, it was evident the artillery barrage had done its job well. Trees were splintered at their bases, and everything seemed unnatural and askew. There was also firm evidence that men had been killed: evidence that included an occasional piece of a limb or an inordinate spot of blood on the ground. No bodies were found, but as in the case of the bunker fighting, there were signs that people had been dragged away.

Farther on, they crossed a slow-moving stream, and Crump, who was in the point squad, was first to notice the blood. It was pooled up in little eddies and backwaters all along the banks of the shallow water, and it expanded and contracted into and out of the lazy current like the fangs of a dark, ferocious animal. Crump hollered for his squad leader; but by then others had seen the blood, and a call was put out on the radio to hold up while two squads were sent to investigate.

An aroma of death hung in the still jungle air as the squads moved up the stream. Soon they found the source.

The bodies of a dozen North Vietnamese soldiers lay along the banks and in the ankle-deep water. All were mutilated horribly, having evidently been caught by one or more artillery rounds as they ran along the stream. It was impossible to say if they had been running away from the fighting or toward it. From their odd positions, the bodies looked as though they might have been dropped from the sky.

While the discovery of the bodies was being relayed back to Kahn, and the rest of the company waited in their tracks, the two squads began gleefully to strip the dead of souvenirs. But nothing of particular interest was found, including weapons, and from this they assumed that other North Vietnamese had stripped them earlier.

It was well into the morning, and Kahn was about to call a smoke break, when they ran into the minefield.

Every so often they had come across a sinister-looking trail. It was much easier to move along the trails than hack through the raw jungle brush, and the men used them whenever possible. Sometimes these trails crisscrossed each other. If a trail turned too far or stopped abruptly, as many of them did, they would simply go plunging off into the brush hoping to find another one ahead.

The man who stepped on the mine, a cheerful oaf they called Moose, was fortunate in a way: It only blew off his foot. If the explosion had set off one of the mortar rounds he was carrying, Moose would have been blown through the tops of the trees. Sharkey was one of the first to reach him. Moose was sitting at the edge of the trail pressing his hands together and breathing heavily. There was an almost curious look on his sweaty face. He did not look down at the stump of his leg.

"I think it blew my boot off, Lieutenant," Moose said nervously. He nodded to a completely intact boot lying on the trail a few feet away. "It don't hurt or anything—it just feels numb. I'm afraid it's going to start hurting in a minute," he said.

"You hang in there, sport," Sharkey said. "We're going to get you out of here." He squatted next to him, cradling his arms and shoulders while someone administered a Syrette of morphine.

Sharkey was speaking to Kahn on the radio when Moose began to scream. He began in deep gasps, then burst into racked sobs which grew into a steady, hysterical high-pitched bleat. Sharkey took the radioman a little farther off down the trail because he couldn't hear what was being said. As he walked, he sighed to himself through his still-missing teeth. It was going to be a long operation.

FOR NINE more days they pushed through, alternating the point, but that didn't seem to make things any better.

Each step forward was taken in terror. The mine that had blown off the foot of Moose the mortarman was only the beginning. As the North Vietnamese withdrew deeper into the forest, they littered the trails and jungle with mines and booby traps. A dozen men had been hurt and two killed, but none from Bravo Company. They were harassed constantly by snipers, which slowed the advance to an antlike crawl.

In between these dangers, a series of running battles took place. The North Vietnamese would set up ahead and open up on them with machine guns and rockets, and for a few minutes the jungle would reverberate with an unearthly racket while invisible men shot at other invisible men. Patch's revised plan, in which the unit under fire would withdraw into the sheath of the pen and wait for Artillery, worked well enough for a couple of days, but the North Vietnamese quickly caught on and would move in behind the withdrawing men into the protected zone and continue to lay down heated fire.

Still they plodded on. Every few days the Air Force would drop a "daisy-cutter" bomb ahead of the advance—a gigantic blockbuster that would blow an enormous hole in the jungle, through which helicopters could descend to resupply them. Still whatever relief was gained when the enemy periodically absented himself from the fighting was quickly replaced by the treachery of the jungle, which was fully as hostile to them as the North Vietnamese.

Beginning the second day, a malicious gray-green mold began to appear on things. First it was noticed on the plastic stocks of rifles and exposed metal of other gear. It appeared on clothing and boots, inside helmet liners and on ammunition clips and bandoliers. It spread itself over radios and constantly had to be wiped off. Finally, the men themselves began to mold. In the mornings when they got up, men could be seen, in addition to their other regimens, scrubbing vigorously at their arms and necks to get rid of the mold.

Other discomforts arose. Skin began to shrivel and peel off. Tiny warts appeared on many of the men, particularly on the fingers and in the region of the crotch.

Medical advice was sought, and word came back over the radio that the warts were the product of a virus that would eventually run its course. Also, after several days, everyone was covered with cuts and scratches from brambles, and these abrasions did not heal normally but became more and more infected. The shrapnel wound on Kahn's hand became inflamed and pussy and started to ache, and he knew it was a matter of time before he would have to do something about it.

Insects and other living things assailed them. Worst were the leeches that crawled under their clothing, silently and unnoticed, and clung, sucking blood, until they created an odd, tingling sensation. These were usually burned off with lit cigarettes, which became another part of their morning duties. They were pestered relentlessly by bugs, the most annoying of which was a fierce winged insect known as "the grabass bug." At dusk, hundreds of these creatures began darting around and smacking into people, sometimes taking a bite of skin.

On the fifth day, a man in Alpha Company was bitten by a snake.

He had accidentally sat down on it during a smoke break, and the snake snapped through his fatigues and punctured his thigh. No one, including the bitten man, actually saw the snake, so consequently no one knew what first-aid treatment to give. If the snake was merely the common bamboo viper variety, the man would begin to suffer a painful but survivable kind of blood poisoning; but on the other hand, if it was a member of the nerve-attacking krait family, the man would soon have no need of medication. It was decided to wait a few minutes to see what symptoms occurred.

Reports that reached Bravo Company later described the victim as catatonic as he was being evacuated, but they never learned of his final dispositon. Later that afternoon, instructions were issued over the radio for every man to take care where he sat and what he touched because there were poisonous snakes in the jungle.

By the ninth day, certain physical and psychological changes were beginning to appear in the men. It went without saying that everyone's nerves were on edge; but there were other signs far more ominous to Kahn and the other officers. Everyone was run-down, and people frequently complained of dizziness and headaches. There were some cases of malaria, but these were mostly mild. However black the humor had been at the beginning of the operation, all signs of it had vanished now. The only thing that improved was the cursing, which seemed the only way the men could describe their condition.

Sometimes a man would go "apeshit" and begin to yell and curse hysterically at everyone else. Usually they would simply let him alone and he would calm down. Other times he would have to be seized and restrained.

Occasionally men could be heard at night talking to themselves or weeping. A man in Spudhead's squad crawled off into the brush every morning and cried for five or ten minutes. Everyone could hear him sobbing, but it was never mentioned.

One day Spudhead encountered the man on his way out to take a crap and decided to ask what was wrong. Red-eyed and puffy-cheeked, the man glared at Spudhead with the air of someone whose deepest privacy had been invaded. *"What's wrong?* I wanna get my ass out of this mutherfucking Boo Hoo Forest—that's what's wrong!" the man cried indignantly. He brushed past Spudhead and began putting his gear in order. He never went off into the bushes again; but also, he stopped speaking to Spudhead entirely.

There was an increasing reluctance to follow orders. Sometimes this manifested itself in out-and-out refusal to obey sergeants and officers. It was as if the men had begun to pick up the rules of the jungle, which were the rules of simple survival. Once, Brill's platoon would not get up from a smoke break. They had run into a heavily mined trail earlier and declared that they would go no farther. Kahn and Trunk arrived at the scene and found the men clustered in little knots, their jaws set in dour, determined expressions.

Shortly after he joined the Company, Kahn had learned that Captain Thurlo had made Brill's outfit sort

of a "goon platoon," filling it with misfits and malcon-
tents who did not perform well elsewhere. Whatever
Thurlo's reasons were, he never explained them to Kahn,
and Kahn never asked, although he would not have done
it that way himself. The inevitable result was that Brill's
platoon had become the seat of whatever trouble there
was in the Company, and a couple of times Kahn had
toyed with the idea of turning it over to Sharkey or
Donovan to shape it up. In the end, he had concluded it
was too late to start mucking around; and it was certainly
too late now.

Trunk strode to the center of the clearing where the
platoon was gathered and surveyed their unhappy faces
while Kahn remained at the edge, trying to look stern.
They had planned it that way at Trunk's suggestion—that
Kahn shouldn't get into a one-on-one in something like
this if he could help it—because if he did, and if it failed,
his authority would be seriously eroded. Kahn had no
idea how Trunk planned to handle it, but whatever it was,
he hoped it would work, because if it didn't then he *would*
have to step in.

"All right, shitheads," Trunk said, "listen up"; but
there was a mellowness in his voice that was almost
soothing. Before saying anything else, Trunk hunkered
down, steadying himself with his rifle, and removed his
helmet, and wiped off a brow full of sweat with the back of
his sleeve.

"Whatever's going on over here," Trunk said, "this
shit's gotta stop." He paused for a moment and searched
the eyes of the platoon. Then he pointed in the direction of
Kahn.

"The Company Commander here asked me to
straighten out you guys. I know what's going on here is
rough—but I ain't driving through here in no jeep myself.
I'm right here with you, and so is Lieutenant Kahn."

Trunk stopped again, and there was some awkward
coughing from his audience.

"Now," he said, "we're all here together, and we've got
to go on ahead together. Otherwise, you shitheads are
going to be left right out here by yourselves alone; and
even if you do manage to find your way out—if the gooks

don't get you first, or the snakes or whatever—you'll be wishing like hell they had, 'cause what the Army'll do to you'll be a hell of a lot worse...."

All the time Trunk was making his little pitch, Brill had been standing silently against a tree, whittling a stick with his knife. Beside him, squatting down, was Sergeant Groutman, a fierce, fathomless grin on his face.

"What we can do now," Trunk said, "is to just sort of forget this happened. Go on and finish your cigarettes— or light another one if you want—but when you're done, you do what the lieutenant here tells you, and get up and go on. You got any complaints about how you're being treated—if you ain't getting enough to eat, or you're hurting—you let me know. That's what I'm here for," Trunk said. "I'll fix it up with Lieutenant Kahn here." He rose to his feet and replaced his steel pot. He fixed his gaze on Crump, who was standing a little way back from the others. Crump still had on his helmet, and his rifle was cradled in his arms.

"What da yah say, soldier?" Trunk said. Crump looked for a moment as though he were going to speak, and then a loud voice boomed out from behind Trunk:

"You dirtballs heard the First Sergeant. He's right. We ain't going to stay here, so let's go."

It was Groutman, on his feet too now, putting on his steel pot and walking to the center toward Trunk.

"C'mon," Groutman shouted, "off your butts!" He made a little rising motion with his hand. "We're getting out of here!" he shouted, and slowly, with some low grumbling, the platoon began to rise and put on their steel pots too, and then Brill stepped forward and began giving orders, and soon they started to form up again and get ready to be on their way.

Kahn was relieved beyond belief. He wasn't sure what he would have done. He would probably have hollered and threatened and they would have stayed put, and—well, anyway, Trunk had fixed it, and again Kahn was goddamn glad to have him around. Still, what had happened here was an ominous sign, and Kahn was afraid they had not seen the last of it.

*   *   *

ALTHOUGH THE officers and men of Bravo Company had no way of knowing it, from the official view point, Operation Western Movie was highly successful.

Since they had entered the Ia Drang region, the four battalions, Four/Seven included, had dispatched a confirmed 477 North Vietnamese killed, and it was estimated at least twice that number had died and three times it had been wounded. They had destroyed several encampment areas and two full field hospitals, captured caches of small arms, ammunition and other equipment and destroyed tons of enemy supplies—at a loss to themselves of 43 men killed and 115 wounded. As Patch put it one afternoon during the general's briefing, "We're just kicking hell out of them."

Most of the men on the ground did not see it quite this way. Crump summed up their position succinctly one night after they had unleashed an artillery barrage following a brutal ambush.

"We ain't nothin' but bait," he said. "Worms dangling on a hook."

Nevertheless, in that late-October week of nineteen sixty-six, the operation was deemed so satisfactory that the information office in Saigon decided to fly up a planeload of reporters to prove that the tide of war was finally turning in favor of the Americans. They arrived on the morning of the twelfth day—television film cameras and crews, notebooks and portable typewriters— accompanied by personable Army information officers and two major generals. After some opening remarks by General Butterworth and the Operational Commander, the briefing was turned over to Captain Sonnebend, the new Public Information Officer, who had been rehearsing his part since the night before.

"Gentlemen," Sonnebend began enthusiastically, "the Ia Drang Valley is a place where civilization has yet to make appreciable inroads...."

AT ABOUT the same time, Bravo Company was moving forward almost eagerly.

Since daybreak they had been pushing toward the

morning's objective: a daisy-cutter hole blown out of the jungle where the Supply helicopters would be landing later to bring them a hot meal and mail. They had the point again, and their particular mission was to secure the landing zone and link up with Second Battalion for the final push. The simple things like the need for mail and a hot meal had grown enormously important, and they were willing to work extra hard for them.

By now most of them had become at least roughly accustomed to the hardships of the jungle. Even the big-city boys were slowly beginning to change from preponderantly indoor creatures to preponderantly outdoor ones, and many signs of their former orientation had already begun to disappear.

SECOND BATTALION had gotten ahead and was already at the landing zone when Bravo Company arrived, and the helicopters had started to land, one at a time. The men sat or lay down at the edge of the jungle, basking in the sunlight. Some of them had removed their clothes to dry, and a few were eating C rations. A detail from Second Battalion emerged from the jungle with the bodies of several dead who had been killed in a firefight the afternoon before. As they walked slowly by, the men of Bravo Company averted their eyes. They still felt a certain embarrassment at seeing their own dead, as though the dead men themselves would be embarrassed at being dead and seen in this undignified position—much the way a man felt embarrassed at being caught in the open taking a shit. But this too was beginning to change—the same way as a man caught taking a shit did not feel quite as embarrassed as he had before they entered the jungle.

Wounded men were different. They could look at wounded men, because there was hope for them. In fact, they would often stare unashamedly at the wounded man and discuss whether or not, in their opinion, he would make it, and if so, what the extent of permanent damage might be. The general assumption was that the wounded could be made whole again after a few months in a hospital, and then be returned to their homes, free men.

Meantime, a further wrinkle had developed. Kahn's hand had been aching for days and had become almost useless to him. It was badly infected, and it was decided, with the concurrence of Colonel Patch, to have it attended to back at the Monkey Mountain hospital.

Kahn was standing in the clearing waiting to board the next helicopter when four men, moving like sleepwalkers, stumbled past him carrying a poncho stretched between them. On the poncho was a man, wounded badly. His knees were tucked up tightly and his eyes were shut. He was very pale. As the little procession went by, Kahn got a glimpse of the man on the poncho. His stomach and chest were covered with his own dried blood, and his fingers twitched occasionally and tapped on the poncho. It was Sergeant Jelkes—the watery-eyed Mess Sergeant; the father of Sally the sex bomb. The bearers looked bleary-eyed and exhausted.

Kahn stepped closer. "How bad is he?" he asked.

The bearers kept their pace, but one of them looked at Kahn. "He's gut-shot, sir. He might of made it if we could of got him out last night," the man said.

Kahn followed them to the helicopter, where they lifted the poncho with Jelkes still on it and gently laid it on the deck. He showed few signs of life except for the spasmodic twitching of his fingers. Kahn leaned inside the door, putting his face very close to Jelkes. "Sergeant Jelkes... Sergeant Jelkes," he said softly; but Jelkes did not move or give any indication that he heard.

Kahn walked away and tried to light a cigarette. Because of his bad hand he fumbled it, and it fell to the ground. A private he had never seen before picked it up and lit it for him. "There you are, sir," the private said. "Hope your hand gets okay."

It was all so fresh in his mind—the night he'd gone to Jelkes's little house and picked up Sally. The look on the sergeant's face, his embarrassment... it didn't seem like a year ago. And the next day, after what had happened... Jelkes's profuse apologies. He'd felt sorry for him....

He had taken her to the officers' club for drinks—not the fancy main officers' club, but an annex that was the hangout of the Airborne division; then early in the evening they had gone, at his suggestion, back to the BOQ, up to his room. There had been heavy petting, and one thing had led to another. She stopped him when he reached under her skirt.

"Why not?" he asked innocently.

"I don't want to—now," she said.

A few minutes later he tried again.

"No," she said, moving his hand, "I told you I don't want to. Not here."

"What's wrong with here? I live here—it's my home," he said.

She sat up on the bed and adjusted her sweater. He lay beside her sullenly, his hands behind his head. "Listen," she said after a while. "I know what you think. You think I'm a good lay, don't you?"

When he protested, she cut him off.

"It just isn't true—I mean, about me going to bed with everybody. I see how they look at me in the PX. They're always trying to get me to sleep with them because they're officers. Well, I don't sleep with people I don't like. I mean, I don't even know you...."

He started to protest again, but she bent over and kissed him softly.

"I really like you. You don't stare at me and say all those things—you know what I mean. You just pay your check.... That's why I went out with you," she said.

He pulled her down beside him, and when he tugged at the elastic again there was only a mild reproach.

A little before midnight they left the BOQ. He drove her to a girlfriend's house where she was to spend the night, and on the way she held his hand in the car. At the door they kissed for a long time, and after she went inside he stood on the porch for a moment to light a cigarette. It was a tiny house in nineteen thirties style—what his father would call a "shotgun house" because of its narrowness. He'd got a whiff of house odor when she'd opened the door—the sickly-sweet smell of food and people in a shut-in place. The stark glow of a television set danced on the walls in a darkened front room. He tried to imagine the girlfriend.

As he walked down the steps he felt warm and satisfied. He was glad he'd met her—there weren't many like her around an Army post—and *what a body*! So what if she wasn't a whiz kid? At least she knew it herself and wasn't ashamed of it. They'd actually had a good time together, and he was going to call her again—maybe tomorrow. . . .

Two boys stepped out of the bushes in front of Kahn as he walked to the street. For an instant he was startled, but they stepped aside to let him pass. His car was beneath a street light in front of the house next door. As he turned down the sidewalk, the larger boy, a tall, rawboned youth of about eighteen, fell into step beside him. The other—shorter, squatter—followed behind.

"Hey, let me ask you somethin'," the tall boy said. His hair was black and slicked down. He was holding a beer.

"You date my sister tonight?" he said. "Your name Lootenant Kahn?"

"Yeah," Kahn said, stopping, feeling relieved. "Are you Sally's brother? It's nice to meet you." He stuck out his hand. The boy did not take it. Instead he looked at Kahn with cold, narrow eyes.

"Yeah, I'm her brother. I look out after her," he said.

Kahn finally dropped his hand to his side. There was an awkward silence. What the hell can this be? he thought. Then he found out.

"I hear you a Joo," the boy said, "That right, Lootenant?"

Kahn felt his face flush. He looked at the boy's mean eyes in astonishment.

"Yes, I am Jewish," he said coolly.

"Well, uh, see . . . my sister, she don't want to go out with Joos," the boy said. "I bet you didn't tell her you was a Joo, did you?"

The other boy leaned against a car on the street and scratched some acne on his face. Kahn realized something was about to happen. Time was moving fast and slowly at once. Both of them were younger—but they were both pretty big.

"Look," he said, "I don't see what difference—"

"It makes a damn lot of difference," the boy cut him

off. "A fucking lot of difference, 'cause Sally, she don't go out with wops, niggers or Joos—even if they are lootenants," the boys said.

"Does your father know you're—"

"Fuck my father," the boy interrupted. "He don't know shit. Joos are dirty people—my sister don't date dirty people. You stay away from my sister, *hear?*"

Kahn had taken several steps toward his car when the beer can hit him in the back. It knocked the breath from his lungs, and he was only vaguely aware of the boy flying through the air at him. They hit the pavement hard, and Kahn landed on his elbow. A ribbon of pain shot through his arm, and he was stunned by the boy's punches on his face.

He rolled and struggled to his knees. He threw a wild right hand, which, to his surprise, caught the boy flush on the nose. Blood spurted out. The boy hollered something unintelligible, and then Kahn felt other arms holding him from behind.

"Don't let him go—hold him," the boy panted.

Kahn struggled frantically. There seemed to be a lot of noise, and time moved very slowly again. The boy hit him twice in the stomach. *This isn't happening*, he thought—*I don't believe this.* Somehow he got an arm free and pulled the acne-faced boy down. The three of them were on the ground cursing and punching. Then other voices were there, and two beefy men jerked them apart. Five or six people were on the sidewalk; a woman was screaming something. One of the men, wearing an undershirt, held the brother tightly by the scruff of the collar. "What the hell is this?" he demanded. The brother continued to hurl incoherent threats at Kahn.

When he was let go, Kahn picked up his cap, which had fallen into the gutter, and wiped his mouth. Blood came off on his sleeve, and he spat a bright red wad onto the ground.

"He'll tell you," Kahn said, jerking his thumb at the brother, who, still held tightly by one of the men, continued to rain curses and threats.

He got into his car, grateful that it started up right

away. As he pulled off, he saw several people standing on the porch of Sally's girlfriend's house, but she was not among them. He thought he saw her inside the door, peering out, but he wasn't sure. He didn't slow down for a second look.

23

A BRILLIANT tropical moon illuminated the heavens and the earth, reflecting the day's sun, which long since had disappeared behind the chain of rugged mountains that lay before them. From its bivouac in some low foothills, Bravo Company could gaze up at the peaks which, bathed in the silver moonglow, appeared as black forbidden castles in the sky.

For six days following Kahn's departure they had forged ahead, with Sharkey in command. The ordeal of the jungle had ended that morning, and the rest of the day they had worked their way through low, dried-out scrub brush to the new Battalion staging area where they would stay the night, then be thrown back into the breach.

For several days there had been savage fighting up and down the rows of mountains at the northeast end of the valley. The North Vietnamese division had miraculously slipped past the Mechanized Infantry regiment and was now firmly entrenched in the mountains. American units had emerged from the jungle in hot pursuit, but the battle was not going well. One group of North Vietnamese, possibly of regimental size, clung tenaciously to the high ground they could see from here, and seemed determined to fight it out. Several assaults, including an attempt by one of the Airborne companies, had been driven pell-mell down the slopes under heavy mortar and machine-gun fire.

Tomorrow it was Bravo Company's turn. Officially they were "in reserve," but they had been told to expect to attack behind Alpha and Charlie companies and secure the crest of a hill known as "The Fake" which was so named because it did not appear on any of their maps. Actually, The Fake was a series of five rolling, successively higher knolls, which was probably why it had been skipped over by the cartographers. But from the perspective of the men below, it was assuredly a difficult and dangerous obstacle.

Their first objective would be to move to the second knoll and relieve a company of the Airborne battalion which had been under heavy fire for a day and a half; then push on to the next knoll and the next. All during the night artillery from far-off batteries had been pounding The Fake and some mountains beyond. Since the staging area had been used by other outfits, there were already holes dug, and Bravo Company simply took them over, grateful they did not have to dig their own.

They lay there during the night, filthy and exhausted, nervously awaiting the dawn, a few sleeping fitfully when they could. Ammunition was running low and they were nearly out of grenades. Somewhere between "Nobody told me to do it" and "I ordered it done," these items had been forgotten, and it was obvious they were going nowhere until they arrived. Some place in the rear, at this very moment, supply sergeants were yelling at beleaguered privates stacking up crates of these munitions for loading aboard the morning helicopters; but not knowing this for sure, Bravo Company sweated in its ratlike holes and prayed silently that the supplies might somehow fail to arrive.

THREE DAYS EARLIER, Kahn had been released from the field hospital with an improved but still tender hand, and he had been going back for treatment twice a day. In the morning he would board one of the Supply helicopters and rejoin the Company. Patch occasionally briefed him on the changing situation, but Kahn could still not picture it completely. At least, he thought, they were out of the jungle. He could not imagine anything as bad as that.

Alone in the officers'-club tent, he was nursing a beer when the first of the "regulars" began to wander in from their staff jobs. They bellied up to the plywood box set up as a bar, paying him no attention. Because he was clean, he thought, they probably assumed he was on a staff too. At the hospital, he had visited the shower tent twice and often three times a day. He had thrown away his ratty fatigues and been issued new ones; still, considering the dirt and grime that seemed impossible to remove from under his fingernails and the patches of skin that peeled off from his arms and neck, he wondered if he would ever be completely clean again.

During his six-day stay in the rear, Kahn had not been preoccupied with thoughts of the Company. On the contrary, he had managed to put it out of his mind, except when he attended the twice-daily briefings on the progress of Operation Western Movie.

He went to these briefings for lack of anything better to do, and would sit quietly near an aisle while the general and other luminaries listened to the clipped assessments of Staff men outlining the features of the campaign. No one had ever asked him for an opinion, and he had not volunteered any. Obviously, back here they were not interested in his opinion. Everything that was done was done on paper; or, when the situation demanded, over the field radio—the reports coming in and out of a black void, orders going out into the void, none of it having much relation to reality.

Kahn knew that the task force had completed its sweep of the Boo Hoo Forest and now, all along a ten-mile stretch of the northern mountains, little battles were taking place, some high in the hills, some down in ravines and some in the bordering jungle. The battles were connected by pinpoint markings on maps in the TOC and the briefing tent, but totally isolated from one another by jungle, high ground and other natural obstacles. Frequently, the enemy broke off contact after a few minutes, vanishing phantomlike into the gloomy forest; other times he would hold ground and make the Americans pay dearly for their assaults.

In the past few days, the focus of it all had become a series of enemy redoubts located on some hills and knolls known collectively as The Fake. Earlier in the day Patch had confirmed to Kahn that when he returned to the Company in the morning, their assignment would to be help break up one of these redoubts.

In the briefing tent, however, Bravo Company was merely an impersonal black square on a map overlay. Each day, the square was dutifully moved around, along with other black squares, by the G-3 Operations staff. There were red squares also on the map, and they were moved around by the G-2 Intelligence people. Sometimes the red and black squares would be moved very close together until it began to remind Kahn of a disorderly kind of checkers game, the red and black hopping wildly about on a board of grids.

In a way, it all made sense here—the black squares chasing the red squares up and down the grids, occasionally landing right on top of one another. The black squares seemed to be winning, because there now were more of them than the red. On the final day he was there, two red squares disappeared entirely from the grid. Really, it was quite funny, and sometimes Kahn felt an urge to laugh out loud. But he didn't dare. These people were playing a high-stakes game here, and he knew it would not be funny to them.

* * *

THE OFFICERS'-CLUB tent was already full of raucous, drinking men when Major Dunn came in. He looked haggard, and when he removed his cap, Kahn thought that his gray hair looked thinner; but this was not surprising, because Kahn had noticed for the first time a few days ago that his own hair was thinner and chunks of it sometimes came out in his comb. Dunn smiled wearily and dropped his cap on the table. "Hi," he said. "I'll get a beer and join you."

The first thing Dunn noticed when he sat down was Kahn's bandaged hand.

"Jeez," he breathed, "got hit, huh—shrapnel?"

"It got infected," Kahn said modestly. It was good to see old Dunn again, even if he did tend to talk a little too much about his personal life.

"Gosh," Dunn said sympathetically, "I hope they took care of it—those things can be dangerous out here."

They drank several beers, and Dunn pressed for news of the fighting. He seemed genuinely interested, and whenever Kahn described a particularly harrowing incident, Dunn would wince in sympathy and shake his head. He seemed happy to have someone to talk with; and finally, he got around to the subject of his wife.

"She doesn't want a divorce—at least, not right now. What she said was the future is 'uncertain.' That's how she put it—*uncertain*," he said.

The letter had arrived two weeks before and was waiting for him when he returned from Firebase Meathead. There was another man, an officer at the post; that was all Dunn knew . . . he had no suspects.

"I didn't want to believe she was fooling around, but I guess I always figured she must have been—she's so damned pretty—a *Fraulein*—a real German beauty," he said.

He had written her back the next day. It was a painful letter, full of thoughts and reminiscences, and he had spent most of the night composing it. He told her how much he loved her. That he felt very helpless being here. That he did not want a divorce. That it would all be different when he came home.

"I'm out after this, you know," Dunn said. "Twenty

years—that's a damned good pension: six hundred a month plus privileges. I'm going to take over my old man's radio shop in Jersey City, do some expanding. Hell, I know radios; it'll be easy to step in."

Kahn listened as Dunn laid out his plan for "the next twenty." He had it all worked out; a house outside of town, the radio store, moving into television—mostly used, reconditioned sets; then perhaps a dealership. The talk went on for half an hour, and more beer was consumed. Finally, Dunn returned to the problem of *the other man.*

"Do you think I'm doing the right thing?" he asked. "I mean, what would you do?" He sucked on the beer. "I bet you'd tell her to fuck off, right?"

Kahn wasn't sure what to say. A sad, quizzical expression crossed Dunn's face. Kahn remembered the same look when they had spoken in the bow of the transport, an almost tormented look. Before Kahn could answer, Dunn slammed down the glass on the table.

"Just tell her to fuck off—that's what you'd do—isn't it?" he cried. His voice was high-pitched and angry.

Some at the bar turned, and the laughter and talk suddenly quieted. Dunn's mouth was pursed, and a black scowl enveloped his brow.

"How do you like it?" he bellowed, slamming the table with the glass again. "The daughter of a goddamn sheep farmer! Where would she be now—shearing goddamn sheep! And look at her—she was nothing before. I suppose if I'd made the list . . ."

Anger spread in waves over his face and voice. He spun around and glowered at the astonished crew at the bar, and they slowly went back to their drinks. The laughter and conversation rose again.

"All of my life," Dunn said in a low, trembling voice, "I have tried to do the right thing, and somehow I've messed up. Do you know how that feels? How could you?"

His voice rose again, and the bar crew quieted down once more.

"Well, I'll tell you this—anybody that wants to hear it!" he roared. "This time, I'm going to look out for old

Number Thirty-seven—*old . . . Number . . . Thirty . . .
seven . . . you hear!*" As Kahn and the others watched
dumbfounded, Dunn got to his feet and with the bent-
over stance of a high school fullback, he hurled himself
through the side of the tent, ripping up pegs and ropes,
bellowing like a stricken cow into the soft, moonlit night.

THE FIRST light of dawn grew from rosy pink to gray, then
blue, and while the last morning stars sparkled in the west
the bombardment of The Fake began. From a gun park
nine miles away, big 175-millimeter guns lobbed a
thunderous barrage up and down the knolls.

The brilliant flashes and trembling of the earth greeted
the early-November morning while Bravo Company
waited in its holes and sweated it out, observing its
objective in daylight for the first time. The artillery tore
overhead like invisible freight trains, ripping the air apart
and exploding with such unimaginable impact that a few
of the men actually thought they had gone deaf. From this
distance, the knolls did not appear particularly hard to
negotiate. The artillery of today and other days had
scorched and shredded the earth, leaving only a few
patches of trees isolated like tiny islands in a bare brown
sea of earth.

The barrage lifted as quickly as it had begun, and they
heard the sound of helicopters flying toward them, low
over the trees. Moments later they came in, dumping out
supplies, their engines still running. The last to land
deposited Kahn and three nervous replacements sent
forward at the last minute after committing certain sins in
the rear.

Alpha Company was milling around in loose platoon
formation, checking its equipment and preparing to move
out. Charlie Company would follow them, and then
Bravo Company. Already there seemed to be a firefight in
progress on the second knoll, but no people were visible,
and Sharkey hurriedly tried to fill Kahn in on the day's
program and the week just past. There had been more
trouble with the men while he had been gone—most of it
in Brill's platoon. Also, a man in Weapons Platoon had

threatened the life of Lieutenant Inge, and Inge was considering proceedings against him. Many of the men were weak with dysentry and other illnesses, and some of their gear was in lousy shape.

"You picked a hell of a time to come back," Sharkey said.

Kahn squinted toward the little firefight on the knoll, and searched his pockets for a pack of cigarettes.

"Now you tell me," he said dejectedly.

Still they waited, and still the order to move out was not received. Trunk, sitting on an ammunition crate, tried to interview the three replacements and at least make sure they had their essential equipment before he decided what to do with them. One of them, a freckled-faced boy with darting eyes and a mischievous smile, was a former jeep driver who had wrecked a major's jeep after loading up on too much beer. The other two were black cooks in the noncom mess whom the Brigade Sergeant Major had banished after they served a disagreeable meal. The Sergeant Major kept a motto above his desk:

> HE WHO TRIFLES HERE SHALL GO
> TO THE FARTHEST RIFLE PLATOON
> IN THE FARTHEST RIFLE COMPANY...
> NEVER AGAIN TO SEE BASE CAMP.

The Sergeant Major was true to his word, and these three frightened men now shifted nervously on their feet as they contemplated the reality of their fate. The jeep driver gingerly fingered a newly issued grenade on his belt as Trunk ran down the checklist of gear he was supposed to have. When he was asked if anything was missing, the driver managed a half-grin and stated that the only thing he had not been supplied with was his own body bag.

Trunk looked up from the checklist and regarded the man ruefully.

"Soldier," he said, "we don't joke about death out here."

HALF AN hour later they were moving up the first of the knolls, following a dusty trail worn down with the footsteps of men who had gone ahead. As they reached the top, they saw ahead and above the long file of Alpha and Charlie companies making their way to the top of the second knoll, where the fighting was. The upward slope, which they had not been able to see until now, was a desolate rubble of brown earth and shattered trees. On an embankment to their left, just below the crest of the first knoll, the mortar platoons of Alpha and Charlie companies were setting up. Although they still could not see any actual fighting ahead, the sounds of battle wafted back, puncturing the morning stillness along the route of march. The plan was that Alpha and Charlie companies were to relieve the beleaguered Airborne company at the top of the second knoll, then press forward as far as they could. Bravo Company was to remain on top of the second knoll and wait for further instructions.

It took nearly an hour to negotiate the downward slope of the first knoll. The trail was slippery, and such short trees as remained kept pulling out at the roots as the men grabbed them for support. As they neared the bottom, the mortars of Alpha and Charlie companies began to fire from behind them. Also as they reached the bottom, the first of the Airborne company began to stumble down toward them. It came as a confused and aimless mob.

All along the ravine between the two knolls the Airborne company streamed past them, cursing, weeping, helping others wearing bloody bandages. Some had no shirts or helmets, and a few even had no weapons. The Commander, a stocky captain with thick Army glasses, was bellowing in rage, trying to pull what was left of his men together. He ran here and there grabbing bewildered, zombie-like soldiers, shoving them into a loose line. There were tears in his eyes, and his face was a mask of anger. "Get down here—Get over there with those men—Where's your platoon?—Don't look at me like that, soldier—Move!" he roared.

Bravo Company was stupefied by this spectacle. They had never seen anything approaching it, even in the Boo Hoo Forest, and they wondered what was going on up there so horrible it could throw the paratroopers into such disarray.

Kahn stopped alongside the trail to study his map as the first elements of Bravo Company began to trudge up the slope of the second knoll. A helmetless man with a blackened lieutenant's bar on his fatigues lurched down toward him dragging his rifle behind by the sling. His face was beet red, and his tongue was lolling out. He looked like a man who had survived a hanging. Because of the narrowness of the trail he could not get by Kahn and stopped short of him, breathing slowly, waiting for him to move.

Kahn stepped back. "What's it like up there?" he asked tentatively.

"Go to hell," the lieutenant said, brushing Kahn with his shoulder as he stumbled past.

A few feet down the trail, the lieutenant stopped and turned. He raised the rifle and slung it on his shoulder.

"Excuse me," he mumbled. Kahn watched him grope down the path, then stepped back into the line uphill.

As they neared the top of the knoll, the ground was littered with the residue of fighting. Ammunition crates, C rations, clothing, bandages, empty cartridge casings, entrenching tools were strewn upon the scorched ground between the splintered trees. The earth had been churned into a soft, dry loam. Below, on the far side of the slope, the corpses of four North Vietnamese soldiers lay baking in the sun where they had fallen. There was a lurid smell in the air.

Alpha Company had already moved out and was at the bottom of the second ravine. Bravo Company could see them walking through the sparse trees. Charlie Company was far to the right still negotiating the downward slope of the second knoll. Every so often there was a burst of small-arms fire.

Already weary from the climb, Bravo Company waited and watched Alpha start up the third knoll. They saw them get as far as midway when a yellowish sheet of gunfire rose in a line above them. Seconds later, a continuous popping of small arms rattled back to Bravo Company. Several Alpha Company men toppled over and lay still; the rest flattened. Explosions burst around them, and the sheet of gunfire continued.

In less than a minute, Alpha was scrambling down the hill to the safety of a line of trees that was somehow untouched by the artillery. The explosions and the sheet of flame ceased. Bravo Company could hear a faint hollering from the treeline. They also saw that Charlie Company had reached the bottom of the ravine and was again moving far to the right, apparently in order to assault the flank of the knoll. Moments later, Bravo Company received new instructions.

The mortars of Alpha and Charlie companies were to be brought up to the second knoll. Bravo Company was to move far to the left, set up its mortars there and work down into the ravine for a left-flank assault on the third knoll. Colonel Patch, who was conducting the operation from the staging area they had left earlier, assured them that artillery had neutralized resistance in the ravine itself and would soon do the same to the third knoll. As Bravo Company walked along the ridgeline, a huge barrage of artillery landed near the top of the crest where the yellowish sheet of gunfire had been seen. It continued for nearly ten minutes, until it appeared to everyone's satisfaction that no living thing could possibly remain there.

Bravo Company was stumbling down into the ravine when Alpha Company again moved out of the line of trees and up the third knoll. They watched disheartenedly as the sheet of gunfire rose up again. In minutes, they too came under fire; machine guns opened up, and everyone dashed for cover in the ravine. As soon as they reached the bottom, mortar shells began falling on them.

Kahn and his Company Headquarters—Trunk; Bateson, the radio operator, and Hepplewhite, the Company Clerk—fell panting into a dry streambed, machine-gun bullets whizzing overhead. On the radio, Patch was involved in a heated conversation with the Alpha Company Commander and Kahn could not break through to him. In the meantime, he called for support from his own mortars, and soon the whistle and crash thundered over the North Vietnamese positions. Momentarily, the whizzing of bullets overhead stopped.

Somehow, Kahn realized, they had to flank those guns

and knock them out. He had no idea how many there were or how they were situated. What he did know was that Patch had been full of shit when he said the ravine was neutralized. It was a ridiculous word, anyway, he thought. In any event, they could not stay here forever, so Kahn took his little three-man cadre down the streambed, crouching against its walls so as to expose only the smallest portions of their bodies. The mortars began to fall around them again.

About fifty yards down, they ran into most of Brill's platoon huddled in the dry clay. Not a single man was firing a rifle, and Brill was nowhere to be seen.

"Where is Lieutenant Brill?" Kahn demanded.

A rifleman, cringing against the wall of the streambed, stammered and pointed ahead.

"I dunno—I think he's up there with some of the second squad," the man said.

Kahn left Brill's men where they were and headed in the direction the rifleman had indicated until the streambed flattened and afforded no further protection. Then they stepped up onto the soft ground and thrashed through some flattened elephant grass. Brill and half a dozen other men were lying behind a broken tree trunk. Kahn and his followers dived in behind them.

"Your men are hiding back there; why aren't you with them?" he asked.

Brill looked at him, amazed. "We're pinned down here; we can't move . . . we . . ."

"Go back and bring them around to the edge of the slope," Kahn said, pointing to the bottom of the slope they had just come down. "I'm sending Sharkey the other way—we've got to get those machine guns. I'll give you all the support I can. Get back to me when you're to their left—understand?"

Brill nodded his head.

"And try to stay with them this time—they're not even firing their weapons," Kahn said.

Brill looked at him darkly and crawled off with his squad. Bateson handed Kahn the handset. It was Sharkey.

"I think I see them just ahead of me—they've only got two guns," Sharkey said. "I'm going to take up two squads and try to knock them out."

"Negative," Kahn replied. "I'm sending the Two Element around to the left. I want to hit them with everything we have at once. Go right as far as you can, then pinch in—got it?"

"Roger, can do," Sharkey said.

Good old Sharkey. Good old West Point. Be careful. Kahn wiped sweat from his eyes.

They waited. The firing had died to an occasional burst. Kahn thought he heard voices from the direction of the North Vietnamese positions. Yes, it was definitely voices—a high-pitched, unintelligible chatter. God, they were that close!

He instructed Third Platoon to lay down covering fire and was about to call in Inge's mortars again when fierce shooting began to the right. Thirty seconds later, the radio crackled with the desperate voice of Sergeant Dreyfuss.

"We're ambushed, sir," Dreyfuss shouted, "pinned flat on both sides. Lieutenant Sharkey and three other men are hit bad—I think we gotta pull back."

Kahn stared into the denseness of the ravine.

"Where are you now?" he said.

"We're behind some kind of bunker about ten meters from that clump of trees. We're all right for a minute, but they got us covered," Dreyfuss panted.

"Wait one—hang on," Kahn said. He put the handset down.

I've got to do something now, he thought. Oh, Lord—Sharkey . . . His mind was cluttered with irrelevant thoughts. He knew he had to sort them out quickly. Everything was happening at once. The whole world was crazy. He could have gone to sleep right there. Slept for hours in the warm, peaceful sun. The radio barked again. It was Dreyfuss.

"Sir, we gotta pull back—we're getting murdered here," he cried.

Kahn had to make his decision. "No, no, you're not

pulling back. You stay put and I'm coming over there with part of Third Platoon. We have to get those guns."

Kahn commandeered two squads from Third Platoon and they went in leaps and bounds toward Dreyfuss' position, where there was a slow but steady firing of small arms. They crawled the final thirty yards through broken tree stumps and burned foliage, bullets kicking dust around them, past the bodies of two Second Platoon men badly mutilated by mortars. It took nearly fifteen minutes to reach Dreyfuss and his little band.

They had holed up behind a wrecked North Vietnamese fortification. Four wounded men lay on the ground. One boy, shot in the stomach, groaned with clenched fists as a medic attended him. Another, hit in the thigh, stared vacantly in shock. A third was unconscious and looked dead. His face was pale gray. Sharkey lay propped against a splintered log.

The bullet had entered just beneath the right armpit, apparently in an instant when his arm was raised. If it had hit him a split second sooner, or later, while his arm was down, it would probably have been absorbed by his flak jacket. Such were the uncertainties of war.

He was still conscious when Kahn got to him, but breathing with difficulty because the bullet had entered his lung and also his kidney. At first, Kahn did not see the ragged hole in his left side where it had come out, spilling part of his insides onto his fatigues and the ground.

Two of Dreyfuss' men suddenly stood up and heaved grenades over the top of the fortification. They exploded somewhere ahead with a dull, heavy thud. Dreyfuss and the radio operator clung to the ground.

Sharkey managed a weak smile when he saw Kahn. His face was filthy, and he was having great trouble breathing. The medic, a frail, dark-complexioned boy named Conway who had been tending the man with the stomach wound, looked at Kahn and shook his head. He pointed to an empty syringe of morphine lying near Sharkey's hand. "I done what I could, sir," Conway said. From somewhere in front, a machine gun blapped nastily, and things zinged above them. Wood from the stump flew into the air.

"Fuck me, Billy," Sharkey said halfheartedly. "This ain't no place for a sanitary man."

"You're out of this," Kahn said. "We're all going back together—hear?"

Sharkey took another labored breath. His tongue was covered with blood, and Kahn noticed blood on his sleeve; he had evidently been wiping it off his mouth whenever it came out.

"Who you kidding, man?" Sharkey said painfully. "My insides are shot out. Just don't move me for a while, all right?"

"Sure, buddy; hang tight, okay?—You want more morphine?"

Sharkey placed a thick, grimy hand on Kahn's knee and sucked hopelessly at the air through the big gap where his teeth used to be.

"Do me a favor," he sighed softly, his big blue eyes cloudy and unseeing. "If them new teeth ever get here, give 'em to the Old Man. Tell him to cram 'em up his ass. . . ."

MORTAR ROUNDS continued to fall around them with maddening regularity. It was clear they could not remain exposed here for long. Kahn spun around to Trunk.

"We have to bust this up," he said. "There's maybe one, two machine guns up there. You go bring up two of those squads from First Platoon and take them around to the left. Send everybody else up here. If there's an extra machine gun, send it up too." Trunk crawled away toward the rear.

"Dreyfuss, you take what's left of these men and move to the right and close in as quick as you can. Use grenades."

Dreyfuss collected his half-dozen men and disappeared into a tangle of downed trees.

Kahn looked over at Sharkey. His eyes were closed, and his face had turned a sallow white. Conway's ear was at Sharkey's chest.

The medic raised his head.

"He's gone, sir," Conway said.

"Cover him," Kahn said weakly. A Second Platoon

radioman turned over and slowly began removing his poncho from its roll on the back of his belt.

The first of the two squads Kahn had told Trunk to send up began to arrive, collapsing behind the fortification, eyes wild and bulging.

"Who's senior man here?" Kahn said. A buck sergeant named Corpusteli raised his hand. "I guess I am," he said faintly.

Kahn looked him in the eye. "I want you to spread these men out in a line on both sides of this bunker and be ready to lay down fire on those machine guns ahead of us. Take off." Corpusteli frowned and then departed on his hands and knees.

"You two, with the M-sixty," Kahn said. "Set up over there where you have a clear field of fire. Keep their heads down." Spudhead Miter and Madman Muntz exchanged furtive glances and slithered off into the brush.

There was really nothing to do now but wait. Brill should be coming up on the far left anytime. A stray bullet whined in the air. *At least, it can't last forever*, Kahn thought exhaustedly; that was what the captain in the hospital had told him, and he was glad to remember it now.

It can't last forever. . . .

The captain had been in the bed next to his the day he came in to have his hand attended to. He was a cheery guy whose company had been overrun somewhere to the south, and he had been shot and left for a corpse. Somehow he had revived himself, plugged a sock into the hole in his chest, wrapped it tight with a binocular strap and walked out of the jungle. He'd been in the hospital for three weeks with a tube running into his nose. After a while Kahn had asked when they were going to take the tube out.

"They say it looks good on me," the captain replied happily. "They say they're going to leave it in."

LATER THAT same day, Kahn had gone looking for Sergeant Jelkes. He left his bed on the pretense of going to the latrine and found a nurse who said Jelkes was probably in the intensive-care ward. Kahn went in unannounced and walked from bed to bed. It was like walking through a nightmare. People moaned and screamed. The first bed he came to was a plastic device filled with air. It contained a wad of bandages, inside which was a man burned black as coal. It really didn't look like a man at all. It looked like a blob of protoplasm struggling to organize itself back into human form. Other beds held other horrors, but Jelkes was not among them. Finally he found a medic who checked a list.

"Yes, he came in here this morning, Lieutenant, but we sent him straight to the morgue. Sorry," the medic said.

THERE WAS firing on the right, but no sign of Brill.

"Where the hell is Second Platoon?" Kahn said to no one in particular. He told Bateman to raise them. For an instant, Sally's face appeared in his mind. I ought to write her about Jelkes, he thought. Both her body and face appeared this time. He remembered the night in the BOQ when she'd pulled off her sweater. Lord, what delicious tits—what an ass. He felt himself getting excited. His mind was racing around. This is ridiculous, he thought; how in hell can I be thinking of something like that at a time like this? . . .

Then Brill was on the radio.

"Where the hell are you?" Kahn said.

There was a long response.

"I don't care about that," Kahn shot back. "I want you moving now."

There was another brief reply.

"Hell, yes I want you to attack—right *goddamn now*. What do you think is going on here?" he yelled into the handset.

There was a short response, and Kahn slammed the handset into Bateman's hand. Suddenly on their right automatic-weapons fire burst across the scorching ravine floor. Everything seemed to erupt at once, and the air was filled with dirt and splinters and steel. On the left he could see Trunk's men leaping and bounding over fallen trees. A burst of fire sent them to the ground. Moments later they were up again. Through the smoke and dust, Kahn thought he saw figures running from the North Vietnamese positions. They're bugging out, he thought calmly.

The squad he'd sent right with Dreyfuss had gotten up and begun to move slowly forward, crouched low. He watched helplessly as a savage fusillade of machine-gun fire swept through them, knocking several men flat. The others fell, hugging dirt.

From a little wrinkle in the ground far behind and to the left of the North Vietnamese came the sound of firing from Brill's platoon. Two grenades sailed up from the spot where Dreyfuss' men had flattened out and floated down on the spot where the enemy machine gun seemed to be. There were two quick explosions, and several more figures scampered off toward the bottom of the third knoll. One of Trunk's squads was on its feet and in seconds had reached the spot where the firing had come from. They disappeared quickly into the bunkers, and Kahn radioed Brill to hold his fire. It was a quarter to two in the afternoon. For the moment, it was over. Now they could move on.

24

FROM THE top of the third knoll, the valley spread out before them like an immense Oriental fan in thin, pastel shades. They had climbed this slope after the ravine fight, molested only by an unrelenting sun—which was nearly as threatening as the enemy, since water was again running short. All of the artillery and mortar preparation had raised an enormous cloud of dust over The Fake and its approaches, and through it, the sun had become a dull red blob in the western sky. The greens of the jungle below and the blues of the mountains on the other side and the silver of the Drang River meandering down the valley had blended into hazy, fragile colors that changed and swirled as the sun sank lower and the dust settled down.

Bravo Company pinched in its flanks, pulled together and took account of itself. The butcher's bill for the day was nine men killed, seventeen wounded and two out of commission for other reasons.

A current of bitterness ran through the men as they dug in for the night. For one thing, they were completely exhausted, hungry and thirsty. For another, they felt the ravine battle should have been avoided, because of Patch's promise that the artillery had wiped out resistance there. But even that aside, many of them were beginning to experience a deep sense of futility about what they were doing. So much of the killing today seemed meaningless; it was take one hill, move to the next—two days later the enemy was back again on the first. It was killing for killing's sake. From the perspective of the third knoll they could see the line of hills stretching into the distance, and it seemed to be endless. Everyone had his own tortured memories of the past weeks, but only the immediate was real. Like the fragments of a satanic dream, the village of the Running Man, the Boo Hoo Forest—even the ravine fight—were remembered clearly but with little connection to time or place. They were drawing their strength out of ruthlessness, and each man had by now developed a sense of this, if he had not had it before.

Above them remained two more knolls of The Fake—each to be taken, then abandoned. And at what cost? Everyone knew that if it went like today, no one would be left to claim the peak, even if they could reach it. As the sun went behind a far-off mountain and the sky faded into a ghostly twilight, the voices of Bravo Company were filled with bitterness and blasphemy—the sour oaths of men who knew they were going to be offered as sacrifices again in the morning. But tomorrow, at least, was another day.

KAHN SAT in the dirt, his rifle in his lap. He too felt the bitterness. Perhaps he most of all. He looked at the top of The Fake. Nothing moved or stirred, but he knew they were there. Waiting. He had come here to pay a debt—a debt his father had said he owed. Owed because everyone owed a couple of years to the service of the country; it was the way they thought—his father and Mr. Bernard and the rest. He wondered if they really understood what was happening.

His own reasons had been different. The debt he saw had less to do with the country than it did with his being a Jew. He knew full well the value of paying his debt. He had never really considered himself an outsider until he had gone out for the football team in high school. He hadn't been very good—second string at best—but they had accepted him for it, and he had begun to realize just how *out* he had been before. After the first year, he really didn't want to try it again, but he did because he dreaded terribly going back to the way it had been before.

He wondered if the people at the country club behind his house would accept him when he returned with a uniform full of ribbons. He was certain to get a Bronze Star—they handed those out like malaria pills. He already was entitled to a Purple Heart; and there would be others—each medal mute testimony to a partial payment on the debt.

Before he came here, he had felt a certain satisfaction in these thoughts. The war was fresh and new then; the nation bright, hopeful and patriotic, welcoming its heroes—and, in fact, creating them. He knew there were rumblings of discontent: actors, academics, writers, students—even a few politicians—screaming about immorality and marching in the streets. What did it mean? On the spot, he concluded he didn't give a fuck what it meant—only his part in it. And that included, at this point, getting out in one piece. Why the hell couldn't they just pack up now and go home? McCrary, the Graves Registration lieutenant, had once proposed it to him and Holden while they were eating ice cream in his morgue.

"We could just announce we've won and clear out," he'd said. "Who in hell would know the difference?"

The more he thought about the debt, the less he felt he owed one at all. His close friend was dead as he could now have been too, or might still be very soon. Here was a terrible place, with steel and lead flying through the air, which in itself was neither anti-Semitic nor racist nor political. Jew or no, he stood about as good a chance of catching some as anyone else, and maybe better. He could have gotten out of it maybe. Gotten married, or left the country, or taken his chances with the draft board—but no. He had joined freely, if reluctantly, the way he had the football, to show them he wasn't some draft-dodging, pawnshop-running Jew who was going to stand for Five Gold Rings on top of his house and his old man having to drive fifteen miles to play golf and himself being put off for dates by girls who attended Baptist and Episcopal churches on Sunday. He wished they knew that out here none of that mattered. This wasn't some yarmulke on top of his head; it was a helmet designed to keep his skull in one piece.

The more Kahn thought about it, sitting alone in the dirt, the madder he got, and if at that moment by some awkward coincidence he had overheard anyone telling a Jewish joke, or perceived *any* kind of insult whatsoever, he would probably have brained him with his gun butt.

SHORTLY BEFORE 10 A.M. they began the assault of the fourth knoll. All night artillery had blasted it raw, and again it appeared that nothing could have withstood that kind of barrage. This time they were right. Cursing, sweating and numb, Bravo Company struggled to the top without a shot's being fired. Charlie Company already occupied an opposite saddle of the same knoll, and they could see them through the gap in the middle. Some Charlie Company men waved across the gap, and Bravo Company waved back. Momentarily there was relief, but it was short-lived. Patch radioed them to set up the mortars there and move on to the fifth and final knoll.

"They are on the run—let's keep pressing it," Patch said. "We may be out of here in a day or so."

The sun was bright in the sky as they climbed higher and higher up the steep slope of the fifth knoll. Behind it loomed the peaks of another chain of mountains, much taller and more forbidding than this one. Along several trails that led to the crest, they would occasionally find a relic of earlier fighting—a helmet, a C-ration tin, a fatigue shirt. They had not been aware that the Airborne battalion had made it up this far.

DiGeorgio was the first to see the head.

It was stuck on a thick tree stump about five feet off the ground. A helmet rested back so that the entire face showed. Its eyes were half open, staring grotesquely across the valley. Clenched in its teeth was a blackened cigar butt.

Tacked beneath the head was a piece of brown rice paper finger-painted in dried blood.

U.S. SOLJERS DIE HERE, it said.

"Jesus Christ!" DiGeorgio said, flinching away.

"Them bastards," Crump said vehemently. "Dirty bastards."

There was nothing to do but press on. Half the company had to walk past the head, but no one made any attempt to remove or cover it. Propaganda leaflets were scattered along the trail. One showed a stack of military coffins reproduced from an issue of *Life* magazine. GOING MY WAY? was its caption. Some of the men picked these up and read them. Most threw them down. A few stuffed them into their pockets.

They had the crest in sight when the machine gun opened up ahead, killing the point man and badly wounding the next man in line. The point man was one of the two black cooks who had been sent out as replacements the day before. He was shot in the throat and flung backward into several other men and was probably dead before he hit the ground.

The fire seemed to come from everywhere—in front and on both sides. Men leaped in panic to what safety they could find, but there wasn't a lot to hide behind up here. Those in the lead element lay flat for a moment, then did the first sane thing that came to mind and scrambled downhill for the protection of a little abutment about thirty yards below. Almost everyone else had taken refuge behind this, and a few brave souls poked out their rifles and fired back, but they were met with such a fusillade they quickly gave it up and shrank down with the rest.

Grenades came tumbling down at the abutment, some exploding over it, some bouncing down and bursting in midair, shrapnel ringing everywhere. Hot pieces of residue floated down like snowflakes.

Predictably, mortars began to land. At first they fell behind them, but the North Vietnamese steadily walked them up the slope toward the abutment. The shells whistled through the air with a high-pitched, inhuman sound, like terrible fingers searching for flesh. Obviously they couldn't stay here, and Kahn organized a withdrawal in the most orderly way he could.

At the bottom, behind the series of rocky hummocks, Bravo Company lay gasping and stunned. Never had they come up against such withering fire. As they tried to regain their breath and wits, the radio hissed and the handset was shoved at Kahn.

"What are you doing? You are supposed to be going up the hill—not down it," Patch said testily.

"Sir, half the North Vietnamese Army is up there. They hit us on all sides. We were getting slaughtered," Kahn said.

"All right, all right, so they're dug in. That's what you get combat pay for, Lieutenant. What you have to do is to flank them, boy, flank them!" Patch said enthusiastically.

"I can't tell where their flank is, sir—they seem to be spread all across the top of the hill. I'll have to send up some kind of patrol," Kahn said weakly.

"There's no time for that now," Patch came back sternly. "You have contact—keep it. I don't want them to slip away again. Finish this up so we can get the hell out of here!"

Kahn looked at Trunk, who was lying beside him wiping blood off of his face from a deep gash he had received when he'd tumbled into a splintered tree. Kahn pointed grimly to the top of the crest and raised his eyebrows.

Trunk shook his head deliberately. "We can't do it, Lieutenant. I don't see how. . . . I think—"

"Damn it, Trunk, I don't either, but that's what the

man says. . . . What the hell am I supposed to do?"

They peered over the rocks and tried to come up with a sensible plan for an assault. Of course, there was none.

Minutes later, Patch's irritated voice came over the speaker. "I don't see you moving down there. Let's get with it," he said.

The receiver still in his hand, Kahn looked around behind him curiously. He glanced at Trunk, then swung his binoculars up to the top of the fourth knoll, where another rifle company was milling around, evidently waiting in reserve. Off to the side of this was a small bunch of men. A figure he recognized as Patch stood out among them, a tiny dot in the distance. The figure was waving its arms violently in what was an apparent signal to move out. How in hell did he get there? Kahn wondered. He's supposed to be back at the staging area.

Kahn got on the Company net and called Brill. "I want you to move right about three hundred meters and then start climbing up," he said. "About halfway, just before that abutment, start to pinch in. Third Platoon will be inside you and a little bit below. I'm taking First Platoon to the left and do the same thing—got it?"

"Right," Brill said. His voice was very faint. Perhaps it was the radio batteries. . . .

Kahn tried to raise Inge on the radio. Unsuccessful, he sent a runner back to tell him to come forward and take over Third Platoon for the attack. Off to the right, he could see part of First Platoon, huddled behind some rocks and boulders, and he was about to make his way over to them when Brill came back on the radio.

"I got trouble here," he said. "They won't do it."

"Well *get* them to do it," Kahn said furiously.

"I think you better come over here and talk to them," Brill said. Kahn could hardly hear him.

BRILL'S PLATOON was lying or sitting behind the rock outcropping with hard, determined looks on their faces. Kahn squatted down in front of them, next to Brill.

"Here's the CO," Brill said. "You bastards better listen up."

"Look," Kahn said, "I know nobody wants to go up there. But the colonel says we are going to do it—and we are going to do it. He also said that when we get up this goddamn hill we can go home—so saddle up; get with it—on the double."

No one said a word or moved. Somewhere above, a sniper's rifle cracked nastily. Everyone looked at Kahn. He paused for long seconds, searching the faces of the men.

"Did you hear what I said?—The colonel says we are out of here soon as we knock off the crest...."

"Yeah, Lieutenant," one man said sarcastically. "Just like he said there wasn't no gooks left in that ravine yesterday."

There was another silence. Someone else spoke up.

"Shit, sir—we go up there—it don't mean nothing. You know that. We just gonna get a bunch of us killed. Them gooks'll be back on this hill the minute we leave," the man said.

The radio crackled, and Bateson shoved it at Kahn.

"Not now—tell him I've got a situation down here," Kahn snapped.

"All right, goddamn it," he said angrily. "This is a direct order to every one of you. Lieutenant Brill and Sergeant Trunk are my witnesses. You men get up, get your gear and move out with Lieutenant Brill in one minute. If you don't, I'm going to take up Second and Third platoons anyway and I'll promise each and every one of you you will spend the next ten years in the stockade at Fort Leavenworth. I am counting now," Kahn said.

He looked down at his watch. The second hand swept toward the bottom, and started upward again. Still they sat.

Once he looked up at Brill and for an instant he thought he saw Brill and Sergeant Groutman exchange glances. Trunk had seen this too, and he raised his eyebrows at Kahn, as though to ask if Kahn wanted him to intercede. Kahn shook his head sharply and returned to the watch. He was in charge here now. He had to see it through. The second hand had returned to the top.

"Okay—that's it," he said. "Trunk, let's get the hell out of here."

They trotted low along the rocks back to where Inge's platoon had joined Third. Kahn gave him new instructions.

Before Kahn reached First Platoon, Inge was on the radio to him.

"I can't get 'em to move. They say if Second Platoon won't go they won't either," Inge said.

"Shit," Kahn growled. He was on his way back to Inge's position when the radio hissed angrily. "It's the colonel . . . says he wants you right now," the operator said. Kahn put the handset to his ear. Patch was irate.

"Colonel," Kahn began, "I have tried everything. They say they won't go up there again—and I can't go with just one platoon."

Patch was mortified. He was standing on the hill with three newspaper reporters, two television crews and a magazine correspondent, who had come to record what the Army was presently billing as the largest single battle of the war—two thousand Americans taking on an entire enemy division and kicking the hell out of them by anyone's standards. Now *this* embarrassment. Men who would not fight? Patch seethed—it could not be permitted.

"Try to pull them together in a single spot," Patch said calmly. "I am on my way down there."

To HIS deep dismay, Patch was followed into the ravine by the entourage of reporters and cameramen, who sniffed a story in this. Men who would not fight? It was good copy. And Patch could not prevent it. As they came up the low slope to the rock outcropping, Patch was in the lead, his sleeves rolled to his elbows, an indignant scowl on his face. In the distance the sounds of rifle fire from another company echoed down the ravine, but as he strode on, he observed with satisfaction that the correspondents were bent over at the waist protectively in a sort of Groucho Marx crouch.

When he reached the outcropping, Patch brushed by
Kahn and addressed the men directly. Some of them
looked a little embarrassed and stared at the ground. His
expression softened.

"Come in here closer," Patch said quietly, motioning
them toward him. He remained standing, most of his
body exposed above the rocks. The men slowly gathered
in and sat back down. The news correspondents backed
up against the rocks and squatted on their haunches and
took out their notepads. The TV film cameras purred.

Patch looked around for a minute before selecting an
antagonist. His choice was a dark-eyed Italian boy from
Providence, Rhode Island, who had been glaring fiercely
at Patch since he had walked up. Patch nodded toward
him.

"Okay, soldier, suppose you tell me what's the matter
here," he asked solicitously.

Kahn was surprised at Patch's tone of voice. It was
certainly not the outraged voice he had expected; the one
he had heard so many times over the radio; the one that
had condemned the men to their bunk rooms aboard the
transport. It was a nice, sweet voice, a sympathetic voice,
a soothing voice. Patch's face had a look of deep concern.

"Well...ah...sir...ah..." the boy stammered. "It's,
ah...like, we been out here almost four weeks now, and,
ah..." He stopped for a moment to collect his thoughts.
The glare on his face melted to a look of awkwardness, as
though he weren't quite sure how to express himself.

"Yes? Go on," Patch said nicely.

"Uh, see, sir...you said yesterday there wasn't gonna
be no NVA in that ravine, and then we got chopped up
bad down there...and, ah..."

"Yes, I know you did, but I was very proud of you, all
of you," Patch said. "Go on."

The TV cameras whirred and clicked, and the
microphone man moved closer to the boy.

"They just murdered us—there wasn't nothing to do
but get down...."

Patch looked at the boy, reserved, waiting for him to
continue.

"You just don't know how bad it was up there, sir. . . . It was . . . it was all over us. . . ." He searched for words. "It was *horrible*," he blurted out.

"Yes, I know it must have been," Patch said sympathetically. "Go on."

"We, ah . . . I don't know, sir. We just don't none of us want to go back up there again. . . . I mean, there ain't been enough artillery up there or something, cause the gooks are set up everyplace, and we go back up now, we just gonna get killed . . . sir . . ." the boy said, almost apologetically.

From above, the sniper's rifle cracked again. Patch did not flinch. The news correspondents reflexively tucked their heads into their necks. A fatherly smile crossed Patch's face. He knew he had them now—or was pretty close to it. He sensed they knew it too. This was a ploy he'd picked up from an old Army manual, and he'd once given a talk on it at Command and General Staff College.

"You want more artillery up there, do you?" Now he was speaking to them all. "Well, we can certainly get that for you. Tom," he said to Captain Flynn, his aide, "raise Wicked Blast. Tell them I want fire on this knoll. Walk it up and down about fifty meters from the top."

The aide summoned the radioman and began speaking into the handset.

"Now," Patch said, drawing himself up. "We are going to put the Big Heat on. But let me say this. You all know we laid fire on these hills for nearly two days and you all saw the results this morning. Obviously they are well dug in up there, and it's going to take infantrymen to dislodge them. It's going to take men like yourselves. . . ." He paused for a moment.

"Part of the problem," he said, "has been that that is a very big ridgeline and until now we didn't know exactly where their strong-points were. Thanks to you, we do. Another problem is that it's been hard to put accurate fire up there because a lot of the guns have been firing ever since this operation started and their bores are smooth as a woman's tits. . . ."

"Ah, sir," another voice came out of the crowd, "maybe

if you put napalm up there it would help."

Patch looked at the voice and spoke again to the whole group.

"Ah, yes, napalm—good thought. We haven't used much of that yet for the same reasons—we weren't sure exactly where they were. Tom, get Air Liaison on the horn. Tell him to put napalm up there after the artillery lifts." The aide spoke again into the radio. The cameras continued to whir.

The sniper had been silent for a while, and Kahn suddenly wondered if he or any of the other North Vietnamese above could see the weird little drama being played out down here. If so, he thought, it must be very puzzling to them—the television cameras, tape recorders and people writing in notebooks. Perhaps they were having a laugh out of it. In other circumstances it might have been quite funny.

"Now," Patch said masterfully. "After we have smashed them with artillery and fried them with napalm, when you men get up there all you should find is bits and pieces and maybe a few halfwitted gooks. But I want you up there. I don't know what Lieutenant Kahn has said to you, but whatever it was, I am wiping the slate clean. I want you to go back to your positions and watch this little show. Then I want you to go back up that hill and mop up whatever is left. When you've done that, I am going to pull you out of here and you'll all get some rest."

As if to punctuate the colonel's closing argument, two artillery rounds thundered overhead and exploded just below the crest of the hill. Everyone looked up. The Big Heat was on. The aide spoke into the handset again, making corrections.

"All right," Patch said cheerfully. "Lieutenant Kahn will take over now and put you where he wants you. You men have done a fine job so far. Good luck on this one." Patch nodded to Kahn. He stepped forward. "Platoon leaders, take your platoons back to their original positions and get ready to move out like I said before," he said.

The TV cameras were still running. The reporters

scribbled furiously in their notebooks. The men did not move.

Slowly out of Brill's platoon a lanky figure uncoiled from the ground. He looked around and said in a Southern drawl, "You heard what the man said; let's go," and Brill's men, following the lead of Pfc. Homer Crump, pulled to their feet and dragged themselves away, talking and muttering to each other and to themselves.

THICK, ACRID smoke and dust wafted down from the crest of The Fake and engulfed them as they hauled themselves painfully upward. Small fires were burning everywhere, ignited by far-flung bits of napalm jelly. There was still no shooting as they reached the abutment where they had taken shelter during the first assault, and they plunged forward with mean, determined thoughts, watching almost hopefully for the first North Vietnamese to poke his head up. An electric sense of victory ran through Bravo Company now, spurred in part by the terrific bombardment of The Fake and also by Patch's appearance on the scene.

Far to the right they heard the faint sounds of some other battle, but it did not concern them. Their own line was spread out perhaps a hundred yards, Brill on the far left, Inge inside him and First Platoon beginning to pinch in from the right.

Spudhead was laboring behind with the boxes of ammo for Muntz's machine gun when the first firing began, ahead of them. It seemed almost halfhearted this time—an automatic rifle or two blapping out of the haze. They crouched lower, but since the bullets were apparently directed elsewhere, they pressed forward. They had reached just about the same spot where the earlier firing had started when Spudhead saw the two North Vietnamese pop out of their hole and lob two black objects toward them.

He tried to scream, "Grenade," but could not think of the word. All he could say was "Oh, hell," and he buried his face in the dirt. Others took the cue and dropped briskly to the ground as though they had suddenly been put to sleep with an amazing nerve gas. There was an explosion, and dirt flew into the air. There was no second explosion. Bright flashes came from the spot where the two heads had popped out. Dirt kicked up behind them. The bunker was about thirty yards away, just below the crest, surrounded by blackened sandbags.

"You see it!" someone yelled.

"Yeah, I see it," Muntz growled back. He was struggling to set up the M-60. Spudhead crawled beside him and took one of the ammunition boxes off his belt. It had been rubbing his backside raw for several days, and he was glad to be rid of the damned thing. The fire rained down on them again from ahead.

"See, there they are," a voice yelled from behind.

"Goddamn it," Muntz screamed back, "don't tell *me*—I *know*!"

Another grenade sailed out of the bunker toward them. Muntz's machine gun barked and caught the pitcher in mid-throw. He disappeared behind the sandbags as though he had been poleaxed. The grenade exploded harmlessly far ahead of them.

"We can't stay here," Hixon, the other ammo bearer, whispered; "there ain't no cover."

"Shut up," Muntz said.

Farther on, Dreyfuss was signaling with his arms from the prone position, motioning several men forward and to the side of the bunker. Two men jumped to their feet and made a dash in the direction Dreyfuss had indicated.

The enemy guns spat nastily again, and Muntz fired off a burst from his M-60. The men Dreyfuss had sent forward rose to their knees and hurled grenades at the bunker. One of them landed inside. Instantly, the grenade flew out again, exploding in midair and sending fragments rattling overhead. The two men threw two more grenades, but before they went off, three ragged men scurried out of the bunker and began clawing up toward the crest. The grenades exploded, and two of the three slid back down. Muntz cut the other one nearly in half with his machine gun, and he slid back with his friends.

There was other firing on both sides, but it wasn't very intense. Then through the smoke, several men appeared at the very top of the hill to their right. Muntz swung the machine gun around and dropped his cheek down.

"No, no!" Spudhead cried. "That's us—that's Americans!"

Dimly, they could see more men steadily walking forward, occasionally shooting down the back slope of The Fake. A cheer slowly began to rise from the men still lying on the forward side, and they got to their feet and dusted themselves and began trudging to the top. As they got closer they could see dozens of strange dark lumps on the ground, some covered with dirt. Closer inspection revealed these to be bodies of North Vietnamese, some incinerated black by the napalm. "Crispy critters," someone called them.

Almost gaily, Bravo Company began picking over the corpses for souvenirs. Anything of possible keeping or trading value was removed. A few pistols were found, and an occasional whistle or knife. These were keepable, as were watches, and wallets, some with photographs in them, if they were still intact. Diaries and official documents had to be turned over to the Intelligence people. They pocketed what they could and then sat down amid the carnage and lit cigarettes or opened C rations. Confidence was as high as it had ever been. They had encountered an enemy as mean as could be imagined and conquered him. In the process, they had worked their will on their Battalion Commander. That Patch had agreed to blast the hill with jets and artillery was a sign to everyone that they had somehow gained a measure of control over their own destiny. However small it was, they did not intend to lose this. They were still cattle, and they knew it, and would never be anything more as long as they remained in the Army. But they were now at least a fierce and organized herd of cattle, and that counted for something.

LATER IN the afternoon, when the sun again hung like a great shimmering ball in the western sky, they waited quietly for the helicopters that would take them back as they had been promised. No one said much, partly because they were tired and shaken by what they had done today, and partly because of the realization that they actually were going home, and for a while it would be over. During the last hour, the jubilation of victory had faded into a welcomed numbness that blotted out the terror of the past weeks. It was a good, light-headed feeling, combined with a sense of satisfaction that at last they had become experts at their grim task.

Somewhere far down the valley the steady *whop-whop-whop* of helicopters broke the mountain silence. All looked in the direction of the sound.

Just above the farthest peaks they could see them, first one flight, then another and another, flying in diamond-shaped formation, little black puffs of smoke spurting rhythmically from their engines. The sun glinted off their windows like dancing spangles, erasing any lingering doubts that Patch might not be true to his word. As they drew closer, the sight of these machines raised a marvelous feeling of joy and relief—much as the sight of land must have raised in seamen who had lived through weeks of storms. They were sailors whose ship had just come in.

Kahn pulled the pin on a green-smoke grenade and tossed it into a clearing where the helicopters could land. People began standing and collecting their gear, but there was still little talk or laughter.

From somewhere in the mob, a voice rose in song. It was a deep, rich Southern voice, belonging to the large Negro, Carruthers.

> Glo-ree, glo-ree, hal-al-luuul-ya,
> Glo-ree, glo-ree, hal-al-luuul-ya,
> Glo-ree, glo-ree, hal-al-luuul-ya,
> His truth is a marchin' on....

It took everyone by surprise, this clear, wonderful voice echoing out across the blistered mountainside like a clarion call. Carruthers began another chorus.

Glo-ree, glo-ree, hal-al-luuul-ya...

Others joined in, struck by a wave of elation despite
the numbness and exhaustion. By the end of the chorus
the entire company was singing, even Kahn—loudly, joy-
ously, reverently, their sweat-stained faces turned upward
toward the dying sun. On a few faces, tears streamed
down making little rivulets that washed away the grime
and filth of their shabby existence. They did not stop
singing even when the first helicopter dropped down and
drowned them out completely. Each squad continued to
sing as it boarded, much to the astonishment of the pilots,
who were convinced all infantrymen were crazy to begin
with. The singing ceased only when the last helicopter
descended into the lengthening shadows and the last man
scrambled aboard. Moments later it jerked skyward in a
fat wash of dust and wind, leaving the mountaintop in the
peace of approaching night.

Part Three

THE
DISMAL
DEEPS

25

EVERYONE KNEW about the inspection before it was announced. It was just one of those things that got around.

They also knew the reason, or thought they did, and it had given them cause for apprehension. They had worked feverishly since midmorning, individually or in small knots, polishing and cleaning, shining and rearranging, and when the word came down that Colonel Patch and the Brigade Sergeant Major were on their way to the Company area, the work slowed but did not stop and was performed in a more orderly manner.

"What is that activity over there?" Patch asked

curiously, pointing to a group of men working in the sandy soil by a row of tents.

The Sergeant Major squinted from the glare and rubbed his chin. "It's uncertain, sir," he said.

"It looks like they're raking the sand," Patch said.

"Yessir, it does," the Sergeant Major said thoughtfully.

"What in hell are they raking sand for?" Patch demanded.

"I'd have to ask the First Sergeant about that, sir," the Sergeant Major replied.

"Why don't you ask the men?"

"Doubt it would do any good, Colonel—they probably don't know."

"Well ask them anyway," Patch said.

The Sergeant Major stepped forward. "Hey, you—come over here!" he said. The men looked up. The Sergeant Major pointed to one of them, who happened to be Spudhead Miter, and motioned him over. Spudhead looked nervously around at the others.

"Yes, you!" the Sergeant Major bawled. "Over here." Spudhead's heart sank. He always seemed to get singled out for something.

THEY HAD been back nearly two weeks. For the first few days they had been visitors in a strange new city.

The old row of billets was now surrounded by dozens of other tents, and the dirt paths between them had been graded and some of them paved with asphalt. Signs identified various units, directed traffic one way or the other and issued assorted standing instructions. A sign at the head of Four/Seven's row of tents proclaimed, DO NOT PISS IN THE COMPANY STREET, and when Bravo Company saw this they knew they were back in the Real Army.

Tin-roofed cinder-block buildings dotted the Operations area where before only tents had stood. The lone exception was the TOC, which remained as it was, isolated atop the little rise. All of the tents and new buildings had been sandbagged, and most were equipped with generator-driven electric lights. To accommodate the influx of new troops and equipment, the perimeter of the encampment had been widely extended on all sides, and beyond its outermost barrier, a second city of native shanties had sprung up, much resembling the Seething Reptile City they had passed the day they got off the transport. In the dim remaining light of their first night back in camp, Bravo Company studied the occupants of this second city through the rolls of barbed wire, uncertain whether they should regard them as friend or foe.

Filthy, hungry and shaken from the fighting, they were herded into a line outside the Supply building and told to strip naked and throw their rags into a row of garbage containers. New fatigues were handed out, along with a towel and a bar of soap, and they were directed to a water tanker with shower nozzles. It was by the numbers again—always by the numbers—but each man did his utmost to scrub himself as fresh and clean as the inside of a new car.

The mess hall was opened specially for them. Hot scrambled eggs and bacon were dished out, with helpings of canned peaches: breakfast food, because there was nothing left from supper—but they couldn't have been happier at a king's banquet. Some returned for thirds and fourths, and Crump, after he devoured the last scrapings from every pan, ate an entire jar of jelly set before him on the table.

Afterward they lay in their cots, satiated and clean and free from the terror that stalked them through the Boo Hoo Forest and the knolls of The Fake. Long after most had slipped into deepest dreams, Crump lay brooding about his banana-cat. He had arranged to go down in the morning convoy to Firebase Meathead and retrieve it, because they knew they were not going back there anytime soon—obviously, since all of their gear had been gathered up and delivered to the billets here. Crump lay back and stared across the blackened paddies with troubled eyes. He was wondering if the Engineers Company men had treated the banana-cat well, and if it would remember him.

*　　*　　*

SPUDHEAD SPRINTED toward Colonel Patch and the Sergeant Major and halted before them, holding his rake at parade rest.

"What are you men doing there?" asked the Sergeant Major.

"Raking sand, Sergeant Major," Spudhead said nervously.

"Who told you to do that?" Patch inquired.

"First Sergeant did, sir," Spudhead said.

"Why did the First Sergeant tell you to rake sand?"

"He didn't say, sir; he just said to go out and rake all the sand around the orderly room and the chow hall."

"Did you ask him why?" Patch said.

"No, sir . . . I mean, yessir—Private Muntz asked him."

"And what did he say?"

"He didn't say anything, sir, but he made Private Muntz go burn the shit barrels in the officers' latrine."

Patch glared at the Sergeant Major, who shrugged his shoulders. Then he looked at Spudhead and his eyes got wide and he seemed to breathe heavily.

"You go back and tell those men to stop raking that fucking sand!" he bellowed. "This is a combat zone! Why the hell should we be raking sand in a combat zone? Is everybody around here crazy?" Patch began pounding himself furiously on the leg.

Spudhead was at once frightened and confused.

He had been in the Army more than a year, but this was the first time he had actually been addressed personally by his Battalion Commander. Rarely, in fact, had he even been this close to him, except in passing, and now it appeared that the colonel was angry at him, and he knew it was a dangerous thing to get on the Battalion Commander's shit list.

The last time Spudhead had had any dealings with Patch was up on The Fake when he had persuaded them to go back up to the top. What Spudhead remembered then was the great empathy and calm and confidence the colonel had exuded, as though he were one of them, and speaking for all.

He still wasn't sure how it had started. He remembered

a heated discussion off to the side between Lieutenant Brill and Sergeant Groutman, and afterward Groutman had crawled over to where some of his buddies were clustered, and a few moments later word had spread that they were ordered to make a suicide attack up the hill, and no one wanted to do that. It had all seemed like some disordered, nightmarish dream—the violent confusion halfway up the slope, the man's head stuck on the tree stump, the terrible fire from above and the pell-mell scramble back down.

But the way he remembered it now, nobody had actually told them to move out the second time. He recalled that Lieutenant Brill had received an order from Lieutenant Kahn, and told them to get ready, but then after he spoke with Groutman, he had told them nothing, and then he'd gone back on the radio to Lieutenant Kahn and said they wouldn't go, and Kahn had come over, and then the Colonel had arrived.... All of it was hazy then, as now, but Spudhead somehow felt that they would probably have gone back up under their own steam if Brill had ordered them. Probably....

Patch's face was craned forward very close to Spudhead's—so close, in fact, that he could see his own reflection in the colonel's black sunglasses.

"What the hell's keeping you, soldier?" Patch bawled, and Spudhead suddenly came to life and ran back with his rake at port arms to deliver the colonel's message to the other sand-rakers, wondering as he did why the Battalion Commander seemed so different here from the way he had been out in the field.

EVERYONE FIGURED the inspection was connected to the potato-throwing melee in the chow hall the night before, and they were prepared to accept the worst. It had started spontaneously and innocently, but somehow had gotten out of hand, and before the MPs arrived a dozen men were bound for the field hospital and the second cook had been stabbed in the groin with a fork.

Patch had been around long enough to know that such things were pretty commonplace, but the version related to him was that the men were protesting because they had been served nothing but potatoes for a week, which news was brought to him by his aide, Captain Kennemer, who had been struck in the face by a flying potato as he walked past the chow tent. Patch mulled it over for a while and decided perhaps he might not be paying enough attention to the welfare of the men and he ought to go down there and find out just what the hell *was* going on.

The fact of it was that while potatoes were the immediate complaint, the incident was the culmination of deep-seated frustrations endured by the Company following the appearance of an article in a national newsmagazine which had been circulating around the Brigade for about a week.

Operation Western Movie was over, and everyone involved in it, down to the last cook and jeep driver, swaggered around the Monkey Mountain camp in a tough, veteranlike way, basking in the admiration of replacement troops, the terror of the fighting having slipped off to a separate place in their minds. The duty Bravo Company drew that first week was ideal. After a few days' rest they were assigned Palace Guard, which consisted of setting up around the perimeter to stave off the enemy in the unlikely case he should choose to attack the camp itself. It got them out of the crud-ball jobs they would have been assigned if they had stayed in the billets and also provided opportunities to trade with the Vietnamese through the wire for a variety of otherwise unobtainable items such as live fowl and the services of prostitutes.

A few days after their return, the official military newspaper, *Stars and Stripes*, had described Operation Western Movie as the "turning point" of the war. In front-page stories and photographs it depicted determined soldiers slaughtering North Vietnamese, smiling commanders and happy infantrymen being fed or catching up on sleep during the action. Individual acts of bravery were cited, and many soldiers singled out by name and hometown. The account was taken as gospel by everyone, including Bravo Company, and the stories were embellished every day.

A week before Thanksgiving, the magazine arrived. On its cover was a stark photograph of men in combat. A medic hovered over a badly wounded man while several others cringed against a blistered mountain slope. A headline slashed across the cover asked: **THE WAR: IS AMERICA REALLY WINNING?** The question itself seemed treasonous.

The story inside detailed the action, but the emphasis was on *American*, not North Vietnamese, casualties. "Heavy losses," it said, were suffered by all four battalions involved, "**raising a possibility that the U.S. Command may have to rethink its strategy of 'Search and Destroy.'**" According to the story, the operation was called off not when the North Vietnamese had been annihilated, but "**when it became apparent that the elusive enemy can fight a protracted battle in the jungle and then retire to sanctuaries across the Cambodian border.**

"**Even though the enemy may have lost the 1,500 dead claimed in Saigon press releases,**" the story went on, "**informed sources concede that the price in American blood was far too high if the United States must look forward to similar battles in the future.**" The story also contained the remarks of a high-ranking general attached to the Saigon Command who described the battle in grand and glowing terms and stated flatly that it was "**more satisfactory than anticipated.**" However, the writer of the article downgraded that opinion with the observation that generals have been known to "**put a good face on bad situations.**"

There was a second story and photograph, margined in red next to the main one, and it was the object of Bravo Company's interest.

The photographer had captured the moment precisely; the faces told the story. Beneath the helmets were gaunt, strained, bewildered, terrorized faces, afraid faces, vacant faces—they recognized themselves: DiGeorgio, Crump, Spudhead, Muntz and all the others—facing the tall, upright back of Colonel Patch. In instantaneous little flashes it began to come back; it had really never gone away. The headline was THE COMPANY THAT WOULDN'T FIGHT.

It was difficult to tell if the story was on their side or not. It described their attempts to negotiate the fifth knoll and also mentioned the fighting in the ravine earlier. It described their enemy as "determined." A small photo inset showed the head of Colonel Patch, and the caption beneath it quoted him as saying, **"They're all good boys."**

The third paragraph was subheadlined **Quelling a Mutiny**. It concluded with the observation that Patch, **"a respected and hard-nosed West Pointer,"** had **"in a fusillade of persuasive rhetoric, skillfully provided the dissidents not only with a carrot, but a donkey as well."**

They felt somehow gypped by the story. Their reasons had not been fully told. The innuendo was that their motives derived solely out of fear or sloth and not futility and that Patch, with his little pep talk, had managed to herd them back up there like so many cattle. Nowhere was it mentioned that they had *forced* him to bombard the hill with artillery and air strikes. Only at the bottom of the story was the Big Heat even mentioned, and it did not seem to relate to the men at all. In fact, it gave the impression the Big Heat was Patch's idea, not theirs, and even then as some patronizing hand job, and not because they demanded it. From their perspective, it was a pretty sorry account of the matter.

In the days that followed, Bravo Company received a merciless ration of grief from other outfits. The swaggers faded, and perhaps by coincidence, they were relieved of the Palace Guard and sent back to the billets to pull regular duty—menial work details under the supervision of sadistic and slave-driving sergeants. Suspicion, enmity and other strong feelings took hold. They were convinced they were being punished for what they had done on The Fake, though Patch had promised they wouldn't be. They became the butt of jokes, and as their mood grew blacker, fistfights broke out with men from other outfits and they began to keep to themselves in their own Company area. They did not see themselves as mutineers; rather, they had simply worked out a very sticky problem with the man in charge, and in the end they *had* gone back up and taken the hill, with no one's help, and with fewer casualties than there would have been otherwise. If other outfits didn't see it that way, fuck them! They could take care of themselves.

All of it had finally erupted with the potato-throwing in the chow tent.

Practically everyone was involved. It had, in fact, started over potatoes, which continued to constitute the largest portion of the meals—powdery, dry-packaged mashed potatoes, frozen-hard French-fried potatoes, soggy overcooked baked potatoes—until people began hoarding C rations and eating them after chow, because the Army had not yet figured a way to include potatoes in them.

It began with chanting and beating on the tables that night, but then a man from Charlie Company had shouted across the tent that perhaps Bravo Company could lead a strike for better food. Madman Muntz immediately rewarded the man with a potato in the face, and all hell broke loose. No one kept score, but it was the consensus of Bravo Company afterward that they had kicked the bejesus out of at least one and a half other companies and also some Engineers men and mechanics and assorted other troops who happened to be eating supper there at the time.

At the height of the action, Trunk had arrived, summoned from his own meal, but when he saw what was going on he stood back and let them continue, and it was left to the MPs to finally put an end to it. There was a grand sense of redemption and relief following the incident, but all of them had been in the Army long enough to realize that such catharsis has a price, and they were preparing to pay it now, beginning with the inspection.

EVERYONE LOOKED useful when the inspection party entered the tent. Patch paced in silence for a while, studying the faces of the men.

"Put them back to work," he said finally. "I'm just going to have a look around."

He poked at the edges of the tent; he tested the strength of the wood floor; he peered at equipment. His interest in human beings seemed to have waned.

"There isn't a tent flap on this side."

"No, sir, there isn't," Kahn said.

"Why not?"

"It wasn't there when we got here—I suppose they forgot it."

"What if it rains?" Patch asked.

"Sir, it hasn't rained in five months, but I suppose they'd get wet."

"Exactly. Have you put in for a flap?"

"I believe the First Sergeant did, sir." Kahn turned to Trunk. "Did you put in for a new flap on this tent?"

"Yessir, the first week we was here. They keep saying it's coming but it ain't here yet."

Patch frowned. "Sergeant, you go back to Supply today and tell them I said find you one." He prodded and poked in a few other places and looked for an instant as if he were ready to leave. Then he stopped in front of a bunk occupied by Madman Muntz, who was cleaning his boots furiously.

"What's your name, soldier?" Patch said hoarsely.

"Muntz, sir." He leaped to attention.

"Muntz, what did you have for supper last night?" Patch was studying a large fresh cut on Muntz's nose.

"Potatoes, sir."

"Do you like potatoes?"

"Oh, yessir, I like them," Muntz said cheerfully.

"Do you like them all the time?"

"Yessir, I do," Muntz replied.

Patch seemed perplexed by the answer. "What I mean, Muntz, is, Do you like potatoes for every meal?"

Muntz looked confused for a moment. He knew he didn't have much time to think about it, because keeping the Colonel waiting was something he knew not to do. But his mind was not working fast enough to figure out the reply Patch might like to hear, so he said what he thought was a prudent thing to say.

"Right, sir." The words were already out when he saw Kahn glaring at him. Patched frowned. "I see," he said, and turned to the next man in the bunk row, Crump, and repeated the question.

Crump, on his feet and at attention, had heard Muntz's

answer and from the corner of his eye had seen Kahn's glare, but was uncertain what it meant. Like Muntz, Crump remembered it was impolitic to complain to high-ranking officers.

Patch's eyes had fallen to dark swollen marks on Crump's right hand. "Well, soldier, do you or don't you?"

"I do, sir," Crump said.

"You do."

"Yessir."

"At every meal?"

"Ah, yessir," Crump said falteringly. Instantaneously it came to him that this was *not* the answer the colonel wished to hear.

But it was too late to change it.

"Then what was all that about in the chow tent last night—that brawling?" Patch said. "Were you in on that?"

Everyone waited for the answer. It was the moment they feared. Tomorrow would begin a spell of latrine digging, or something equally bad.

"Yessir, I was," Crump said sheepishly.

"And was it about potatoes?"

"Well, sir . . . it was . . . uh . . . some people was banging on the tables with their knives and forks, and then somebody started throwing potatoes, and then all hell broke loose . . . sir."

"Then it *was* about potatoes," Patch said, very detectivelike.

"Yessir, I guess it was," Crump said, as lightly as he could.

Patch spun around to Kahn and was about to say something when his mouth dropped open in astonishment.

On a duffel bag near the tent fly sat the banana-cat, tied to a rope, calmly watching the proceedings and scratching itself. Earlier, Crump had secured it to one of the tent pilings and shooed it under the floor outside, where it liked to stay in that heat of the day anyway. Evidently it had heard Crump's voice and decided to come up for a look.

"What in hell is that?" Patch bawled. "Is it some kind of monkey?"

"It is a banana-cat, sir," Crump said helpfully—and before Kahn could say anything.

"Where did you get it? In the jungle?" Patch's eyes were large—quizzical.

"No, sir," Crump said. "I bought it."

"Bought it," Patch repeated. "From whom? What for?"

"Sir," Kahn injected, "the men sometimes buy things from the Vietnamese—chickens and ducks; they use them to supplement their meals."

Patch's whole face seemed to swell like an overripe tomato. He turned on Kahn furiously. "Do you mean to tell me this man is going to eat that goddamned thing? The chow is that bad?"

"No, sir," Kahn stammered. "I mean . . . I don't know if he plans to eat it or not, but what I'm saying is that that is probably where he got it—from where they buy the ducks and chickens in the local market. The Vietnamese sell them through the barbed wire. . . ."

"I won't have it!" Patch roared. "The United States Army is committed to provide every soldier with decent, edible food. I will not have them purchasing monkeys or ducks or any other goddamn thing instead of it." He was waving his arms wildly. His mouth seemed to open enormously. "If the chow is that bad, I want to know about it!"

"Yessir," Kahn said.

"Well," Patch said, regaining some of his composure. "I am personally going to eat my lunch in the enlisted mess today, and if they can't serve proper food, then by God they'll all go out to the boondocks and I'll bring in some people who can." He looked around the room at the men staring blankly at him. The Sergeant Major was looking at Crump and shaking his head sadly.

"And get that thing out of here," Patch said crossly. "It belongs in a zoo." He stormed out of the tent, and as they watched him go down toward the chow hall they could catch an occasional loud expletive and see him shaking his fist at the Sergeant Major.

THE LETTERS came the same week—the one from Julie and the one from Spudhead's father—and they had a profound effect on Spudhead's morale, which up until now had been no better, or worse, than anyone else's.

Hers came first. He squirreled it away in a pocket and took it back to the billet to read on his bunk while everyone else was at lunch. He opened it carefully so as to save the envelope, and removed the thin airmail sheets.

It was a long letter, handwritten in her small, neat style, with a few underlinings here and there. The first two pages were about how much she loved and missed him and chatty talk about things she was doing. She had gone to the homecoming game with friends in her dormitory. He pictured her in the student section on a cool, bright afternoon, rust and gold autumn leaves falling gently outside the stadium, screaming cheers and chants and fierce, fast action on the field below.

As he visualized the scene in the heat and dust of a quiet tropical afternoon, a feeling of helplessness overtook him. For an instant he wanted to scream, or curse, but he didn't. He had had the same impulse absolutely everyone had. But nobody actually did it unless it was absolutely necessary.

He read on: two pages—three; stopped. Reread, foggily trying to comprehend what she was telling him. Something about a peace rally. Something about the wrongness of the war. She was trying to explain something. A group of girls had come to her room a few nights before with a petition against the war. She had refused to sign it on account of him. But it had set her to thinking. She hated it, the war, because it frightened her. But she hadn't given it much thought, except for hating it, until now.

There had been someone speaking on campus, a man named Widenfield, a professor from a New England women's college. She had stopped to listen for a while. What he said had made sense. He had spoken of the arrogance of power. Of the fallibility of total American involvement in revolutionary situations. Not only was our history against it, but common sense was against it. "What interests," he had demanded, "are Americans trying to protect? Do we have extensive economic ties with this country? Does the war affect our immediate security? Do we have close bonds of friendship? What right, then, does one man have, without the full and open consent of Congress, to commit the flower of American youth to a bloodthirsty, senseless war on the Asian continent?"

Widenfield bad been persuasive. He spoke in convincing tones. He did not rant and rave. When he touched the moral question, his approach was rooted more in logic than in emotion. War, all war, by its own nature was immoral. There were no good wars; only necessary ones. Some were more necessary than others. For a variety of reasons, he declared, this war ranked very low on the necessity scale.

Julie was deeply affected by what she heard, and she had thought about it for several days. It had been necessary to make a decision. It was too important a thing to shunt away. Widenfield had called for commitments, personal commitments, which, he said, were the only means of stopping what was going on because the government was too clumsy, the bureaucratic machinery too rusty, to make an impression on the man in the White House, whose fault was arrogance, not maliciousness.

The speech had been well received for a conservative, Mid-western university. Of course—and Julie could not know this—it was not the same speech the man gave when he visited more liberal, or radical, schools in the East or on the West Coast. But she had become a convert. It had not happened immediately, but had taken place over the course of a few days, the kernel of her decision growing rapidly in her mind. She knew the man was right, and she had made a thoughtful decision, which was very important to her because of Spudhead's involvement. She did not want to denigrate what he was doing—she was clear about that. But she had to do what she knew was right, and hoped he would understand. She thought he ought to know.

Spudhead's reaction was different from what she might have expected. At first, there was no reaction at all, just a melancholy curiosity. She was talking about it; he was doing it. Simple as that. He really didn't know why she had spent so much time trying to explain it all.

For the next few days he toyed with the idea of Julie the Peace Freak. It did not outrage him. He couldn't imagine her going berserk and laying siege to buildings, or marching by torchlight singing songs. He knew she was wrong, but he couldn't say exactly why. He had been told to come here and fight for ideals that had been drummed into his head ever since he was old enough to think reasonable thoughts, and he had never had serious cause to question them. Americans fought good wars. They did not lose them. For peace and freedom. They fought noble wars. This was ingrained in him and as much a part of him as his nose. He tried to think up arguments to give her. The same arguments he had heard all his life—peace, freedom, liberty—who could argue against that? A month ago he might have been convincing; but he had seen too much in the tangled, twisted, bloodscreaming, hatefilled, fearstruck death-stinking weeks in the jungle to even want to try. It was easier not to think about it at all.

The letter from his father arrived three days later.

"Dear Harold," it began:

Your mother and I hope everything is going well and that you are safely out of harm's way by this time. In your last letter you described the details of the fighting in which your company took part very graphically. I realize it must have been a trying and difficult experience—especially seeing some of your friends hurt and killed. As you know, I was in a war myself, so I am well versed in the tragedies and high emotions connected with military combat. However, your mother is not, and as you know she is given to the normal female weaknesses when it comes to violent or disagreeable subject matter—and especially so when you are involved. I think it would be a good idea, therefore, that when you write to us both you would refrain from such scenes as you described in your last two letters because it upsets her greatly. Naturally you may say whatever you wish to me personally if you feel a need to get it out of your system. Just write me at the office so your mother won't be involved....

Spudhead tried for a moment to recall the things he had written. It was the day after they returned from The Fake. He had tried to set it all down so that they would know, his father anyway, that he wasn't sitting on his ass in the rear getting a suntan, but out there doing something important—the biggest thing he had ever done in his life; putting his life on the line—and he wanted somebody to know it. But now he pictured them sitting in the living room and reading the letter over cocktails—about the killing and the fighting up the mountainside; the napalmed bodies of the North Vietnamese—all of it must have seemed strange and gory.

Why would he write such things? They must have wondered about it. He should have known better. He had spared much of it in the letters to Julie, because he didn't want to upset her. What did that mean? That he didn't think his own parents were worried? Or that he didn't care? He read on:

As a member of Congress and the Armed Services Committee, I have seen and heard things in recent months deeply disturbing to the future of America and our quest for peace and freedom. There are forces at work in this country—some of them in the Congress itself—that would destroy all America has stood for and built up for two decades.

Some of these people are well meaning; others are probably subversive; but they have banded in an attempt to force the government of the United States to abandon her commitment to her allies. I am sure you realize that should we pursue such a foolish course, the Communists would be in control of Asia in a matter of months and in time would be lurking at our very doorstep.

The seeds of dissention have appeared most visibly in the universities and among certain misguided clerics, who believe that by sticking its head in the sand, the ostrich can avoid its fate....

The letter continued in this vein for a while. The war was part of a vast global struggle to contain a fanatical

and evil-minded political movement and to protect
helpless allies from being crushed against their will. But it
was the last paragraph—a P.S., handwritten—that
gripped Spudhead's attention:

Today, before I mailed this the President
of the United States came to the Capitol
to address a joint session of the Congress.
As he was leaving he stopped at my
seat and asked how you were. I
was not aware that he even knew you
were in the service or engaged in the
fighting, but I told him what I knew
from your last letter, and afterward he
touched me on the arm and said I should
be very proud. I want you to know son
that I am. I realize that my political
life has sometimes kept me from being as
close as a father should be to his son.
Perhaps when you return we can make it
up. You are making great sacrifices for
the cause of peace, and I have the
utmost confidence that you will continue
to do your duty in an honorable and
proper way and if by chance it is
the Almighty's will that something should
happen to you, you may take with you
the sure and certain knowledge that the
sacrifices you have made are in the
name of freedom and liberty, and that
I love you very much as does your
mother and that you have made me
and your President very proud.

Love,
Dad

Spudhead carefully tucked the letter inside the envelope and slipped it into his duffel bag. He reached for his rifle and began wiping it down mechanically with an oily cloth, sitting on the edge of his cot. The tent was empty, and a hot, dusty wind was blowing off the rice fields.

How about that—the President of the United States...And in quick little flashes he pictured the President pinning a medal on him while his father and mother and hundreds of others looked on...and just as quickly there came a vision of a row of empty black body bags—he had passed such a sight earlier that morning—waiting to be filled...and it shifted again, the vision, and he saw dead men, hundreds of them, lying quietly in a field, the hot sun beating down; waiting to be put into the body bags and zipped up into the darkness, never again to see, or to feel or screw or laugh...just a black void forever...down in the body bag:

> Down in the bod-ee bag,
> Down in the bod-ee bag,
> I'm gonna meet my little sweetheart girl
> Down in the bod-ee bag—
> Down in—the bod-deeee bag....

Humming the tune silently, over and over, rubbing the oily cloth up and down the rifle barrel—maniacally, in cadence with the beat, as though it were a slide trombone...and then he put it to his mouth—muzzle first, as a mouthpiece—and saw the field of dead again; he tried to tell if he was among them, but he could not recognize anyone among these peaceful dead...and he felt dizzy and strange and somehow possessed by something he could not identify...and standing there in a corner of the field, surveying it quietly, was the President of the United States—with his father; sadly shaking their heads, but looking very proud—and be continued playing crazily, working the slide of the rifle like a trombone—backward and forward, Jack Teagarden style, the noiseless tune coming out of the black stock/bell, metal cool on his lips, raising the instrument into the air for the final notes, the oily cloth hanging down...We gonna dadadadadadada—down in the body bag, down in...and the field of baking dead, a peaceful audience, along with the President of the United States of America: who would *here highly resolve that these dead shall not have died in vain*...Down in the bod-ee bag...*But in a larger sense we cannot dedicate, we cannot consecrate, we cannot hallow*...Down in the body bag...PEACE AND FREEDOM!...and dying for it...Down in... well, hell, they didn't die for it, did they? They were killed for it, maybe—but they didn't die for it... Down ... down ... down ... down down ... nosiree— they didn't die for it—they just died....He suddenly remembered the dying face of Lieutenant Donovan, lying in the peaceful creeping vine—and like him—Him!— HIM—down in the shuddering emptiness...Down in the black, waiting, open nothingness, proudly zipped up by the President of the United States...who had convened a necessary war...not good, but necessary...in the name of peace and freedom, to murder gooks, by the hundreds, by the thousands—who didn't even have body bags...Down in the...and get murdered back, too— wasn't that a part of it? Wouldn't be fair otherwise...not sporting...not...not anything...as he played madly on by himself in the hot, sticky tent, entertaining his first serious thoughts about trying to get the hell out of all this....

26

CARRUTHERS SLUMPED into his chair at the Duc Twan Bar and reached across the table for his glass of warm native beer. There was hurt and bitterness set deeply in his great black face. He turned and glared at the girl sitting in the back of the room.

Off in a corner, Madman Muntz and DiGeorgio were dancing with two Vietnamese bar girls, and Spudhead and Crump were seated at the table with Carruthers, trying to have a conversation above the blaring radio music. The girl was sitting on a stool at the end of the bar, alternately sipping her glass of the watered-down whiskey they called "Saigon tea" and running her fingers through her waist-long black hair. Occasionally she would glance over at Carruthers, then turn away haughtily, and he continued to glare, and his countenance seemed to turn blacker and blacker and corresponded with his mood.

Crump leaned over the table. "Thought you was gonna dance with her, Carruthers."

Carruthers said nothing; he continued to glare.

Nobody knew much about Carruthers, except that he was big, and black, and quiet and Southern, and that he was the one who had led them in song the afternoon they were relieved up on The Fake. And until then nobody had paid him much attention, but afterward there was some brief curiosity about him, during which time it was rumored that he had never worn shoes until the Army gave him a pair; that he practiced a weird voodoo cult and that he was a descendant of a fierce tribe of Negroes who, because of their intense blackness, were sometimes referred to as Blue Gum Niggers.

"Hey, what'd she say, huh? She don't wanta dance?" Crump had put down his beer and was leaning across the table.

"She nofin bu a ho!" Carruthers said, lapsing into an all-but-incomprehensible dialect. There was something scary in Carruthers' face. In his anger it seemed to suck into a black hole inside of which two red eyes burned, and the eyes seemed not like part of the face but like separate things that lived in the hole.

"Well, what'd she say, man? Whatdaya mean she spit on you? Say, huh?"

"Yeah, say what happened," Spudhead chimed in.

Carruthers' huge fist was balled up tightly and he was massaging it with his right hand, looking down angrily at the floor.

"Ho," he said. "I ough cuttah."

"Well, what in hell happened?" Crump said in frustration.

"Axed er ta daince—you know she don daince wid blacks..." His voice trailed off.

The girl had drawn herself up like royalty and was looking straight ahead, her delicate features glowing in the dim lantern light. She was far and away the prettiest girl in the bar, and maybe along the whole row of dives and brothels in the shantytown that had sprung up around the base camp at Monkey Mountain.

It was a place of filth and squalor, peopled by camp followers and other displaced persons who found it easier to live off the Americans than to try to scrape out an existence in the war-torn countryside. They slept in tin-roofed shanties or beneath straw-topped lean-tos, and mostly they were women and children and a few old men, the younger men having already been killed or conscripted by one side or the other. Their sole belongings usually consisted of a brace of pots and pans, a straw sleeping mat and the clothes on their backs.

In the daytime, the women squatted over open fires tending pots of rice or fish or water buffalo meat, chattering like magpies—or spent their time begging from the soldiers or scavenging food and other things from the land. A small cottage industry had developed, utilizing waste materials left behind by the Army, of which the most notable aspect was the transformation by old men with pointed white beards of artillery-shell casings into brass ashtrays and other useful items, which were immediately sold back to the Americans at exorbitant prices.

As prostitutes arrived in droves, entrepreneurs erected ramshackle bars, and every night these bars and the dirty streets outside them were filled with drunken, brawling soldiers from the Brigade; men willing to put up with filth and wretchedness just to get away from the Army for an hour or so.

Bravo Company had not been allowed to patronize this encampment until a few days before, and then thanks only to a directive by General Butterworth himself, who had learned, quite by accident, that Patch, fearing God-only-knew-what-kind-of trouble, had restricted Four/Seven to Base Camp the moment they returned from the field.

It happened when Chaplain Greaves got up to give his weekly report on morale at the daily briefing.

As usual, morale was high, he said, offering statistics

that so many men were attending church services—or so many had reported such and such problems, but the indications were good. The last item on his agenda was a report on the rate of venereal disease within the various battalions—a function the Army had at some point lumped among the duties of its chaplains because high VD rate was considered an indication of low morale. General Butterworth usually tolerated the Chaplain's report without comment, but that day he rose to his feet.

"Wait a minute, read that again," the general said.

The Chaplain repeated the figures. In three battalions the rate of VD was approximately thirty cases per one hundred men—relatively high—but in Four/Seven, the Chaplain proudly reported, the rate was barely five cases per one hundred.

"There is something wrong here, Chaplain," the general said. "How is it that these men have such a low rate of VD?"

"Sir," the Chaplain replied knowledgeably, "I believe it is because the Battalion Commander has restricted them to the Base Camp."

The general looked at Patch, who was seated in the front row. "Is that true, Jason? Your men are not allowed out?"

"That is correct, General," Patch said, getting to his feet. "As you know, they have been through some very rough combat, and I am concerned about turning them loose on the civilian population at this point."

The general pondered this for a moment. "Well, how do you explain that five of your men still reported in with venereal disease last week, then?"

"I am afraid," Patch said gravely, "that some of them are having liaisons with prostitutes through the barbed wire. I am told it goes on late at night."

The general's face seemed to screw up into a knot. "You mean to say your troops line up to receive sex through a barricade of barbed wire—they're doing it standing up while everyone else can go to town?"

"It is what I have been told," Patch said. "It seems to be the only logical explanation."

"Good God," the general sighed. "I don't think it

would hurt anything to let them out—if you put some limitations on it—especially if everyone else can."

"Well, I could certainly..."

"Hell," the general said, a twinkle suddenly in his eye, "that VD rate ought not to be five—it oughta be a hundred and five."

"Yessir," Patch said obediently.

"You know," the general continued, "when I was in Korea there wasn't a Red Cross girl who'd come within fifty miles of our division."

"Begging your pardon, General," the Chaplain interjected meekly, "but if I may say so, incidence of venereal disease is quite high in this area, and as you know, the Army considers it an important morale factor..."

General Butterworth eyed the Chaplain impatiently. "Those poor devils," he said, "will go through a lot before they get back home to Palookaville, U.S.A., and I believe they are entitled to a piece of ass when they have the opportunity."

The Chaplain's mind raced for a counterpoint. Certainly there must be one. Sex outside of marriage was sinful. Obviously, if that many men had gotten VD, they must all be doing it. The entire Brigade was sinning, and nobody cared and they were even encouraging it. Lamely, though, he returned to a more practical argument.

"With your indulgence, sir, the manuals are very explicit regarding morale problems associated with venereal disease...."

"Chaplain," the general said, "those manuals were written long ago—probably before I was in the Army and certainly before you were. Maybe then we were fighting to preserve some high sense of honor. Perhaps even with some kind of divine guidance. But I can assure you that is not the case in this lousy war. Sometimes late at night I wonder why we are in it. The bastards themselves who live here don't give a damn. The people back home don't seem to either, and every day I'm sending out boys not much older than my own kids to get blown all over the landscape while we sit here powerless to raise a finger against the principal cause of the trouble Up North.

"Give me three armored divisions and I would roll across the DMZ and put an end to this foolishness in a couple of weeks. Then we could go home. But it's not going to work out like that. So if you want to do something useful, go and pray for those boys who are going to do the fighting—and they are going to have to do it, because that is the way things are—and they're going to do a good job of it, too. And as far as this VD thing goes, if there is one thing I am convinced of after twenty-three years of military service it is this: men that won't fuck won't fight."

There was a long pause, during which no one even coughed or breathed heavily, and then the general left the tent and stalked up the little hill where his own quarters were. He had his supper brought to him, and he did not come out until the following day. But that same night, Four/Seven received the good news that they could leave the encampment and visit all but a few off-limits places in the native village.

THE FORWARD encampment of an Infantry brigade is a bustling, teeming place of decisions and preparations. It has been so since the days of Alexander the Great and the legions of Caesar. Day begins before dawn, and night never ends but simply enmeshes itself with the next day, and the next and the next, and at any time the whole affair is likely to just up and move some place else. But while it is stationary, life goes on as it does in any great city: there are many things to be attended to; there is confusion and laughter and tragedy and foolishness and heartbreak—for the inhabitants are, of course, mere mortal men trying to do the best they can, and in some cases more and in some cases less... and it was so on a given week at the place called Monkey Mountain in the late autumn of nineteen hundred and sixty-six:

A corporal with a reputation for scrounging was provided a truck by his commander and sent forty miles away to a Supply depot to see if he could steal some sets of new jungle fatigues. Six hours later he returned with a huge CONEX container which, when pried open, was found to contain approximately one hundred fifty thousand tent pegs. He was told to "get rid of it," and reassigned a week later to a forward line unit.

A family of Vietnamese was badly afflicted after they cooked their food in some helicopter fuel mistakenly left at the site where the Brigade kitchen staff normally dumped their leftover grease. The Office of Civil Affairs quickly paid them off and the incident was forgotten.

A lieutenant colonel who had caught the clap was told to provide the hospital with samples of urine and semen. As he sat on the latrine attempting to produce the semen, a private first class assigned to clean the commode accidentally walked in on him, thereby earning the officer an unfortunate nickname that remained with him for the rest of his tour.

A terse message was received at Headquarters announcing that a certain Supply lieutenant who had been sent to the coast to supervise the off-loading of matériel had inadvertently been sunning himself aboard an aircraft carrier when it weighed anchor and he would have to be flown back when the ship reached Guam.

A twenty-year-old draftee who had studied concert piano cried for four hours from his hospital bed after seeing that his hand had been amputated.

Several thousand board feet of lumber were delivered to a nearby village by the U.S. Aid Mission for reconstruction of a burned-out church. Three hours later the sample pile of lumber was observed in the back of a Vietnamese Army truck, bound for the black market in Saigon.

A master sergeant who had just consumed a fifth of bourbon accidentally shot himself to death while cleaning his .45.

A private first class was given a seven-and-one-half-minute break from KP after receiving notice that his wife had given birth to a seven-and-a-half-pound girl.

A newly commissioned captain on his way to an artillery outpost forgot to gas up his jeep and was found shot by the roadside as he walked back with a jerry can.

A Thanksgiving dinner planned by the Chaplain for

children at a nearby orphanage almost turned into an international incident when the orphans, surrounded by cardboard cutouts of turkeys, Pilgrims and Indians, became violently ill after eating the meal. A doctor was summoned, and after a hasty examination he declared that nothing was wrong except that the American food was too rich for children accustomed to a diet of rice and fish.

A nineteen-year-old helicopter pilot was grounded for a week for flying into a tree and shattering his windscreen.

An Air Force major who had received the Silver Star for heroism got drunk the night before he was to be shipped back to the States and decided it would be a good thing to sing to the men before leaving. After being hooted out of the officers'-club tent, he made his way to the enlisted men's beer hall and, unaccompanied, sang all three verses of "America the Beautiful," and would have sung more if the MPs had not arrived and suggested, politely, that he leave.

Two cooks got into a knife fight over what ingredients should be put into a bean soup. One was sent to the hospital, and the other was chained to a tree overnight. Both were back in the kitchen the next morning. The bean soup had been consumed with no extraordinary complaints.

A battery of 105-millimeter howitzers was instructed to test-fire a Korean War-vintage propaganda-leaflet shell to see if it could still be used. When the lanyard was pulled, the roll of leaflets flew out in a gigantic flaming wad, immolating three native huts and severely frightening their occupants.

A Vietnamese child who had been trampled nearly to death by a water buffalo was patched up in the camp hospital. Afterward, his family tried to sue the Army.

A four-foot-long cobra wandered into the TOC by mistake, and thirty-seven fully armed officers and men ran out into the night. The snake wound itself around the Sergeant Major's chair and was finally dispatched by the Sergeant Major himself with a 12-gauge shotgun borrowed from the MPs. The chair also did not survive.

A captain sat down to write his wife that their application to adopt a war orphan had been turned down by the bureaucracy in Saigon. No reason had been stated. Halfway, he stopped and took out some photographs of the child and began to cry uncontrollably.

A scandalous court-martial was averted by the reassignment of the Mess Sergeant and his assistant following a meal in the enlisted men's mess served to Colonel Patch and the Brigade Sergeant Major. The colonel's investigation revealed that the Mess Sergeant had been selling off the best of the Army-supplied food on the Vietnamese black market and substituting a heavy diet of potatoes in its place. The offenders were called in by the Sergeant Major, who pointed to the dictum above his desk and ordered them to report to a rifle company operating deep in enemy territory, "...and never again return to base camp...."

The Chaplain wrote eighteen letters of condolence at one sitting to the families of dead soldiers, making each one of them sound different.

The expression "Sorry about that" was repeated at least six thousand times between Reveille and Taps.

A Negro soldier named Carruthers was arrested by the MPs after he was found weeping hysterically at a table in a bar in the native village. A bloody six-inch switchblade knife was in his hand, and bystanders said he had used it to stab one of the girls who worked in the bar.

THE FIELD telephone in Kahn's tent growled twice, and he groped out foggily for the handset.

"Is this Bravo Company, Four/Seven?" a voice asked.

"This is Lieutenant Kahn, yeah."

The voice identified itself as that of a sergeant from the MP detachment. "We got a man down here name of Carruthers says he belongs to you."

Kahn thought sleepily for a moment. Carruthers? Carruthers? "Ah, yeah...mortar platoon...big black guy?"

"Black as the ace of spades," the voice said, "and he's in a world of shit."

"What'd he do?"

"Want me to read the charges?"

"Go ahead."

"First off, he's charged with assault with a deadly weapon, carrying a deadly weapon, assault with intent to do bodily harm, assault with intent to commit murder, mayhem, disfigurement and so forth; being present at an off-limits establishment and attacking a foreign national—and that ain't all. They're typing up some more more stuff now."

Kahn was beginning to come awake. "What in hell did he do?"

"Cut a bar girl with a knife."

"Jesus, he must have worked her over bad."

"Don't know about that yet, Lieutenant; she took off and went to the doctor," the sergeant said.

"What do you want me to do?" Kahn asked.

"Up to you, sir—he's your man."

"Will he keep till morning?"

"Oh, yes, sir—we got him cuffed to a CONEX container. He's still pretty drunk and kind of wild. Might be good to let him calm down a bit."

"Okay, sergeant—thanks. I'll come down first thing in the morning." Kahn hung up the phone and lay back down on his cot. In the darkness the paperwork lay stacked before his eyes like a tall white chimney.

At fifteen minutes after seven in the morning the field telephone rang again. Kahn was shaving when someone called out his name.

"Lieutenant Kahn," he said into the mouthpiece. From the other end a voice demanded gruffly, "Do you speak Nigger?"

"I beg your pardon?" Kahn said. He wasn't sure if he had heard the question. It sounded like Colonel Patch.

"I asked if you speak Nigger," the voice said again.

It was Patch. Kahn stumbled for a second. "Ah, well, sir, I uh ... am from the South. I have spoken with a lot of Negroes."

"Then get the hell down here and translate for me," Patch said. "This is your problem too." He hung up the phone.

When Kahn arrived in Patch's headquarters, Carruthers was standing at attention in front of the colonel's desk. Two MPs were waiting outside. Patch was scowling.

"Kahn," Patch said, "this man has apparently done something terrible. I am trying to find out what his version is. I have asked him three times and I haven't understood a goddamn word he says."

Kahn looked at Carruthers. His eyes were bloodshot, and even though he was at attention he was blubbering quietly and trembling from head to toe.

"Carruthers," Kahn said gently, "I want you to tell me very slowly what happened."

"I already said that," Patch grumbled in a low voice in the background.

Carruthers suddenly seemed to hyperventilate. He gasped a few times and then spewed out a glub of words, which sounded to Patch like this:

"Wellsuhlutent... Isndis bah wivsom gazn axed fadis gult' daince wibme'n... 'n she said she ont daincewib no nigras'n she... a sayed ta me ta githail awayfrum er'n I's clean'n my fangernells wibma naf'n it slipt'n cutuh... bud I dint meen't isware...."

Carruthers' big beefy hands were rolled into tight balls, and he began to choke and sob.

Patch glowered at Kahn. "Can you make sense out of that?"

"I believe so, Colonel," Kahn said, looking at Carruthers. "He says he and some other men were at a bar and he asked a girl—a bar girl—to dance with him and she refused because he's black, and she told him to leave and—I'm not exactly sure about this part, but I believe he was cleaning his fingernails with a knife and it slipped and cut her but it was unintentional." Somewhat composed, Carruthers nodded his head in agreement.

"That is amazing," Patch exclaimed. I ought to put you in for a medal." He ordered Carruthers out of the room.

"Well," Patch said, clearing his throat, "we're going to have to do something about all this. These are pretty serious charges. I'll have to appoint an investigating officer.... Any suggestions?"

Kahn held his breath. "Uh, no, sir... but maybe we should look outside of Battalion... I mean, since the charges are serious..."

"Good idea," Patch said solemnly. "Uh, how about that guy on the Old Man's staff?—one of the aides—I've seen you with him in the officers' club a few times."

"Maybe you mean Lieutenant Holden."

"Yeah—Holden, that's it." Patch smiled. He relished the idea of bogging that cocky guy down in a nightmare like this. "Get hold of him and tell him to report to me," Patch said.

Kahn walked out light-headed. He couldn't wait to see the expression on Holden's face. It was like beating him at poker. Almost as good.

HOLDEN LOOKED at the girl across the table. He could see why Carruthers might have been taken with her. Her almond eyes were tantalizing. Her complexion was clear—unlike the faces of most of the women, who had ugly scars from smallpox. This one was different. She wore pretty clothes, and he bet she didn't shit in the street like the others.

A cast extended from her wrist to her elbow and was set in a sling of silk cloth. She remained aloof while a small, smiling one-legged Vietnamese man tried to explain the consequences of what had happened to her.

"You see," the man said in a thick but clear accent, "she no can work for long time—two, maybe three months. Regular customers—they not wait so long, so she lose ten, maybe twenty thousand piaster. Also, some maybe find new girl—not come back even after arm well—she lose from this too. She also have to buy new dress—other one ruined—bloodstains." The man seemed genuinely concerned.

"What does she want?" Holden asked.

"Here is list," the man said, handing Holden a slip of paper. "She asked me to write for her. She say if Ahmercan soldier pay, she forget everything."

Holden studied the list. The total for lost trade, future losses and the dress came to seventy-eight thousand piasters—about four hundred dollars. She asked no punitive damages.

"I see," Holden said. "Uh...let me ask you this, Mr....ah...ah..."

"Bac," the man replied. "My name is Bac. I am her friend. I was soldier under Marshal Ky—until I lose leg."

"Let me ask you, Mr. Bac, who was the lady's doctor?"

Bac spoke to the girl and she gave a long answer.

"She say she go to doctor in Xuan Lap village, but, uh, he now gone to Qui Nhon. She not remember name—she say she was very upset."

"Why did she go all the way to Xuan Lap? Why didn't she go to the hospital at Tuy Than?" Holden said.

Bac spoke to the girl again.

"She say she not trust hospital at Tuy Than. Say they too busy with soldiers—not take good care of her."

"And she says the soldier attacked her without warning—she did not say anything to him at all—is that correct?"

Bac turned to the girl.

"She say she did not speak to him. He stab her for no reason."

"I see," Holden said. He wrote in his notebook. "Well," he said finally, "tell her, please, that I will get this information back to the commander of the soldier involved and I will let you know what the decision is."

Bac relayed the message. The girl did not look at Holden, but she nodded her head and turned toward the bar.

"By the way," Holden said, "could I see the dress—the one she was wearing?"

Bac translated.

"Ah...she say dress thrown away—no good now—too much blood."

"Okay," Holden said. "I'll get back to you, and...ah, tell her I'm sorry about what happened."

He walked into the dusty street, where his jeep was waiting. The odor of raw sewage assailed him. This whole little incident assailed him. His girl had assailed him. The Army assailed him. He figured Patch had done this just to twist the knife. A little bit more. What an asshole—even the general thought so, but even he couldn't do anything. Patch had managed to marry himself up with the daughter of a three-star who was running things in Europe and would probably be running them over here pretty soon, so what the hell could Butterworth do but be nice to him?—though privately—and Holden knew this—privately the old man thought Patch was a little bit off his gourd, the way he carried on about the old-time Cavalry and Indian fighting and how it was all the same over here, just a hundred years misplaced; and the general had said once, to his Chief of Staff, noticing that Patch had allowed his blond moustache to droop a little longer, Custer style, that maybe it was Patch who was a hundred years misplaced.

"He's a pretty damned good officer," the general had said, and Holden had overheard this, "except he carries some of this Cavalry bunk a little too far," and the Chief of Staff had thought for a moment and said, "Well, do you think he really believes it?" and the general had said, "I'm not sure—but I wouldn't be surprised," and the Chief of Staff had said, "That is not a good way to be," and the general had agreed.

A dozen ragged children surrounded Holden's jeep, begging and chattering, while the driver did his best to see that they did not steal anything, and when they drove off, bouncing through the potholed streets, Holden tried to keep his mind off Becky's final letter—which was like trying to keep his mind off a toothache.

"Where to, Lieutenant?" the driver asked.

"Tuy Than—the Vietnamese hospital," Holden said.

The driver looked across at him. "Tuy Than—that's a tough ten clicks, sir. There's a Condition Red on that road—they've had some mines..."

"Drive on," Holden said.

"Sir, shouldn't we better call the Engineers and see it's been cleared?"

"Live dangerously," he said.

IF BOTTICELLI had somehow missed out on painting Dante's Inferno, he might have made up for it by drawing scenes from the hospital at Tuy Than. Vietnamese

soldiers and civilians littered the corridors on every floor
of the dingy three-story building, some near death, some
in great pain, most staring blankly ahead. Hope was
absent from their faces. There was an awful smell from an
open-air incinerator into which arms, legs, livers, spleens
and the other human parts shattered by the war were
thrown at irregular intervals. Families of the wounded
and sick squatted over their loved ones, ministering to
them as best they could. Doctors and nurses dealt only
with the most complicated treatments.

There was an administration desk of sorts, where
Holden employed a combination of sign language and
rough Vietnamese to persuade a harried clerk to search
the records for a woman with a knife cut on her arm. He
had a suspicion. If the cuts were serious, why would she
have gone all the way to Xuan Lap? And this business of
the disappearing doctor—and the missing dress...He
was damned tired of deceiving women.

The clerk's fingers stopped at a line of his ledger book,
and he nodded his head and turned it for Holden to see.
Holden asked to see the doctor and was led into a small
room where a man was sprawled on an operating table,
with the doctor working alone over him. The doctor
stopped what he was doing and looked up when Holden
walked in.

"Uh, excuse me," Holden said, "I didn't mean..."

"May I help you?" the doctor interrupted in perfect
English. He put down a needle he was using to stitch up a
tear in the man's back.

"Ah, I...er...understand you treated a young
woman...two days ago. She was cut on the arm,"
Holden said uncomfortably. The man on the table
groaned.

"I have treated a good many people in the last few
days," the doctor said stoically. "As you can see, we are
quite busy here."

"Yes, of course—but I thought you might remember
her. She would have come late at night. The records say
you treated her for knife wounds. You put her arm in a
cast."

The doctor thought momentarily. The man on the table groaned again and started to move, and the doctor pressed his shoulder back down.

"Oh, yes, I believe I remember now—a very pretty girl—just a small cut on her arm, but she asked me to make a cast. And why not?—it was a slow night."

"Then the injury was not bad—it was superficial. Is that true?"

"Superficial—yes. Very minor. But she wanted a cast anyway. She said...it was something to do with her work—and, well, she was very persuasive and *very* pretty." The doctor smiled.

"Would you recognize her if you saw her again?"

"Of course," the doctor said.

"Thank you very much," Holden said. "You will be here if I need to talk to you again?"

The doctor picked up the needle and returned to the man on the table. "I will probably die here," he said.

Holden walked outside into the sunlight, and it felt good on his arms and face and the back of his neck. At least, she wasn't going to get away with it, even if...even if Becky...God! she could always sense things, and when they were together she would say she could feel it when he was in pain or feeling low, hundreds of miles away....He thought he might reach her...maybe she could feel it now...and he thought very hard, hoping the the waves might reach her through all the distance and she would know and feel it back—how much he loved her.

But he didn't feel anything back, as the jeep rocked crazily down the road back to base camp, yet he kept on thinking, deeper, and deeper, sucking down into his brain as hard as he possibly could...Please, Becky, please, baby, please...

A WEEK later they received orders to move out. No one was particularly surprised, because for days rumors had been circulating that something was up—and only a few men were genuinely upset, because the Mickey Mouse at Monkey Mountain had been driving them all nuts. They had been restricted again after the Carruthers incident.

From sunup to sundown they toiled at a number of disagreeable chores, mostly in the capacity of common laborers—loading and unloading, digging, performing maintenance and upkeep—all in the withering heat, with few breaks and less compassion.

Back in the field, at least they could enjoy a little autonomy. The operation this time seemed far more palatable than the Ia Drang campaign: they were to perform security duty and run patrols in a valley of rice fields about twenty miles to the south. It didn't sound too bad, and in the end they went along happily. But they would have gone anyway, happy or not.

KAHN WAS worried about the company's status. Replacements had been promised, but only a half a dozen had arrived, and they were down to less than two-thirds authorized strength—but so was the entire Battalion. Nine of its twenty-two lieutenants had been lost to the Ia Drang, and they were light on noncommissioned officers too. Two new lieutenants had been assigned to replace Sharkey and Donovan, but Kahn still had no Executive Officer.

The new lieutenants, Range and Peck, were odd ducks who had been classmates at a well-established Southern military college. Both were tall and skinny, and they hung together like Tweedle-Dee and Tweedle-Dum. They even acted alike; they giggled and took things as a joke and sometimes behaved almost effeminately. Trunk was convinced they were homosexual, and one day he raised the subject to Kahn.

"There's talk about them two new lieutenants, sir," Trunk said. "Uh—that they're, um, sort of peculiar...." Trunk had been making out the morning report and sipping coffee from his battered cup. Kahn was reading the file on the Carruthers incident.

"They just stick to themselves, Sergeant," Kahn said. "They haven't been here long enough to feel they're a part of the Company."

He returned to reading the file.

"What I mean is, sir, is that...ah...some of the men

have—are—talking about them—like they was fairies. There's a rumor they go off by themselves at night and—"

Kahn slammed the file shut.

"No, Sergeant, I don't know what you mean. And if you hear any more of that kind of talk, you put a stop to it. I've got enough trouble in this goddamned Company without a bunch of crap like that getting started."

And he did have trouble in the Company. It was nothing he could put his finger on, but there was something off. When he'd taken over aboard the transport at Okinawa, Kahn hadn't know his ass from third base—but now ... now he was past first base, and second too, and rounding third. Somewhere between the Village of the Running Man and the final knoll of The Fake, Kahn had become the Company Commander. He realized this when he realized that his fears, and his comforts, and his debt, and everything else had become subordinate to the Company, and even though there was the same sick knot in his stomach every day, he was out there, he did not cater to it, but went about his job running the Company.

Somehow, through the random happenstance of a sour appendix, he had been entrusted with a hundred-odd souls, and most of them looked to him to get them through, and maybe some hated him, and some mistrusted him, but in the end he was responsible for their day-to-day life-and-death crime-and-punishment eating-sleeping-living-defecating-fighting-crying-and-whining. A couple of years ago, he thought, if someone had tried to tell him this—he was running around the fraternity house guzzling beer and waiting for night so he could try to get some girl into bed—he never would have believed them. All in all, he decided, he was doing pretty good.

Except for control.

He had hoped that that would somehow smooth out too, once he got settled into things—but now he wasn't sure. There were some things beyond control, like driving a car too fast, even if you were the best driver around and everyone said you could do it. The Book gave him control on paper, but in practice it was something else.

The Book didn't take into account what things like the enemy and weather and terrain and Lieutenant Brill could really do to control; it simply assumed you had control and proceeded from there.

When he thought of the balking on The Fake, and earlier, and of some of the people like Groutman and Brill and Patch, he worried about control. Once recently he had discussed it with Sergeant Trunk, and Trunk, sensing what he meant, had told him he had often felt the same thing in other outfits and not to worry, but then he had said something that bothered Kahn even more after he'd thought about it. "The thing is, Lieutenant," Trunk said, "some of these shitheads are getting a little crazy."

CARRUTHERS PRESENTED his giant carcass to Kahn at 0800 hours on the morning of the day before they were to move out. He stood at attention before the little field desk, prepared to take whatever whipping the Massa planned to dish out.

Kahn put him at ease.

Spread out before him was Carruthers' 201 file, the Army's singular view of the man Carruthers, beginning with his serial number—which, in the military mind, was at least on an equal footing with his name. Besides the typed results of Holden's investigation of the Duc Twan Bar incident, the file provided some other insights into Carruthers' background—the most interesting of which to Kahn was that he was from Kahn's own hometown, Savannah, Georgia.

Curious, Kahn had kept on reading. Carruthers lived with his mother and two sisters and a brother—no father was mentioned—on a little street near where Kahn's father's junk company was.

As Kahn remembered that street and the Negro shanties along it, which he had not thought about for a long time, he suddenly felt warm and good, and a little closer to home, just knowing this.

He considered mentioning it to Carruthers when he came in; but suddenly it dawned on Kahn that in Savannah—where everybody knew everybody—nobody knew Negroes but other Negroes, except perhaps by their first names, and looking at this file before him, ten thousand miles from home, he realized for the first time in his life that the distances between the races where he had grown up were as incomprehensible as the distances between galaxies. He pondered this for a while and shortly before Carruthers arrived decided that Carruthers was coming here for punishment anyway, so whatever he wanted to do, awkward or not, it wouldn't be the proper time or place.

"I SUPPOSE," Kahn said sternly, "you know why you're here?"

Carruthers seemed forlorn and looked as if he wished Kahn would get on with it.

"Yessir, Lieutenant—I know," he said.

"Well, what the hell do you think I ought to do with you, Carruthers? You have any suggestions?"

Carruthers said nothing. He twisted his fatigue cap in his hands. Kahn stared at him, letting the moment build. In a way, he was enjoying it. He knew what he was going to do, and the hot seat was a part of it.

"Okay," Kahn said finally, fingering the sheet of paper from Holden's report. "I've read this and I've talked to the Battalion Commander, and he has authorized me to deal with you as I see fit."

Carruthers nodded his head.

"According to these findings, you were present at an off-limits establishment and you cut this girl with a knife—is that correct?"

Carruthers looked away, out through the tent flap.

"Goddamn it!—stop looking around. Stand at attention.

"And because of what you did, this girl is now demanding that the United States Government pay her hundreds of dollars in damages—did you know that?"

Carruthers shook his head.

"And do you realize what this sort of thing does to our relations with the people of this country?"

Carruthers shook his head again. He seemed totally downcast.

"All right, you can stand at ease," Kahn said. The huge

body seemed to slump outward. An awkward silence followed.

"Carruthers," Kahn said at last, "I said before that I have talked all this over with the Battalion Commander. I hope you realize you could go to the stockade for a good many years. . . .

"However," Kahn continued, "It has been decided that instead of recommending you for court-martial, I will administer Company punishment. There are two reasons for that. First, you didn't hurt the girl badly, and second, I need every man I can lay my hands on. . . .

"But," Kahn said as sternly as possible, "I want you to promise me right now that you will never carry a knife again when you are off duty and that you won't go into any place that is off limits during the rest of your tour here. Is that clear?"

Gratitude flowed from Carruthers like flour down a chute, and he began to burble his assent in the same dialect that had given Colonel Patch so much difficulty.

"All right, all right," Kahn waved him off. "Now I have to do something about you, so I'm going to put you on KP for two weeks. Report to the mess sergeant first thing in the morning."

"Thank you, sir," Carruthers said. If he had had a forelock, he would probably have tugged it.

"Okay, that's it—go on back to your platoon."

Carruthers stopped at the tent flap and turned around. He opened his mouth for a second, but nothing came out.

"Something else?" Kahn said.

"I wanta axe you sompin . . . Lieutenant . . . ah."

"Well, what is it?"

"Ain't you from Savannah?"

Kahn was dumbfounded.

"Yes, I am," he barked. "Now get the hell out of here."

27

THREE MEN sat in the trench—two of them eating
a C-ration breakfast, the other smoking a damp cigarette
and gently fingering his rifle. The sky was white and glum,
and long banks of gray, rain-laden clouds billowed
threateningly above the distant mountains at the end of
the valley.

"Fuckin' rain," one of the men said crossly, tossing an
empty can outside the trench. "I gotta get outta this
dump."

"It could always be worse," the second man said.

"Oh, yeah?" said the first. "Whatta they gonna do, send
me to Vietnam?"

Below in the inundated rice paddy, two listless farmers, their baggy black trousers rolled to the knee, slogged toward a tiny hamlet half hidden by tall coconut palms. All morning the three in the trench had watched them working the field, stooping over in their peculiar, jerky way, the first guiding a rude plow behind a plodding water buffalo, the second following behind, sticking small rice plants into the ankle-deep muck.

It was infuriating to the men in the trench.

Never once—either from fear or from ignorance—had the two Vietnamese acknowledged the presence of the armed encampment above.

"Lookit them bastards," the man with the cigarette said.

"Yeah," said the other. "What they got to worry about, huh?"

"Squat," said the third. "They don't worry about squat."

SOMETIME EARLIER, Bravo Company had emerged from its rain-soaked burrows on the scrubby hillside and with a sure sense of futility, the men set about hanging and drying their clothing and gear, knowing well that the effort would be undone with the next rain. The rains had been intermittent for the past week—sharp, torrential showers two or three times a day that left everything a sodden, clammy mess. With the onset of the monsoon season, the rains would eventually take over everything, and in time it would be the brief absence of rain that would seem unusual.

The men sat around in uninspired little knots, griping, joking, passing time until the day's patrol order was issued. The piece of terrain they were situated on was referred to as "The Tit," because when viewed from the side it resembled a large, well-shaped breast. At the very peak there was a rock outcropping where they had set up an observation post that commanded a view of the whole valley. Naturally, this was called "The Nipple." On the backside of The Nipple, The Tit broke off to an almost sheer escarpment down seventy or eighty feet into dense jungle. The front side, which faced the valley, was a gradual slope of five or six hundred yards, broken occasionally by gentle terraced rises, and it was between the last of these rises and The Nipple that Kahn had placed his command post.

Everyone was aware that eight months earlier, an Airborne company had been overrun on this same hill by a large but still unidentified force of Vietcong. Nevertheless, Bravo Company now eagerly occupied their vacated holes and makeshift shelters—grateful that it saved them the trouble of constructing their own. When it had first been suggested that Hill 67—its official designation— resembled a tit, exhaustive jokes had been made for several days, and Kahn himself got into the spirit when, at the end of the first week, he was required to change his radio call sign and declared that henceforth he would be known as "Big Tit" and his platoons as "Tit-One," "Tit-Two" and so on. What with the rain and other discomforts, it was hard to raise a laugh of any kind out of this bunch.

THE TWO rice farmers were passing directly beneath the three men in the trench. They observed that one of them had lost a leg, and hobbled along on a makeshift crutch.

"If those two ain't VC, I'll kiss yore ass," the first man said.

"Hell, they *all* VC," replied the second. He spat on the wet earth beside him. "Only thing's to catch 'em at it."

"Two ways you can tell for sure," the man with the cigarette said.

"What's that?"

"If he runs, he's VC—if he's dead, he's VC. Them's two good ways," the man said with a fierce grin.

"Yeah?"

"Yeah. You wanta find out?" the man with the cigarette said.

"Do what—kill them?" the first man said. "Old Brill'ud have your ass hanging high for that, I'll bet."

"Brill—shit," interrupted the second man. "He'd like to do it himself, he got the chance. That is one mean sombitch, that Lieutenant Brill...."

"Nah, I ain't talkin' about killing 'em; I said there's *two*

ways to find out," the man with the cigarette said. He
chambered a round into the rifle and peered down over
the top of the trench. "I'm jest talkin' about a little
experiment, that's all. Just to see if they run."

He giggled indifferently, and then a dark, brooding
look came over his face as he pointed the rifle toward the
plodding men, aiming it just a little ahead of the water
buffalo.

The single shot cracked the stillness of the morning,
and a tiny geyser of water flew up a few yards in front of
the buffalo. All three—the two farmers and the
buffalo—stopped in their tracks. The farmers looked at
each other, the one-legged one resting heavily on his
crutch. The buffalo looked from side to side. None looked
up to where the shot had come from. Then methodically,
as though nothing had happened, they plodded forward
again, infuriatingly, toward the tiny hamlet in the coconut
trees.

"Shit," said one of the men in the trench. "That don't
prove nothin'." He looked back up the hill at several
figures, including a scowling Sergeant Trunk hurrying
down at them to find out what had happened.

"Hell it don't," said the man who had fired the rifle.
"Proves them bastards smarter than we think."

SUCH WAS the mood of Bravo Company in Christmas
week, nineteen hundred and sixty-six: halfway around the
world from home, half-way through its yearlong tour of
duty. For three weeks the men had languished on the hill,
which in another time might have been called the "front,"
except that here there was no front. There was a "rear,"
and everybody spoke of it, but no front, because once you
left the rear they were at not only your front but your back
and sides and top and bottom as well.

Since early morning they had been waiting for orders
for today's patrols, faces hollow and cadaverous beneath
sodden camouflaged helmets, voices ticking out a
monotonous litany of boredom and unrest. As they had
been told it would be, this was indeed a far cry from the
fighting in the Ia Drang; but as it turned out, even more

maddening because it wasn't really fighting at all, but more like a daily game of Russian roulette—and all the more frustrating because here they had time on their hands to think about it.

Each morning, one or more platoons would be sent out to work their way through a section of the valley on a "search and destroy" mission. In time it became obvious that the word "search" under these circumstances was idiotic. Whatever VC there were would long since have been waved off by the villagers, most of whom were known sympathizers if not part-time VC themselves. What remained was a web of mines and booby traps and an occasional sniper. The people they had been sent here to protect were evidently not interested in their protection, and the Company soon came to regard them as worthless.

They spoke with bitterness of the fact that few if any inhabitants of the valley ever stepped on a mine or set off a booby trap, while they encountered these dreaded obstacles day upon day. If shots were fired at them from a hamlet, they were invariably greeted with a silent, resentful, know-nothing reception when they arrived to investigate. And if by chance they happened to see and kill the sniper, chances were his body would be dragged away later by one or more wailing women.

For young men who a few scant months before had been repairing automobiles, mending sewer pipe, studying in high school or slinging hash for a living, it was a difficult situation to comprehend. The ultimate effect was to inspire a bullyish attitude—different from, but somehow related to, the ruthlessness they had felt during the Ia Drang fight—and if a few of them were comfortable with it, others were not, and yet it overtook them just the same.

This was illustrated by an incident that happened a few weeks before in another company of the Battalion operating in a valley nearby.

Colonel Patch had been on his way to visit the Command Post when his helicopter was fired on from a tiny hamlet. When he arrived at the CP, the colonel was livid and decreed that the hamlet should be evacuated immediately and then wiped off the face of the earth by artillery and air strikes. As the story went, Patch first secured permission from Headquarters to declare the hamlet a "free-fire zone," then requested a helicopter equipped with loudspeakers to fly over and announce to its inhabitants that they had three hours to gather their belongings and leave. Patch considered this a sort of updated version of the ancient practice of plowing up the site of a conquered city and sowing the ground with salt.

As the time period drew to a close and the batteries of artillery prepared high-intensity phosphorous rounds and the big Phantom fighters boiled on their runways, Patch received a message from the helicopter pilot circling overhead that no one had been observed leaving the hamlet. The people who lived there, he reported seemed to be coming and going as though nothing had happened or were going to happen.

The story at this point had several variants, but the most common was that Patch had gone into a wild rage and said to "Burn 'em out, then," and when the Company Commander timidly reminded him that there were women and children in the hamlet, Patch retorted that *Women and children burn like anything else!"* and ordered the destruction to proceed on schedule.

In the fact, Patch did postpone the strike until the villagers were forcibly evacuated, but his now famous declaration, *"Women and children burn like anything else!"* circulated throughout the Battalion to the tune of dry, black laughter, a bonus contribution to the callousness they were all beginning to feel toward the Vietnamese, and in time toughness became synonymous with meanness, and not a few civilians fell victim to this attitude.

Back at higher headquarters, the hoped-for result was that the Battalion's presence would deter the enemy from availing himself of the rice crop in these fertile valleys. But not being privy to the Big Picture, Bravo Company, like the rest, could only wonder why it was here being nickled and dimed to bits, and curse and rage against the immemorial usage of the foot soldier.

*   *   *

SHORTLY BEFORE NOON, the radioman poked his head into the Command tent where Kahn was poring over a map with his other officers.

"The Old Man's on his way over here, sir."

Kahn dropped his grease pencil and looked up. His face was haggard and his eyes sunken from lack of sleep. There were lines around the corners of his mouth and nose that hadn't been there six months ago.

"When?" he asked tiredly.

"He's airborne now from LZ Horse—so's I guess in just a few minutes," the RTO said.

Kahn turned to the others. "Let's sack this for now. I'll put it to him when he gets here and see how it flies."

"Jesus Christ, I should hope so," exclaimed Lieutenant Peck. Kahn ignored him and walked out of the tent. In a few seconds the foolish look faded from Peck's face and he turned on Brill, who had been shaving bark off a stick with his Randall knife.

"Why is *he* in such a pissy mood? He's not the one who has to keep going out there day after day," Peck said defensively. Brill stared at the other darkly, a smile of relish on his face, but he did not say anything and he did not stop shaving the bark off the stick.

A few tiny drops of rain began falling, and the clouds in the west had grown darker and more ominous. Somewhere in the distance, two claps of artillery thundered in well-spaced succession. Kahn walked down the forward slope of The Tit into the cleared space on one of the terraces and watched the sky to the north.

He heard the helicopter before he saw it, flying low through a pass between the hills. It circled once overhead, just low enough to scatter anything that wasn't tied down, then dropped gently into the landing zone. Colonel Patch, wearing a wide-brimmed bush hat and a .45 slung on his hip and the small, dark glasses perched on his nose, bounded out, ducking beneath the rotors, and returned Kahn's salute.

"Welcome to The Tit, sir," Kahn said, forcing cheerfulness. He was a little taken aback by the comic cowboy look Patch had affected.

"Hello, Billy," Patch said, "How's it going?" He gazed around, hands on hips, surveying the emplacements and the panorama of the valley below. "I'd say you've done a pretty good job since I was here last."

"It's not bad except for the rain," Kahn said. "I think we might best be relocating pretty soon, though—we've been up here nearly three weeks now."

Patch peered over the dark glasses as though he had heard something unexpected.

"I wouldn't worry much about that," he said. "Hasn't been any large-scale activity here in—what is it—eight or nine months? You've got the best defensive position in the whole Area of Operations; and that ARVN company down in the valley—been there two or three months and haven't been touched." Patch began walking uphill.

"That's because they don't do shit," Kahn said drily, and Patch looked at him in that same abrupt way.

They walked the rest of the way up the hill in silence, past the rolls of barbed wire and the machine-gun emplacements and make-shift living quarters of the troops. Men who had been sitting or lying down rose to their feet and saluted when the colonel passed, and others, if they were far enough away, altered their courses from his path. Halfway up, Patch thought he saw a tall soldier far ahead dart into some bushes carrying a monkeylike creature under his arm, but he wasn't sure and decided not to make an issue of it.

Inside the CP, Kahn gave Patch the single folding chair and sat down himself on an empty ammunition crate.

"Like some Cs, Colonel?" Kahn offered. "I think we've got some canned peaches here."

"No, thanks, Billy. I'll get something back at Monkey Mountain. Can't stay here but a few minutes, anyway—there's an early briefing today. Take some coffee, though."

"Coming right up," Kahn said. He put on a heat tab and dug around in a C-ration crate. "Just the old Army stuff, sir; isn't too good."

"It's fine, Billy—fine," Patch said. "Now let's talk about your deployment." Then, remembering he had forgotten something, he removed the sunglasses and blinked in the darkness of the tent. Outside, the rain had picked up, coming down in needlelike bites, and a sharp, moist breeze blew in through the open flap.

"First off, I noticed your mortars up there to the right," Patch said. "Don't you think they're a bit too close?"

Kahn reached for a cigarette. Patch took out a cigar and chewed on it, unlit. "I thought about that, Colonel, but it's about the only place I can think of to put them—it's the farthest spot up the hill. That backside drops straight down, and about the only other thing I could do is put them down in the jungle or up on another hill, and that wouldn't be very secure."

"I guess not," Patch said thoughtfully, "but if you do get hit they won't be able to help you much those last two or three hundred meters—it's where you'll need it, you know." He stopped for a moment and pondered the problem. "How about if you move your perimeter down the slope a hundred or so meters—that ought to do it, huh?" Patch said, sounding pleased at his suggestion.

"Well... I thought about that too, Colonel, but it just seemed to me that if we go down there... I mean, if they're going to hit us here, they've got to come all the way up here to do it." Damn, Kahn thought, he always sounded so ineffective when he talked to Patch. The truth was—and he knew it—that he was afraid of the man; or rather, of that silver eagle on his collar, which had such control over his life; which could decide if he was to live or die or shovel shit or be disgraced or become a hero... or maybe it *was* the man.... He thought of the business with Carruthers and wondered what Patch thought of Jews.

"I know what you're saying, Kahn, but sometimes you have to sacrifice position for coverage. You have to weigh the advantages, and I'll tell you this, if it were my company, I'd move on down that slope and make room for the mortars."

Once he had seen Patch out of uniform, at a party off post, and he remembered thinking then how civilian clothes diminished him. But when he was wearing the uniform he was a frightening man... dangerous....

"Colonel, you're probably right, but...like I said before, I think we're gonna have to get off this hill pretty soon anyway—I think we're stretching it now as far as—"

"Nonsense," Patch declared. He took a long, disapproving look at Kahn. "This is the best spot in the valley to defend from. That is why I put you up here. Reconnoitered this hill myself. Couldn't do any better. Main thing is, it commands the road to Bong Tien. Besides, they're not going to hit a reinforced company up here. It'd take two battalions."

"Well...ahm...I just..." Kahn faltered momentarily. "Maybe not...."

"Now, what else?" Patch said sternly. "How's your supply?"

"Rotten, sir," Kahn said, relieved to be off the hook, though nothing was resolved. "We're becoming beggars. The men are trading things with the chopper crews—we ask for everything and get nothing."

"Humm..." Patch said, mulling it over. "Tell you what: you make up a list of what you need and send it on the chopper in the morning. I'll take it to Supply personally and kick ass—okay? Well, I ought to be heading out if I'm going to make that briefing." He stood up and put on his bush hat.

"There's something else I'd like to speak to you about, sir," Kahn said. He had said he would. The others expected it. Now he had to.

"Yes? What's that?"

"It's about the two-platoon-a-day patrols." He noticed Patch's eyebrows rise. This wasn't going to go down well.

"What I mean is, we're getting chewed to bits by these damned mines and booby traps and snipers, and...well, we don't have shit to show for it." Kahn fumbled for another cigarette. Patch looked at him impatiently.

"I've lost sixteen men these three weeks, and it's getting worse. If we keep this up much longer, I'm going to be down to cooks and jeep drivers...."

"I know what your losses are," Patch said tersely. "Replacements are building up, though. As soon as they go through orientation we'll be able to get you back somewhere near normal."

Kahn pressed on anyway—haltingly, but on.

"It's not so much the replacements; it's . . . well, it's getting to be a problem with the men. There's a lot of reluctance on their part to go out and get blown away every day with nothing to show for it, and . . . well, bluntly, Colonel, they don't like it, and . . . I . . . I think I have to say that I agree with them. . . ." Kahn felt Patch's hard, cold stare on his face. "What I mean is, I've given this a lot of thought, and I believe I have a solution that might save some lives and bag some game. Why couldn't we run just one patrol of, say, a single platoon every other day?—mix it up so they wouldn't know where to expect us. It would keep them off balance, and . . . it certainly would cut down on the casualties."

Patch had lit the cigar and stuck it in his mouth. He removed it and looked Kahn in the eye.

"First of all," he said, "I have my assignment just like you have yours. The whole Battalion's spread out in these valleys, and it's the same for every company. It's messy business, but we have a big AO and that's how I've decided to cover it—saturation patrols. Old Fifth Cavalry did the same thing back in the eighteen nineties against the Indians in the Southwest. Very effective—keeps a high visibility." He glanced out the open tent flap toward the waiting helicopter and took a puff of the cigar.

"Look, Bill," he said, "the general staff has considered these problems and calculated the risks. I'm sure you are right—we would avoid casualties if we cut back patrolling, or simply stopped it altogether. It's what a lot of people back home would like to see us do—move into goddamn enclaves or something—but that's neither here nor there. That's not what Saigon wants us to do and it's not what the Commanding General wants to do and it's not what I want to do. We're here for one thing—Search and Destroy. Search and Destroy the enemy, Billy." Kahn could tell Patch was getting worked up. He'd seen it before.

"Just remember this," Patch said: "your men are *your* problem. You're running the show, and I'm telling you how to do it. If they're getting blown away by booby traps, tell 'em to go after the guys who make them. It isn't

Little Red Riding Hood who's putting them there.

"Well," he said, "I gotta go—looks like the weather's closing in." Kahn followed him outside.

"By the way, what's all this stuff they've put on the bushes?" Patch said, indicating a dozen or so scrubby trees festooned with the tops of C-ration tins, empty cartridge brass and other bright and decorative items.

"Christmas trees, Colonel," said Kahn. "It's Christmas this week, you know, and—"

"Have them get rid of them," Patch interrupted. "Sooner the better."

Kahn was stunned. "Sir, may I ask why? The men have worked hard on them for a week now—and it's put them in pretty good spirits. . . ."

"I think you're wrong. It only makes them more lonely. Hurts morale. Saw it in Korea. In this battalion there's not going to be any outward celebration of Christmas. Doesn't mean they can't recognize Christmas, but no dog-and-pony show. They all know about it, but there's no need to dwell on it. Plenty of time to celebrate when they get back home." The colonel started downhill for the helicopter, and Kahn fell in beside him.

"Colonel," he said pleadingly, "I know these men. And if I have to go out there with my thumb up my ass and—"

"Better than a sharp stick, my boy—better than a sharp stick." Patch grinned drily.

"By the way, I'm sending you a new Executive Officer in a few days." He stepped up his pace and was gone.

THE HOURS dissolved into days and the days into weeks, and always there was the rain.

Sometimes it would last for days on end, a relentless drizzle blowing down from the north; sometimes it would pour down in torrents out of the west, with brief periods of cessation during which the sky would hang heavy with dark, sullen clouds.

The mood of the men matched the weather. They had been resentful over the curtailing of their Christmas but finally took it in stride like everything else. They had gotten better at their jobs, and casualties began to drop.

Everyone kept his own DEROS calendar—an Army anacronym for Date Effective Return from Overseas—to mark his remaining time, and through this hopeful practice the days settled into a crazy kind of routine in which each man lived for the particular hour he had set for himself to strike off another day. And before them lay the valley, a patchwork sea of thin brown mud alive now with thousands of bright green rice shoots. Around its edges the jungle lapped out in poison green, beckoning maddeningly for their presence. And always there was the rain....

If it had not been for Sergeant Trunk, Kahn's troubles would have been worse than they were. The two of them had lapsed into sort of father-mother roles—Kahn giving the orders, and expecting them to be carried out; Trunk dealing with the day-to-day gripes, fuck-ups and confusion. He scolded and blustered around the company area, putting things as he wanted them, trying to keep the place as habitable as possible, handing out discipline and trying to keep supply moving. In between all this he somehow found time to help the men with personal problems; arrange their R&R leaves; see to their general health and welfare, in such ways as getting a hot meal flown out once in a while, and do other things to keep the Company running. Supply, however, remained a major problem.

Patch had done what he could, but because of the weather, helicopter pilots were often as not unable or unwilling to fly, and the Company had to make do with what was on hand. Beyond that, because of the huge buildup of new troop units all over the country, most items of necessity were in hot demand and short supply. In time, after sending in requisition slips and engaging in repeated arguments via the field radio, Kahn turned to the time-honored military practice of cannibalization.

He instructed Trunk to inventory their available gear, whatever the condition, matched it with the company Table of Organization and Equipment and arrived at a formula for stripping one piece of equipment to make another functional again. If, for instance, a mortar was out of commission because the aiming sight was busted and another down because it had no baseplate, he would cannibalize a third to repair the other two. If a machine gun's sear was worn down or its spring loose, he would strip it down and allocate the parts to guns with other problems. This worked well enough for a while, but the supply famine persisted, and in the end Kahn resorted to the ultimate cannibalization. He cannibalized a man.

The man was named Dunbar, a rifleman in Peck's platoon whom no one considered very useful anyway. One day, after listening to a series of desperate pleas for this item or that, Kahn stormed out of his tent, and the first person he saw was Dunbar, lounging stupidly under his shelter half.

"Come in here for a minute," Kahn said. Dunbar looked at him dully, then rose up and followed his commander inside.

"Dunbar," Kahn said, "is your equipment in good order?"

Dunbar replied that it was.

"Good," Kahn said. "Now, what I am going to say to you is strictly between the two of us—understand?"

Dunbar nodded his head.

"With any luck at all," Kahn said, "A chopper with water and C-rats is going to land here in an hour. When it leaves, I want you on it."

Dunbar looked at Kahn blankly for a moment, seeming not to comprehend what he had been told.

Kahn took out a piece of paper and sat down at his desk and began writing on it.

"When you get to Monkey Mountain, go to the hospital and give them this note. It says you have been sick. It says you probably have a bad case of malaria or some other strange tropical ailment and you are unfit for duty. It says this illness comes and goes every few weeks and I, your Company Commander, request that you be observed for at least that length of time and not be allowed to return to the field until you're well. Got it?"

"Uh, Lieutenant," Dunbar protested, "I ain't sick—I ain't been nothin' but wet since I come out here."

Kahn overrode him. "This is your chance for a few

weeks in the rear. Just do as I say. Don't argue with me."

"Yessir," Dunbar said, his face brightening.

"Now what I want you to do is gather up all your gear and take it to Sergeant Trunk. Everything you've got—your rifle, your pack, your poncho liner, grenades, fatigues, boots—everything. Leave it all here. Understand?"

A befuddled look filled Dunbar's face. "My fatigues, sir—and my boots?"

"That's right, Dunbar. When you get on that chopper I don't want you wearing anything but skivvies and dog tags. Leave everything else with Sergeant Trunk—we need it." Kahn continued to write.

"But, sir," Dunbar said pleadingly, "I...I can't go back to base camp like that—in my underwear." He sounded as if he might begin to cry.

"Why not?" Kahn said acidly.

"Because, uh..." Dunbar thought for a moment. He knew there must be a reason. "Uh...because I'll get into trouble," he said.

"No, you won't," Kahn said. He bore down again with the pen. "I'm going to say in this note that your illness prevents you from wearing clothes. They...ah...irritate your skin. Just show it to anyone who questions you."

"But, sir—" Dunbar protested.

"Listen, Dunbar," Kahn cut in, "I am going to tell you a secret." He beckoned him closer. "You are being cannibalized."

"Cannibalized, sir?..." Dunbar repeated the word, and then said it a second time, a little proudly, as though he suddenly understood an honor was being bestowed upon him.

"Cannibalized," Kahn said majestically. "I figure you're the best man for the job."

Dunbar straightened out of his slouch. "Okay, sir. I'll get them things over to First Sergeant right now," he said. There was a touch of giddiness in his voice.

"Good." Kahn handed him the note. "And good luck."

Dunbar bounced out of the tent, and Kahn leaned back in his chair. Not long afterward, two men passing by the tent heard what sounded to them like hysterical laughter from inside. They pulled up short and looked at each other. The laughter continued—a weird, nutty laughter like that of a crazy person. The two men shook their heads and resumed walking. The way everything else had been going lately, it was not inconceivable that the Company Commander himself had gone Asiatic.

IT WAS a Thursday early in January, but it could have been any day of the week, for none but a very few ever cared about days of the week; most counted time only as it applied to the magical DEROS date. Yet this particular Thursday marked the beginning of a strange and terrifying new atmosphere that descended on Bravo Company and eased it into a morale twilight from which it would never fully recover.

Two things happened that day: the first was the death of Sergeant Trunk, and the second, though of lesser import, was the arrival of the new Company Exec—First Lieutenant C. Francis Holden.

HOLDEN ARRIVED on the mail chopper, early in the morning, fatigues freshly starched and lugging his gear bundled in three packs. The rifle slung over his shoulder was new and unscratched as though it had never fired a shot in anger, which in fact it had not. Trudging up the hill from the landing zone, Holden passed by scruffy-looking soldiers who might have been taken for wild animals in their rain-soaked, seedy, unshaven state. They watched him too, curiously and suspiciously, as they would have watched anyone who would soon have a bit of control over their lives.

Kahn was in his tent, stretched out on the cot asleep in his skivvies, when Holden poked his head in.

"Pardon me," he announced very loudly, "I am looking for Epsom Downs."

Kahn snapped bolt upright as though he had received a hotfoot, eyes wide as saucers. A feeble "huh" issued from his throat as he stared dumbly at the figure standing over him.

"Jesus, Billy, I didn't mean to give you a scare," Holden said. "Say hello to your new Exec."

Kahn shook his head to clear the sleep away.

"Frank Holden—you're kidding me.... How in the hell..." He swung his legs off the cot and sat on the edge rubbing his eyes. "Well I'll be damned ... Uh ... put your gear down." Kahn stuck out his hand. "I was just catching up on a few, uh ... was up most of the night ..." He stood up and extended a hand.

"So you're it, huh? Well, how in hell did you get yourself assigned to a busted-up outfit like this?"

"Lucky, I guess," Holden said. "Here, I brought you something." He reached into his pack and took out a black woolen sock, from which he removed a still-cold can of beer.

"An appreciation for our boys at the front," he said cheerfully.

Kahn accepted the beer groggily. "Manna from Heaven. You bring one for you?"

"Whole pack of it," Holden said. "Figured the beer hall closed early out here."

"The beer hall is now open," Kahn said authoritatively, punching a hole in the can with his knife. "Welcome to Disneyland."

28

THE DEATH of Trunk seemed to crystallize the men into sullen, animalistic bands, isolated from the Army, the war and in some cases from one another. There was no explanation for this, except that for all his bellowing and bluster, the First Sergeant had—like a human ball of green tape—managed to hold the Company together.

Trunk had died quietly, and with dignity, the morning Holden arrived, victim of a land mine tripped off by a man in Peck's platoon walking ahead of him on a patrol near An Lap hamlet, which lay in the center of the valley. An Lap had been a hotbed of trouble since the day they had come—mines, booby traps and sniper fire spread outward from it in ever-widening circles—and the purpose of the patrol that day had been to move the occupants and destroy it.

The mine that killed Trunk was what was called a "bouncing Betty"—an ingenious invention whose parts are supplied, unwillingly or unwittingly, by the opposing side. An empty C-ration can, for instance, is filled with explosive from a dud artillery shell and buried carefully in the ground. The man who trips its cord will hear a small pop as it rises a few feet into the air, and perhaps a slight hissing for a couple of seconds before it annihilates him. Trunk heard such a sound moments before he died.

It interrupted a chorus of the "Missouri Waltz" he had been humming softly between his teeth; and afterward, as he lay on the ground, his bottom half nearly severed from the top, looking upward, beyond the men hovering over him, delivered his parting words: "Them shitheads—oh, them shitheads..." contemptuously, in bewildered rage against a war so strange a man could be killed by a device so simple a ten-year-old child could make one—and probably *had* made it—and if there had been time, and he had not been dying, more than likely Trunk would have utilized the occasion as an instructive example to the others, for there were many dangerous things to watch out for out here....

Half an hour later, the rest of the patrol stormed into An Lap hamlet in a carnival of boiling vengeance and burned it to the ground. Fearful beatings were administered to the inhabitants, and Lieutenant Peck was powerless to stop them. He and his sergeant ran here and there breaking up gangs of men laying into someone, but no sooner had they separated them than another incident would break out. Some of the Vietnamese accepted this stoically, as though they were aware of what had precipitated it; others, however, shrank into terrified little groups and squatted on the ground.

LATER THAT DAY, just before dusk, Kahn was sitting on the edge of his cot, bare except for undershorts, when

Holden walked in. The patter of rain drummed against the canvas tent top, and the dank, acrid odor of unwashed bedding and moldy clothes hung heavily in the air. A kerosene lantern sputtered above the field desk, on which the contents of two field packs had been spread out and sorted. In a corner, a can of C-ration stew was cooking over a heat tab.

"It was really tough about your First, Billy," Holden said glumly. "I heard he was a good soldier."

"He was a thoroughly good soldier," Kahn said. He leaned back on the bunk, thin and pale-looking to Holden. It was the first time he had seen him without a shirt.

"This is his stuff, huh?" Holden said, picking up a photograph. It was a picture of a man and woman copulating.

"Yeah. He never had much use for the junk most guys pick up—cameras and that kind of crap. I think the most valuable thing he owned was this." Kahn handed him the preposterously battered coffee cup. Holden turned it in his hands.

"He got it in Korea after some kind of brawl with the Air Force," Kahn said. "Look inside; you ever seen anything like it?"

Holden peered down inside the cup and winced. "Ugh," he said, and put it on the desk.

"He never washed it," Kahn said, "just poured in water and it turned into coffee. Said it would lift you right off the ground."

"You ever try it?" Holden smiled.

"I took his word for it."

The rain kept up its drumming against the top of the tent. The flap opened suddenly and the radio operator stuck his head in, dripping wet. "Artillery called, Lieutenant. They're putting heat on Hill Two Forty in fifteen minutes. ARVN company may have spotted something—want to let you know."

"Right," Kahn said. He bent over and stirred the C-ration stew with his knife. "Damned ARVN, always seeing ghosts. You want some chow?"

"What we got?"

"Trout almondine with asparagus tips and butter sauce—look for yourself."

Holden selected a dinner of meat loaf, circa 1957, and lit a heat tab for himself.

"You get a look around this afternoon?" Kahn asked.

"Pretty good."

"Sorry I couldn't go with you," Kahn said.

"What about operations?" Holden said.

"Sucks. And that's the best you can say for it." Kahn lit up a cigarette.

"Bad, huh?"

"Terrible. But there's not much we can do. Patch is all gung ho about running these damned two-platoon patrols every day, and...you saw what happened today—scratch one first-rate top sergeant. But what can I do? Every time we go out there somebody gets blown away, and we don't have ding-dong to show for it. I've never heard of a place mined like this."

"Hmmm..."

"What I'd like to do is run a single patrol every other day—mix 'em up a bit—and ambush at night sometimes: catch the bastards moving. The way it is now, we might as well mail them a schedule."

"What's the Old Man say?"

"He says to keep smiling."

Holden pulled two beer cans from his pack, and they dined on the C-ration supper while Kahn pointed out the tactical situation on a map laid out between them.

I wonder, he thought, I really wonder...Fucking Patch...sent out an exec with no field experience when there must be a dozen platoon leaders from other companies...What's he trying to do?

He was of course glad to see Holden, because it had been depressing and lonely after Sharkey and Donovan—and now Trunk—were gone. But what he needed most right now wasn't a friend. Right now he needed a solid hand who could step in and take over certain duties in the Company.

From the blackness across the valley a rumble of

artillery shuddered through the gloom, its flashes visible through the open flap like fireflies fluttering against the mountainside.

"How about the platoon leaders? Anything I should know?"

Kahn lit another heat tab for coffee and stood at the opening staring out at the little show.

"Well, there's Peck, First Platoon, and Range, he's got Third. They came about the same time, and they both went to, uh…" He thought for a moment before remembering the name of the school.

"Lord," said Holden, "that's worse than the Academy."

He gave Holden a rundown on the other officers. He told him what he knew about Peck and Range, leaving out the still persistent rumors that they were queer. He filled him in on Lieutenant Inge and the reserved, studious way he ran the mortar platoon. He told him as much as he could about the noncoms, and that he had decided to make Sergeant Dreyfuss the new First Sergeant. Outside, the artillery continued to gnash and tear at the neighboring hillside. Finally he got around to Lieutenant Brill, and since it was fresh in his mind, Kahn told Holden about the incident with the ear.

Three days before, Brill had returned from patrol with an ear. He had strung it around his neck with a piece of commo wire: a brownish, shriveling, disgusting human ear. Kahn had noticed it while Brill was making his report to him, and when he asked him what it was, Brill cheerfully reported that he had taken it from a man "who didn't need it anymore."

Kahn hit the ceiling.

"Damn it!" he'd said, "You know the standing orders about mutilations—and here you are, an officer, wearing that thing in front of your platoon."

Brill sullenly protested that it wasn't anything but a fucking gook anyway—and one that had sniped at them at that; but Kahn cut him short.

"Look," Kahn said, "you know we don't go for that kind of shit out here. Get rid of it." Afterward, he'd told

Trunk to put out the word again that there were to be no mutilations. It was just like Brill, he thought, to pull some kind of maniac thing like that.

Holden did not seem surprised. He recalled a case back at Monkey Mountain of a man who was court-martialed when he was found with a tentful of anatomical parts, pickled in various containers. Word had gotten out that the man was "building himself a gook."

"The thing about Brill," Kahn said, "is nobody pays much attention to him. I guess I'm as guilty as the rest."

"He sounds kind of crazy to me," Holden offered.

"I guess maybe all of us are," Kahn said.

They talked a little while longer about other things, and Kahn promised Holden he would take him on a thorough tour of the area the next day.

The artillery fire had ceased, and the overhead lantern flickered for a few seconds and went out. Holden put on his helmet and stood up. "Think I'll turn in and start out fresh in the morning—with my thumb up my ass."

"Better than a sharp stick," Kahn said knowingly. They both laughed.

IN THE week that followed, the mood of the men did not improve.

Insolence, sometimes bordering on insubordination, fist fighting and general malaise marked the company spirit. The two new lieutenants, Range and Peck, complained on different occasions that they were unable to get their platoons to move into preassigned positions and, worse, had heard vague, unsettling rumors against their lives, none of which could be proved.

The discontent was so general that Kahn was completely baffled as to how to deal with it. Punishing a man or a couple of men was one thing, but the problem became infinitely more complex when it involved practically the whole Company. It wasn't so much a concerted stand against the officers or their orders; it was more a kind of mobocracy in which the officers were still loosely in control. How much of it had to do directly with Trunk's death was hard to tell. There was the rain, too, and the boredom spliced in with the nerve-scraping, screaming heebie-jeebies of the daily patrols and the tasteless food and having to piss and defecate into open holes in the ground and the absence of women and other things.

But Trunk's death had made it all the worse, and the brutality inflicted on the Vietnamese in the valley was henceforth done in his name.

Of course, not everyone felt this way, and at least one man was deeply troubled by it.

Ever since the letters from Julie and his father, Spudhead had been walking a pretty shaky plank between sanity and the horrors, but now he felt himself sliding slowly off. First there were physical symptoms: headaches, dizziness, the stomach sickness—he almost always felt like throwing up—but beyond that something else was wrong...wrong, wrong, wrong...and he couldn't quite put his finger on what it was except that, basically, he felt sad.

At first he mistook his sadness for the regular depression that troubled everyone. But finally he came to him that what he was actually feeling was sorrow. Sorrow for his dead companymates—and sorrow for the Vietnamese who were being killed, and sorrow for Julie, who was worried about him. He remembered the ponchos lined up on the Blood Alley Road where the personnel carrier had been mined. He was sorry for the men who had been inside it. He was sorry for the Running Man they had killed outside the village, and for Sergeant Trunk and Lieutenant Donovan and the soldier whose head had been cut off and stuck on the stump up on The Fake, and for the blackened "crispy critters"...and for Lieutenant Sharkey and Moose, the mortarman, and for the people in the An Lap hamlet whose houses had been burned. It was very different from the regular depression, which was temporary and was sometimes even replaced by a strong euphoria which made him feel very fierce and powerful and self-righteous.

But the sorrow was different.

It did not come and go. It came and stayed and got worse. Sometimes he could put it out of his thoughts by thinking other things. But it was still there, somewhere. It was not the war itself that made him sorry—he still believed in it, even after Julie's letter; it had to do with his being in the war. But he still couldn't quite figure it out. He knew he wasn't very smart—but he wasn't dumb either. And it didn't take any great brains to see that there was an enemy who was trying to kill him and who was against his country.

To complicate things more, fear began to creep into his life. Not the animal terror he had felt in the Boo Hoo Forest and on The Fake, but plain, simple fear which, like the sorrow, did not come and go but stayed in varying degrees all the time. He had a singular vision of himself dead. He was being carried off in a poncho, his muddy boots dangling out of one end. Rain would drip down on his face, which was tranquil and unmutilated. He could not tell what had killed him, because he could not see inside the poncho, except for the face and feet, and they were unmarked. He had this vision at least several times a day. Each time he would squint deeper into his mind to try to find out what had killed him, but he never could. Some other soldiers were standing around while the poncho was carried past, but every time he tried to ask them what had killed him, the poncho would disappear from his view like a character walking offstage—and then, slowly, the whole vision would fade out and he would be forced to conjure it up all over again.

It got so bad Spudhead stopped talking to people. Even his close friend Madman Muntz told him he was an asshole. Finally he decided he was going to have to talk to somebody or he would go crazy—if he wasn't already. There were a lot of things to think about these days. And a lot of hours to think them!

THE PROBE came just before midnight, two weeks to the day after Trunk's death. In the intervening time, five men had been lost, and the atmosphere of malevolence remained over Bravo Company like the smell of rotting cabbages.

It was a light probe—although they could not know this and at first treated it like a full-scale assault; but it achieved its purpose of checking out the Company defenses so that a full and detailed map could be made, and when the enemy digested this information he must have been surprised to learn that the positions marked were almost identical to those gleaned from a similar probe eight months earlier, a few days before the Airborne company was overrun.

Kahn had spent the day in the field, with Holden shadowing him around. It surprised Kahn how quickly Holden was picking up on things, and he was already beginning to turn over some duties to him.

And the nights, which before had been scary and depressing and lonely, he now almost looked forward to. Once they had gotten the Company settled in, the two of them would sit in Kahn's Command Post tent and cook their supper and talk about things far removed from the war and the Valley of The Tit. Kahn learned, for instance, about Holden's family background, and his sister, Cory, and his tennis game, and, of course about Becky, and even though Holden frequently said their relationship was finished, Kahn suspected he had not seen the last of it. Kahn told Holden about himself too. About the geology and Savannah and the South, which seemed to fascinate Holden. Several times he said that when all this was over he would like to come South and the two of them could maybe take off on a trip to Atlanta and New Orleans and other places—and also, if Kahn ever wanted to come to New York...

Tonight they had been feeling better than usual, because of the phosphate discovery and an unexpected bottle of bourbon.

That morning Kahn and Holden had been flying over the far end of the valley, looking for one of the patrols that had gone out the day before, and as they passed over a series of jagged craters made months before during a B-52 strike, Kahn punched his intercom button, and asked

Lieutenant Spivey, the pilot, to circle around again, lower.

They made a pass, and then Kahn asked Spivey if he would mind setting her down in the paddy.

"Aw, for the love of God," the big slack-jawed Irishman said, "I'm supposed to be taking supplies out here, not landing all over the place."

"You can leave her running," Kahn said. "It won't take me two minutes—I want to look at something in one of those craters." Spivey shrugged and dropped down into the rice field. Kahn hopped out and was back minutes later with two handfuls of rocks and dirt.

"What was that all about?" asked Holden, as Spivey hauled air again.

"Phosphate," Kahn declared.

"No kidding?" Spivey broke in.

"I think so," Kahn said, "I want to look at these samples."

"What is it?" Holden said in a perplexed voice.

"They use it in mineral fertilizers," Spivey interjected. "It's hard to come by, at least in the U.S."

"You know phosphate?" Kahn said.

"Got an uncle who's a mining engineer. I used to work for him before this came up," Spivey said.

They had made contact with the patrol, and afterward Spivey delivered them back to The Tit. It had not rained since early that morning, and the three of them sat outside on some logs and ate lunch, and as they drank coffee, Kahn delivered his opinion of the phosphate find.

"No way to tell without drilling and that sort of thing; but just looking at the stratification in that crater and these samples, I'd be willing to bet this whole valley floor is made of phosphate. Maybe other valleys around here too."

"Maybe you can get the Army to ship it home in your trunk," Holden said. "Or sell it at the PX."

"Listen," Kahn said, "the war ain't going to last forever, right? And when it's over there'll still be a great big field of phosphate ore ready to come out of the ground."

"Yeah, but who owns it?" Spivey said.

"There seems to be a big dispute about that now," Holden chimed in cheerfully.

Kahn ignored him. "Probably nobody," he said. "I mean, the damned Vietnamese own it, I guess, but they don't know it's there. Suppose you went down to Saigon and said, 'Somewhere in your country there is a big vein of phosphate and I would like the rights to mine it and give you such-and-such of the profits.' How could they lose? They don't know where it is and they'd never find it on their own. We could set up a fertilizer plant right here, with local labor. Mix the stuff with nitrate and peddle it all over Asia. It could maybe double a rice crop in a year or so."

"How do you know you'll be dealing with Saigon?" Holden said darkly. "You might have to go to Hanoi, you know."

"Fat chance," Kahn said. "You guys interested?"

"Huh?" Spivey said.

"In what?" Holden asked.

"The Far East Phosphate Company," Kahn replied awesomely.

"Look," he said. "Spivey—you've got mining experience, right? And Holden, your family is into banking..."

"Brokerage," Holden reminded him.

"Same thing." Kahn said. "It's going to take money, and it's going to take experience and time too. But can you imagine what this country's going to be like when the war's over? This could be a once-in-a-lifetime chance..." As he spoke, the words of Mr. Bernard suddenly flashed in Kahn's mind. *"You will be in a good position. . . . You may see certain opportunities. . . ."*

They discussed it for another half-hour, becoming more enthusiastic, until Spivey had to leave.

"I'll be back in a minute," he said, and walked over to his helicopter, on the side of which was emblazoned the slogan YOU CRY—WE FLY. He removed from beneath the seat an unopened bottle of Jack Daniel's Sour Mash Whiskey. Each of them took a slug to seal the deal, and Spivey left the bottle with them when he took off.

That night in the tent, Kahn and Holden sat around

drinking the whiskey, and Holden confided to Kahn that Becky was still very much on his mind. "I guess it's the real reason I raised hell to get off Staff. I thought it would be better out here. Get it off my mind. . . ."

The tent flap flew open and Sergeant Dreyfuss, bare-chested, poked in his head.

"Lieutenant, listening post says they think they saw movement. They want to blow off a flare."

Kahn got to his feet. "Yeah—okay; roust out a crew. Where was it?"

"In the draw just to the right of the Second Squad machine-gun pit."

"What'd they see?"

"Not sure—just something moving, they think. Probably, ain't nothin'."

"Yeah. Better safe than sorry—tell 'em to keep their eyes peeled." Dreyfuss disappeared, and Kahn poured himself a cup of coffee. "Those bastards are getting like the Vietnamese. They keep seeing things—it's the third time this week." He sat back down and lit a cigarette, drew a lungful of smoke and coughed violently. "These damned things are going to kill me yet. I'm up to three packs a day."

Holden was fiddling with a compass on the field desk, turning it this way and that, watching the needle spin.

"It's the pits about your girl, Frank," Kahn said. "She sounded pretty sharp till this guy Widenfield got hold of her. Why the hell they fall for the older guys I don't know—but they do. You know, I had a girl once myself—or at least, I thought I did—just before we shipped out. She was a . . . ah . . . aw, hell—that's another story. You want some coffee?"

"Billy," Holden said. He put the compass aside. "If you're serious about this phosphate thing . . . you know, I would like to try it. It sounds crazy as hell, but at this point—"

The crack of the mortar interrupted him, and they both turned toward the tent opening. The flare cast an eerie glow over the hillside, floating gently into the paddy fields, where it extinguished itself in the muck.

"Seeing ghosts again," Kahn said crossly. He ground

out the cigarette on the dirt floor. "We still gotta get this damned hill..."

"You think so?"

"I know so. There's three or four thousand people in that valley—all rice farmers—except maybe for one night a year. Then they stop being rice farmers and start being VC. Ol' Papa-san and Mamma-san and Baby-san all got a rifle or grenade buried somewhere, and when they get the word they dig 'em up and come out of the woodwork and *whammo*, no more Bravo Company. Sun comes up next day and they're rice farmers again—till the next time."

"Doesn't sound too encouraging for the Far East Phosphate Company," Holden said.

"I guess not," Kahn said.

RIFLE FIRE shattered the stillness, and seconds later a spate of excited unintelligible words were shouted out in the night. There was more rifle fire, but it was impossible to tell who was shooting at what. Kahn leaped up and ran outside, Holden close behind him. People were running everywhere and cursing in the darkness. Quick little yellow flashes were coming from half a dozen places on the forward slope. An explosion burst on the right side of the perimeter. Dreyfuss came panting up to Kahn, weaponless and still naked except for his underwear. "We're being hit, sir," he said.

"I can see that," Sergeant," Kahn said irritably. "What have you done about it?"

"First Platoon's got the right, and ...ah... I can't really tell what's going on yet.... They—"

"Get on down there and find out," Kahn barked. Two grenades burst far downhill. The tiny yellow flashes continued in periodic staccato.

"What can I do?" Holden said loudly. He was standing in sort of a half-crouch.

"Hang tight—let's see what we've got." Kahn grabbed a frantic-looking soldier running past him. "Go up and tell Lieutenant Range I want two of his squads to take up positions down there—on the left. Take off." The man disappeared uphill.

"Mortars! Where the hell are the mortars?" Kahn bellowed upslope.

"Waiting for data," a voice called down out of the blackness.

"Fuck that!" Kahn roared. "Line of sight. Walk 'em up." He turned to Holden.

"Go raise Battalion—they're probably already on the horn. Tell them what's happening and stand by. Goddamn it!" he spat, "I knew we should have got our asses off this hill."

Holden took off for the radio tent. The first mortar rounds went off with their peculiar clanking sound. As he passed the mortar pits, he could barely make out half-naked men working feverishly over the tubes, sweating and cursing. The amount of profanity required to operate a mortar astonished him.

In his first real combat, Holden was satisfyingly relieved—if not pleasantly surprised—not to be frozen stiff with fear. From time to time, he had worried about it—that when it got down to the real nitty-gritty he wouldn't be able to stand the gaff and would disgrace in one humiliating moment two hundred years of Holden military honor. But he was doing all right, even though he was scared. And as he trotted along, he realized he was going to be able to function and perhaps perform a useful service.

The first mortar volley burst downslope, and the second rounds were firing off. Fearful cursing issued from the pits and elsewhere. Holden had the radiotelephone in his hand and pressed the bar to speak. Hot damn, he thought, this is really something! He wished Becky could see him now.

"WHAT STARTED IT?" Patch asked imperturbably. He leaned back in his chair, a cigar clenched in his teeth. Behind him through the tiny window of the Quonset hut, Kahn watched the banks of gray rain clouds, but there had been no rain today.

"LP asked for illumination; then all hell broke loose. I think maybe we fired first."

"What makes you think it was a probe, then? How do you know it wasn't just a patrol caught with their pants down?"

"Well, they were halfway up the slope."

"And you weren't mortared?"

"No, sir."

"Rockets?"

"No, sir."

"Grenades?"

"I believe there were grenades. We were throwing them too—I'm not actually sure that—"

"And they fired only in your right sector, that right?"

"Yessir."

"And broke off after, what? Five, ten minutes?"

"That's about right."

Patch pushed the black eyeglasses to the top of his head and squinted at his Company Commander. "Well, that doesn't sound like much of a probe to me," he said peevishly. "Sounds like your boys caught some of them going to pay a visit to their women or—"

"Sir, they were halfway up the slope . . ."

"That slope cuts off half the distance to that first string of hamlets—does it not? They probably didn't want to get caught out in the paddies. So they could have been trying to save time, right?"

"Colonel," Kahn said, determined to stand his ground. "I believe we were probed last night and that within a few days we are going to be hit hard. I ask your permission to move my men off that hill and set up farther down the valley."

Patch removed the cigar and knocked off a fat ash.

"Billy, this is well-plowed ground. I put you on that hill for a very specific purpose: because it is strategic to the valley. It commands the approach to the only road in and gives a clear view of the AO, and there isn't another spot in the area that does that. Besides, I want to leave the gooks with a clear impression that we are there to stay."

"Sir, I have got some problems out there. The hill is one of them. I am concerned about a full-scale attack and our ability to—"

"Damn it, now," Patch said irritably, "you have what is in effect an American rifle company reinforced with the whole array of artillery and air support, and you are situated on some of the finest fighting terrain in this country. You could stand off an entire regiment—let alone whatever raggedy-assed VC might be floating around out there. The only thing you haven't done is take my suggestion to move your CP farther down so you can blanket the perimeter with mortars. Am I going to have to order you to do that, or what?"

"No, sir, you won't have to order me to do it. But that's not the only problem. I've been having some trouble with the men...."

He told Patch about the mood since Trunk had died. The threats and the insubordination and the unwillingness to pitch in and the rest of it.

"I just think it might help if we were to move somewheres else—kind of a fresh start. It's gotten so bad I've got men wanting to come in and see the Chaplain."

"Chaplain—what about?" Patch seemed to take interest.

"About the war...I guess, and whatever they're doing....What I'm saying is that morale is pretty low....This morning I had a man who I just found out is the son of a Congressman asking to see the Chaplain; he—"

"Congressman—what Congressman?" Patch exclaimed. "What's his name?"

"Miter. He's an ammo—"

"I don't care what he does. Jesus Christ—who's his father?"

"He's a Congressman, like I say—he didn't say where from or anything. He just wanted to see the Chaplain."

"What's his problem?"

"I'm not sure exactly. I think he's just lost his stomach for the Army—"

"He has, has he?" Patch interrupted. "Well that's just dandy—a Congressman's son. So where is he now?"

"I suppose he's with the Chaplain. I brought him in with me on the chopper this morning."

"Well, I don't like anybody seeing the damned Chaplain," Patch said crossly. "If they got that kind of problem, send them to me. This could mean real trouble, Kahn." Patch stood up and looked out the window, puffing on the cigar.

"Sir, it's every man's right to see the Chaplain. . . ."

"Yes, yes, I know that. What I mean is, you don't have to encourage it."

Kahn said nothing, and there followed a long and annoying silence during which Patch puffed on the cigar and raised a dense cloud of blue smoke.

"All right," he said finally. "I want you to keep me posted on this boy. No special treatment. Just keep me posted."

"Yessir," Kahn said.

"Now," Patch said. He reached into a drawer behind him and drew out a large terrain map, unrolled it and placed an ashtray over one corner, flattening the other two edges with his hand.

"I was going to save this for a few days, but so long as you are here I might as well let you in on it now. Since you're so anxious to get the hell off that hill, I'm going to give you a chance—at least, some of you. How would you like to lead a patrol on a special job outside the valley—a nice long patrol?"

Kahn looked at Patch. He was still slightly afraid of him, and disliked himself for it. God only knew what he had in store now. But there was still only one answer.

"Sir, I'd take them to Rangoon if it would get us out of that valley," he said hopefully. It was a lie, but what else could he say?

"You won't have to go that far," Patch said cheerfully, "and you'll still have to defend the hill with whatever you leave behind. But it might be a pleasant little expedition."

29

SINCE FIRST gray light they had been climbing higher and higher through the mean tangle of growth that covered the mountain slope like the fur of some bush-dwelling animal. Aside from an occasional burst of profanity, the slip-and-stumble progress of Kahn's little party had been free of banal chatter as they struggled to crest the hill by noon and meet their next objective: to work through the mysterious, unnamed valley that lay on the other side.

They were to engage any "targets of opportunity," but the mission was largely exploratory. The valley had been charted only roughly on the current maps. Aerial reconnaisance revealed no signs of population or enemy activity, but it was designated "suspicious" for that very reason. It was approximately eight miles long and three miles wide and there was a river running through it, but beyond that it remained a mystery—a condition especially annoying to military commanders—and General Butterworth had decreed it should not be so any longer. A week earlier, he had ordered Patch to detach a warrant officer from the Topographical Engineers and get up a party to go out there and find out what the hell was going on. Out of this was born The Crazy Horse Patrol.

As Kahn stumbled over a slippery mush of rotting logs and vines, he was wondering how Brill was going to make out back on The Tit. Once he had decided to bring Holden along there hadn't been much choice, since Brill was senior to the other officers, and aside from the balking incident on The Fake and his occasional unpredictability, Brill had become a pretty tough platoon commander. He inspired an odd kind of loyalty in his own men and handled most of his discipline problems himself, which was more than could be said for the others. But sometimes Kahn wondered about Brill and the balking incident. There were times when he suspected Brill might have put them up to it—or if not, had at least winked at it. He remembered the exchange of glances between Brill and Groutman. But there was no way of proving this, and he had other things to worry about anyway.

"Lieutenant," a muffled voice said from ahead, "point's got to the top." The column had stopped, breathing heavily, looking on both sides into the dark woods. Kahn turned to Hepplewhite, the Clerk.

"Go back and get Lieutenant Holden up here. And pass the word there'll be a smoke break." Just as he said it, the sun broke through the tops of the trees—the first time anyone had seen it in weeks. Little patches of brightness grew on the forest floor and danced on the dripping fronds of vines and ferns.

Looking down, Kahn watched his new Executive Officer hauling up the steep slope, rifle slung over his shoulder, .45 strapped on his hip—thin and spare, lean

and mean as he climbed past the line of idle men. He
certainly did *look* like an Infantry officer.

THE VIEW from the crest of the hill was not what anyone
had expected.

Instead of a sinister hellhole of twisted jungle, they
looked down on an open, green glade, surrounded by
majestic jagged mountain peaks, some of them cliff-faced,
from which occasional waterfalls cascaded down, pooling
up at the bottom, then running in narrow streams into the
slow-moving river that meandered down the center of the
valley.

Tall pine trees ringed the edge of the valley, and there
were clusters of smaller trees around the pools. The earth
looked green and solid in the sparkling sunlight, and they
saw no signs of cultivation or other human presence.
Below them, but still high above the valley, an eagle
soared and dipped, casting its shadow on the ground.

"Just look at that, Lieutenant," Crump said, standing
at the edge, looking down. On his shoulder the
banana-cat perched precariously, and cheeped and
chattered.

"Will you shut that damned thing up!" Kahn said
peevishly.

Crump stroked the banana-cat's head and it fell silent.
At the last minute he had decided to bring it along. There
was no need to tie it up anymore, because it had become
quite tame and was deeply devoted to Crump. Most of the
time, not even Lieutenant Kahn seemed to mind having it
around. They fed it C rations and it also foraged for mice
and frogs that lived in the foxholes, and when Crump
took it to the field it liked to ride inside his pack and sleep.

The boulder-strewn slope provided many footholds,
and in less than an hour they had descended single file into
the pine grove. The valley floor was a plush, spongy
carpet of mossy grass, and the sky was bright blue and
clear now except for a few wispy cumuli that sailed
overhead in the direction from which they had marched.
The sunshine was bright and warm but not at all hot, and
the air in the valley was as still and fresh as a spring

morning. As they moved into the open ground, they heard the barking of deer from the pine grove and came upon various fruit-bearing trees, some containing parrots and parakeets and even an occasional monkey. They stopped for a break at the first pond—a shallow pool with a pebble bottom. In the shadows of reeds around the edges they glimpsed the forms of some large, orange-colored carplike fish.

The men lay around in the sunshine, smoking, some eating C rations, talking and laughing and filling their canteens from the clear mountain water. The change in the weather and the benevolent lushness were acting as a marvelous restorative serum, and they began to resemble the rough-and-tough nineteen-year-olds Kahn remembered from when he had first joined the Company—so long ago it seemed, but only a little more than a year. There were some new faces now, and ones missing, but even the familiar ones had changed. Perhaps it was the light of the sun, which had not shone upon them for so long. It gave a burnished, glowing cast to the skin and made them squint. Still, there was something in those faces that no amount of sunshine could have put there—or taken away: a dark, almost haunted look of an animal that has slaughtered its first prey.

Kahn yawned. The sun felt good on his face. The warrant officer from the Office of Topographical Services walked up beside him with a folding drawing board on which he had taped the old map of the valley.

"See that hill range over there?" the warrant officer said. "Now look at it here on this map: they only got four crests—and you can see at least seven from here."

Kahn looked at the chain of mountains stretching westward. They glowed a deep blue-green.

"And see this river here: they say here 'fifty meters'—couldn't be more than twenty."

"What's this?" Kahn asked, indicating a grease-pencil notation on the face of the map.

"Just clowning around a little," the warrant officer said. "Thought I'd give the place a working name."

Under the legend, he had written in the name "Happy Valley." He had also given names to the major terrain features.

The stand of tall pines was called the "Yum-Yum Woods," and the stream running through the center was the "Crystal River." The peaks to the right were the "Sugar Plum Mountains," and the long, wavering hill to the south he had named "Candy Cane Ridge."

"We never really get to name stuff in my shop," the warrant officer said—"just numbers is all. Can't go on the update, but it might stick for you guys."

Kahn nodded and told the warrant officer about naming The Tit, and the various other names they had thought up for the valleys and ravines around it.

"That's one thing they're real serious about in my shop," the warrant officer said. "You can't name anything dirty or obscene."

"What's so obscene about a tit?" Kahn frowned.

"I don't know," the warrant officer said, "but they wouldn't let you put it on a map."

THEY PRESSED on into the afternoon sun, and the farther they marched, the lovelier the valley seemed to be.

Exquisite orchidlike wild flowers grew in abundance, and some of the men began adorning their clothing and gear with them. After a mile or so, many were festooned as if in an Easter parade, and there was laughter and whistling and horseplay, and several times Kahn had to bawl them out about keeping discipline in ranks.

Even so, he felt the carnival spirit himself. The mood of blackness that had hung over them for so long seemed to have lifted. No longer were they acting like press-ganged laborers; now they were behaving more like a troop of Boy Scouts on a day's outing. But they were not, of course. They were infantrymen with mortars and rifles and hand grenades, and that was how they would have looked, despite how they might have felt, to anyone watching them move across the valley from above.

They saw great flocks of a large, pinkish heronlike bird

poking at the edges of the pools. Occasionally one of these would flap its wings and strut around almost as if it were making a gesture of welcome.

Kahn had been toying with a geologic explanation for the valley. His theory at this point was that at one time it had probably been filled with water—a huge mountain lake fed by the springs that now tumbled down from the Sugar Plum Mountains. Some time ago, perhaps less than a hundred years, the water had eaten through some permeable rock—probably limestone—at the base of Candy Cane Ridge and the lake had drained westward beneath the mountains, leaving only the Crystal River, which he was certain would disappear underground as they reached the end of the valley.

Near sundown they stopped by a clear, shallow pool. The sky had turned deeper blue, and the sun still cast a warm glow over the mountains. Kahn gave permission to go swimming and even took a dip himself in the cool water. They discovered that the sluggish carplike fish in the shallows could be caught by hand, and that night they dined on delicious fried fish and cooked bananas and wild date nuts, and the war seemed very far away.

As darkness came, a sliver of moon appeared above the jagged peaks and the sky filled with billions of bright stars. Lying on his back looking up at the spectacle, Kahn felt a peculiar surge in his brain; a sudden, startling tremor of knowledge that he had seen this place sometime, somewhere before, but could not remember where or when.

In all of us, he thought, there must be some long-forgotten cell that carries a wisp of the past; a legacy transmitted from our progenitors fifteen million years ago....

In that instant he had seen the picture so clearly, the same one they had seen then: this moon, these stars above the ragged peaks. It had finally penetrated after millions of years, an infinitesimal impulse; flashed once, then receded forever into the electric-charged tissue of his brain....

But why now? Why here?

And the picture of a huge ship appeared, it's gray belly churning relentlessly across a bottomless ocean chasm, propellers throbbing—soundless in the depths...but recordable and recorded nonetheless in the mind's eye of some Devonian creature fishtailing its way in the opposite direction...

...and passed on, an impulse of fragmented light and heat—protons and electrons spinning in their own chaotic order, embedding themselves deeply in a single cell among billions...and some small part of that, a tiny glimmer, would find its way out at a later time by way of a process so old and terrifying it could not be understood collectively but only individually by someone who has actually experienced it....

The tropic stars looked cold and hard, and Kahn closed his eyes. Soon he was sleeping as peacefully as a baby.

30

    LIEUTENANT BRILL had been doing some patrolling of his own. The same morning Kahn and Holden took off with the Crazy Horse Patrol, Brill had returned jubilantly from the largest single action the Company had seen since the fighting in the Ia Drang. He brought with him three prisoners: a man who had been carrying documents and two young nurses with medical supplies. The bodies of five more had been left behind on a trail.

    They had walked into Brill's ambush bold as brass. Madman Muntz, hiding in a clump of bamboo, had heard them first, chattering loudly as they rounded a bend. Without consultation, he depressed the trigger of his machine gun and dispatched the first three men in line. Two others fled down a branch of the trail where another section of the ambush party was waiting. The three they took prisoner had dived for some bushes and begun calling out, *"Chieu hoi,"* the accepted meaning of which was to turn oneself in voluntarily; and even though that was not exactly the case, Brill brought them in anyway and was glad he had because the man with the documents looked as if he might possess vaulable information. The nurses, on the other hand, were fourteen or fifteen years old and apparently worthless, except that they had been carrying enough medical supplies to tend a full-sized platoon.

A mood of dark satisfaction swept the encampment as news of Brill's massacre got around, not unlike the agitation that runs through schoolboy groups when two of their number engage in a fistfight. Practically all the men who had not participated in the ambush formed up around the prisoners to gawk at them, laughing and gesturing as if they had gathered at a pier to witness the display of prizewinning fish. The man, a scrawny specimen, appeared frightened as he was nudged along at rifle point, but the girls seemed placid by comparison, and perhaps even a little curious in the presence of so many youthful men.

BRILL COULD hardly contain himself. In nearly two months Bravo Company had succeeded in killing fewer than a dozen VC and had never taken one alive, and now on a single operation he had annihilated a main-force enemy squad and captured three prisoners, one of them with obviously valuable information. He was determined to find out just what this information was.

He would do this, First Lieutenant Victor Brill, and not some jerk-off back at Monkey Mountain. He wasn't just going to phone it in to any Spec./4 radio operator, either. He would wait till he had it all wrapped up in a neat little action report and give it to the colonel himself. But first, he was going to have to get the information out of these people, one way or another.

*   *   *

INSIDE THE TENT, the pressure lantern hissed furiously like a self-contained little storm. The interpreter, a boyish-looking Vietnamese, was seated at the edge of a cot, eyeing the toothless scarecrow prisoner. Brill sat at the field desk, carving up a stick of wood with the Randall knife. For nearly a minute no one had spoken.

"Ask him what his unit is again," Brill said.

The interpreter spoke, more sharply this time, and received the same reply.

"He still say he come from Nag Ho hamlet. He say VC come last night and make him go with them."

"Tell him he's lying," Brill said masterfully. The interpreter translated.

On the field desk a map of the valley was spread out, the position of the ambush marked in red grease pencil. Brill extended a cigarette, and the prisoner accepted it with a gummy grin. Brill let him take a few drags before continuing. He hadn't interrogated a prisoner in this kind of situation before, and his idea of how it might be done was drawn mostly from movies he had seen. He remembered Japs and Germans offering cigarettes to poker-faced, battle-wise American soldiers, who, of course, revealed nothing more than name, rank and serial number. But he figured the method was probably as good as any.

"Ask him where the VC are," Brill said.

The interpreter spoke with the prisoner.

"He say VC in the mountains. He say VC come into his house yesterday and take him along."

"Ask him exactly where in the mountains," Brill said impatiently. "Tell him to show me on this map."

The prisoner and interpreter conversed for a moment. "He say he not know where they are, Lieutenant. He say he not VC. . . ."

"Fuck that!" Brill roared. He jumped up and slammed the knife into the top of the desk. The prisoner seemed impressed by this display, and his eyes darted back and forth between Brill and the interpreter.

Brill leaned across the desk so that his nose was only inches from the prisoner's.

"Where?" he howled.

Breathing in the prisoner's face, Brill reached down and worked the Randall knife out of the desk. The man's eyes followed pleadingly as Brill brought the blade upward toward his bare stomach so that the point just touched the man's navel.

Slowly the prisoner shifted his gaze to the terrain map on the desk, looking as though he had been asked to comprehend an immensely complicated mathematical problem.

"Tell him again," Brill said. "I want to know where his unit is located." As the interpreter spoke, Brill gently inserted the blade into the hollow of the navel until he felt it touch the knubby skin inside. The prisoner tensed and made a choked-off animal-like sound, more of fear than of pain. They stood there that way for nearly a minute. Finally the man spoke.

"He say they in the mountains," the interpreter said.

"I know they're in the mountains!" Brill hissed, still glaring into the prisoner's face. "Does he suppose I think they're bivouacked in the goddamn rice paddies?" He jabbed the point of the knife a little harder and twisted. The prisoner flinched, and a thin trickle of blood appeared at the lip of the navel and ran down into his pants. The prisoner said something very terse, but a smile came across the interpreter's face.

"Ah," he said, "he say they in mountain by Hung Lap hamlet. Have camp there."

"Good," Brill said. "Now we're getting somewhere. . . ."

The navel torture went on for nearly an hour. Each time Brill asked a question he gave the knife a little flick, and the prisoner got more and more specific in his answers until Brill had ascertained that he was a low-ranking sergeant in a VC company that had been terrorizing the valley for years and that the company was equipped with mortars and heavy machine guns, and took its orders from a North Vietnamese cadre, and other interesting things.

Brill would have liked nothing better than to saddle up and go after them, but he knew Patch would never approve of it. It would have been the perfect operation, from start to finish, provided this bastard wasn't lying—but what kind of man would lie when his navel was being cut out?

IT HAD started to rain, a downpour that trickled off into a sprinkle and promised to annoy them through the night. Brill was finishing his interrogation of the prisoner when he heard his name called from outside the tent.

"Yeah?" Brill said, and a drenched soldier entered and stood before him in the dim lantern light.

"Ah, Lieutenant, I, uh, was just down at your platoon, and, ah, I think you . . . might want to go down there, sir." The soldier looked embarrassed and took off his helmet. He saw the prisoner, but did not look at him.

"Oh, yeah? What for?" Brill said icily.

"Well, sir, it's them nurses. The ones they captured today. . . . Ah, I ain't sure, 'cause I was just by there to see a buddy and it was dark and all, but I think somebody might be, uh . . . fooling with them or something. . . ."

Brill was standing in front of the prisoner, but had dropped the knife to his side. "What's that supposed to mean?"

"Well, sir, like I say . . . I was just down there to see a buddy and I didn't see nothing, except that there was some talk and I heard some sounds, ah, woman sounds . . . coming from in one of the foxholes. But I think you better get down there, sir, that's all I came up here to say."

"What's your name, soldier?" Brill said.

"Poats, sir—Weapons Platoon," he said apologetically.

"I'll tell you what, Poats: if I were you I wouldn't worry about what's going on in Second Platoon. I'm running this company now and I know what the hell is going on in it, and everything's under control. Whatever you saw or heard down there is Second Platoon's business and not yours."

"Yessir, ah . . . I'm sorry, sir, I just thought you might want to go down there and ah . . ." Poats stopped and began fidgeting with the helmet in his hands. "Sir, I'll be getting on back to the mortars now," he said, and disappeared into the darkness and rain.

Brill put the knife down on the table and told the interpreter to take the prisoner outside and tie him up. He'd found out what he wanted to know. After they had gone, he lit a cigarette and settled back on Kahn's cot, one arm folded behind his head. The lantern hissed and sputtered out, but he made no effort to relight it. As he lay in the darkness he tried to imagine what kind of fun his guys were having with the two nurses. To hell with it, he thought. They're entitled. They did well for him today—his men, his friends!

So what if people like Kahn, and that asshole Inge, and those two new queers, Range and Peck—and that snotty new Exec, Holden—so what if they treated him like shit? He'd tried to be friendly. He'd tried talking to them. But he wasn't going to kiss ass for anything.

Brill knew how that kind of thing went. When he was in military school they had ignored him too. They'd all go out weekends, and the ones with cars all said, "We don't have no room, Brill." And like shit they hadn't! He'd seen them—two, three people in the cars—and when his old man finally gave him money to buy his own car himself, it had been the same. They all said, "Well, I told so-and-so I'd go out with them," and finally he'd started hanging around with freshmen who weren't old enough to drive and didn't give a damn who they went with—but even they didn't pay him any attention, and as soon as they got their licenses they abandoned him too, and the last couple of years he'd spent his time with townies who went to the public school sometimes and hung around the pool hall and got into fights, and he'd even gotten into a few himself.

Yeah, screw them—screw 'em all, Brill thought. There were guys like Ed Groutman and Harley, and Maranto—*they* were his friends. He could sit around with them and tell stories and they didn't act like they didn't want him around. So tonight, by God, he'd given them a present . . . some present, too. . . . And tomorrow assholes like Patch and the others would all know what kind of officer Victor Brill was. They might even give him a medal. Ha! fuck medals—he didn't want any. He just wanted them to know...

Outside he heard a noise: a shrill, high-pitched cry too far away for him to tell the source or reason. Brill closed his eyes and returned to what was probably going on down there. Those two girls. Those two murdering zip cunts. Just thinking about it made him excited, and he opened his fly and began to stroke himself.

"What do you want us to do with these two?" Sergeant Groutman had asked.

And hadn't he told them: "They look pretty dangerous to me, Ed—they'd kill you as soon as look at you, all you boys...."

And everyone had laughed, and Groutman said, "Mind if we 'interrogate' 'em, Lieutenant?" and Brill said, "You guys do what you want," and walked away smiling, as if he had given a dog a bone.

31

CRYSTALLINE DROPLETS of morning dew sparkled on the grass and flowers in Happy Valley as the sun appeared fresh and blood red above the Sugar Plum Mountains. The Crazy Horse Patrol had been stirring around for half an hour, and there was a smell of coffee in the air and the sounds of people splashing at the edges of the pond they had camped beside. The sense of serenity had lasted through the night, and as they sorted and adjusted things in preparation for the day's work, their mood was that of adventurers rather than manhunters.

Two hours later they had covered more than four miles of ground, and it had been easy going, with frequent breaks for the officer of Topographical Services to make notations. They were preparing to move on from one of these rest periods when someone saw the house.

It was hidden in dense foliage and partly covered with giant creeping vines. The sides and thatched roof were a weathered chocolate, and it seemed strange and out of place in the noonday sun. They moved on it cautiously, rifles at the ready, and inevitably the tenseness began to seep back. There were things to worry about again, all related directly to the house and what it stood for.

Quickly they discovered two things: first, it was not merely a single house, but part of a tiny village of half a dozen buried deep in the thicket; second, the village had been deserted for a long time. There were few clues as to why it was here or what had become of its occupants.

There was no evidence of farming, so the former residents must have been hunters—yet it was unusual for hunters to contruct such elaborate houses. Moreover, there departure must have been very hasty, because of the sundry things left behind. Articles of clothing and other household items were hanging on the walls or left lying about as though they had been in use moments before the previous tenants departed. Various utensils surrounded the blackened ashes of cooking fires, and pots and pans were ringed with some long-ossified substance of food as though the inhabitants had simply dropped everything they were doing in a mad dash to get away.

Foliage had all but swallowed some of the ghost-town huts, but they brushed this aside and searched in a workmanlike way until it was established that there was nothing there to harm them, and afterward began automatically congregating in the clearing at the center of the village around a small pond covered with smelly green slime. The officer from Topographical Services had been moving around busily, pacing off distances, measuring angles and writing on his map when Kahn walked up to him.

"About done?"

"Just about," he said, and showed Kahn the map, on which he had penciled in the words "Gingerbread Village."

"Still at it, huh?"

The warrant officer nodded and smiled.

"What do you make of this?" Kahn asked, pointing to an arrow under which had been written, "The Ghost Town Trail."

"I walked down it a little ways. I'm not sure if it was made by animals or people; seems to lead toward the river."

"The Crystal River," Kahn said wryly.

"Yeah, Crystal River," said the officer of Topographical Services. "I'd be curious to see where it goes."

THEY HAD not been on the Ghost Town Trail for long when the blood bees found them.

The midday sun was whiter and seemed hotter than the day before, and the sky had turned a hazy blue-gray. Yet the air remained still and cool beneath the treetops above the trail. They still had not encountered any dense jungle and could see forty or fifty yards on both sides and ahead, where the forest floor was green with ferns and low-lying flora. The blood bees appeared from nowhere.

All at once there was a thin humming in the air and a sense of flying things, and within minutes everyone in the column had been bitten several times. In a curtain of profanity they began rolling down their sleeves and swatting wildly around their faces. The bees were small, perhaps half the size of a normal bee, but they descended on human skin like mosquitoes, sucking blood until they were either squashed or brushed away. They seemed to come from everywhere, millions of them, buzzing, hovering and darting all across the forest floor. It was maddening—but no one had promised it was going to be easy.

It took an hour to reach the Crystal River, and the blood bees remained with them along the way. The point squad stopped short when they heard the gurgling of the stream ahead and then crept slowly up to the bank while the rest held up in their tracks along the trail. Kahn sent for Holden to join him and go up for a look.

They hadn't walked ten steps when a burst of gunfire crushed such hopes as remained that the war had somehow overlooked their newfound paradise.

The point squad had been standing quietly in some thick plants near the riverbank when the North Vietnamese soldier appeared on the other side. He hadn't even bothered to look around, but simply emerged from the bushes and strolled to the water's edge. He was weaponless but unmistakably enemy, pith helmet and all, and his trousers were neat and clean as though they might even have been recently pressed. He dropped them and squatted into the stream to defecate.

Crump spotted him first, and then the others did, but they were all too startled to do anything. Recovering, Crump laid down his blooker and snatched a rifle from the man nearest him.

"Hate to do this to anybody in that position, but he oughtn't be fouling the river," Crump whispered as he flicked off the safety.

The first shot struck the man in his back, and the other hit him in the neck. He teetered precariously for a second or two before toppling into his own mess, thrashing around like a speared fish, then floating gently downstream toward them—the penultimate "target of opportunity."

Kahn and Holden arrived in time to see the body float by. By now the point squad had spread out warily in the bushes, anticipating more trouble.

"Caught him with his pants down, Lieutenant," Crump said matter-of-factly. He pointed the muzzle of his blooker gun toward where the man had fallen.

Kahn gazed at the spot for a few seconds, dimly aware that he was in charge. "Well, we can't stay the hell here now," he said to Holden. "Let's wheel it upstream and cross there . . . and, uh, you'd better get Battalion on the horn and tell them we've made contact and they should stand by." He looked again at the spot where the man had taken his final constitutional. "Whoever they are, they know we're here—thanks to the efforts of Private Crump," he said grimly, but without disapproval.

They waded across the river and moved stealthily through a grove of banana trees, and found themselves at the edge of a large horseshoe-shaped clearing overgrown in elephant grass. Except for the man by the river they had seen no signs of the enemy, but it would have been high folly to assume he had been alone. A bank of grayish clouds was gathering above the Candy Cane Ridge, and the air had become sluggish, but not oppressive. The blood bees, though fewer now, still buzzed and stung. It was nothing to compare with the surprises of the Ia Drang or the Valley of The Tit, but neither was it as comfortable as yesterday, or even today, before they had entered the abandoned Gingerbread Village. That was where it had all started to change, almost as if their presence there had violently disturbed some evil thing.

Holden was near the rear of the formation, close to a radio and to the officer from Topographical Services, as they crossed the open space. Ahead, the lead elements moved nakedly through the waist-high grass, shoulders hunched over and slightly bent, as if they wanted to go into a crouch but were embarrassed to do so without so much as a shot's being fired. A short, pale-complexioned soldier at Holden's side was moving his head from side to side as if he were watching a tennis match. His eyes blinked rhythmically, as though they were gulping for air.

Holden fought to keep down a burble of hot stomach fluid that was rising in his throat like mercury. Even in the midst of fifty heavily armed men he felt very much alone. Not scared, but alone. At least, not scared in any way he had known before. Maybe he was too frightened to be scared. Maybe he wasn't scared at all—who knew? Who cared? The line of trees danced and shimmered in the sun, and her face appeared as it had been doing, on and off, all morning. He had come all the way out here to take his medicine, but she followed him anyway—her face. Her body . . .

It was not always unpleasant. Sometimes when he pictured her he remembered the good times they had had, and he would forget that she had decided to go with Widenfield. But sooner or later that fact returned. He saw her hanging on to Widenfield, having breakfast with him, lying beside the fire with him. The one thing he *never* allowed himself to imagine was her actually screwing him. Frequently he would see her face—hair spread out, tossing her head from side to side, eyes open to tiny slits, her tongue flickering out of her mouth; big breasts heaving, her nipples stiff and wonderful, passionate sounds coming from her mouth, her legs curled up around... HIM!—not Widenfield, but *him*—and that was the way he always remembered it. Him and not Widenfield. If only he could get to her right now, he thought, to tell her... he knew he could put it right! He had written so many letters, but sent none of them....

Maybe Kahn was right. Maybe he should just write her off as tough shit and think about other things—like joining the Far East Phosphate Company—and stop worrying about love and marriage and getting locked into an office job and a house in Scarsdale—solemn thoughts anyway, when you were twenty-four years old. He scanned the fanned-out sweating men ahead, and suddenly it occurred to him that if an army could be conscripted of no one but jilted men, there wouldn't be a force on earth that could beat them, because they would be the meanest sonsofbitches in the world.

IT STARTED up ahead—a ferocious tearing sound all around, and ripping, whizzing noises in the air. As he dropped to his knees looking for a place to hide, Holden caught a glimpse of a man falling ahead. A bullet had caught him in front and spun him completely around. He seemed to hang in the air for a moment before crashing down. His eyes were shut, and his mouth was a great black hole, but no sound had come from it—at least, no sound that could be heard. His rifle preceded him to the ground, and his elbows were drawn in to his sides and elevated high in the air as though he had been caught in the middle of a chin-up.

Holden slithered over to a hummock, which turned out to be an anthill, and hid there wondering what to do next. All worries of love and rejection had vanished. His world was suddenly reduced to minuscule proportions no broader than the distance between nose and dirt. Around

him a zillion insects scampered here and there, the peace
of their day disturbed by the transactions of men at war.
So far as he could tell, nobody on either side of him was
doing anything more than he was. The air above his head
was filled with deadly projectiles, and there was nothing
to do but hang on, which he did for what seemed like a
long time but was actually only a minute or so. During
that period he was in a good position to observe the
frantic comings and goings of the ant colony, of which he
was now practically a part—as were the others, pressed to
the ground with the ants and other crawling things. They
had become—Holden thought mirthlessly—a company
of ant-men, who by definition had very low horizons.

"Horse Two, Horse Two, what is your location?"

Holden suddenly realized that the violent tugging at his
sleeve was the RTO, who had jammed the handset into his
face. It carried the voice of Kahn.

"Horse One, this is Horse Two," Holden said back into
the device.

"Horse Two, what is your location? Over." Kahn
sounded very businesslike.

"Uh. I'm, ah, behind an anthill." He knew that sounded
dumb as soon as the words left his mouth.

"Horse Two, can you see me? Over." Kahn said,
ignoring the remark.

"Negative, Horse One. I am pinned down here—I can't
tell where from yet—I think it's coming from the tree
line."

"Well, it's coming all around us up here," Kahn replied
gruffly. "Can you move two squads to my right toward
the tree line and lay down some fire?—We have to get the
hell out of here." Holden thought Kahn sounded
remarkably calm for someone in his predicament. He
sounded almost as if he were falling asleep, which was
frustrating for Holden and almost made him mad.

"Ah, roger, Horse One, wait one." Holden extended
the handset back to the RTO, who was flattened down
beside him. He hadn't stuck his head up since the first
shots were fired, and since he was an officer his job was to
do exactly that.

Cautiously he peeked above the anthill and looked around, but could see nothing except grass. Pulling his knees under him, he rose behind the anthill as far as he could, then sprang upward like a jumping jack, took two quick looks around and threw himself to the earth again, motioning for the radio.

He caught a glimpse of Kahn's men lying maybe fifty yards ahead, deep inside the end of the horseshoe-shaped clearing. He had seen no enemy, but they were obviously firing from the line of trees, which extended in front and on both sides of the spot where Kahn was, and Holden figured that if they weren't in it all the way back here, he could probably get to within twenty yards of Kahn... maybe closer... without being spotted.

"I think so," he said.

"No 'I think so'!" Kahn barked. "You'll have to do it. Try to move straight to the tree line and then come forward about thirty meters. Really pour it on them—and shake it up; I've got to pull back quick."

Holden crawled off to the left, where he remembered a couple of squads had disappeared when the shooting started. He came on three men lying in a little indentation beside the unassembled components of a mortar. Lying on his belly, Holden addressed them from about five yards away: "I need you people. Get the rest of your squad and follow me. We have to move up."

"Sir," came a muffled response, "that's way too close. We couldn't do no more good there with mortars than we could here."

"I don't care about mortars; I need a fire team," Holden said loudly.

The three men looked at each other darkly. "Sir," one of them said, "We're the mortar squad; what are we gonna do with the mortars? We can't take 'em with us."

"Screw it—leave 'em here," Holden said. He was beginning to feel panicky. A bullet kicked up dust behind him.

The man who had spoken looked at him as though he had just been told to take a flying leap off a high place. "Lieutenant, we can't leave 'em here—these are the mortars..."

Holden glared at the man, suddenly realizing he was right and trying to figure out what to do next. The RTO solved the problem by handing him the handset.

"Jesus God, where are you?" Kahn screamed. "We're being penetrated up here!"

"With the mortar squad," Holden shouted back. His face felt flushed and tingled. Again he had said the wrong thing. A longer explanation was required.

"For chrissake, we can't . . ." There was a lull as Kahn's voice trailed off. The sound of a heavy machine gun came from the trees and there were several explosions. Holden rose on his elbows and tried to see what was going on, but his view was limited to the tops of the grass and the white, sickly sky. Ant-men, he thought.

Kahn came back on the radio. "Okay, forget it—we've got to pull back right now. Get everybody you can to pour it on that tree line ahead of us—and keep it a little high—but everything they've got—and forget about mortars—got it?"

"Roger," Holden said, and took off on his belly to give The Word.

In less than a minute they came pouring back, some crawling, some flat on their stomachs, some loping apelike. The covering fire Holden had instigated was doing its job. Panting, bug-eyed, dragging his rifle behind him, Kahn collapsed behind the indentation in the ground and lay on his back, trying to catch his breath.

"Air strike coming," he said between gasps. "Let's get our asses back across the damned river." He looked at Holden's grime-covered face and grinned. "How ya like the Real Army, Princeton?"

"I'd rather be digging phosphate," Holden croaked.

THE MORTAR SQUAD, the officer of Topographical Services and assorted other elements were sent to ford the river and set up a defensive position on the other side. The plan was that the rest would shoot like crazy and then the jets would swoop down and blast the line of trees and they could retire. It was the standard school solution—except that the North Vietnamese had thoughtfully sent some people around to flank the riverbank ahead of them.

Kahn realized what had happened the instant he heard firing from behind and was already working on a new plan when a terrified red-haired private with a blood-soaked ankle collapsed into the Headquarters party with news that the enemy had not only flanked them, but *were* on the other side of the river, and in force. The River Blindness again, Kahn thought, and then the jets began to scream overhead.

Kahn was talking over the radio with a foreward air controller cruising somewhere overhead when he saw the North Vietnamese moving toward them out of the treeline.

Everyone else saw them at about the same time, and there was a rising crackle of rifle fire. About twenty yards ahead, a man stood up and hurled a grenade at the advancing force. In mid-throw he was hit by one or more bullets and flew backward through the air as though he had been struck in the face with a bat. Everyone in the Headquarters party saw this. Judging the instantaneous strike of the bullet, it was probable that the shot had not actually been aimed at the man, but that by some stroke of bad luck he had simply risen up into it. In either case, he was now sprawled on the ground—whether wounded or dead no one knew.

Meanwhile, the two machine guns attached to the Crazy Horse Patrol had come to life and temporarily stalled the enemy attack. Kahn was craning over the top of the indentation when he saw a soldier rushing toward the spot where the hapless grenadier had fallen.

It was Carruthers, the giant Negro from Savannah—recognizable by his huge form; out of some unfathomable impulse he had gone to aid the wounded, or dead, man. He got to within five yards of him when he was sent reeling sideways by a burst of automatic-weapons fire. "Lookit that dumb nigger," Bateson, the RTO, said. "He's gonna get his ass wasted." Still on his feet, Carruthers resumed course and was struck a second time and knocked flat on his butt. He sat staring for a moment before staggering to his feet and continuing toward the fallen man. A third burst of fire caught him in the chest, virtually lifting the huge body off the ground, and this time he did not get up. "Aw, shit," said Bateson. He said it for all of them.

"Red smoke," Kahn said into the handset, and received some kind of acknowledgment from the air controller above. The plume of red smoke was already rising above the trees, but things had changed since he had ordered it fired.

"Hang on a minute, Skyking," he said. He craned out toward the spot where the North Vietnamese had vanished into some tall grass, just ahead of where Carruthers and the man who threw the grenade had gone down. Kahn could see nothing. For an instant he thought about the old, dilapidated row of houses in Savannah where Carruthers had grown up. He had known those old houses down on Broad Street, only a block or so from his father's junkyard, all of them long gone now, replaced by empty lots—and Carruthers; he wondered if he had ever seen him playing around there. Sometimes he used to go down to the salvage yard and wait for his father and sometimes watch the Negro children playing in the street, but he was not allowed to play with them. . . . "Dumb nigger" was what Bateson had said. . . . "Aw, shit" was right. . . .

"He can't stay up there all day, Horse One," the air controller said. "Gotta go home, chop-chop."

"Like hell he will!" Kahn thundered. "I've got a real situation down here and I need support—you hang on."

"Negative, Horse One," the pilot of the control plane said. "My boy's gotta feed his bird or down he goes—crash and burn."

"Don't give me that shit," Kahn roared. "You get me another one up there on the double, then. I'm fighting for my ass down here."

"Listen, buster"—the voice from the sky was cool and deliberate—"this is Lieutenant Colonel Stonebreaker. I assume you are *captain* somebody, so just keep your shirt on; I'm doing everything I can."

Kahn was looking out toward where the bunch of North Vietnamese had disappeared into the grass. He caught a glimpse of half a dozen more of them running in a crouch around to his left. Others spotted them too, and there was a flurry of rifle fire.

"I don't care who you are," Kahn snapped coolly into the handset. "If you don't get me a plane up there I'm not going to have any shirt left to keep on. Do you read me?"

"Loud and clear, Horse One," the airman replied. Someone handed Kahn the handset from the other radio. "It's the Old Man, sir," the someone said.

"I've got some gunships and a Medevac on the way and we're rounding up an assault force. Can you hang on?" Patch said.

"I'm not sure," Kahn replied. "All I can tell now is that we're straddled on three flanks and maybe four, and I've got Charlies damned near close enough to spit at. Only thing they haven't done yet is mortar us, and I expect that's next."

"Gunships'll be there in ten or fifteen minutes. I think we can get reinforcements in half an hour or so. Do what you can."

Kahn acknowledged the transmission and put the handset back. Another fierce burst of firing broke out in the direction where the line of North Vietnamese disappeared into the grass, and there was periodic firing all around. It didn't look good, but they were a tough bunch of boys, these boys of his.

For the next five minutes they sweated it out. The occasional firing continued, but by and large both forces simply lay hugging the ground, warily, each waiting for the other to make a move. It came soon enough when the North Vietnamese decided to close the ring.

KAHN COULDN'T get his mind off Carruthers' gallant impulse to reach the injured grenade thrower. Out of what reasoning had he decided to do it? *Hit three times—three times—and kept on going . . .* was it out of love for the man? Or that he didn't think he was going to get hurt? Or just reckless bravado? . . . He scanned the field beyond the spot where Carruthers had fallen. Nothing stirred, not even the faintest wind. No, it was none of those. It was

something else Carruthers must have felt, something
Kahn himself felt at times, had felt first during the
counterattack in the Boo Hoo Forest and was feeling
now, too. It was a crazy kind of insanity that swells in the
brain—and must have swelled in Carruthers' brain, now
freshly spilled on the dirt ahead—a short-circuiting of the
instinctive kernel of self-preservation by an impulse
which convinces an otherwise sane man that he is already
dead, so nothing matters anymore and he can operate in a
fear-free little world of his own. It was not a bad feeling,
this feeling, for it eclipsed the awful fear, and some men
were so glad to be rid of it that they would do foolhardy
things just to prove it wasn't there anymore.

Naturally, no one would explain this to Carruthers'
mother when they gave the medal to her. The citation
would read: "For an act of valor in that he, blah, blah,
blah . . ." or some such as that. Kahn would have to write
it himself, and some clerk-typist back at Headquarters
would put the finishing touches on it, standardize the
language, condense it into a paragraph or two, requisition
the medal and forward the whole business through
channels in sextuplicate so that there would be a copy for
everybody's file—Battalion's, Brigade's, Division's, Department of the Army's back in Washington, Carruthers'
own 201 file and finally one for his mother down in
Savannah, and that would be the end of that—a neat little
salutation for the dumb nigger so his mother and brothers
and sisters would have something to show people when
they came around to convey their respects.

THREE SUCCESSIVE explosions announced the enemy
assault, and the air cracked and sang with skimming
bullets. It was an act of madness to raise one's head more
than a few inches from the ground, but Kahn chanced a
look. Just then he saw three North Vietnamese in
bluish-green uniforms get up and start running toward
the outer line of their defensive perimeter. Each carried
something in his hand—a large brownish object—and
Kahn watched them for four or five seconds, bobbing his
head up and down to present a less favorable target;

reason told him this gesture was futile, but it made him feel safer to do it. The first of the North Vietnamese men was hit by a bullet and spun down into the grass. The two others hurled their objects toward the line, and a single explosion followed. Off to the right other North Vietnamese were running too, some forward and some down toward the river. Everyone was shooting like a madman.

"Green Smoke! Green Smoke! Do you roger?" Kahn shouted into the handset.

"I roger, Horse One," the air controller said. "Target is Green Smoke."

"White Smoke is me," Kahn said loudly. "I say again, White Smoke is me!"

"Roger that," the controller droned. "White Smoke is you."

Moments later he was back on the line, sounding perplexed.

"Horse One, this is Skyking—do you read?"

"Go ahead, Skyking." Kahn had been trying to dig a hole with his feet and the butt of his rifle so as to hunker down a little more. *Lord, let this work*, he thought.

"Your smoke is all mixed together, Horse One. Can you give me visual from your location? Over."

"I know it's mixed, goddamn it!" Kahn growled. "They're all in here with us. Just try to keep him to the outside edge of the white."

There was a pause on the other end.

"Wilco, Horse One," the controller said. "I hope you know what you're doing. He's going to be coming in pretty fast...."

Bateson handed Kahn the other handset.

"Horse One—Do I understand correctly that you are requesting napalm on your own position?" There was a ring of disbelief in Patch's voice—or was it disapproval?

"Negative—but very close," Kahn said. "We are in very close contact." *Negative*—what a stupid word, he thought. Why couldn't you just say "no"?

"Are you being overrun?"

"Not yet," Kahn said. He was still digging with his feet, thankful that the ground was not very hard.

"Wait one," Patch said tersely.

Wait One! WAIT ONE!—what the hell was that supposed to mean? If they didn't hurry up and . . .

Patch came back: "The general says to tell you 'good luck.'"

THE CONCUSSION of the bomb was not an earsplitting blast but an awesome volcanic tumult of roaring heat, and the gigantic orange fireball seethed and roiled upward and outward. The air became furnacelike, and for a moment Kahn thought his hands and face were on fire. In fact, they did turn reddish, and his breath was partially sucked from his mouth. The bomb must have landed a good seventy-five yards from where Kahn's Headquarters party was, and perhaps twenty-five yards from the outer edge of the perimeter, but it expanded toward them with an awful growling sound, and for a horrifying moment they all thought they were going to be consumed. Then it receded and died down, leaving small gobs of flaming jelly everywhere—some landing on men, some burning harmlessly on the ground. The whole thing took less than thirty seconds, but no one there would ever forget it as long as he lived.

As the fire died down, an uncanny silence enveloped the battlefield. Well and wounded alike were too stupefied to do anything but thank their lucky stars they had survived it. Then through the smoke and haze they heard the sounds of rotors—followed shortly by the screaming hiss of rockets and brilliant explosions all around the line of trees where the North Vietnamese had dug in. Kahn and Holden pulled together such men as were available to begin pouring fire in that direction, and for the next few minutes the field shook with the sounds of heavy battle. At some point, a helicopter pilot radioed down that he was chasing several dozen North Vietnamese fleeing toward Candy Cane Ridge, and the air controller reported that a dozen or so more had taken off in the opposite direction. Despite this information, and the fact that even from the ground it looked as if the enemy had broken contact, the Crazy Horse Patrol kept up heavy fire until Kahn got them organized and set the

mortars to laying fire along the apparent routes of retreat.
The assault force Patch had thrown together was diverted
to these areas also, to pursue and kill as many enemy as
they could.

Although they would not find this out until later, an
entire operation with a name of its own was born that
afternoon, based on their firefight at the Crystal River. It
would involve not only the Brigade, but the entire
Division and elements from other divisions, in a
two-month running battle that would be heralded in
Army press releases as the "turning point of the war."
Hundreds of enemy would die, medals would be handed
out, promotions secured, headlines made—all set into
motion by their chance encounter with the North
Vietnamese soldier who had felt an urge to relieve himself
in a stream.

But this was all to come, and there was other work to be
done. Sometime during the cleanup and evacuation of the
wounded and dead and the other tasks attendant to the
removal of the patrol from Happy Valley, Colonel Patch
informed Kahn via the field radio that he was putting him
in for a Silver Star.

NEAR DUSK, they were deposited back on The Tit—bone-
tired, but grateful to be home and out of the fighting.
Kahn was too exhausted to do much more than fall into
his cot and pass out, but something he had seen from the
helicopter as they were landing had to be cleared up first.

He trudged up the hill to the CP and dropped his gear
on the floor, except for his rifle, which he laid on his bunk,
and was going to look for Brill when Brill entered the tent
and sat down on the ammo crate.

"Hey, you guys really had some action out there, huh?"
Brill said. He seemed very animated.

"Uh-huh," Kahn said wearily, "but never mind that.
What the hell went on here?"

"Oh," Brill said, "I, ah, guess you saw the bodies, huh?"
He waited expectantly for Kahn to respond, but Kahn
merely sat looking at him, so Brill continued.

"We had a time ourselves—after you left. I guess you haven't heard, but we bagged ourselves a main-force squad yesterday...." He began telling Kahn about the ambush, and the interrogation of the prisoner, until Kahn cut him short.

"We can get back to that. What about those bodies?" Kahn fixed his gaze directly into Brill's eyes.

"I was coming to that," Brill said. "Like I say, the gook sang us a nice song, and then I got a couple of guys to tie him up for the night and I went on to sleep.

"Sometime during the night," Brill said, "the prisoner managed to get loose, but he waited till morning to make his move, probably because he felt they were less alert then. It happened about zero nine hundred," Brill said.

"The girls were with Second Platoon, and suddenly the goddamn gook pops up out of nowhere and grabs somebody's M-sixteen and he doesn't say a word, he just blasts the girls and runs off into the brush. Time my guys got it together the bastard's disappeared. I sent out a patrol, but they didn't find a trace except that he dropped the M-sixteen about twenty-five meters outside the perimeter."

Kahn eyed Brill suspiciously. What he had just heard sounded incomprehensible—but not impossible. What he had been through this afternoon would sound incomprehensible too if he had had to explain it to someone who hadn't been there.

"Why would he do that?" Kahn asked.

"Do what—kill them? I don't know, I guess—"

"No," Kahn said quietly. "Why would he drop the rifle?"

Brill seemed confused, and he stumbled for an explanation. "I guess, er, maybe he didn't want to carry it because it weighted him down or something. Who knows why these fuckers do things?"

"All right, then, why would he shoot them?" Kahn said. "He didn't shoot anyone else, right?"

"I've been trying to figure that one out myself," Brill said nervously. "The only reason I can think of is he didn't want them to go back to MI, or maybe he was afraid they knew he'd spilled his guts and they might get loose and tell his buddies or something."

"Why are they way down there outside the perimeter?" Kahn asked.

"Well, ah, I didn't want to just leave them lying there—they're gonna start to smell pretty soon and I thought it was better to get them away . . . and, ah, there's something else. . . ." He paused and shifted nervously on the crates.

"Some of the men last night, ah, they started messing around with them a little, you know. I think it started out harmless enough, but they got to messing with them, and I, ah, think the, um, less that's said about this the better, you know."

"Battalion know about this yet?" Kahn asked.

"Not yet; I was waiting to talk to you about it first. I thought . . . I mean, if they are going to get their bowels in an uproar, we might try to smooth it over a little. . . ."

"In other words, you waited so I would have to do it, huh?"

"Oh, hell, no—I just thought you'd like to get the story first so you would know what went on before the . . . ah, shit hits the fan—if it does. . . . I mean, I bet this whole thing just blows over if we don't make too much of it."

"Too much of what?" Kahn said.

"Well, the whole business—I mean, it's too bad it all happened, but there are a lot of guys involved. . . ."

"Let me tell you this," Kahn said. He felt a sudden surge of anger and cold fear through the tiredness. "Whatever happened with those girls—and I'm not even sure if I want to know—I hope you're telling the truth about it, because if you're not, and Battalion gets wind of it, we're all going to swing."

Brill nodded his head in agreement.

DURING THE next forty-eight hours, Kahn's sense of right, wrong and duty—to himself, his men and the Army— were taxed beyond anything he had known to that point in his life. Having just faced death in its pure, primitive form, he was now forced to grapple with its more sinister implications, and in so doing, he found himself enmeshed, deeper by the hour, in a web of half-truths, prevarications and lies revolving around the events of the previous night and the machinations of Lieutenant Brill.

As the monsoon gloom closed over the Valley of The Tit, he had tried to quiz Brill further about the killings of the girls, but Brill stuck to his vague story and suggested to Kahn that they simply bury them and forget about it. Before anything further could be said on the subject, they were mortared.

Only a few rounds came in, but it was enough to send the encampment into chaos and cause a general alert until the wee, early hours, after which Kahn returned to his tent, exhausted, and fell asleep, wondering when the attack would come. He was sleeping at 0800 the next morning when Colonel Patch arrived, and would have slept longer if Hepplewhite, the Clerk, had not poked his head into the tent and told him the Old Man was walking up the hill. Kahn hastily threw on his fatigue blouse and was lacing his boots when the colonel entered the tent.

"A little late to be getting up, isn't it, Billy?" But there was a smile on Patch's face when he said it. "I'll be outside when you're finished."

Kahn joined him on a knoll overlooking the northern perimeter of the positions. Below, the colonel's aide waited patiently beside the helicopter. "I'm sorry, sir; I didn't realize you were coming out. I would have—"

Patch waved him off. "No need to apologize. I was just on my way over to LZ Horse and decided to drop in to see how you were. Those mortars didn't do much damage last night, did they?"

"No, sir, they didn't," Kahn said. "Only six rounds—but I figure they were just registering. Colonel, we're going to be hit up here very soon, I'm afraid. All the signs—"

"I doubt it," Patch interrupted. "There's not a shred of evidence that a large enough VC force exists in this area to pull off any attack like that. Besides, the way you performed yesterday you shouldn't have to worry about anything. You don't know this, but when the general heard me say I was putting you in for a Silver Star, he said he would endorse it. Now, how about that?"

Kahn was still groggy from sleep, but a Silver Star was a Silver Star, and for the moment his interest changed.

"Well, Colonel, I . . . I'm grateful, but I don't think I deserve it."

"Nonsense," Patch said, "You did a very impressive thing out there, calling for napalm damned near on your own positions. You don't know this either, but what your patrol ran into was part of an NVA division. They were using the valley for their R and R. The Two Corps Commander has put two battalions in there after them, and they're fixing to throw in a whole brigade from down at Phan Rang."

"No, sir, I didn't know that," Kahn said.

When he looked at the colonel again, Kahn saw that his expression had changed.

"By the way," Patch said matter-of-factly, what are all those bodies doing down there?" He nodded downhill.

A sharp, gloomy impulse shivered up and down Kahn's spine as he suddenly remembered the interrupted conversation with Brill. "I'm really not, ah, sure, Colonel, but from what I gather, those two were prisoners, and there was a third prisoner who got loose night before last and got hold of a weapon and shot them."   -

A perplexed look crossed Patch's face. "Well, how in hell did that happen?" he said. "I don't remember any POW reports from here."

"Like I said, I'm not really sure. I haven't had time to look into it," Kahn said. His mind was spinning with impulses now: to tell the colonel what troubled him about Brill's explanation; to keep quiet about it and see what the Colonel did; to lay it off as Brill's problem . . .

"That's the damnedest thing I've ever heard," Patch said. "You people ought to be more careful out here." The colonel looked back down the hill again, the puzzled expression still on his face. From where the two of them were standing, it was just possible to make out the dark shapes of the two bodies lying outside the barbed wire in the brush.

Patch seemed about to speak again when Kahn seized the moment to change the subject.

"Colonel, I hate to keep bringing this up, but I honestly believe we should be relocating off this hill now. With the mortars last night, we—"

Patch spun around sharply.

"Look," he said, "I told you all along you are going to have to hold this hill. My plan, the general's plan and the Two Corps Commander's plan is to make the presence of this Battalion be felt very vividly among the people in these valleys around here—and the way to do that is to stay put and not jump around all over the place, and to run patrols as much as possible. Anyway, look out there. There isn't another hill in sight as tactically or strategically located as this one. I reconnoitered it myself. Every day the people in this valley pass along that road right down there on their way to the market, and the simple fact that you are here gives them a sense of well-being. That's part of the mission here, you know.

"Now," Patch said, "when the hell are you going to move this perimeter down so you can cover it properly with your mortars? I don't know why you haven't done it yet, but now I'm telling you to do it—and you can get started today."

"Colonel," Kahn started to protest, but Patch continued, "If they want a firefight, we'll give it to them. I wouldn't have put you on this hill if I didn't know you could defend it. You might get started by putting your claymores out first; then move the wire down, and dig in good and tight."

Moments later Patch was gone, striding down toward his helicopter, which was already warming up, leaving Kahn with the sinking feeling that something was drastically, and irrevocably, out of control. He was returning to his tent to brush his teeth when Brill came up to him, dressed in full field gear.

"Listen," Brill said, "I'm taking off now, and I thought—"

"Taking of where?" Kahn asked.

"I have the patrol today," Brill said, sounding surprised.

"Says who?" Kahn demanded.

"It's my turn," Brill replied. "I rotated them while you were gone like you said. It's my platoon's turn again."

Kahn studied him for a moment. "You and I," he said, "have got to have a talk about those goddamn bodies out there. Nobody's going anywhere until we do."

"That's what I came to see you about," Brill protested.

"Okay, let's have it, then," Kahn said.

"Well, what I want to do is, when we go out, we'll take them along with us and leave them down on those trails where we captured them to begin with. The VC'll come and police 'em up and it'll get them off our hands."

"That isn't what I mean, Brill. I want to hear what happened to them. Why in hell are they here in the first place?" Kahn fumed.

"I *told* you last night," Brill said indignantly. "We brought back three prisoners, the—"

"I know what you told me last night," Kahn said, "and that's just what I told the Old Man. I don't know if he bought it, but that's what I told him because I didn't have anything else to tell him, but now I want to know what the fuck happened!"

"All right," Brill said sullenly, "I'll tell you what I know."

Brill set forth much the same story he had given Kahn the night before, though more elaborately. He was especially graphic when it came to the condition of the girls after the men got through with them. "I don't know if they were raped, or how it started, but they were a mess," he said. He also insisted that the male prisoner had shot the other two in the way he had described before, adding that, "If he hadn't, we'd really be in a world of shit, because they would have had to go back to MI looking the way they were."

"Who were the guys?" Kahn demanded angrily.

"I don't have any idea," Brill said. "Nobody's talking; but I'll tell you this—it must have been a whole lot of them. If we open this can of worms, the whole company's in for it. We're gonna be screwed right down to the last man. You know how those bastards in the rear are; they got nothing better to do—"

"Damn it!" Kahn cried furiously, slamming his fatigue hat to the ground. "How could you let something like this happen? I'm going to have to do something. Where was your ass when all this was going on?"

"I told you," Brill said, "I was interrogating the gook."

Kahn reached down and retrieved his hat and stood shaking his head painfully, looking down at the cluster of Brill's men waiting to go out on patrol. Among them he saw Crump's lanky frame towering above the rest, the banana-cat cradled in his arms.

"Listen," Brill said, "what's happened, happened—I say let's don't stir up a shitpile. Those bodies are going to start to smell pretty soon anyway and we're going to have to do something about them. Like I say, I can take them out now and dump them and at least we'll have them off our hands. How about it?"

Kahn sighed deeply. The valley below them was shrouded in smoky morning mists, peaceful and green— yet the hand of death lay heavily across it. He had seen so much killing these past few months, what difference did a few more make, one way or the other? The policies differed from company to company, and from time to time: take prisoners, take no prisoners. War! War! War!—rape, pillage, burn—they had done all these things. "If he runs, he's VC—if he's dead, he's VC. War! War! War!" The thought was monstrous, but he thought it just the same. The way Kahn's mind was turning now, the question before him had little to do with killing or rape, but with what to do next: to go by The Book or not.

In the end, he put it off again.

"All right, go ahead," he told Brill. "But this isn't going to be the last of it. When you get back, you and I are going to find out who's responsible—and they're going to have to answer to me."

Brill replied with a dark, knowing look and trotted away toward his platoon. A chilling tremor ran through Kahn as he stood alone on the hillside, realizing for the first time that he was in this thing himself now. A few minutes later, he was on his way to Sergeant Dreyfuss' tent to get him started on the move downhill.

*   *   *

TWICE MORE after Patch's visit the subject of the prisoners was raised, and twice more Kahn shunted it aside. That same afternoon he had a brief exchange with Spudhead, who gave him a different version of the story from Brill's, and the next morning a man from the Army Criminal Investigation Division flew all the way up from Nha Trang for a longer conversation. The following day, two helicopters of MPs arrived at The Tit and arrested Brill, Sergeant Groutman and six members of Brill's platoon. Also advised of his rights, but not taken into custody, was the Commanding Officer of Bravo Company, First Lieutenant Billy Kahn.

Part Four

THE
RIVER
BLINDNESS

32

"PLEASE SHUT the door and sit down," the man behind the cluttered desk said. He turned from the window through which he had been gazing across the red-tile rooftops of the lovely and once-tranquil city of Nha Trang, and rising, motioned Kahn toward a battered wooden chair.

He was a thin, hawkish man, shorter than Kahn, with dark curly hair and thick black-rimmed glasses set low on his nose, over which he peered like a fighter fixing his opponent, chin tucked down, eyes moving from side to side to take in as much as possible. "I am Captain Gore," he said.

Kahn collapsed into the chair miserably as Gore flipped through a large brown folder for the papers he wanted, muttering, "Kahn, Kahn, Kahn" to himself. Kahn had been chewed out so many times in the last few days he was beginning to flinch at the mere mention of his name.

"Saw the Judge Advocate this morning, right?" Gore asked.

"I saw him—he gave me this. . . ." Kahn handed Gore a sheaf of mimeographed papers.

"Already sent me a copy earlier," Gore said. "Did you read it?"

"I read it."

"Is there anything in it you don't think is fair?"

"A couple of things."

"Like what?" Gore said, looking over the rims of his eyeglasses.

"Like number four—and maybe number two," Kahn said.

Gore glanced at the papers.

"Number four is crap; no way they can hang you for failing to take adequate safeguards to protect prisoners when you weren't even there. Number two I don't know about. . . . They'll have trouble proving it, though, if what you told the investigating officer is correct."

"It is," said Kahn.

"Even so," Gore said, "I don't have to tell you you're in a lot of trouble. Once you make a false statement, then the whole goddamn report is suspect—and you can bet they're going to make as much of that as they can."

"I told him," Kahn said, "just what I told the other guy."

"The investigating officer?"

"Yeah, that guy."

Gore studied the papers a few seconds longer, then got up and sat on the windowsill. Behind him, Kahn watched a truck convoy rumbling down the dusty tree-lined street, packed with fresh replacements. They were eagerly taking in the sights—the schoolgirls in their flowing white *ao dais*, the cyclo-boys passing in their pedicabs. Some of the soldiers waved and called out, and there was a look of innocence in their faces, and inquisitiveness, as though they were tourists in a bus.

Captain Gore regarded Kahn dourly.

"Let me start by saying this: this whole affair is shocking and disgusting if this investigation report can be half-believed. If I had my way, I would be trying this case instead of defending it." Then Gore looked over the glasses a little more hopefully. "But there are certain things about the way it's being pushed that bother me.

"One of them is that they're determined to hang all of you. Some of those fools probably deserve it, but a few don't and you might be one of them. Anyway, whether you know it or not, they're gunning for you—mostly because of your boy, whatisname . . . Brill. You heard what happened to him, I suppose?"

"They said he's a psycho case or something," Kahn said.

"More than that," said Gore. "He's been diagnosed as mentally incompetent to stand trial. Right now he's on his way back to the States to get discharged. He's completely out of it. If that hadn't happened, it might not be so bad for you, but the way it stands now they want an officer's ass and you're it."

"Great," Kahn said.

"It's not funny," Gore said. "The Commanding General of Two Corps is in a goddamned fit. He's scared to death the papers'll get hold of this, and he wants to move fast so they don't. That doesn't help you or the other guys."

"I don't understand," Kahn said. "You mean Brill's not going to be tried at all?"

"You've got it," Gore said.

"But how the hell can they not . . . he's the one . . ."

"Look, military law is very complicated. When a member of the Armed Forces commits a crime against a civilian in a foreign country he's tried by the military. That's so U.S. soldiers get the protection of our own Constitution. If this had happened in civilian life back in the States, they probably would have held Brill in an institution until he was fit to stand trial—and he would stay there until he was—even if it took fifty years. Trouble is, the Army doesn't have institutions for that kind of thing. Being mentally incompetent doesn't mean he's insane—or even that he was when he did this. It just means he isn't up to assisting in his own defense. It could be a temporary thing or last for the rest of his life. The Army doesn't want to chance being stuck with him for that long."

Kahn shook his head. "Well, there're about ten men who were standing there watching when—"

"Doesn't make any difference," Gore cut in. "As of now he isn't guilty of anything because he hasn't been tried and convicted, and it's just easier for them to get rid of him."

"That's the craziest thing I've ever heard of," Kahn said.

"Listen, that's the way it is. Right now, you're the next available scapegoat—and I gather you aren't exactly innocent in all of this yourself, so we'd better concentrate on getting you the best deal possible."

"Yeah," said Kahn, "like ten years in the stockade."

"Let's level with each other," Gore said, leaning against the sill. "I'm a damned good lawyer. I graduated top of my class at UCLA and was on the verge of making a lot of money before I had to come into the Army. I've been a prosecutor, and I conducted defenses in which I've walked people out of courtrooms who did a hell of a lot worse things than what you did. If this wasn't the Army, your case would never go to trial. But it is, and it's going to, so you'd better tell me everything you know, as honestly as you can, so I can figure some way to get you off the hook. Besides," he said with a twinkle, "most you can get is five years and a dishonorable discharge."

Kahn spent the next two hours telling Gore what had happened. He began with his return after the firefight in Happy Valley and seeing the bodies of the girls from the helicopter and his conversation with Brill and what had occurred the next day when Colonel Patch arrived and saw the bodies too. Gore occasionally interrupted with a question.

"Did he seem overly surprised?" Gore asked. "I mean, did he bring it up first?"

"Not right away," Kahn said. "We talked about a couple of other things for a minute and then he asked about it."

"What exactly did he say?"

Kahn thought for a moment. "He said something like 'By the way, what are all those bodies out there?' and I told him what Brill told me—that a male prisoner had gotten loose and shot the two girls—and he said, 'Well, how the hell did that happen?'—I believe those were the words he used—and I told him just what Brill told me."

"What did he say then?"

"He shook his head and said, 'That's the damndest thing I've ever heard of.'"

"And nothing more?"

"No, that was it. We talked about other things and he boarded the chopper and took off."

"What other things?" Gore asked.

"He and I had sort of an argument."

"About the girls?"

"No—about getting off that goddamn hill. We'd already been probed once and mortared—I figure they were just registering; but he wasn't having any of it."

"So he never mentioned it again—about the bodies?"

"Nope," said Kahn. "Not until he called me in after they found out what happened and started reading me the riot act."

"And you say you considered that 'Making a Report'?—just what you said to him that day after it happened?" Gore said testily. "You call that proper military procedure?"

"Look, if I did everything the way The Book says I'd either be dead or in the stockade by now—or at least relieved of my command...."

"You're already relieved of command, and you might wind up in the stockade anyway," Gore retorted. "The Army takes a pretty dim view of raping and murdering teen-age girls. As the officer in charge, you—"

"Listen," Kahn said fiercely, "I never even saw those girls alive—but I'll tell you this: they weren't nice little schoolgirls like you see walking around here; they were goddamn VC—caught red-handed, and they'd as soon have killed you as looked at you—and if you think those men didn't know that—"

"Okay, okay." Gore waved him off.

"No, damn it, let me finish!" Kahn shouted. "You can sit on your fat asses back here and drink Kool-Aid and tell me I'm an animal or something—so maybe I am, because I'll tell you this: I don't feel one goddamn thing for those girls. Not one little twinge. I'm not saying it's right—but I don't feel anything, nothing! And those guys who did this—and I know them because they're my men—and they'd sweat their asses for me—they didn't feel it either, so lay off the morality crap!"

Kahn was flushed and straining forward at Gore. The lawyer peered down over his glasses and said nothing for a few moments, and Kahn leaned back in his chair and looked out the window.

"You cooled off now?" Gore asked finally.

"Yeah," Kahn said. He studied his shoes.

"You're right," said Gore; "closest I get to the shooting is the five o'clock salute gun. But I'll tell you something. The kinds of questions I've been asking you are baby talk compared to what Mr. Carter Fox, the Judge Advocate, is going to put you through. That court will be regular Army, and they're not going to feel sorry for you because you've been in combat. They are going to go by The Book, and The Book doesn't provide that as an excuse. You get what I'm saying?"

Kahn nodded dismally.

"Listen, maybe you've got a right to be sore," Gore said gently. "But keep it with me—not with them. From now on, you and I have no secrets. Now, how about let's mosey on over to the Air Force Base club and have a drink and you can tell me the rest there."

"So MUCH brass around here you have to be at least a brigadier to get a jeep," Captain Gore said apologetically as they stood trying to thumb a ride to the airfield that lay on the outskirts of the city.

Seconds later, two privates on their way to the motor

pool picked them up, and they bounced along a busy thoroughfare beside the bay; past white sparkling beaches dotted with off-duty soldiers and civilians basking or swimming in the late-afternoon sun. The opposite side of the road was lined with lovely stucco villas with red slate or tile roofs, cool beneath spreading mahogany trees. Once the summer places of elite Vietnamese families, they now served as living quarters for American officers, some of whom could be seen lounging and drinking beer on the wide front porches. Farther on, they passed a row of dingy bars and nightclubs all with American-sounding names whose spelling was thoroughly wrong and inconsistent. Gore waited until the privates in the front seat began a conversation of their own before opening the subject.

"When did you first know about this thing?" he asked.

"I'm not sure, really," Kahn said. "I know that sounds crazy, but, well, I guess I knew something was wrong the minute I got back and saw the bodies. You just don't come across two dead girls without thinking something is wrong. Then I suppose after what Brill said—that some of the guys had 'messed around with them'—I suppose I had an inkling of the rapes, anyway. He suggested we try to play it down."

"How did he suggest that?"

"Well, he said we might just bury them and forget about it."

"What did you say?"

"Understand," Kahn said, "I was pretty beat. We'd just come back from...a pretty long afternoon. I said, I forget exactly what, but something like 'I don't want to do anything now. We'll talk about it tomorrow.' I wanted to wait till I had a clear head to find out what...what it was."

"Did you have any idea they had been murdered?"

"Not then—I didn't know what the hell had happened."

"Ummmmmmmmm," said Gore. The jeep was jerking along a side street clogged with Vietnamese riding bicycles. The driver was cursing at them and blowing his horn furiously.

"When did you first know it—or maybe I should say,

when did you first suspect it?"

"I guess it was the next day, after Colonel Patch came
out. By then I had just about put it out of my mind—I
suppose I was trying to, anyway. We had a lot of things to
do. I told you the Colonel wanted me to move the whole
laager down the hillside, and he started making us run
those goddamned patrols again too."

The jeep was weaving in and out among the bicycles,
and both privates in the front were yelling at the riders. A
fender of the jeep touched the rear end of one, and the
man on it tumbled into the dirt. Apparently unhurt, he
picked himself up and mounted the bicycle again, silent,
but with a dark, angry look on his face. The jeep drove on.

"That afternoon," Kahn said, "a guy from Brill's
platoon came up and asked if he could see me for a
minute. I was checking positions and asked him what
about, and he said, 'The girls.' And I said, 'What about
them?' and he said, 'Do you know what happened?' I told
him that Lieutenant Brill had filled me in, and he just
stood there looking at me, and finally I said, 'What is it
you want to say?' and he said, 'Well, I don't think he told
you the truth.'"

They were cruising on a newly paved road toward a
guard-post entrance to the air base. Dozens of tin-roofed
buildings lined both sides of the road, and a multitude of
aircraft occupied the runway—jet fighters, propeller-
driven fighters, helicopters, light observation planes, big
transports.

"Go on," Gore said.

"Well, I think I said something like, ah, 'How do you
know what Lieutenant Brill told me?' and he said,
'Because I heard what he's been saying.' And I said,
'What's that?' and he gave me the story Brill had told me
that first night."

"What did you say to that?"

"I said that if that wasn't the truth, then what was? And
he said the lieutenant killed the girls and that some other
men had raped and hurt them earlier. Then I asked who
these men were, and he sort of stumbled around and
wouldn't tell me, so I told him I'd look into it and to go
back to his unit."

"And that was the last you heard of him?"

"Yes—well, until when the chopper came in, just about dusk. We were always sending people back and forth to the rear, and I had a rule that anyone who wanted to go in for anything had to clear it with me personally, or with the First Sergeant. The chopper had already left, and the First Sergeant came up with a list of three or four people he'd okayed to go back to Monkey Mountain. One of them was this guy. He'd told the First Sergeant he wanted to see the Chaplain."

"Did he say what about? Didn't it surprise you?" Gore said.

"Not really. I'd had some problems with him before—not problems, exactly; he had trouble adjusting. He'd asked to see the Chaplain a few times before this."

"What was this man's name?" Gore asked.

"Miter," Kahn said. "His father is a Congressman."

"I know," said Gore.

THEY PASSED through the gate to the air base, and the privates dropped them off in front of the officers' club, a large white building with glass windows looking westward over the rice fields to a chain of bluish mountains. The first thing Kahn noticed was cold air on his face and hands. Air conditioning, he marveled—they had air conditioning here.

The varnished wood bar was lined with loud, drinking Air Force and Army officers, many of them high-ranking. Outside, on a large roof-covered patio, a mob of eager officers had gathered around a small stage to watch a blond stripper perform. Gore and Kahn ordered drinks at the bar and found an empty table in a corner.

"Australian," Gore said authoritatively of the stripper. "They're the best-looking ones. The ones the USO sends all look like they just got deported from Lower Slobbovia." So far, the girl had removed none of her clothes. She was young and pretty, and Kahn regarded her wistfully.

"Let's talk about what you said to the investigating officer," Gore said. "When did he come out?"

"It was the next morning—two days after the,

ah . . . killings. The morning after Miter went to see the Chaplain. He showed up at the CP and looked me up."

"What did he say?"

"That he was there to investigate a report of nonbattle deaths of two civilian women, and I said, 'Well, I guess I knew you were going to come sooner or later.' Then I said, 'They weren't civilians; they were VC.'"

"How did he react?"

"He said it 'remained to be seen,' or something like that."

Gore waited for him to continue.

"We went into my tent and sat down, and he said this was an 'official investigation' and that I was under oath, and he took out a pad to write on and started asking questions.

"First he asked me if I was aware the girls had been raped and molested, as he put it, before they died, and I told him I really was not aware of that.

"Then he asked if I knew exactly how they died, and I told him I understood that there was another, male prisoner and that he had gotten loose and managed to shoot them. Then he said did anyone tell me a story to the contrary, and I said I thought I might have heard something to that effect but I wasn't sure."

Gore took a long swallow from his drink and waited.

"Well, then he said, 'Did you investigate this incident and make a report?' and I said, I did make a report. He said, 'To whom?' and I said to the Battalion Commander, and told him about the conversation the morning when the colonel came to the CP. He asked was that the only report I made and I told him it was.

"He wrote it all down and said he was going to question some of the other men and named their names, and he asked me to tell him where to find them. He said he was going to get back to me later, but he never did. The next thing I knew—and that was late that next afternoon, after he left—I got a message from Battalion to get my ass on the next chopper to Monkey Mountain and report to the Chief of Staff, and when I got there he said I was relieved of command pending an investigation and possible court-martial."

"All right," Gore said. "Now, don't take offense at what I'm going to ask you. As your counsel I need to know the truth. When the investigating officer asked if you were aware that the girls had been raped and molested, you answered you were not, and that was a lie, wasn't it?"

"Well, yes, I suppose it was," Kahn said. "I really wasn't 'aware' of it, because I hadn't seen it. But Brill told me they'd been 'messed with,' and then Miter clinched it, and I guess I pretty much knew it, or at least suspected it."

"And when he asked if you knew how they died and you gave him Brill's story, you suspected then that that was not the truth, correct?"

"I suppose I did—all right, yes I did, but it wasn't an out-and-out lie. I told him what I had heard from one of my officers."

"But it was a prevarication, wasn't it?" Gore said.

"Yes, it was that, but not a lie, except . . . Oh hell," Kahn said, "sure I knew it was a lie." He stared at his drink and stirred the ice with his fingers. "I know I'm sunk," he said miserably. "Why don't I just plead guilty and take what's coming to me?"

"Nonsense," Gore said, "that's exactly what they expect you to do. It'll follow you around the rest of your life—dismissed from the service and all that. There's no such thing as throwing yourself on the mercy of this court—they'll be hand-picked by the general himself, so you may as well make them sweat for it. Besides, like I told you before, I'm a pretty damned good lawyer." Gore smiled. "Let's have another drink up at the bar."

They bellied up to an empty spot where they could see the stripper through the glass picture window. She had gotten down to a G-string and pasties and was teasing the men in front with bumps and grinds. A large crowd had gathered, and some in back were standing on chairs to get a better view. All were hooting and laughing.

"We start in the morning at oh eight hundred," Gore said casually. "You may as well sit in and try to pick up something from the testimony—it might help you." Kahn looked extremely surprised. "You mean they'll let me listen?" he asked.

"Can't stop you. This isn't your show yet. They'll get to you when we're finished with the enlisted men."

There was a sudden commotion outside the patio. All heads that had been watching the stripper were now turned to a bunch of men clustered about a prostrate form in the center of the crowd, next to a large table. Gore and Kahn couldn't see what was going on, but the stripper kept up her gyrations, and had removed both pasties by now and thrown them to the audience.

"Happens every time," groaned a crusty Air Force major standing beside them at the bar. "Some damned fool always decides to stand up on that table for a better look and gets his head caught in the fan."

They finished their drinks, and Gore walked Kahn to the door.

"Sure you don't want to stay for supper here?" he said. "Chow's pretty good—it's Air Force."

"Thanks anyway," Kahn said, "but I told somebody I'd meet them back at my hotel. By the way, I don't have anything but fatigues to wear—didn't have time to dig out my khakis before I left."

"You're better off without them," Gore said. "Like I told you, we're not going to make any speeches about your being a field soldier, but it's little things like that that'll let them know."

THERE WAS an Army truck that served as a shuttle between the air base and the city, and Kahn caught a ride back on it. From the drop-off point he walked five or six blocks down quiet side streets and up the hill where the hotel was.

Since no one had specified where he was to stay, he found out about a small French hotel, the Maison Dupont, and after the deprivations of The Tit, he figured it would be money well spent—the more so since his fate after the court-martial was in considerable doubt.

In his room, Kahn stripped down and stood under the old-style bowl shower in a corner of the room, letting the tepid, sun-heated water drain over his head and shoulders. After a while he stepped out onto the tile floor, dried and wrapped the towel around his waist and walked to the louvered doors that opened into a long covered portico overlooking the shimmering Bay of Nha Trang and the great green-hued mountains that marked the entrance to its harbor. He stood for quite a long while, thinking about what was really going on out there, deep in the vaporous jungles and mountains, and in the little villages at night: murder, pain, treachery—and for what? Capitalism? Communism? Chauvinism? Jingoism? Or some other ism nobody but Political Science professors understood?

There had been a time he thought he knew.

When they were piping across the Dismal Deeps of the big Pacific ocean, once then, during the boxing matches on deck, he had watched old Crump take his beating, take the blond boy's best shots, then rally and bear in on him. Lean and mean American Crump, sailing into battle, flags flying, banner raised . . . He had seen it all so clearly then, and it had been almost grand.

At a quarter past seven he dressed and walked through the hotel to the veranda, where a dozen or so guests, mostly American or European, were seated at tables for drinks and dinner. The sun had dropped behind the mountains, and a dark mass of rain clouds was gathering on the western horizon. There was a little outdoor bar with four stools, and seated at one of them, in baggy seersucker pants and a Hawaiian shirt, was Major Dunn.

"Hello there, young man." Dunn said, grinning cheerfully. "What'll you have?"

"Hi, Major—Scotch and soda, I guess," Kahn said. The Vietnamese behind the bar smiled apologetically. "Sorry, sir, we have no Scotch whiskey. A brandy maybe?"

"Yeah, all right—with soda water," Kahn said. "Been here long, Major?"

"Not at all, just half a drink. God, it's pretty here, almost like Hong Kong. Bill, you wouldn't believe that place. . . . The girls there—oooooh, boy!"

"When do you have to be back in your cage?"

"First flight in the morning—so I ain't through yet."

For the next ten minutes the major gave Kahn a blow-by-blow account of Hong Kong delights.

"I've never done anything like that in my life," Dunn said wonderously, "even before I was married. . . . I don't suppose I told you—I'm divorcing her. Right out of the picture. . . ."

They took the drinks to a small table. The menu described in both French and English several types of fresh fish, lobster and cold soups and salads.

"So tell me, what are you doing down here?" Dunn said. "I didn't quite understand what you said before. You're not transferred, are you?"

"Not exactly," Kahn said. He took a deep breath and told Dunn the story. They were midway through the main course of dinner when he finished.

"Oh, boy, oh, boy," Dunn said shaking his head sympathetically. "You do what you think is right and then get screwed over for it. Whew!"

"I don't know about that, Major," Kahn said ruefully. "I'm afraid . . ." His voice trailed off. "The way it looks now, it was one of the dumbest things I've done in my dumb young life."

After dinner the major tried to persuade Kahn to join him for a night of Oriental pleasures in the town, but Kahn begged off. Sitting alone, he finished a cup of coffee, then strolled over to the outdoor bar, where a tanned balding man in white shirt and black trousers was having a Pernod and smoking a Gauloise cigarette.

"Glass of brandy and soda please," Kahn said. "Yes, sir," said the bartender, smiling. . . . They always smiled that same smile, all of them—shopkeepers, farmers, cyclo-boys, soldiers, old women, children—as though they knew something you didn't know. And, he thought, they probably did.

It had been painful to tell Dunn. Almost more for Dunn's sake than his own, because halfway through, there was a haunted, heart-wrenched understanding in the major's face as he ran through the memories of his own little horror: that split-second decision—careless, stupid—that didn't seem so at the time; then, whammo! . . .

Kahn took a deep swallow of brandy and looked out toward the bay. Below, the city lights were beginning to come alive, misty spots of brightness in the twilight.

... He should have known, damn it! No matter what he'd thought at the time, there was always The Book, and if he had gone by it he wouldn't be in this fix. All of his life he had gone by The Book—some Book or other. Because The Book was The Word, and The Word was all set out there in The Book—the right and wrong, and punishments for those who disobeyed. The Book did not care if those men had become so brutalized they probably hadn't even known what they did was wrong—or not very wrong, anyway. It didn't give a hoot if he felt a certain protectiveness toward them because *he* understood it—if that was what he really *had* felt. Nor was The Book interested that the two dead girls had probably spent the day before they died tying fuses to mines that would wreck the lives and limbs of the very men who had savaged them.

The Book was not concerned with these things.

The Book was his enemy now. Not the general, or the officers on the court, or Patch—they didn't give a good goddamn about those girls. And no matter the killing and carnage and terror and frustration and the living like swine... The Book had to be followed, because without it, it would only be worse, and he had not followed it, and now he was going to be convicted because that was what The Book said. And there was a Book...

"Have you enjoyed your dinner, monsieur?" the man next to him asked.

"Oh, yes. It was very good, delicious," Kahn said.

"Ah, I am glad," the man said. "Allow me to introduce myself. I am Paul Chogny, proprietor of the hotel. I see your friend has deserted you."

"Not exactly," said Kahn. "He went into the town for... uh... a little fun...."

"Yes," Chogny said, "there is fun to be had there now. For more than a year. It used to be so quiet."

"You've been here for a while, then, I guess."

"A long while, my friend—for more than thirty years. I suppose you could call that a while."

"No kidding?" said Kahn. "You've owned this hotel all that time?"

"Oh, no, only for a few years—five, to be exact. Originally I came here with the army."

"Thirty years—that's before the, ah..."

"Yes, before the Second World War. I was here first in nineteen thirty-six."

"And you've stayed on ever since?"

"Ah," Chogny said, sipping his Pernod, "not exactly. You see, when the Japanese came in nineteen forty, I managed to get across to Burma and fought with the British there until the war ended."

"And then you came back?"

"Theoretically, I was still in the army. By that time we were having trouble with Ho Chi Minh, and so I got back with my old unit, and fought with them until Dien Bien Phu. After that, I came down here and married a Vietnamese—you may have seen her behind the counter inside. I worked at this hotel as manager and finally borrowed enough money to buy it." Chogny turned to the bartender. "I would like to buy my friend a drink," he said. The smile faded slightly from the bartender's face, but he took the glass from Kahn and filled it again.

"It's a very nice hotel," Kahn said. "The food is excellent."

"Ah," said Chogny, "last week we had the good lobster, and a wine from Bordeaux. It is hard to get some of this these days."

"I suppose the war is affecting you, isn't it?"

"Of course—but not always in a bad way. I mean, you could see we had a good business tonight. Every night, now that the Americans are here. But it is not easy to serve the best dinners. Still, they come."

"What about the VC?" asked Kahn. "Do they give you trouble?"

Chogny shook his head disdainfully. "They leave us alone. I don't know why...." He finished off his Pernod and ordered another. "I think," he said, "it could be because I know someone—I once knew him, anyway. He is very important in the Vietcong here. In fact, I hear he runs not only this province but the area you call Two Corps."

Regarding Kahn's raised eyebrows, Chogny continued:

"I haven't seen him for years, but I hear things, you know? He and I were old friends once."

"Have you told someone about this?" Kahn asked, "I mean, if you know him..."

"Oh, they all know him. He is very well known."

"I take it, then, he's out with the VC somewhere. I mean, he doesn't live here or anything."

"Oh, no." Chogny laughed. "If they could catch him, what a prize he would make! They'd take him to Saigon and skin him in the middle of Tu Do Street. But he's a shrewd fellow—I know. We were on the same side all the way to Dien Bien Phu. He lost his leg there—to artillery, you know; right off at the knee."

"But you don't see him anymore?"

Chogny laughed. "Oh, no! Five, maybe six years ago, I think. On the street in Phan Rang; we had a drink together in a little café. He was under the name of Vinh."

"That's not his real name?"

"Sacre bleu!" Chogny exclaimed. "No. I think his real name is Trung, something like that—all these Asian devils' names sound alike, eh? Last I heard he was going by the name of Bac or Boc—I can't remember which. Slippery fellow—they'll have a hard time catching that one...."

Kahn savored the warmth of the brandy as it drained into his stomach. He felt good. He almost wished the court-martial could be right now. His mind felt clear. He could tell them what he felt....

Below, the city lights sparkled gaily and the fishing boats twinkled like fireflies around the ragged islands in the bay.

"This must have been a lovely place before the war," Kahn said.

"Ah, *mais oui,* Lieutenant," Chogny said, leaning back on the stool to catch a rising breeze. "But there has always been a war."

33

THE COURT-MARTIAL opened promptly at 0800 hours in a small, airless room on the first floor of the II Corps Field Force Headquarters building in a compound near the center of the city. The president of the court was a stern-faced colonel named Maitland, whose most distinguishing feature was a pair of enormous black eyebrows that peaked up at the ends to give him an apelike countenance. At either side of him sat the rest of the court—a major, two captains, two master sergeants and a sergeant major of Japanese descent who wore, on his immaculately pressed khakis, the ribbon for the Congressional Medal of Honor. Set out on the long table were seven yellow legal tablets, each with a pencil laid neatly across its top. An American flag drooped listlessly on a wall.

Before them sat the accused—six melancholy and frightened men—postured respectfully behind a desk at which their defense counsel, Captain Gore, was poring over some papers.

The Judge Advocate, an earnest-faced captain named Carter Fox, rose at a nod from Colonel Maitland and swore in the court in a rich Virginia accent. He ran his fingers through his longer-than-regulation blond hair, then grimly ticked off the charges and specifications against each of the accused: "That on the sixth day of February at the Company laager on Hill Sixty-seven, Sergeants Groutman and Maranto, Specialists Fourth Class Trent, Harley and Mullen and Private Acquino did with malice aforethought assault, rape and commit other wrongful sexual acts against two Oriental human beings known as Co Vin Duc and Co Ba Duc, aged approximately sixteen and fourteen years old, now deceased." The complete readings against each of the six took nearly half an hour. Then Maitland indicated he was ready for the Judge Advocate's opening statement, and the six accused shifted uneasily in their seats.

During this time, Kahn had watched passively from the rear of the room, studying the faces of the six. Groutman had not surprised him. He could almost have predicted it. Even before he had gotten the company, even back at Bragg, Kahn had disliked Groutman, even feared him a little, and made a point of staying away from him, and when Brill had come to him and wanted to make Groutman Platoon Sergeant, Kahn had reluctantly gone along, but he had never liked him. Never. The others he barely knew. They were faces and names among dozens and dozens of others in the Company. But, he thought, maybe he should have known them better. The fact was that he had pretty much stayed away from Brill's platoon. Just shunted it aside and let things take their course. Once he had thought of letting Sharkey and Donovan, or even Inge, step in and shape it up. What if he had? If, if, if . . . maybe things would be different now.

Captain Fox exuded a sense of outrage as he outlined the prosecution's version of the crime. "My main regret," he declared, "is that the officer apparently responsible for these events will not go to trial."

The court listened with interest, and occasionally one of them would shoot a glance at the table where the accused were seated. It was not a pretty story, and as summed up by Captain Fox it was exactly the kind of thing the Army takes a very dim view of.

"Very well, then," Maitland said when Fox had finished, "you may call your witness," and Pfc. Harold N. Miter, Jr., was summoned to the chair.

FOX WASTED no time getting to the matter at hand.

"Private Miter, did anything of an unusual nature occur the night of February sixth at your company position?"

"Some guys raped the girls," Spudhead said nervously.

"What girls?"

"The two detainees. They were VC nurses, Lieutenant Brill's patrol had brought them in earlier that day."

"Lieutenant Brill—was he your platoon leader?"

"Yessir."

"Now, you say 'some guys' raped them. Can you tell me who they were?"

"I don't know who all of them were. I wasn't there for the whole time. It went on most of the night."

"Do you know who any of them were? Are any of them present in this room?"

"Yessir," Spudhead said.

"Will you identify them for the court, please?"

"Sergeants Groutman and Maranto were the only ones I saw, sir."

"And what were they doing?"

"They were raping them."

"Simultaneously?"

"Well, they were both doing it. Groutman was on top of the little girl and Maranto was with the big one."

"What hour of the day was this?"

"It was about twenty-one hundred hours."

"So it was dark?"

"Yes, sir."

"And where were you positioned?"

"I was right next to them. They were out on the ground under poncho liners."

"Tell us what you saw."

"I saw the poncho liners go up and down for a while."

"What did you conclude from that?"

"Uh, I don't understand your question," Spudhead said meekly.

"I mean, when you were standing there watching these poncho liners going up and down with men and girls beneath them what did you think was going on?"

"I thought . . . I thought that the men were raping the girls."

"How do you know the men were raping them?"

"Ah . . . well, there had been a rumor earlier that some of the men were going to rape them."

"And you inferred from this and from what you saw that that was what was happening—is that correct?"

"Yessir."

"Did you see anyone else raping the girls?"

"Not exactly."

"Can you be more specific?"

"Well, all during the night men came and went. I don't know how many of them there were—or really who they were. I heard some of them talking about it later, but I didn't actually see them raping."

"Who talked about it later? Are any of them in this room?"

"Yessir, there was Harley and Acquino and Mullen—and Trent. They all talked about it."

"How did they talk about it?"

"They just talked. They said they had had sex with the girls. They were laughing about it."

"I see," Fox said, stepping back to his desk. He picked up a legal pad and examined it for a moment, letting Spudhead's testimony sink in.

"Now, Private Miter, going to the next day. In the morning, what events occurred?"

"It was about oh nine hundred, I think, and Lieutenant Brill came down to the positions with the man prisoner and—"

"Just a moment. You say there was a male prisoner. Who was he?"

"They caught him the same time they caught the girls. He had been tied up all night back up the hill."

"And Lieutenant Brill came down and he had this man with him?"

"That's right. There were two other guys who were actually leading the VC; Lieutenant Brill was walking in front of them."

"Go on."

"Well, when the lieutenant got there he bent over and looked at the girls, and he looked very mad, and then he told the VC he could have a choice of shooting them or he would be shot."

"Just like that?"

"There was other talk—a lot of people standing around—but that's what Lieutenant Brill said."

"He said this directly to the prisoner?"

"He said it through the interpreter."

"What happened then?"

"Lieutenant Brill got the interpreter to get the girls on their feet. They were in pretty bad shape. Their clothes were torn, and the older one had blood all over her... pants. She looked like she was having trouble standing up. The VC didn't want to do it."

"Why do you say that?"

"Because at first he didn't want to take the weapon. He wouldn't hold out his hand."

"What weapon was this?"

"It was an M-sixteen rifle."

"Whose was it?"

"I don't know. It was somebody's in the crowd. Lieutenant Brill just grabbed it from somebody."

"Please continue."

"Lieutenant Brill took out his forty-five and pointed it at the VC and told him—had the interpreter tell him—to shoot the girls. The VC took the weapon and he started to aim it, but he was having trouble with the safety. He couldn't get it to go off. I guess he'd never shot one before. But Lieutenant Brill helped him with it and he said something to him, but I don't know what it was because it was in Vietnamese."

"What happened then?"

"I don't know, sir. I turned away and went back to my position. I knew what was going to happen and I couldn't watch."

"I see. Can you describe for the court, then, the mood of the men who were standing around. How were they behaving?"

"They were just standing there. They weren't laughing or talking or anything. They looked kind of funny."

"What do you mean, 'funny'?"

"They looked like they wanted to be somewhere else."

"I have no more questions, Private Miter. Thank you."

Gore rose up slowly and approached the witness chair looking over his glasses at Spudhead Miter.

"You say it was about twenty-one hundred hours when you witnessed what you believe was raping of the two girls—is that right?"

"Yessir, it was about that exactly, because I had just come off guard duty."

"And you were right at the scene of the alleged incident, I believe you said?"

"Yessir."

"How did you come to find yourself there?"

"I . . . uh . . . just went down there, after I got off guard duty."

"You went there for no reason? Wasn't it nearly thirty yards from your position?"

"Well, sir, like I said, there was this rumor going around . . ."

"That the men were going to rape the girls."

"Yessir. They said it was a revenge for Sergeant Trunk, who had been killed a couple of weeks before."

"And you heard it and decided to go on down there yourself—isn't that correct?"

"I—ah, I heard it, yes. And I just . . . went down there."

"And you watched while Groutman and Maranto had sexual relations with these two women?"

"Yessir."

"You watched the entire time?"

"Yessir."

"And when they were finished, what did you do then? Didn't you do something with the girls yourself?"

"No, sir—I mean, I just went to look at them."

"Didn't you do more than that? Didn't you touch them? Didn't you get down there with them?"

"I did not do anything wrong."

"Isn't it true that some of your buddies teased you and said you were afraid to do anything with those girls?"

"Yessir, they did that."

"Suppose you tell us about it."

Spudhead slouched down in the chair and looked at Captain Fox, but the Judge Advocate nodded to him to answer the question.

"They did tease me. But I did not go down there to do anything wrong. After Groutman had finished with the younger girl he got off of her, and after a minute or two she got up and went over and got into the foxhole. The foxhole gave her a little warmness. There was a bunch of people standing around laughing about something, and they pushed me toward her—in the foxhole—so I got down in it too. She was lying there very quiet and holding herself, and I put my arms around her and put her head on my shoulder. She didn't cry or anything. She just lay there. I felt sorry for her."

"How long did you lie there together?"

"I don't know exactly; maybe ten or fifteen minutes."

"And that was all you did? You were there in the foxhole in the dark with that girl for ten or fifteen minutes and you simply held her in your arms?"

"Sir, I was very lonely. I miss my girl. I was feeling very bad. I had felt bad for a long time now, but that was all I ever did with her. I swear it to God."

"I have no more questions," Gore said brusquely.

Captain Fox introduced into evidence a number of items at this point, including an aerial photograph of the murder site, and some drawings of the scene to scale. His next witness was Private Edward Poats of Weapons Platoon.

"Did you, on the night of February sixth, Private Poats, have occasion to visit the headquarters of First Lieutenant Brill?"

"Yessir, I did," Poats said.

"What was that occasion?"

"It was because of something that was going on down on the perimeter, sir."

"What was going on there?"

"I believe there was some raping of the girls who had been taken prisoner."

"How do you know that?"

"At the time I didn't know it. I had gone down there to see a buddy and talk to him and I heard some sounds from that area."

"Sounds?"

"They was woman sounds. Like somebody was being injured."

"And you investigated?"

"I went over there and saw a bunch of guys standing around a foxhole."

"What time of day was this?"

"It was about twenty-one hundred hours, sir."

"What were the men doing?"

"They was watching one of the girls being raped."

"Who was raping her?"

"That, sir, I cannot say, because I did not stand there and watch."

"But you heard the girl making sounds. Weren't you close enough to see who was with her?"

"No, sir; it was dark and there was a bunch of men around them."

"And they were just watching quietly?"

"No, sir, they were laughing and cheering on the man with the girl."

"What did you do then?"

"I left the area, sir, and I went back up to the mortars."

"Straight back?"

"Oh, no, sir. I was going to, but I started up and I got to thinking that it wasn't right, so I stopped into Lieutenant Brill's tent because I didn't think he knew what was going on and that he would like to know."

"You didn't think *what* was not right?"

"The raping. I mean, they was just little girls . . ."

"So you saw Lieutenant Brill? In his tent?"

"Yessir."

"What was he doing?"

"He was interrogating the VC prisoner."

"How was he interrogating him?"

"With a knife."

"He was cutting him?"

"Yessir."

"Where did he cut him?"

"It looked to me like in the navel, sir."

"I see," Fox said. He stepped back a few feet and paused, glancing at the court members. All were leaning forward on the table, and the eyebrows of Colonel Maitland had furrowed to dark, arborlike arches.

"What did you say to Lieutenant Brill?"

"I told him some people was molesting the girls and that he should go down there."

"And how did he respond to that?"

"I beg your pardon, sir?"

"What did he say?"

"He said, ah, for me to mind my own business and let Second Platoon take care of themselves."

"And then you left?"

"I did, sir."

"Thank you, Private Poats," Fox said. He sat back down at his table.

Gore stood and backed up as far as he could until he was on the edge of the waist-high partition that separated the dock from the spectator section.

"Private Poats, have you ever molested a Vietnamese female?" he said loudly.

"Objection!" Fox was on his feet looking astonished and angry.

"I'll rephrase the question," Gore said. "Have you ever had sexual intercourse with a Vietnamese woman?"

"Objection!" Fox cried. "What possible connection does that question have to this case?"

"*Well*, Captain Gore?" Maitland said, the eyebrows raised.

"Sir, it has every connection. This man testified that he saw a rape in progress, although he cannot tell us who was involved. This line of questioning is to determine if Private Poats knows a rape when he sees one."

"Mister President," protested Fox, "this is not only a rape case, but murder as well, and in a murder case you always lose your best witness. What Private Poats has told us is what he observed. He stated plainly that in his opinion what he saw was rape. I submit that the court is intelligent enough to decide for itself if a crime was committed after hearing all the testimony." Fox glared at Gore, who returned the look disdainfully.

"These men," Gore said, gesturing toward the table, "are accused of the most serious of crimes. The Judge Advocate has introduced testimony by a man who claims he saw a rape. As Captain Fox astutely points out, there is no complaining witness, because both of them were murdered. Nor are their bodies to be examined, because they were apparently dragged off at some point. The defense asserts no contention to the contrary. But in the absence of the direct corroboration of the two women who were allegedly raped, the defense respectfully suggests that this is essential to find out exactly how this witness knows that what he saw was rape."

Maitland leaned back in his chair and considered the argument, then spoke in a measured tone:

"All right, Captain, I will let you proceed so long as it has bearing on the issue you have just presented. But be advised that I believe you are on shaky ground."

"Thank you, sir," Gore said, and walked briskly back to the partition.

"I ask you again, Private Poats, have you ever witnessed, or been a part of, sexual intercourse with a Vietnamese woman?"

Poats seemed embarrassed, and his answer was spoken weakly.

"Yes, sir."

"Please tell us about it."

"Well, there was a time at Monkey Mountain when they let us go into the town. There was—"

"I'm talking about a more recent incident, Private Poats. I am talking about a certain patrol about three weeks ago near a hamlet in the valley where your company was positioned. Was there a woman in the rice field on that patrol?"

Poats looked absolutely shamefaced. "Yes, sir," he said.

"Can you speak a little louder, Private Poats?"

"Yessir, there was a woman," he said.

"What was this woman doing?"

"She was having sex with the men."

"How was she doing that?"

Poats looked confused. "She was just doing it, sir."

"With how many men?"

"I don't know exactly, sir. It was Melcher's squad and some of my own—and there was a couple of guys from First Platoon there too."

"So this woman was having sex with perhaps—what would you say, fifteen or twenty men?"

"Maybe."

"And were other men gathered around her, laughing and watching?"

"They was, sir."

"Were you involved in this affair?"

"Yessir," Poats said meekly.

"You'll have to speak up please," Gore said.

"Yessir," Poats said.

"Who was this woman?"

"She was just a peasant, sir. She lived in the hamlet."

"And she came out into the rice field and had sex with twenty men?"

"Well, sir, it was Melcher's squad that paid her. I think they must have took up a collection or something."

"How did you know this?"

"Somebody said it."

"Who said it?"

"I don't remember who exactly said it. It was just what everybody said."

"So you availed yourself of the services of this woman on the strength of a statement by a person whose name you can't even remember that her sexual favors had been bargained for and paid for in advance—is that correct?"

"Huh?" Poats said. "I mean, uh... I don't exactly understand what you said," he stammered.

"I mean," Gore said, "did you have sex with this woman without actually paying her any money yourself while a crew of your buddies stood around and watched?"

Poats looked blankly at the court and at Fox, and then, very downcast, at the floor. "I guess I did, sir."

"And you did not consider that rape, did you?"

"No, *sir*," Poats said indignantly. "It was paid for!"

"But not by you."

"No, sir."

"And you can't tell us by whom, can you?"

"I can't remember, but everybody said—"

"That's all, Private Poats," Gore said.

"PLEASE CALL Master Sergeant Rollie I. Moon," Fox said. Into the courtroom stepped a tall, thin, craggy-faced man about forty years old, wearing starched khakis and an unhappy look.

"Please be seated, Sergeant, and state your name and unit."

"Master Sergeant Rollie I. Moon, Weapons Platoon, Bravo Company, Fourth Battalion, Seventh Cavalry."

After Moon was sworn in, Fox paced back and forth, running his fingers through his longish blond hair.

"Sergeant Moon, on the night of February sixth, nineteen sixty-seven, did you have occasion to visit the Second Platoon positions on Hill Sixty-seven?"

"Yessir, I did."

"For what reason did you go there?"

"Well, sir, I was finished checking my night positions and I just sort of took a walk around and I heard sort of a moaning sound. I thought somebody might be sick. It was dark and I couldn't tell who it was, so I went down to check that it was none of my people."

"What was it, then, Sergeant?"

"It was some kind of sexual thing going on between the

persons in Second Platoon and the two VC girls they had captured earlier in the day."

"What kind of sexual thing?"

"They was screwing them."

"You saw this?"

"Yessir, I did."

"What did you see?"

"Sir, I seen an individual having sexual relations with one of the girls. I made sure it wasn't one of my people. I told my people to get back to their position, and then I went back to my platoon CP."

"What did you do there?"

"I told my people to stay away from down there. I told them whatever was going on was Second Platoon's business and for them to stay out of it. I was there for a while and then I went back and seen the individual still on the girl."

"The same individual?"

"Yessir."

"What was he doing?"

"Sir, he did have his dick in her cunt, but I would say he wasn't having sexual relations with her—it was more like he was torturing her."

"Sergeant," Colonel Maitland interjected, "I realize the need to be specific, but the court would appreciate it if you could be a little less graphic in your descriptions, since the transcript of these proceedings will ultimately wind up in front of some authority in Washington. You may continue."

"I am very sorry sir, I..."

"Go ahead, Sergeant," Maitland said.

"Sergeant Moon," Fox said, "do you recognize the individual you saw having relations with the girl? Is he in this room?"

"He is, sir. It was Sergeant Groutman. He is sitting over there."

"I have no more questions," Fox said.

Gore walked close to the witness chair.

"From the groaning—I take it it was the girl groaning—and from what you saw, what did you conclude was going on?"

"I didn't conclude nothing, sir. I just wanted to make sure it was none of my people."

"But you must have formed an opinion of what was going on, didn't you?"

"I did not, sir."

"All right, Sergeant, you saw all this and you did not form any opinion whatsoever. Now what about the groaning? What did you make of that?"

"It did not last long. It was very brief."

"How so?"

"Well, Groutman there stated to the girl to '*im lang*,' which means 'shut up' in English."

"You mean it is 'shut up' in Vietnamese."

"Yessir, that's what it means."

"And did the girl shut up?"

"She did, sir."

"Didn't you think after hearing that that Sergeant Groutman might have been forcing himself on the girl?"

"Sir, I did not think anything. It was nighttime, and we was on a hill where many things could happen."

"But you must have thought something," Gore said.

"The Army does not pay me to think about things that happen in other platoons than mine," Moon said defensively. "Sergeant Groutman was there. That was his responsibility."

"Where was the First Sergeant all this time—Sergeant Dreyfuss?"

"He was asleep, sir. He had been up most of the night before."

"Did you consider waking him up?"

"No, sir. Sergeant Dreyfuss did not like to be got up when he was sleeping."

"If you had known that what you had witnessed was a rape, would you have taken measures to stop it?"

"Objection," said Fox.

"Let him answer," Maitland said.

"If I had known it for sure, sir, I believe I would have done something."

"But you did not do anything—is that correct?"

"That is right, sir," Moon said. Gore returned to his seat.

The last prosecution witness was Conway, one of the Bravo Company medics. Kahn remembered how his face had looked when he lifted it from Sharkey's chest, back at The Fake. Fox established through questioning that he had gone to the Second Platoon positions in the morning after someone told him the two girls were in bad shape.

"Both of them were lying in a foxhole, and they didn't seem like they could move much at all. The older one, she was just like a dishrag when you throw it against the wall," Conway said.

"Did you examine them?" Fox asked.

"Yessir, sort of. There wasn't much for me to do. They didn't teach us about those kinds of problems—ah, female problems."

"But you did examine them?"

"Yes, I did. The older girl was the worst. Her stomach was distended like a three-months-pregnant woman. I didn't want to touch her, she was so sloppy."

"What about the younger girl?"

"She was pretty bad off too. Her blouse was open, her breasts were exposed and her pants were torn at the crotch. There was a lot of blood on them."

"Did you try to aid them?"

"Yessir, I was about to give the older one a shot of morphine because she seemed to be in a lot of pain, but then Lieutenant Brill came down and he said for the girls to get up and go with him and the interpreter."

"Where did he take them?"

"Just down the path a little ways. There was a bare space where the bushes had all been beaten down."

"And you followed them?"

"Everybody did, sir."

Fox led Conway through a line of questions similar to those he had asked Spudhead, establishing that Brill had told the prisoner to shoot the girls. Twice Gore stood up and objected on grounds that what had happened to the girls at the hands of Lieutenant Brill was not material to the Army's case against these defendants, but Maitland allowed Fox to proceed. Conway reached the point at which the prisoner was having trouble with the safety on the M-16.

"What were the girls doing all this time?" Fox asked.

"The older one, she was barely able to stand up and she was looking at the ground. The young girl was just standing there holding her blouse together where it was torn."

"Did the prisoner shoot them?"

"Yessir, he did. He shot the older girl first."

"What happened to the girl after she was shot?"

"Her head flew back and she fell to the ground."

"Was she dead?"

"I do not know, sir. She twitched a little bit, but she did not move."

"And did the prisoner then shoot the other girl?"

"Not right away. He looked over at Lieutenant Brill. The lieutenant had his pistol out, not pointing at him, but he had it out and cocked."

"But the prisoner eventually did shoot her?"

"He did, sir. He shot her twice, and I believe one of the shots missed but the other hit her in the chest and she went down hard."

"What did you do then?"

"I went over to her. Everybody was just standing there, not saying anything. I think they were very shocked. I looked at her. It appeared her chest was rising and falling, and her eyes were like when you look up at the sun—she wanted to open them but the sun was too bright."

"Did you try to assist her?"

"No, sir, I did not. I did not know what to do. I might have been able to help her, but Lieutenant Brill was the one who had gotten her shot, and so I guessed he wanted her dead. I have never been in a situation like that before, sir. It wouldn't have done any good to try to help her."

"What happened then?"

"The lieutenant took back the rifle from the prisoner and he looked at the girl himself. He was standing over her. Then he pointed the rifle at her and braced it on his hip and he fired it twice into her."

"And this killed her?"

"Yessir. The first round made her head jump. Then he fired a second round and her head looked just like a hole. It had exploded. It spread brain matter all over the ground in the area."

"And then what happened?"

"Then everyone just sort of drifted away. I went back up to my positions. I guess everybody else did too."

"I have no more questions," Fox said acidly. Some of the court members were looking with open hostility at the table of the accused.

"Private Conway," Gore said walking to the witness chair, "when you examined these two women at first, you said they had been raped. What made you conclude that?"

"From the way they looked, sir; they were pretty badly worked over."

"What do you mean worked over? Had they been beaten? Were there any indications that they had been injured aside from their sexual organs?"

"No, sir, not that I saw."

"Did either of them state to you that she had been raped?"

"They did not say anything to me, sir. But even if they had I wouldn't have understood it."

"So you base your conclusion on the fact that their sexual organs were strained from too much sex—is that correct?"

"You would have had to have seen it to know what I mean, sir. I mean they really did a job on them, like I said . . ."

"But you only based your conclusion on your examination of their sexual condition—right?"

"That is right, sir."

"I have nothing further," Gore said.

Fox was already on his feet.

"Private Conway, you described earlier the condition of the girls' clothing. Would you repeat that for the court."

"It was very torn. The younger girl, her blouse was like it had been ripped. And the older one was torn in the crotch."

"At the time, what did you make of that? Did it suggest to you that the girls might have been forcibly assaulted?"

"It did, sir."

"Thank you, Private Conway. I have no further questions," Fox said. He turned to Maitland. "The Army has concluded its presentation, sir."

"Very well," Maitland said. "Does the defense wish to call witnesses or introduce evidence?"

Gore rose halfway out of his chair. "No, sir," he said calmly.

"Very well, then," Maitland said. "It's nearly lunch-time. We will resume at fourteen hundred hours for closing arguments."

KAHN CAUGHT up with Gore in the hallway outside the courtroom. "Like what you heard in there?" the lawyer said.

Stung by the coldness in his voice, Kahn looked Gore hard in the eye. "You were the one who told me I should be here," he said.

Gore smiled a creaky grin. "Right. Wanta get a cup of coffee?"

They walked through the packed-dirt streets to the coffee shop and ordered two cups, which they took out to a table beneath a banyan tree. The sun was hot and the air humid but not stifling, since it had rained sometime during the morning while they were in the courtroom.

"What do you think?" Kahn said.

"Hard to say. It's better than I thought it would be."

"God, I don't see how."

"I'll tell you something," Gore said with just a hint of bitter satisfaction. "It's all appearances. What you see in a criminal trial—or any kind of trial, for that matter—most times it doesn't bear a whole lot of resemblance to what really happened.

"Take this guy Poats, for example."

"Yeah, how did you know about that?" Kahn asked. "I never knew about it."

"Groutman told me—I think—or maybe one of the others—doesn't make any difference. Anyway, he and the rest of them banged some village whore. He doesn't think there's anything wrong with it, right?—he'd never have gone to Brill to blow the whistle in this thing, if he had. In fact, there wasn't anything wrong with it, I suppose, but you make it look like there was. See what I mean? Appearances—all appearances," Gore said. "Their weak point is they don't have any documentary evidence to show rape. To the court it sure looks like rape, but proving it's another thing."

"Well, everybody knows what went on—there must have been two dozen wit—"

"Doesn't make any difference," Gore said matter-of-factly. "Fox is a damned good lawyer. I know—we went through JAG school together. But he's up Shit's Creek in this one because the general screamed so much about getting it tried fast and wouldn't let him let one of my guys off the hook on a lesser charge so he could testify against the others—at least, I guess that's what happened, because Fox is too good a lawyer to go into court with the case he just put on. You can imagine what would have happened if one of my guys had gotten up there and started implicating the others. But it didn't happen, so there you go—anyway, it looks bad enough now."

HOSTILITY AND outrage were exuded by Captain Fox when he addressed the court with his final argument.

"The defense will apparently try to persuade you that a rape never happened." He gestured toward the table of the accused. "The *defense*," he said, barely disguising contempt, "would like you to believe that those two little girls—who were murdered in cold blood according to the testimony of several witnesses—gave themselves willingly to the abuse of these men, and others so far unidentified. But you have all heard the account of the witnesses this morning. That their clothing was torn and bloody. That they were hardly able to stand. That they moaned and whimpered while being assaulted. I ask you gentlemen to recall the testimony of the company medic who examined these girls shortly before they died. Can you honestly believe that these two girls, sixteen and fourteen years old, actually volunteered for and agreed to acts which left them in that horrible condition?"

Fox made much of the "rumor" that had circulated

that the girls were to be raped to avenge Sergeant Trunk and leaned heavily on Spudhead's testimony that some of the accused had joked about the rapes afterward.

"Two elements must be present to convict in a crime of this nature," Fox said. "Motive and opportunity. There can be no doubt that the opportunity was there, and as for the motive..."

Fox hammered a few more points home and then sprang his conclusion.

"There is no more plain or eloquent statement to put the crimes of these men into perspective," Fox said, "than these words by the late General Douglas MacArthur. regarding the trial of General Tomoyuki Yamashita, the Butcher of Bataan."

He stepped back and read loudly to the court:

"'Rarely has so cruel and wanton a record been spread to public gaze. Revolting as this may be in itself, it pales before the sinister and far-reaching implication thereby attached to the profession of arms. The soldier, be he friend or foe, is charged with the protection of the weak and unarmed. It is the very essence of reason for his being. When he violates that sacred trust he not only profanes the entire cult but threatens the fabric of international society.

"'The traditions of fighting men are long and honorable. They are based on the noblest of human traits—sacrifice. These men,'" Fox said, and as he said it, pointed a finger directly at the table of the accused, "'have failed this irrevocable standard; they failed their duty to their country, to their enemy, to mankind; have failed utterly to their soldier faith.

"'The transgressions resulting therefrom are a blot upon the military profession, a stain upon civilization and constitute a memory of shame and dishonor that can never be forgotten,'" Fox's face was flushed when he sat down, and to emphasize his own personal sense of outrage he did not look at the court but stared angrily above them at the American flag hanging on the wall. Groutman and the others stared at their table sullenly.

"Captain?" Maitland said.

Gore rose up slowly, his glasses lower than usual on his nose. In his hand was a copy of the United States *Manual for Courts-Martial*, and he began his closing argument by reading a passage from it:

"*It is true that rape is a most detestable crime . . . but it must be remembered that it is an accusation easy to be made, hard to be proved but harder to be defended by the party accused, though innocent. . . .*"

Laying the book aside, Gore said, "That, gentlemen, is the kernel of what you must decide in this case—not whether these soldiers sitting here committed rape, but whether rape was actually committed at all.

"The witnesses you have heard have been inconsistent about whether what they saw was rape. Only two of them have actually stated that they saw any of the accused having sexual relations with the alleged victims. The rest are implicated only through conversation. Ask yourselves—is it not common for men to boast of sexual exploits even though they did not actually perform them?"

Gore recounted the testimony of Sergeant Moon, "a senior noncommissioned officer with an honorable record who was at the scene—not once, but twice—and stated emphatically that he did not conclude that what he saw was rape." The defense lawyer also chipped away at the testimony of Spudhead and Poats, who had initially labeled the activity rape, then waffled under cross-examination. He painted a picture of the accused as all-American boys, nineteen and twenty years old, some of whom had been wounded and received decorations. Finally he attacked the prosecutor's "rumor"-motive theory as wholly inadequate evidence.

"Men must not be sent to prison on hearsay!" Gore proclaimed righteously. "The defense does not discount that such a rumor might have been spread in the encampment; but if these accused talked of foul deeds, they spoke as men who had seen so much killing and human suffering that it made little difference to them to discuss it in conversation.

"The question here is rape, and no firm evidence has

been presented, in witness' testimony or otherwise, that a rape actually occurred. The witness, Private Miter, who spent some time himself in the foxhole with those women, testified that what he saw was rape. Yet his conclusion was by inference only. The witness, Private Poats, who admitted being engaged in a sexual group thing with a Vietnamese woman two weeks earlier, was unable to identify a single one of the accused as being present on his visit to the Second Platoon positions. Sergeant Moon, who went down to check, did not think it was rape, and the medic, Conway, freely admitted that his training was inadequate for him to form a decision as to whether or not a rape had occurred.

"Reasonable doubt," Gore said, letting the words hang on his tongue while he surveyed the court. "If these soldiers are to be found guilty of this most serious of crimes, it must be proved *beyond a reasonable doubt*.

"It is not incumbent on them to explain what happened out there that dark rainy night. It is up to the prosecution to prove *beyond a reasonable doubt* that rape did occur. So far what the prosecution has done is throw up a smoke screen of 'torn clothing' and 'moaning.' How do we know *beyond a reasonable doubt* that these were not signs of ecstasy? *Beyond a reasonable doubt*.

"No matter how repugnant the idea may be, it is necessary for you to consider the character of the women in question. The fact that they were killed has no bearing on the case at hand. These men are charged in a rape—not in murder—and no evidence whatsoever suggests that they were in any way involved in the killings. These two females were in custody as Viet Cong prisoners—not innocent civilians as the prosecution has suggested. All of you are aware that teen-aged males and females can be as dangerous to the American soldier here as the most hardened North Vietnamese. Perhaps more so because their danger is insidious and unexpected.

"Finally, I ask you to consider the character of the female population of this very town. The entire country has been referred to as 'a vast brothel.' Is it not true that every night hundreds if not thousands of young

women—many of them barely in their teens—emerge to
solicit money for sex from the troops stationed here—and
that on a given night, they might take on all comers in
exchange for a prostitute's fee?

"What I am suggesting is that a reasonable doubt
exists. The prosecution has not established rape; it has
only hinted at it. And hints are not enough to send men to
prison and ruin their future lives."

Captain Gore returned to his chair. He did not look at
the six men at his table, or at the glare he received from the
Judge Advocate, Captain Fox.

TWO HOURS later the verdict was returned. Kahn was not
present in the courtroom when it was announced and
received word of it from Gore in his office later in the
afternoon. The court had found Groutman and Maranto
guilty of "taking lewd and indecent liberties with the
person of a female," a lesser included charge, and
sentenced them to three years each at hard labor,
forfeiture of pay and bad-conduct discharges. The rest
were acquitted and sent back to the Company. No one
was convicted of rape, and the case was officially closed
except for the trial of Kahn, which was scheduled for the
following afternoon.

"It's hard to believe," Kahn said, but Gore ignored the
comment and remained uncommunicative during the
conversation except to go over some of the questions he
planned to ask him on the witness stand. When he was
satisfied, he put away his note pad and shut the filing
cabinet, turning over a sign that read OPEN so that it said
CLOSED.

"I'll see you tomorrow," he said. "It's at thirteen
hundred, but be a little early." He turned off the light and
preceded Kahn to the door.

"You going for a drink?" Kahn asked.

"Yeah."

"The air base?"

"I guess so."

"Want some company?"

"Not really," Gore said. He removed his glasses and

began wiping them with a handkerchief. "I think I'm going to drink by myself tonight."

"Oh," Kahn said. He followed Gore down the hall, walking just a pace behind. "Listen," he said, "I didn't do anything to piss you off, did I?"

Gore put the glasses on again and tried to smile. "No, you didn't piss me off. I just don't feel very good right now. As a matter of fact, I think I feel sick," he said.

34

THE SAME day Kahn went to trial, the new
Commander of Bravo Company, Lieutenant C. Francis
Holden III, was inspecting his forward positions. He was
passing by one of the observation posts when DiGeorgio
pointed out something he had been observing with
puzzlement most of the afternoon.

"I don't know if it means nothin', sir," DiGeorgio said,
"but they been comin' and goin' down there for three, four
hours."

Holden brought the binoculars down on a cluster of
huts at the edge of the paddy, about five hundred yards
away. He focused on perhaps a dozen women with rice

baskets balanced on their heads, walking along a dike. Each woman would enter one of the huts and emerge minutes later with an empty basket, then return along the dike.

"What do you make of it?" Holden said curiously.

"Beats me, sir," DiGeorgio said. "Looks like they storing the rice down there. I don't know; they never done this before."

Holden zeroed in again. It seemed harmless enough. He raised the glasses to the far end of the valley where a dark mass of rain clouds was gathering above the mountains, blotting out the sun which had shone most of the morning and part of the afternoon. Then he swept across the valley floor. Everything seemed normal. A few people were moving around in the large hamlet, and there was a stillness in the air of the kind that sometimes precedes a storm, and the black clouds on the horizon gave every indication that they were in for weather during the night.

"Let's keep an eye on them," Holden said to the men in the lookout. "It's a little late now; in the morning I'll get a squad together to go down there and find out what plays."

HOLDEN HAD taken over a company in limbo. Ever since the murders, the collective behavior of Bravo Company had resembled that of a person with inner-ear trouble—things were thoroughly and seriously off. Although the mood of violence and hostility had diminished in the aftermath, it had been replaced by a hazy twilight of guilt. Anyone who had been near the scene was affected by this, and it spread in the days following to almost everyone in the Company. Those on trial had become sour martyrs of a sort. If no one was guilty, everyone was guilty; if everyone was guilty, no one was guilty. The shame existed on various levels, and no small amount of it was due to the knowledge that they were all on Battalion's shit list and probably would be for some time to come.

Holden, nevertheless, was enjoying his role as Commanding Officer. On Patch's orders, he had engineered the moving of the Company position downhill, and finally was beginning to feel that he was in the war. In all these months he had never really come to grips with its essential scheme; the politics, the strategy, the viciousness: none of it had ever really jogged his interest. What did intrigue him was whether or not he would be able to function honorably and well. Moreover, Becky was dominating his thoughts less and less now. She was still there, of course, and he knew it wasn't finished entirely. He would have to do something himself to break it off for good, and once he had, she would be gone forever. In the meantime, running the Company gave him something to keep his mind off it.

Two shirtless men were digging in a trench in the new positions beside a disassembled machine gun. One of them stopped Holden as he passed by.

"Hey, sir, we talk to you a minute?"

"What's up?" Holden said.

"See that little rise over there, Lieutenant?"

"Yeah," Holden said, squinting downhill where the man was pointing.

"You said to hold up the perimeter here, but we ain't going to have no interlocking fire if we do. We put out the aiming stakes a while ago, and that rise defilades a big hole coming uphill."

"Yes," Holden said, "I see what you mean. You... ah... what's your name, by the way?"

"Muntz, sir."

"Well, Muntz, you bring up a good point. What do you think we ought to do about it?"

"Only thing I can think of is to move the perimeter down some or either to get some people to shave off that rise with shovels or something."

"That's a good idea, Muntz—better than disturbing the integrity of the perimeter. How long do you think it would take?"

"Dunno, sir; maybe three, four hours, if we had a squad on it."

"Okay, Muntz," Holden said. "Good idea. I'll send some people down first thing in the morning and I want you to get it done. First thing, all right?"

"Right, sir," Muntz said darkly, and after Holden walked away he threw down his entrenching tool in disgust and said to the other man, "What'd I tell you?—Them fucking jerk-off officers—say to do something one minute and change it the next. Lookit that goddamned Brill—we ain't ever gonna get outta here because of the shit he pulled. Officers don't know their asses from live steam."

"Whatya expect?" the other man said. "You such a dumb bastard you think officers know what they're doing?"

Muntz snatched up the shovel and resumed furious digging. After a while he stopped and turned to the other man as though he had had a revelation.

"That's *Mister* Bastard to you, scumbag."

IN THE eyes of the United States Army, Lieutenant William Kahn had sinned, and sinned mightily, and what remained was the formality of establishing his guilt beyond a reasonable doubt and punishing him. The *Manual for Courts-Martial* contains a depressing list of charges and specifications ranging from minor offenses, such as drinking liquor with a prisoner or using provoking words and gestures, to major ones, such as being a spy or murderer. In between are a hundred and nine other offenses covering practically every vice known to man, and it was from among these that Captain Fox selected the four issues he intended to prove at trial.

The former Commander of Bravo Company stood at attention before the same court that had tried the other six (except that the three sergeants had been replaced by two captains and a major) while Fox intoned his crimes:

"One—Dereliction of his duties during the period six February by negligently failing to enforce adequate safeguards to protect female Oriental prisoners then in custody of his unit from physical maltreatment.

"Two—Failure to obey a lawful regulation—paragraph three, USARV regulation thirty-three dash three: Failure to report the nonbattle death of an Oriental human being.

"Three—Making false statements under oath to an officer lawfully investigating a crime.

"Four—Misprision of a felony, to wit: having knowledge that a member of or members of his command had committed a felony and wrongfully concealing such felony by failing to make same known to authorities."

A fifth charge, "Conduct Unbecoming an Officer and a Gentleman," had been dropped by Fox the morning after Gore chided him for overkill.

Many of the witnesses who had testified at the earlier trial were put on the stand by Fox to establish that crimes against the girls had been committed. They told the same grisly story of the rape-murders for the benefit of the new members of the court. In addition, Spudhead Miter recounted his conversation with Kahn several days after the incident, and the investigating officer testified that Kahn had sworn to him that he had no knowledge of rapes and murders. Finally, Fox introduced into evidence a deposition taken by Colonel Patch which attested that he had never received a formal report of the incident from Kahn and that his knowledge of it was limited to a cursory exchange the day afterward when he had come to inspect the Company.

Gore let all of this pass without comment and cross-examination. The light outside was fading through the lone little window in the courtroom when he rose to his feet to present his case. His first and only witness was the accused.

"Going back several weeks before the incident with the prisoners, how would you describe the mood of your men, Lieutenant?" Gore said.

"It was very bad. Morale was rock bottom."

"To what did you attribute this?"

"A lot of things, but I think when the First Sergeant was killed and then we were losing a lot of men and that started the real—"

"Objection! Fox exclaimed. "We are talking about alleged misconduct by this officer on and after February sixth—not the 'mood' of anybody weeks before."

"Can you indicate what you're driving at, Captain Gore?" Colonel Maitland said patiently.

"Sir, I am trying to show that Lieutenant Kahn was under incredible pressure at the time these events occurred and that this behavior was most assuredly colored by that condition."

"Is counsel trying to raise an insanity defense?" Fox asked.

"Not at all. I'm simply trying to put the action in its proper context."

Maitland turned to Gore. "Defense counsel well knows that at this time we are attempting to establish facts: did this officer do what he is charged with, or did he not? Any extraneous subject matter can be brought up later, but first let's find out what happened. Resume your questioning in a different vein."

"All right," Gore said. "Let's move to six February. What were you doing that day?"

"We were in a firefight ... in a valley about fifty kilometers from where the Company laager was. Part of the Company was on patrol—"

"Objection," Fox said. "Defense counsel continues to pursue irrelevant matters."

"Colonel," Gore said, "I am simply trying to establish where the lieutenant was at the time the crimes were committed. We cannot simply open up in a vacuum."

"Proceed," Maitland said peevishly.

"So you were in this firefight. When it ended what happened?"

"We were lifted back to The Ti—to Hill Sixty-seven."

"What time was this?"

"About twenty hundred hours."

"What was your physical condition then?"

"I was very tired—exhausted."

"Please the court," Fox said, on his feet again, "if the lieutenant would like to plead guilty because he was tired, then let him do so and spare us the rest."

"I withdraw the question," Gore said. "Lieutenant Kahn, when you returned to your Company laager, did you notice anything unusual?"

Gore led Kahn through his discovery of the bodies and the conversation with Brill and the arrival of Colonel Patch the next day.

"When the colonel came up to you on the hill, what did he say?"

"He said, 'What are all those bodies down there?'"

"And you said?"

"I told him what Brill had told me. That the male prisoner got loose and shot them."

"What was his reaction to that?"

"He said 'Well, how the hell did that happen?' I believe those were the words he used."

"What did you reply?"

"I said I wasn't sure, that it was still sort of confused."

"Did he tell you to make a written report?"

"No, sir."

"Do you believe the colonel did not want a written report?"

"Objection!" Fox cried. "Counsel knows perfectly well that would be pure conjecture by the witness."

"Mister President," Gore said, "as the court is fully aware, I have attempted in every way possible to have the colonel present at this trial, but my requests have been denied. The prosecution has introduced a deposition from him, but under the circumstances of his absence it is only fair that my witness be allowed to present his views on the colonel's thinking."

"Captain Gore," Maitland said, "as I stated earlier, the colonel is presently engaged in a large field operation from which he cannot be detailed. His sworn deposition is more than enough to suffice. I think you could rephrase the question so that it does not violate the rules of evidence."

"May I approach the court?" Gore said. Maitland nodded, and Gore and Fox stepped forward. The court members huddled in for a conference.

It was nearly dark outside and the dust had settled down. Wishing he had a cigarette, Kahn sat forlornly in the witness chair and pondered the answer he would have given to Gore's question. Did he really believe Patch had wanted no written report? He wanted desperately to think so, but in the last few days the truth had become murky and obscured, and in a way it became whatever he said it was. . . .

The bench conference continued, with heated whispering between Gore and Fox.

That morning, Kahn had thought he had it all sorted out. But the testimony of Spudhead and the others pulled him back to the daily rising fear and frustration and loneliness and self-doubt and self-pity too, and the animal-like living and ultimately animal-like thinking.... As he had listened to it, a nauseating knot rose in his stomach, the same familiar knot that had plagued him every day whenever he was out there and had become so much a part of him that it seemed normal, except at times like this, when just listening to somebody else talk about it brought it back....

Without realizing it, Kahn had been gripping the witness chair with both hands, and his legs were tucked tightly into the rungs as though he were holding on to it for dear life, which in a way he was, because despite the awful reason he was sitting here, at least it was safe and secure, and his responsibility was only to himself—not like out there ... not like out there ... For a brief moments his mind darted around in a tight panic as he realized he was going back out there, and if anyone had come up to him, just then, and ordered him to leave that chair, or tried to pry him from it, he would have defended his right to sit there very fiercely.

"All right," said Gore. "Did there come a time when Private Miter spoke with you about what had happened to the prisoners?" Kahn was startled to discover that the conference was over and the questioning had resumed.

"Uh, yes, there did," he said shakily.

"Tell the court about that encounter."

"He, ah, came up to me about three days afterward and asked if he could talk to me. He said, 'Do you know what happened?' and I told him I did because Lieutenant Brill had told me, and he said that he did not believe Brill told me the truth and asked if I wanted to hear the real truth, and then he told me the same thing he testified to this afternoon."

"Did you believe him then?"

Kahn looked past Gore to the table where the earnest-faced Virginian, Captain Fox, was chewing on his pencil and watching him with a barely disguised look of contempt, as though he thoroughly anticipated that Kahn was going to wriggle off the hook by giving the answer he and Gore had discussed earlier—that Miter was an unstable soldier who frequently needed to visit the Chaplain and was against the war and could not be depended upon. Kahn imagined that as he said this, the expression on Fox's face would dissolve into a look of full-fledged disgust.

"Could you answer the question, please?" Gore said in a slightly bewildered voice.

"Did I believe him?" Kahn said calmly. "I'll have to answer it this way—yes and no. I guess I did believe him... but... I didn't want to, and I suppose I made up excuses in my own mind why I shouldn't, and I—"

A pained look shot across Gore's face. "Ah, when was the next time you spoke to anyone about the incident of February sixth?" he interrupted hurriedly.

"Please the court," Fox said rising quickly to his feet, "I believe the witness has not finished answering the first question."

"He answered it," Gore said nervously. "I don't want to get into it too deeply. I have my line of questions all drawn out."

"I'm sure you do," Maitland said condescendingly. "However," he said, turning to Kahn, "Lieutenant, did you have something more to say on the question you were just asked?"

Kahn swallowed hard. Gore was staring at him sternly.

"Yessir, I do," he said.

"Please go on."

"Well, what I was trying to say is that... uh... I knew deep down the first time I talked to Brill that something wasn't right about it. I'm trying to be as honest as I can. I was going to look into it the next morning. But after the colonel came, and he didn't seem very interested, I just sort of let it drop. I pretty much knew what happened after I talked to Miter, but all I wanted then was not to have to deal with it.... I guess that's how low I had gotten."

Kahn paused for a moment. All the while he had been talking he had stared straight ahead, and now he looked at the court. They were leaning forward attentively, all of them.

And it *was* low, he thought. Raping little girls. Killing little girls. War! War! War! Rape, pillage, burn—the words came back to him now the way they had that day on the Tit. A few months ago, this time of day, he might have been playing bridge at the fraternity house, or guzzling beer, or studying for a test in Intermediate Light ...instead of sitting here stark bareass alone before a court-martial. At the age of twenty-four, he'd come a long way. Yet in the instant he had begun to tell the truth—and he knew this time it was the truth, not his truth, or anyone else's, but the real, honest truth—he had felt a quick flashing revelation, much like the glimmer he had felt once out in Happy Valley looking up at the stars and mountain peaks. A few seconds ago, when he'd answered Gore's question truthfully, the ring of self-preservation around Billy Kahn began to collapse like a house of cards, and a shiver ran up his spine like steam in a riser pipe until he felt his face flush and tingle. He also knew instinctively that he had set a trap for himself, into which he would not proceed, wittingly, the best way he could.

"I'm not trying to make excuses, but dead people...get to where they don't mean much after a while; they're just like hunks of meat. Mostly, the best thing you can do is to go on with whatever you're doing and forget about it."

Captain Gore had returned to his seat and was slumped motionless in the chair looking over his glasses at Kahn with a wan expression. Colonel Maitland, his eyebrows raised, cleared his throat.

"Does the defense wish to make a statement at this time?" he asked.

Gore replied, half-rising, "I believe he's making it, sir."

Maitland turned to Kahn.

"What about what you told the investigating officer when he came out to question you?"

"It was a lie, sir," Kahn said. "He asked me if I had heard the girls were raped and murdered and I told him that all I knew was what Brill told me. That wasn't the truth. I don't know why I said it, except that I knew we were all in for a hell of a lot of trouble if I said the truth—just like I knew I'd be opening a big can of worms if I had gone down there and started asking questions. Once you start to lie, it goes on and on. I guess this is where it ends, though."

Kahn noticed that Fox had been looking across at Gore almost sympathetically.

"Does defense counsel wish to question the witness further?" Maitland asked.

"No, sir," Gore said.

"Would you, Captain Fox?"

"No, I think not, sir."

"Very well," Maitland said. "What we have just heard has saved us all a great deal of time. You may step down, Lieutenant Kahn; thank you." He looked at the other court members.

"The court will now go into closed session. It's getting late, but if you gentlemen would like to wait out in the hall I don't think this will take very long."

THE THREE of them—Kahn, his defense counsel and the prosecutor—filed out into the hallway. The MP stepped out behind them and assumed a wooden position in front of the door.

Gore marched straight to a windowsill and stared out at the sunset. Fox and Kahn lit up cigarettes at opposite ends of the hall. After a while, Fox went up to Gore and the two began a muffled conversation. At first the prosecutor did most of the talking and Gore occasionally nodded his head. Then the defense counsel began talking and Fox began nodding, and at one point there was a bitter, stifled laugh from Captain Gore.

The door to the courtroom opened suddenly, and one of the new captains on the court said something to the MP, who had snapped to attention. "They're ready for you, sirs," he said to the lawyers. As he walked back into the courtroom, Kahn felt weak and sick. He had a flash of how Carruthers must have felt entering his tent for punishment.

THE THREE of them stood before the court: Fox off to the right; Kahn squarely in front, with Gore at his side. Maitland got right to the point.

"Lieutenant William Kahn, it is my duty as President of this court to advise you that the court in closed session and upon secret written ballot has found you guilty or not guilty as follows:

"Of the charge of Misprision of a Felony—not guilty.

"Of the charge Dereliction of Duties, failing to enforce adequate safeguards for prisoners—not guilty.

"Of the charge Failure to Obey a Lawful Regulation—not reporting a nonbattle death—guilty.

"Of the charge Making False Statements Under Oath—guilty.

"Do you wish to make a statement before court passes sentence?"

Gore glanced at Kahn. "None, Mister President," he said.

"Very well, then." Maitland returned to the sheet of paper before him.

"Lieutenant Kahn, you have been duly convicted on charges of Failure to Obey a Lawful Regulation and Making False Statements Under Oath. It is my duty to advise you that the court has adjudged that you shall receive a reprimand in your officer's personnel file and pay a fine of fifteen hundred dollars to be deducted from your pay at the rate of two hundred dollars a month until paid, or paid in full before you may be separated from the service. Is there anything else from counsel?"

When no one spoke, Maitland looked directly at Kahn, his eyebrows furrowed down so that he resembled a neolithic primate. "This proceeding is closed," he said.

A COOL breeze was flowing in off the South China Sea and the sky was low and overcast when they stepped out into the dirt street. A stream of raucous servicemen was pouring past the compound, riding in cyclos or jeeps or on foot, headed toward the old center of town, where the action was. At the bottom of the steps, Captain Fox turned and waved at Gore, nodded politely to Kahn and disappeared into the night. The accused, now convicted, and his counsel walked without speaking for a while. Then Gore turned to him, as always peering over his glasses. "You are certainly not my ideal client," he said, to which Kahn rpelied, "No, I suppose not," and Gore said, "You use a drink? I could," and Kahn said, "Yeah, a drink would be good."

THE RAIN that night came out of the west and spread over the Valley of The Tit in a steady, pin-prickling drizzle that would not reach Nha Trang before morning. Huddled in its shelters on the hillside, Bravo Company waited sullenly through the storm, gripped in a state of agitation for which there was no explicable reason.

Far down the valley the reason moved.

It shuddered in the jungle-covered hills beneath dripping leaves, vexed to savage fury by weeks of cold anticipation, hard-won calculations and somber plans. At last its orders came. A core of scraggly, raggedy-assed brown-skinned men with vague and inarticulate hopes and dreams moved across the valley floor and into the first hamlet, where mothers and fathers and children squatted by candlelight or cooking fires in dirt-floored huts—into which The Reason entered and said that it was Time. Weapons wrapped in oilcloth or cellophane were dutifully removed from secret places, and The Reason moved again—larger, more powerful—into the rain.

By the light of the pressure lantern in his leaking tent, the new Commander of Bravo Company had concluded a letter which began *"Dear Becky"*:

> *I've torn up every letter I tried to write you until this one, but it's going out in the morning mail.*
> *It has been more than four months since you wrote that you were dumping our relationship to go with Widenfield and do all that silly crap you and he are*

involved with. I don't know if you planned it that way or not, but your letter arrived exactly a year to the day we met at Cory's party. Nice timing.

All those months we were seeing each other before I left I kept my mouth shut about what you were doing. I figured you would come to your senses sooner or later, but in fact, you only got worse. I don't know why I put up with it for so long, except that I loved you and hoped you would change.

It has taken me a long time to get used to the idea, but at last I can truthfully say it is finished between you and me. Not that you'd give a damn. I'm sorry, but not sad, because there are things more important than merely loving somebody and I'm just beginning to understand them.

I'm really in the war now—not just running errands for the general. I am commanding a rifle company in the field, and for the first time in my life I can honestly say that I feel completely and totally in control—of myself, of the Company, and of where I fit into this world.

I needed to write this letter, so I did. Now the radio is squawking and I'd better go out and see what's up. Before I do, I'd like to say good luck, and goodbye.

> *Regards,*
> *Frank*

He left the letter on the field table and walked outside. Bateson, the RTO, was hurrying toward him, and they met halfway in the rain.

"Lieutenant, sir," Bateson said breathlessly, "LZ Horse is getting zapped, and so is an ARVN compound up by Tien Trang. Battalion put out a Condition Red as of now. They've overrun some Artillery battery too. The colonel says to be ready to help out if he gives the word and for us not to call unless it's bad because they got all the traffic they can handle right now."

Holden stood motionless for a moment, the rain dripping off his helmet.

"All right; go stand by the radio and get me some runners to keep me posted," he said. "And get somebody to tell Sergeant Dreyfuss to start putting out the word and then tell him to find me—I'll be down on the perimeter somewhere."

Holden walked back into the tent and picked up the letter. He folded it neatly and tucked it into his top pocket. Then he slipped on his poncho, strapped on his .45 and picked up his rifle and several clips of ammunition, which he stuck into the pistol belt. One last look around the tent; then he turned out the lantern. As he walked out into the wetness, there was a faint, featureless grumbling of artillery. It seemed far away but fairly constant, and through the rain he could make out the flashes, pink and low behind the mountains. Below him, an unseen tidal wave was swelling across the valley, gathering strength from hamlet to hamlet.

No ONE saw the flash, but the single *crump* of a mortar incoming reverberated up the hillside. People began to shout and curse, and in the few seconds before it landed, Holden suddenly realized he'd made his first mistake a few hours earlier by not looking into the comings and goings of the women carrying the rice into the huts at the bottom of the hill—because, damn it, there wasn't any harvest yet, so why should . . . ? In that same instant there was the sigh of the incoming round, and he went to ground cursing himself again for not having dealt with the rise on the perimeter where the machine guns couldn't get to—Damn, damn, I should have done it! I should have!

The round burst behind him, far uphill where the old positions had been. Holden got to his feet and dashed back to the CP, grabbing the telephone to the mortar section, screaming for illumination flares, which came almost instantaneously because they had anticipated the call. Bateson had Battalion standing by as Holden yelled into another phone linked to the listening post down the hillside. As the flares lit up, the garbled cursing at the other end communicated a dark picture of what was yet to come. Then Holden heard the bugles too.

Madman Muntz, squinting over the top of his hole,

could barely make out the moving forms below, but he saw enough in the eerie light to know that this was no ordinary probe. There seemed to be several groups; in one he counted about fifty people, in another twice that number and in a third, which had already reached the base of the hill, there were about two dozen men.

Then, as his eyes adjusted to the light, his breath caught up in his throat. Behind the three groups there seemed to be a huge mob stretching as far as he could see in the fast-fading flare. Among them he thought he even saw women and small children carrying boxes and baskets. And people were blowing whistles and bugles.

Muntz depressed the barrel of his machine gun to the first wave, but they were still too far away for him to open fire. They were plodding uphill very slowly and deliberately, and all at once he thought of rats: a horde of rats—or something like rats—that gathered in groups once a year to make their way to seaside cliffs over which they plunged to their deaths, apparently happily, stopping for nothing. That in itself was very scary.

By now the mortar section had begun to plop shells down into the rice paddy, but they seemed ineffective as the ratlike horde continued its advance. Holden was still in the CP tent, feeling a little panicky because he didn't know if he should remain there by the phones and radios or be outside directing the fight. He could think of about ten things he ought to be doing—and even then he still didn't have a clear idea of what was going on. Bateson had the Artillery Section on the radio, and Holden requested firing of Defensive Targets, which had been preset some time before. All four field phones were ringing like crazy, and while waiting for an answer, Holden screamed at three of the worried-looking runners Bateson had selected, "Don't just stand there—answer the goddamn phones!" and the runners gratefully leaped for the phone table and began taking calls.

The popping of small-arms fire below grew steadily as the fighting joined. Holden glanced at his watch: exactly 9 P.M. He closed his eyes. "When I open them . . . this will be gone." He knew when he thought it, it was silly. Then the incoming mortars began raining down on them, and were answered by their own mortars and by the first of the DTs, which cracked and split violently in the valley.

In his hole on the perimeter, Crump had been taking an occasional well-aimed shot at the advancing enemy, but there were so many of them now, he was having difficulty deciding whom to shoot at. They were coming up in long files, through the sheets of rain, taking cover wherever they could, but always coming. As another flare lit up, Crump rapidly squeezed off three rounds, and several men in one of the files toppled in a dominolike heap. Others clambered over or around them.

Off to one side, standing plainly in the open, one man was spurring the others on by waving a pistol and yelling.

He was standing in an odd way, bent over a little to one side, and in the dimming light Crump saw that one of his trouser legs was pinned up at the knee and he was leaning on a crutch. As the flare flickered out, Crump got a look at the man's face, which seemed terribly familiar, and as he lined his sights directly at the trunk of the one-legged man, the flare died out. Another burst, but the man was gone, and Crump was left to curse his luck and wonder if he'd been right.

THE TONE of the call that came into the TOC from Bravo Company, even through the radio jargon, was so desperate that any officer or enlisted man in hearing distance stopped what he was doing and turned to listen. They too were alert at Monkey Mountain, but what the caller said—*"I think we're being overrun"*—pierced the tent like a distant scream in the night. For an hour Patch and his staff had been directing support for the fighting, but as the attacks on their tentacles mounted, more men and equipment were being consumed than could be marshaled. Captain Flynn, the aide, was trying to soothe the frightened voice on the radio when Patch took the handset.

"What is you situation? Over."

"Sir, Lieutenant Range is dead and so is Lieutenant Peck, and the CO—I don't know where he is...."

"And the First Sergeant?"

"He's in pretty bad shape. Most everybody's hurt or killed. Everything's falling apart—we gotta have help fast, sir."

"Who's running things now?"

"Lieutenant Inge. He's out now trying to pull the men together so we can make a stand if we have to. Please hurry, sir. Over."

Patch digested this information grimly. Everyone who had been listening was now looking at him.

"Okay," he said, "we're on the way. It'll take about a half an hour—maybe forty-five minutes, though. You hang on down there, hear? Over."

There was a pause, and the person at the other end was depressing the transmit bar so Patch could not get through. Then the radio crackled again.

"Sir... my name is DiGeorgio..."

"Roger, DiGeorgio—you hang on there, now. And one more thing: we'll be coming up on your right flank. I guess you'll tell those guys to watch who they shoot? Over."

"Roger, sir," DiGeorgio said. Something else was said, but it got garbled in the transmission.

"Goddamn it!" Patch spat, "we've got to pull some kind of relief together. What in hell have we got?"

"Colonel," said Flynn, "there are about half a dozen APCs in motor pool—down for something—but I'll bet most of them'll run. We might be able to scare up a tank, and there's that platoon from C Company and a lot of straphangers waiting around for something. I could take them down there myself."

"Right—good," Patch said. "Get the APCs and I'll take care of the tank. Round up every cook and shitkicker you can find. You sure they can get down that road? We don't want 'em to get stuck five miles away."

"I'm pretty sure, sir—I flew over it a few days ago."

"All right—but look, I can't spare you to go, so we'll have to find somebody else. Think of somebody—quick."

A look of relief disguised in disappointment filled Flynn's face. "Ah, the only one I can think of is Lieutenant Styles in MPs."

"Colonel Patch," said a voice from behind, "I can take that column down there."

Patch looked over his shoulder directly into the face of Major Dunn, who had been standing by his bank of radios most of the night.

"Major," Patch said curtly, "that is very admirable, but with the communications situation we have here—"

"Colonel, there isn't a goddamn thing I can do for the communications station at this point. These men are perfectly competent technicians and they have everything under control. I'm just in the way here. I would appreciate it very much if you were to permit me to do this. I have friends there."

They looked at each other closely, the West Point colonel and the bootstrap major with the sad eyes and graying hair, and for an instant Patch saw a fierce determination in Dunn's eyes which he had recognized before in certain officers of proven field merit.

"Major, you're in charge. Captain Flynn will go with you to motor pool." He turned to Flynn. "Brief him on what to do, Tom—and try to scare up some NCOs."

MAJOR DUNN's relief column had been grinding down the rain-swept, pitted spur with nightmare slowness for half an hour, lights out since they had turned off the main road. Locked in the darkness of the steel personnel carriers was a nervous grab bag of jeep drivers, mechanics, KPs, new arrivals, men going to R&R—or returning from it—and others unfortunate enough to have been swept up in Captain Flynn's dragnet.

"I think I see it, sir," the driver of the second vehicle called back into the cabin. Major Dunn crawled forward, and through the viewing slit could take out pale flashes against the lowered sky. The driver resumed his radio conversation with the big tank ahead. Dunn punched him on the shoulder. "Try to raise them again—maybe we're close enough now." The driver reached over and switched frequencies. A minute later he turned and shook his head.

"Nothing, sir," he shouted back. "I'll see if the tank can get them—he's got better radio...JEEZUS!" A searing flash of hot light burst through the slit, and the carrier jolted sideways and slammed to a stop. There was another awful explosion, and through the observation slit Dunn could see flames and smoke silhouetted against the blackness.

"Jesus God," the driver shrieked, "the tank..."

"Back it up! Back it up!" an Armor lieutenant was screaming. "Tell them to back it up back there!"

"What the hell's this?" Dunn exclaimed. The vehicle had gone into reverse and was backing up as fast as it could go. "What are you doing?" He grabbed the lieutenant's shoulder.

"We're backing up—They got the tank—Get the hell out of here!" the lieutenant cried.

"You can't do that!" Dunn said. "We'll have to go around it."

"SOP," the lieutenant said. "We get fire, we back up—C'mon, Red, move it!"

"Screw SOP!" Dunn bellowed. "Get this goddamn thing going forward again. Do you know what's going on up there?"

"Sir, I am not going to put this vehicle in that kind of situation. I'm doing what I'm supposed to do," the lieutenant said.

Dunn grabbed the driver and screamed in his face, "I am ordering you to get this thing out of reverse and move out. I am a major—do you hear me, soldier?"

The driver eased off the accelerator, and the APC came to a throbbing halt. He looked at the lieutenant of Armor.

"What do I do now, sir?" he said.

"Do what he says," the lieutenant mumbled helplessly. "Major," he said, "you must be out of your fucking mind."

Just as the APC lurched forward, a terrific explosion lifted it up on one side and shuddered through every inch of metal, dashing men to the floor in a terrified tangled pile.

"Get back—back up!" the lieutenant screamed again, but the driver had already opened the top hatch and was standing ready to scramble out. "She's dead, sir: we gotta get..." His words were lost in another explosion, worse than the first, which filled the inside of the cabin with thick awful smoke and heat and knocked Major Dunn hard against the side. He felt his hand break at the wrist, felt it crush and give way and the stab of pain, and when he looked into the cabin he could see nothing, nor hear a sound, but there were people in there, because he could glimpse them through the faint smoky light.

Dunn got to his feet dizzily, stepped up on the seat and started crawling out through the hatch. Outside, there was firing from both sides of the road and ahead, and the APC behind them was engulfed in broiling flames. Several bodies were lying on the road, and he heard a lot of yelling. His head was spinning, but his thoughts were clear and condensed into a knot of disappointment. Dear God, he thought, everything I touch...everything I touch...

He felt only a numbness when the bullet slammed into his chest—a numbness that spread quickly.

The pain he waited for never came. Instead, things simply got dimmer. He had a sense of being on his back looking up at the sky, but it was very dark: so dark he couldn't tell if it really was the sky, or perhaps he had closed his eyes—no, they were open, so maybe it was dark. Then, slowly, it began to brighten, and he was aware of a terrific noise, the noise of thousands of people—and the sky brightened into brilliant blue with a few wispy clouds high overhead. It was chilly, but not unpleasant for a clear November day in a football stadium.

He had a sudden surge of energy, and elation as he remembered clearly...so clearly through the years... because he had never done anything, *anything*, so satisfying as that run...that bolting, ripping, slashing sixty-five-yard touchdown run, straight out of the backfield, through waves of would-be tacklers, until he was free with only the goal ahead. Everyone had been behind him. Oh, how the crowd had cheered! As he turned in the end zone, the siren blew and they were all running toward him and he had never felt such a wonderful, satisfying feeling—never again, in all these years—and when they were all over him, hugging and whooping, for an instant he'd closed his eyes and felt himself trembling—aware of nothing, aware of everything—not actually seeing, or hearing, just feeling... Old Dick Dunn... Old Number Thirty-seven... slipping back across the years into a dark and dreamless sleep....

As THE clean white rays of the aurora spread over the misty hills and fields of the Valley of The Tit, the stillness of a perfect morning was broken by the sound of a single helicopter circling overhead. Slowly it descended, the pilot nervously squinting through the haze until the ground came into view. Even before it touched down, Patch could see where Holden had gone wrong.

There were roughly three groups of bodies, all of them bunched closely together as if three separate things had been going on at once. From fifty feet and closing, they looked like peaceful sleepers. He had an urge to cry out, "Get up! On your feet!" but this passed quickly. Patch waited for the machine to shut off before stepping out with his aide. Nearby, several other helicopters were parked idly, blades drooping, pilots still inside. A tall, gaunt lieutenant began walking downhill from where he had been supervising a party of men who remained at their work, silently and methodically bending over each corpse and lifting it into a large bag.

"Tom, this is terrible," Patch said to the aide. His face was strained and white.

"Yes, it is terrible, sir; it is."

"But they made a gallant stand, didn't they, Tom?"

"They did that, sir. Yes, they did," the aide said ashenly.

Digger McCrary, the Graves Registration officer, approached Patch and saluted. "Sir," he said, "we've counted them first—there's forty-two. I only counted the ones on the hill. There's one at the bottom where it drops off up there, and we counted him too, but I haven't sent my men down there because I'm not sure what we may run into. We found a Morning Report that shows there were a hundred and fifteen men here as of yesterday. All those are dead—they made sure of that. Got most of the weapons, too. The Quartermaster people haven't found any machine guns or mortars and only a few sixteens. They even made off with C rations and the phones and radios."

Patch grunted, and stared at the carnage.

"They're still picking up stragglers," he said. "A lot of them managed to get down into the jungle and make their way through. Make your tally after we police everybody up—figure out if anybody's missing from that. Have you found the Company Commander?"

"Yessir, he's up there," McCrary said. "He was in one of the mortar pits. Tube isn't there, but it looked like he had been firing it himself until they got him."

Patch nodded grimly.

"Tom," he said, "let's have a look around." They walked past the first group of bodies, which was spread along twenty yards of freshly dug trench in the middle sector of the perimeter.

"You see that little rise over there?" Patch said. "Now, that can't be enfiladed. Why in hell he ever set in a gun there I don't know. You see what I mean, don't you?"

"Yessir."

"And look at this—when the shit hit the fan, they all started to bunch up. Look at the goddamn space here—you could drive a tank through it."

They walked in silence for a while, along the edge of the wire.

"I'd sure like to know how many of the bastards they took with them," Patch said. "We're going to have to make a guess. I don't see a single one, do you?"

The aide shook his head. "Must have been in the hundreds from the look of things, sir. You can see all the blood trails down there."

"Yes, hundreds—at least. We ought to settle on a figure. . . ."

Suddenly, from the corner of his eye the colonel

glimpsed something—a small animal, monkeylike, sitting on the side of a hole in which lay a single body. It sat absolutely motionless, as though it were guarding the lanky, still form, and fixed its eyes on the two approaching men.

"Hey, what's this?" Patch said. "Hey, little fellow—whoa, there—nobody's going to hurt you," he clucked.

"That's one of those banana-cats, sir," the aide said.

"Yes, yes I know," the colonel said; "I've seen them before. Hey, there—look, it even has on a collar."

Patch stooped to his knees and snapped his fingers as though he were dealing with a dog. "Hey, come 'ere, little fellow," he said gently, but the banana-cat remained motionless and bared its teeth as Patch drew nearer, looking fearful and very much alone.

35

THERE WAS a song that year, the quixotic, fateful year nineteen hundred sixty-seven, that began:

> It's a long, long way from Cam Ranh Bay,
> To the air strip at Pleiku...
> Where many a man has lost his life,
> From doing what he must do...

Which song was widely sung—despite the fact that it never appeared on any charts, or was even recorded, to anyone's knowledge—by pilots, convoy operators, tank crews, Infantry and artillerymen, especially after a few

rounds of beer, and in time it was picked up in Signal
Corps sections and Navy barracks and maintenance
shops and ultimately in replacement depots, which were
overflowing late that winter with a seemingly inexhaust-
able stream of soldiers and sailors and airmen all keenly
geared for the fight that lay ahead. So it was not
surprising that this song was hummed on that gray, misty
morning by the aviator of a helicopter flying into Monkey
Mountain with a load of mail and a lieutenant named
Kahn who had hitched a ride the morning after his
court-martial.

"You hear about all that out here last night?" the pilot
called back over the intercom.

At seven thousand feet the air was cold and bumpy,
and the endless mountains of the Annamese Cordillera
harsh and forbidding. "They were talking about it in the
Flight Section this morning," Kahn said. "Nobody
seemed to have any real poop, though."

The pilot kept his eyes glued ahead. "All I know is that
they overran a company and an Artillery battery, and
some ARVN too, I think. We were on standby the whole
goddamn night."

"Hear what company it was?"

"Didn't hear. But whoever they were, they had to go it
alone. We were socked in from about eighteen hundred
until this morning."

"Yeah," the copilot added; "even the flare ships
couldn't get up—and they'll fly in damned near
anything."

"Who're you with?" Kahn asked.

"Two-thirteenth Aviation."

"Yeah? You know a guy named Spivey flew out to LZ
Horse a lot?"

"Spivey—sure. You heard what happened to him, I
guess?"

"Something happen?"

"'Fraid so—you didn't hear, then. A fucking brigadier
up at Qui Nhon got him to fly down to Tuy Son to one of
those little fishing villages to buy up some fresh lobster for
his goddamned lunch. They zapped him when he was

coming in—never had a chance. They must have been waiting. He took over a hundred holes in the fuselage."

For a few moments, the steady clatter of the rotors was all that could be heard. The pilot went on:

"Happened about a week ago. Worst of it is that this fucking brigadier calls up the CO and says he wants to put all of them in for Silver Stars. He tells the Old Man to write it up with stuff like 'above and beyond the call of duty.' The Old Man just hangs up in his face."

Ahead a dark, grayish peak loomed out of the mist. Sprawled around its base like a strip-mining camp was the Brigade Headquarters at Monkey Mountain.

"We fixed that bastard, though," the copilot said. "Whole damned squadron sits down one night and composes a citation for him to sign—even got an artist to draw a picture for it. It starts out, 'For Heroism: Concerning the Delivery of a Lobster....'"

The aircraft descended sharply. As they drew nearer to the ground, it seemed the whole encampment was abuzz with some kind of activity, but Kahn was thinking of the motto Spivey had painted on the side of his helicopter:

YOU CRY—WE FLY

which was what he remembered most clearly about him now, as he conducted his own private little funeral service in his mind. He wondered what the crazy, slack-jawed Irishman's last thoughts might have been as they opened up on him. Kahn decided they had not been about phosphate. He had probably thought something like "Aw, for the love of God." He used to say it all the time.

The helicopter settled onto the landing pad, and Kahn thanked the pilots and got out. The air was sticky and hot, and the sun beating down mercilessly through a hole in the clouds. Everything seemed different—even the color of the landscape. High on its pole, the flag above the TOC twitched occasionally in a faint breeze.

There was feverish coming and going around the field hospital at the far end of the runway. Carrying his AWOL bag, Kahn set out toward the Administration tent to check back in—and then he noticed a short, sorrowful figure, hatless and wearing mud-stained fatigues, standing rigidly beside the tarmac runway, wringing his hands and making a high, wailing noise. As he came nearer to him, Kahn recognized the face of Private Louis DiGeorgio.

"DiGeorgio, hey, what happened?" Kahn said, trotting over to him. "Were we in that last night?"

DiGeorgio nodded his head.

"We got hit? What is it?"

DiGeorgio nodded again; then he began to choke up. His breath came in quick little gasps, and he put his tightly clenched hands up to his mouth as though he wanted to jam them inside it. He began to sob pathetically.

Kahn touched his shoulder. "Easy, now—it's over. Where's Lieutenant Holden? Is he here?" DiGeorgio bit on his lip and nodded in the direction of the hospital.

"He's hurt? Is he in the hospital?"

DiGeorgio shook his head and pointed to a small cinder-block building set off in the rear and to the side of the hospital. A building Kahn knew well, because he used to go there sometimes and eat ice cream. Suddenly his face flushed and a sick dizziness came over him.

"Dead!"

DiGeorgio nodded again.

"Who else?" he asked painfully.

DiGeorgio didn't answer. He had put his hands back over his mouth as if to stifle some terrible cry, and stood looking at Kahn with tearless, pleading eyes.

The former Commander of Bravo Company took a deep breath and headed up toward the hospital and the morgue. Halfway there, he was intercepted by a private in fresh fatigues and shined boots.

"Are you Lieutenant Kahn, sir?"

"Right," Kahn said, slowing down but not stopping.

"The colonel sent me to tell you to go see him in his tent on the double when you came in."

"Okay. Thanks," Kahn said, continuing toward the hospital.

"Sir," said the private, following along, "he said to tel you, 'on the *double*.'"

"I heard you the first time," Kahn said crisply.

Kahn waded into the milling mob around the hospita and the morgue, and the first person he recognized wa Inge—mud-covered, red-eyed, holding a gauze compres over a large gash in his hand.

"What in hell happened, Inge?" Kahn said. H recognized a few other faces, drawn and filthy, seated o the ground or leaning against the hospital wall. A doze or more poncho-covered bodies were lying neatly outsid the entrance to the morgue, waiting to be stripped washed down and pronounced dead when one of th doctors found time.

Inge did not reply. Like DiGeorgio, he simply stare vacantly past Kahn, off into the distance, miles and mile and miles.

"Inge!" Kahn cried. "How bad is it?"

Several news correspondents, who had gotten wind o the action and flown in earlier, stopped their othe interviews when they heard Kahn's voice and closed i around him. Captain Sonnebend, who had been escortin them, hurried over too.

"Inge," Kahn pleaded. "For God's sake, can't you tel me?"

"Who are you, Lieutenant?" one of the correspondent asked. "Are you with this company?"

"No, he's not; he used to be," Sonnebend said abruptly stepping in close. He put a hand on Kahn's arm. "Kahn, want you to leave the area now. I want it clear for th reporters and authorized personnel."

Kahn tore his arm away. "Get away from me, yo creep!" he shouted. He turned back to Inge and seized hin by the lapels. "God! Say something, Inge, will yo please?"

Digger McCrary had come out of his morgue, an when he saw what was going on he took Kahn gently b the arm and led him away into the cluttered little offic where he did his paperwork.

"What in hell happened, Mac—will you tell me, fo crissakes!" Kahn exclaimed. "Is Holden dead?"

"Sit down a minute," McCrary said. "You want a beer or something?"

"Hell, no! I want to know what's going on."

"All right, I'll tell you. I've tagged forty-three bodies and the hospital's got a couple of more they've just put aside to die. And there're still some missing. Inge led the rest of them out."

"Jesus God, Jesus God," Kahn groaned, burying his head in his hands.

"It was the worst I've ever seen for one company. They ambushed a relief column that Major Dunn took down there, too. He never made it past Surgery. We got him over here about an hour ago."

"And Holden too, right?" Kahn said angrily.

We got him out on the first load. By the way, there was something in his effects..." McCrary produced a mud-stained, wrinkled sheet of stationery.

"It was in his pocket all wadded up like he'd maybe thrown it away and then picked it up again."

Kahn read over the first lines of the letter.

"It's hard to know what to do with something like this," McCrary said. "Ordinarily we'd just send it along, but...ah, do you know the girl?"

"He was having some trouble with her," Kahn said softly.

"Maybe he would have wanted her to get it, then."

"I don't know. I can't think straight right now, Digger. Why don't you let me keep this? I'll see the right thing gets done with it."

McCrary nodded. "No sweat," he said. "And listen, Billy, I'm real sorry about your company."

"What company? There isn't any more company," Kahn said.

KAHN STORMED into Patch's tent like a man flying into a brawl. The Battalion Commander was sitting ramrod straight, wearing the dark sunglasses, his hands folded on the desk in front of him. A cigar smoldered in the ashtray.

"Did the Colonel wish to see me?" Kahn said, addressing him in the old, formal Army style.

"I certainly do," Patch said coldly. "The results of your

court-martial were received here this morning." Kahn said nothing and stared at the face behind the dark glasses.

"I also understand," Patch said, "that you tried to get me dragged into the goddamn mess somehow." Kahn remained at attention and did not reply.

"I have to tell you," Patch went on, "that I have never had such a disgraceful episode occur under my command. Because of the circumstances, I am going to transfer you out of this unit. It will be better for everyone concerned."

Kahn was still at attention, but his fists were clenched. Whatever fear he had once had of Patch had completely vanished. "Does the Colonel's concern extend to a Board of Inquiry?" he said icily.

The Battalion Commander did not flinch. "I don't know what you're talking about, Lieutenant."

"What the Lieutenant means is, is the Colonel concerned that the Lieutenant might testify against him at a Board of Inquiry?"

"What Board of Inquiry?" Patch bristled. "I don't know what you're talking about."

"I'm talking about a goddamn company of men that got wiped out because you're so fucking dumb you wouldn't move them, Colonel!" Kahn exploded. "That's what I'm talking about."

Patch drew himself up like an adder. "There will be no Boards of Inquiry about anything, *Lieutenant*!" he thundered. "And you'd better the hell keep a respectful attitude or I'll have you court-martialed again!"

"There will be, *Colonel*, if I tell the Division Commander I begged you for three goddamn weeks to let me take them off that hill—they were sitting ducks up there. You knew it!"

Something seemed to deflate in Patch. He was still stiffly ensconced behind the desk, eyes hidden by the glasses, but he was working his lips and tongue and teeth together as though he had just been fed a very bitter pill. He stared at Kahn quite a long time before answering, and when he did, he spoke in the tone of a man seeing something precious slip away.

"It's easy for you to try to blame me," he said, "but I'll tell you something, Kahn. When I went out there this morning and saw it, I came back here and I wept, right here at this desk, for two hours. . . ."

"Who wouldn't?" Kahn said acidly. Patch let the remark pass, and went on.

"I had to hold that hill. There was no way around it. Besides, they were reinforced. Something went wrong— they should have been able to hold off a whole army from there—"

"Yeah, like hell—" Kahn started to interrupt, but Patch cut him off.

"All right, go ahead and stir up a Board of Inquiry if you think you can. But I'll beat it. Everything I did was with the approval of the General Staff—and they aren't about to announce to anyone that they were wrong. Go ahead—and I'll walk out of there, and where will that leave you?"

"No worse than I am right now," Kahn said angrily.

"Don't be too sure of that," Patch said. "There have been cases of first lieutenants who have found themselves walking point man in the shooting gallery for the rest of their tours." He let that sink in for a moment.

"Colonel," Kahn said, "you are really one of the sorriest bastards I have ever known."

Patch picked up the cigar and took a puff. Outside, a truck growled in the mud, and the driver's curses wafted into the tent.

"I'll ignore that last comment, Lieutenant, because I think I have learned something from this little conversation. There are some people, and I have met them from time to time throughout my career—and that includes a few at the Academy—who simply are not suited to the military. I believe you are one of them, Kahn. The Army isn't your cup of tea—and you're not the Army's either. So I'm going to suggest something to you. You were working on some kind of advanced college degree before, weren't you? I was reading your Two-oh-one file earlier."

Kahn did not answer.

"You've got about four months left here, and you were

in the field mostly, up till now, right? . . . so I suppose we would fairly say you've pretty much served your time. . . ."

The oaths of the bogged-down truck driver filled the tent as Patch reached across the desk for a note pad and a pen.

"The Army understands these things, Kahn. You're familiar with the 'Early Out' program—you must be. If you wish to apply to go back to finish your degree . . . well, you aren't eligible for another two months . . . but I have good connections in Saigon. I could scrape you under the wire and you could be out of here tomorrow, maybe even today—maybe even *this afternoon*." Patch leaned across the desk, pen in hand.

The truck driver had gotten himself unstuck and roared off in a flood of profanity, leaving a thick, ugly silence in the Battalion Commander's tent. Kahn's brain throbbed and pounded and seemed locked tightly away from the discussion.

"Well, that's it," Patch said, standing and putting on his helmet. "I'll drop this note off at S-One on my way over to the briefing. They will draw up the forms. There's no need to tell me what you decide; just go over there and tell them. You should make up your mind this afternoon, though."

He walked out of the tent leaving Kahn still at attention, facing the empty desk and crushed cigar, and he stood there that way. For a long, long time.

THE STORAGE tent was dark and sweltering as Kahn sat on a cot sorting through his footlocker. He had already turned in his issue gear, and what remained was his—though there wasn't very much; far less, in fact, than he had come over with. There were some pottery bowls he had picked up from a vendor somewhere along the way—his mother would like them; and some snapshots that someone had given him. He would take those too. One of them in particular he liked: a picture of himself and Holden taken sometime before Holden joined the Company. They had been laughing about something, but he had long since forgotten what it was.

Rummaging down to the bottom of the locker, he retrieved one of his two pairs of khakis which had lain undisturbed all through the fighting in the Ia Drang and The Fake and the court-martial. They were still neatly folded, but the months of dampness and heat had caused them to mold slightly—and worse, they had somehow been permeated by the shitsmoke from the latrines. But they were all he had, so they would have to do, and he shook them out and laid them on the cot.

A large, potato-shaped face appeared in the tent opening and searched the darkness.

"Lieutenant Kahn, sir, are you in here?"

"Over here," Kahn said, and Spudhead Miter groped his way inside.

"Lieutenant—ah, somebody said you were leaving. I . . . ah . . . wanted to talk to you."

Kahn had already taken off his boots and was unbuttoning his shirt. "What's up?" he said.

"I . . . just wanted to say that, ah, I'm sorry if I caused any . . . trouble . . . for you, Lieutenant."

"Forget it, Miter. It didn't cause me anything that wouldn't have happened sooner or later anyway. In a way, I'm glad you did. I'm getting out of here now."

"Well, sir, I just want you to know that I . . . you—you and Lieutenant Donovan—were the best officers I've ever had, and I'm going to write my father . . . he's on the, ah, Armed Services Committee . . . and see if he can help you . . ."

"That's nice of you, Miter, but let's just let it go, huh? I'll be Stateside and out of the Army in a few days. I'd rather not stir anything up."

Spudhead thought about it.

"Well, maybe you're right, sir. I wouldn't want to mess up your going home. But I'll be glad to write about the, ah . . . court-martial anyway. . . ."

"There's nothing to write about. Whatever they said I did, I did. There is one thing, though. . . ."

He slipped off the fatigue blouse while Spudhead stood waiting for the rest. But in the end, he did not say it. There might have been a letter to someone, he had thought, asking them to look into forty-some-odd dead men who had been left sitting on the same hill for two months waiting to be massacred. Somebody ought to be asking *why*—and this was the perfect chance; but...

...he couldn't do it, because the second he had accepted the chance to go home, he had entered into a kind of unspoken bargain with Patch, though he hadn't quite realized it at the time. But that was what he had done, and he sure as hell saw it now, and a man couldn't go back on that sort of deal, even if it meant letting the whole thing pass forever.... Besides, it couldn't bring them back. And maybe Patch had been right. He just wanted to get the hell away from here.

"Forget it," Kahn said. "Listen, I appreciate you coming here, Miter, I really do. Don't worry about it. I, er... have to get ready to go now, okay?"

"You sure, sir? I mean, I'd be glad to write him—if you want."

Kahn looked through the brightness of the tent flap. He could hear the roar of helicopters and see groups of men from another battalion, wearing full battle dress, forming up on the landing strip.

"I'll tell you what, Miter," Kahn said. "Why don't you just give me your father's address? Don't you write him or anything. Just let me have it. Maybe I'll stop in and see him, or call, when I get back."

"Sure, sir," Spudhead said. He scribbled it down on a piece of paper and handed it to Kahn, who put it into his wallet. "Well, I just wanted to say goodbye," Spudhead said, and he turned to go.

"Wait a second," Kahn said, extending his hand. "Thanks again—and good luck."

"They said something about making me a clerk, sir," Spudhead said.

"Great. You'll be out of here yourself in a few months, then," Kahn said. "So long."

After Spudhead left, Kahn put on the sour khakis and walked out to the airstrip. The helicopter that would take him away for the last time was warming up in a whining, dusty cloud. The crew chief even took his AWOL bag for him and stowed it in a safe place on the floor.

*   *   *

WHATEVER PATCH'S connections were in Saigon, they must have been very high up and important, because Kahn's departure was arranged so quickly and thoroughly he was gone that very day.

He breezed through the debarkation depot in less than an hour, then was taken by special bus to the air base at Long Binh, and the jet he was ushered aboard was not just any jet but one apparently reserved for generals, State Department and business executives and their wives.

It was a little past midnight when the big 707 roared off the runway and climbed sharply into the tropic sky. From his seat in the front section, First Lieutenant Billy Kahn took his last look at the Land of the River Blindness. The glow of a full moon illuminated shimmering rivers and flat rice fields in the short distance from the air base to the shore of the South China Sea—beyond which he would be safely and totally away from it all. As the plane gained altitude, he could also make out the flickering and flashing of flares and artillery across the darkened land. But he was out of it now—or would be, at least, in a few minutes' time.

It was cold in the cabin, since the air-conditioning system had not yet adjusted to the steep ascent, and Kahn furtively slipped his hands beneath him to keep them warm, hoping the person seated next to him, a middle-aged, bespectacled man who was shuffling through a briefcase on his lap, wouldn't notice. Far ahead the ocean appeared, vast and calm in the moonlight.

The man with the briefcase rose without comment and moved to a seat nearer the back of the cabin, and Kahn stretched his legs across the vacated seat and leaned back. He had a sudden, strange impression that his neighboring passengers had been looking at him; possibly, he thought, they were wondering why a lowly lieutenant was flying in such fancy company. There was one, elderly and important-looking, sitting opposite him in the other aisle. Once Kahn caught him glancing across at him as though he were some unbelievable freak. After a while, he too relocated to the rear, and Kahn was very much relieved to see him go.

The jet airliner was flying peacefully over the ocean, high above and beyond the turmoil that had consumed his life these past months. It still seemed cold in the cabin, and he considered asking the stewardess if she would turn up the heat. But nobody else seemed to mind, so why should he? Strange, he thought; he was the only one left in this section, except for a woman in front of him. Perhaps it was warmer in the rear....

It wasn't that, of course; the reason came to him quickly enough: it was *him* they were moving from. He hadn't noticed it until now, but his khakis, which had lain for months in the shitsmoke and rot, *stank!*—the more so to people like these, who were used to the villas and hotels of Saigon.

There was some shaving lotion in his AWOL bag, and he considered going into the lavatory and dousing himself with it. But that would only make it worse, he decided. He wished he had a blanket, it was so cold. He was starting to shiver a little. Cold like the cold in the jungle at night when you don't expect it...cold as in a damp, cold vault...cold like dead men...like Holden, Crump, Sharkey, Muntz, Major Dunn...all of them, fiercely cold...and he was going home.

He might have done that one thing for them...might have gone to the general and demanded a Board of Inquiry...might have simply told Spudhead to write his father...might have, might have...it was always "might have."...

Somewhere in his brain the debt-bird flapped its wings. What now? he thought. There must be something else...being in a war, living through it was not enough!

The woman in front had put down her magazine and was fiddling with her handbag. Kahn leaned forward a little between the seats. She was going to leave! Oh, please don't...he hoped. Please stay...but she slipped quickly past him, and then he was alone.

He reached up and turned out the light and slouched down in the seat. He had to go to the bathroom too, but was embarrassed to get up.

Somehow, he had let them down. His men. His friends.

His! He felt awfully, terribly helpless. There must be something... at least write a letter to their parents... or call them... or go to the funerals. It was not over yet. They were still his men—alive or dead, it didn't matter.

They were whistling their way northeastward, far out to sea, beneath which lay a nether world of silent stillness. And yet if such things could be recorded, somewhere deep below there might have been heard a sound of soft crying.

He tried to stop the tears—tried quite hard, in fact—but they flooded upward from a tightly gripped heart. In the dark, Kahn sobbed quietly and alone, and though it was partly from relief and partly from sorrow, it was partly from shame too. Because he *was* ashamed—of what he hadn't done; and embarrassed too, because he smelled so bad.

36

BILLY KAHN picked up the phone and dialed the Holdens' number. From his hotel window he could see the open fields of Central Park, little patches of snow dotting the ground beneath barren trees. But the day looked fresh and crisp, and there were people in the park, walking dogs or hurrying to work.

"Holden residence," someone answered.

"Is Mr. Holden in?"

"Who's calling, please?" the voice asked.

"My name is Kahn. I was . . . in the same company with Frank Holden. I'm in New York City."

"Just a moment, please," the answerer said.

It had taken him a week to get out of the Army, since Patch's pull apparently did not extend much beyond the flight line at Long Binh. It had been a week of interminable form-filling, physical examinations and orientations—in between which he lived in one of the BOQs at Fort Dix, New Jersey.

For the first day or so he had spent his spare time hanging around the officers' club, where he could buy a meal and a drink. Even though he was a stranger, people frequently engaged him in conversation about the war as soon as they noticed the division insigne he was wearing, and that it was on his right shoulder, indicating he had served in a combat zone. He quickly discovered, however, that the questions were often tedious and sometimes painful and that, in fact, he did not want to talk about it, and so he started staying around his BOQ.

In the mornings he would walk to the commissary and buy sandwich fixings, which he prepared himself in his room, and he also purchased a couple of bottles of whiskey. Darkness came early in the month of February over the flat New Jersey plains, and after he had made himself a sandwich he would go and sit in a chair by the window and have a drink and look out over the empty parade ground. When the whiskey began to make him feel good, he would have another drink, and when he felt good he would begin to think about it . . . but only then. . . .

Once, the day before he received his discharge, he had walked through the lobby of the BOQ past a television set showing the news. The story was of a big antiwar demonstration in Washington, and he stopped to watch it. The other officers, mostly second lieutenants, jeered and swore—but he did not. When the commentator switched to some real war footage, he went back up to his room and poured himself a larger-than-usual drink of whiskey.

"HELLO," a woman said. "Mr. Holden is unable to come to the phone right now. May I help you? This is Mrs. Holden."

"Yes, ma'am," Kahn said, faltering a little.

"I...ah...knew your son, Frank. I was the...the Company Commander just before he took over."

There was a pause at the other end.

"Are you in New York?" she asked.

"Yes, ma'am—I'm in a hotel near the Central Park."

"Would you hold on a moment, please?"

The previous afternoon he had taken the train out of Fort Dix, sitting next to a haggard-looking woman in a blond wig who said she was a dancer and invited him to the club where she worked. Paying off the court-martial fine had left him with savings of eight hundred dollars, more or less, with which to begin the rest of his life, and the first thing he realized was that he needed some clothes. He had bought some slacks and a windbreaker at the post PX, but today he planned to go down to one of the shops along the street and buy himself a suit or sports coat.

"Hello," a man's voice said. "This is Francis Holden. I understand you knew our son."

"Yessir," Kahn said. "We were friends. He was my Executive Officer."

"Where are you staying?"

"I'm in the Filmore Hotel...on Seventy-second Street—West, I think. It's near the park."

"If you didn't know it, the funeral is today—at two," Mr. Holden said. "But won't you come over here a little before? We're having some people in."

He sounded slightly stiff, but very polite, Kahn thought, and thoroughly in control. Not at all like Mrs. Crump, whom he had phoned earlier down in Mississippi. But these were a different kind of people from the Crumps...and from himself, too.

"Please, Mr. Kahn," Mrs. Holden said from another phone. "We aren't too far away.... You knew Frank. We'd like to see you very much—won't you come over?"

"Yes, ma'am, I'd like to very much."

"We're on East Sixty-second Street," the elder Holden said. "You can catch the crosstown bus or take a cab..."

After he hung up, Kahn went to the window and looked down at the busy sidewalks. The racket of automobile horns and other city noises drifted ten stories up to meet him, and he wondered if they knew, any of them down there. If they had any idea at all...

A few minutes later the phone rang. It was the long-distance operator. "I have your party now," she said.

"Hello, is this Mrs. Dunn?"

The voice at the other end sounded pleasant and young, and with a trace of an accent.

"My name's Kahn, ma'am. You don't know me, but I was a friend of your husband's...

"Yes, we met on the ship going over. Oh, he wrote you? I didn't know that....

"...Well, I was wondering when...the funeral was going to be. I'm in New York City now, but I'd like to try to come down for it....

"...It has...already?...Oh, at Arlington Cemetery....

"...With full military honors.... I see.... It must have been very nice. Yes...of course—I just didn't think he...

"...Oh, of course.... I had just been wondering if there was anything I could do, to be of help. It must be very hard...

"...Well, if you think of anything, please don't worry about calling. I'm at the Filmore Hotel in New York City, at least for another day or so...

"...No bother at all, ma'am. I, ah, I want to tell you something, though. Your...husband, Major Dunn... was a fine man. Very fine....

"...No, ma'am, I'm out of the Army now. My time was up...."

He put on the windbreaker and went to the elevator. It was nearly 11 A.M., and if he wanted to get over to the Holdens' house he was going to have to hurry up and buy that sports coat and put it on.

THE CHURCH was a gray Gothic spire situated at the confluence of the great and powerful avenues of Wall Street and Broadway. Former First Lieutenant Billy Kahn arrived jammed in a limousine with an aunt, an uncle and two cousins of the Holden family. They went straight inside, but he stood on the sidewalk for a while, watching other limos, taxicabs and private automobiles disgorging serious-faced, proper-looking people in front of the church. He thought he recognized some of the faces, but wasn't sure. In any case, he thought, the Holden family were certainly well connected.

An icy gust deviled down the canyon of skyscrapers and needled his eyes, and he clutched the front of his new tweed jacket together against the cold—and also to make it fit better, since when he bought it he had simply asked for his old size, forgetting that he had lost weight. He hadn't noticed how loosely it hung until he stopped in front of a plate-glass window on his way to the Holdens', and by then it was too late to do anything about it.

They had ushered him warmly into the Holden household, offering food and drink, and taken him into the big living room where everyone was gathered and introduced him around. All eyes were on him, and the room fell silent when the Holdens began asking questions about their son. He had answered delicately but truthfully, and given as close an account as he could of the final battle—leaving out, however, any mention of Patch's refusal to relocate the company. During this time, most—except for the Holdens themselves—looked down at the floor, and a few had shaken their heads sorrowfully from time to time. In the end, though, all seemed relieved to have been carried back through the last moments by someone who had been especially close to it.

When he had finished, only Holden's sister, Cory, was moved to tears, and as she sobbed quietly in a chair, Holden's father said to him, "Billy, do you believe Frank had any idea of what he died for?" Kahn thought about it briefly, then said, "Mr. Holden, he had a whole company to look after, and from everything I heard, he did the best he could. That's the only answer I can give you."

THE HONOR guard arrived in their dress blue uniforms and formed up alongside the church. They received mostly passing, awkward glances from those filing in—with the exception of a tall, pretty girl standing on the steps, and she stared at them with such a narrowed fierceness in her bright green eyes that Kahn had a sudden inkling he knew who she was. He walked over and said, "Excuse me—is your name Becky?"

She continued to stare at the honor guard—six lieutenants and a captain, who were talking together quietly. "Yes," she said.

"I guess I thought so. Frank told me about you."

She looked at him. Her eyes were slightly red as though from crying, but not for a while.

"I'm Bill... Billy Kahn. Frank and I were in the same outfit."

"Oh," she said flatly, then added, "Why are you here?"

He stumbled for words for an instant. "I am... well, because... he was my friend...."

"Oh, no, I didn't mean that," she said, softening. "I mean, how did you get here... if you were just over there with him?"

He was about to answer when a tall, slightly graying man joined them. He was craggy and handsome and almost fatherly-looking, but he took Becky's hand.

"Sorry I'm a little late—something came up," he said. She leaned over and kissed him lightly on the cheek.

"Richard," she said, "this is... Billy. He knew Frank... over there."

The man extended his hand. "Hi, I'm Dick Widenfield," he said. They shook hands, and Kahn fished around for a cigarette. In his pocket was Holden's unsent letter; he had read it again this morning, and yet had no more idea what to do with it now than he had had the day he got it.

"You're in the Army, then?" Widenfield asked.

"Until two days ago."

"Oh, so you just came—"

"Oh, God! It's stupid!" Becky suddenly blurted out. "Why did he have to die? For *what*?"

It was the second time that day someone had asked that question. He knew that the answer he had given before wouldn't do this time... different people, different answer. Maybe there wasn't a single answer. Maybe there wasn't an answer at all... so he stood there dumbly and said nothing.

"Do you know our group?" Widenfield interceded.

"We're trying to stop this thing before it goes any further. There are some veterans organizing too—you could be of . . . you could help us, if you want to. . . ."

Becky was watching him curiously, and he suddenly felt awkward and uncomfortable in the ill-fitting tweed jacket and his short, Army-cut hair.

"I don't know what I'm going to do right now," he said. "I haven't been here very long."

"Of course," Widenfield said, "but look, why don't you take this card? Give a call sometime—even if you just want to talk. Tell whoever answers I said to put you 'straight through.'"

Kahn took the card and put it into his pocket along with Holden's letter and Congressman Miter's address. There were only a few people trickling into the church now, and the honor guard had formed up at the curb.

"I guess we should go in," Widenfield said.

As they walked into the church, Becky dropped back beside Kahn.

"Did he say anything about me . . . before, I mean?"

"I wasn't there; I didn't see him for about a week or so before."

"I hope he knew," she said, "that I loved him," and in a lower voice she added, "I was going to marry him. . . ." Then she stepped quickly up beside Widenfield and took his arm to walk down the aisle.

KAHN TOOK a seat alone in one of the hard, wooden pews in the back of the church beneath the high beams and buttresses. The organist had been playing low, funereal music, but as he sat the tempo built into a powerful, uplifting throb. It must be, he thought, the hymn they were discussing in the car; the family had requested the old Episcopal prayer of thanksgiving because it was "hopeful." The sweet melodic strains swept high into the rafters of the church, until after a while they seemed to become a part of the old building itself—as did he, and the others—caught up, all of them, in the spirit of hope and thankfulness. . . .

There came to him now something he had not

understood before: that there was in fact a strength in the dead; it was their legacy to the living. Somewhere, he realized, in other churches in towns and cities all over the country where the war dead were being buried, this sad, bittersweet legacy was being passed along . . . to those like himself who had come through it and would go on to become bankers, or salesmen, or service-station attendants, or farmers, or forklift operators or geologists—and husbands and fathers—and spend their Friday nights swapping the truths and lies down at a VFW hall or in a bar until in time it wouldn't matter which; the important thing would be to have a place to go and be with people like themselves, since anyone who hadn't been there probably wouldn't know what in hell you were talking about.

At the altar a young priest sat meditating, his head slightly bowed. He, Kahn had also learned from the conversation in the car, was chaplain of Holden's old prep school, summoned down to New York by the family to deliver the final, parting words.

The organist continued to ring out the powerful joyous message of the hymn . . . A Prayer of Thanksgiving, he thought. It was very beautiful. How odd . . .

. . . Even the others, the ones with missing arms and legs and perforated intestines and steel plates and rearranged faces, he marveled—all of them, including the ones who would lie for years in hospital beds hoping to get well enough someday to walk outside and sit in the garden—they at least were still capable of pondering why it had happened to them; and for this they too could be thankful to the legacy of the dead.

The organist had gone through the hymn once and changed into a higher, more forceful key. From a balcony above, a lone voice rang out the hopeful words of the song:

> We gath-er to-geth-er
> To ask . . . the Lord's bless-ing;
> And pray that thou still
> Our de-fend-er wilt be . . .

...and what a strong, wonderful voice! Clear and sweet—belonging, Kahn knew, to a member of the Metropolitan Opera Company: another touch added by the family.

When the singer finished, the organist returned to a deep prelude, building more power this time, preparing for a huge radiant burst which came as the great doors of the church opened and the captain of the honor guard stepped in. Behind him, the six lieutenants stood on either side of the casket, and as the organist plunged into the final stanza they stepped in perfect cadence as the people rose to their feet.

Kahn felt a swelling in his chest. He soared with the music. As the honor guard passed by, a single tear came, and rolled down his face and quickly dried on his cheek, but he made no move to brush it away. It made no difference. He knew that he could go home now to the life that lay in front of him—even though the biggest thing that probably would ever happen was already behind.

He had only one stop along the way, and that would be in Washington, to look up Spudhead's father and tell him his son was doing fine—and also discuss with him the matter of a certain brigade commander and the deaths of fifty men.

Soon afterward, although he could not possibly know it now, the debt bird would fly away forever, leaving in its place a shadowy, begging void of doubts and questions. Why? What on earth was it had dragged him through the knothole onto the playing fields of hell, then brought him back again and left him here? He had seen many terrible things; yet now they seemed far away and growing dimmer. All he knew for certain was that somehow, he was close to the end of it.

The music exploded into a great ringing crescendo as the organist pulled out the stops; bells and cymbals trembled in the rafters and floors of this venerable house of God.

The little procession was far down the aisle, and the young priest behind the altar looked reverent and grave. Everyone watched the honor guard as it drew to a halt precisely at the close of the hymn, so none of them saw the former commander of Bravo Company raise his right hand to his forehead, bring it down again quickly and then slip out quietly into the cold February sun.

MEN AT WAR!

Gritty, gutsy, fascinating, real, here are stories of World War II and Vietnam— -and the men who fought in them.

WAR
BOOKS
FROM JOVE